STORMING THE
BLACK
ICE

DON BROWN

STORMING THE
BLACK
ICE

PACIFIC RIM SERIES

ZONDERVAN®

Zondervan

Storming the Black Ice
Copyright © 2014 by Don Brown

This title is also available as a Zondervan ebook. Visit www.zondervan.com/ebooks.

This title is also available in a Zondervan audio edition. Visit www.zondervan.fm.

Requests for information should be addressed to:

Zondervan, *Grand Rapids, Michigan 49530*

Library of Congress Cataloging-in-Publication Data

Brown, Don, 1960-
  Storming the Black Ice / Don Brown.
      pages cm. — (Pacific Rim Series)
  ISBN 978-0-310-33016-5 (softcover)
  1. Submarines (Ships)—Fiction. 2. International relations—Fiction. 3. Suspense fiction. 4. Christian
      fiction. I. Title.
  PS3602.R6947S76 2013
  813'.6—dc23   2013035595

Maps created by Jane Haradine, Copyright © Don Brown

Cover design: Curt Diepenhorst
Cover photograph: Deborah Zabarenka, Corbis Images
Interior design: Michelle Espinoza
Printed in the United States of America

---

14 15 16 17 18 19 20 /RRD/ 20 19 18 17 16 15 14 13 12 11 10 9 8 7 6 5 4 3 2 1

Dedicated to the memory of

Todd Allan Overgaard

May 23, 1964 – June 24, 2010

504th Parachute Infantry Regiment

82nd Airborne Division

United States Army

"All the way!"

ACKNOWLEDGMENTS

For his superb editorial assistance, a special thanks to US Army veteran Jack Miller of La Mesa, California, who, along with his wife, Linda, are generous benefactors of the San Diego Zoo and the Lambs Theatre of Coronado, California. With grateful appreciation for the behind-the-scenes tours with the giraffes and the magical musical performances by the Pacific, and for hosting fabulous Super Bowl parties during my February trips to San Diego.

As always, a special and warm thanks to Sue Brower, acquisitions editor of Zondervan, and to Jane Haradine for her patience with me and tedious dedication in the editorial process.

Finally, I offer a special tribute to my astute literary agent, Steve Laube of Phoenix, who came up with the idea for this book, gave me his thoughts, and encouraged me to write it.

PROLOGUE

Belgrano II base camp
Argentine outpost
Antarctica

8:18 p.m. local time
early twenty-first century
in the reign of King Charles III of England

Belgrano Base. This is *FAA* C-130. We are on final approach for cargo drop. Estimated time . . . ten minutes. Stand by."

The announcement from the aircraft, transmitted over the base camp's loudspeakers, sent the handful of scientists and Army officers scrambling off their foldout canvas chairs and makeshift cots.

Yanking thermal gloves from drawers, they grabbed heavy jackets from lockers and tossed snow boots and flashlights to each other. The weapons officer rushed to the arms locker and began passing automatic rifles to the men.

Lieutenant Fernando Sosa zipped his thermal jacket and swung open the door of the geodesic dome. Frigid Antarctic air blasted through the cozy warmth inside the research station as Sosa stepped outside ahead of the others.

The snow had started when he arrived at base camp one week ago. And it kept snowing—until an hour ago. Out in the cold of the night, Sosa took five steps and stopped.

He gazed up at the sky. How could he not?

At the bottom of the world, the magnificent sight that spread across the heavens could stop any man in his tracks.

Greenish bands glowed against the starry sky, arcing in a broad swath across the heavens. Behind the celestial green, God had painted a tapestry of pink, mixing in light green and red, sprinkled with yellow, and a pure blue.

Aurora Australis. The Southern Lights.

The panorama triggered memories of the priest's words from mass last month.

The heavens declare the glory of the Lord.

Photographs could serve no justice to actually witnessing the brilliant colors of *Aurora Australis* for the first time. If only Carolina could witness this.

They were still newlyweds, married for six months, and he hoped she would soon bear him a son. But on this top secret mission, Carolina had no clue of his whereabouts.

Blinding searchlights lit the night.

"Move . . . move!" The colonel's command snapped him from his gaze.

Powerful white beams crisscrossed the skies.

"Keep moving!" the colonel shouted.

Through deep snow they trudged, out to an icy tundra, away from the comforting warmth of the geodesic dome.

Armed riflemen fanned into a defensive perimeter as a faint whir of aircraft propellers sounded in the distance and grew louder as the military cargo plane approached from somewhere in the night.

"Spread out!" the colonel ordered. "Rifles ready!"

"There!" The first sergeant pointed to the sky.

Sosa looked up. Crisscrossing spotlights clipped the four-engine aircraft, an Argentine Air Force C-130, passing low over the camp.

Then the plane disappeared, its roaring engines still audible in the distance, its blinking tail and wing lights vanishing last.

"Parachute! Parachute!" someone shouted.

Searchlights shifted to the left, illuminating a white parachute floating from the sky. The wooden crate at the bottom of the chute drifted back and forth in the wind, gliding at a shallow angle toward the ground. It landed in a snowbank a hundred yards downrange.

"Let's go! Secure that position!" the colonel snapped.

Riflemen dashed through the snow toward the box as the parachute floated to the ground. Two men slipped and fell, then got back up and joined the others as they formed a tight circle around the crate.

"Are you ready, Lieutenant?" The colonel looked Sosa in the eye.

"Yes, sir," Sosa said. "I have been training for months for this."

"Let's go."

They headed out toward the drop zone, through wind so cold that Sosa's nose and eyes ached with throbbing pain.

The ring of soldiers guarding the crate moved aside as the colonel stepped through.

Sosa followed the base commander into the armed perimeter. Off to the right two soldiers were bent over, rolling the parachute and stuffing it into a canvas bag.

"Light it up," the colonel said.

The staff sergeant lit the night with a blinding flashlight beam.

The wooden crate, about a four-foot cube, had an ominous warning painted in Spanish:

¡Secreto superior!
¡Propiedad de la Fuerzas Armadas de la Republica Argentina
¡Advertencia!
¡Pegarán un tiro a cualquiera que no tenga autoridad para abrir!

Which in English translated into:

Top Secret!
Property of the Armed Forces of the Argentine Republic
Warning!
Anyone who opens without authority will be shot!

CHAPTER 1

The silver Beamer hugged the curve along Moanalua Road, racing under the bright, warm sunshine and deep blue skies of an early Hawaiian afternoon. The driver slowed when the sea of brake lights flashed up ahead in front of the entrance of St. Timothy's Episcopal Church on the right. He cursed under his breath, then checked his watch.

His problem—bad timing.

Pearl Ridge Elementary School over to the left was letting out, attracting a sea of open-top convertibles and snub-nosed vans jammed in a long line at the entrance of the school, backing up traffic for a quarter of a mile. Even without the traffic jam, getting to Commander Pete Miranda's appointment with the admiral would be a tight squeeze.

"Why didn't I take the H1?" He hit the brakes, coming to a stop in bumper-to-bumper traffic. Pete checked the time, then let out an expletive. "I need some air." He pushed the button on the dash to open the retractable top of the brand-new BMW 650i. "I fork out all this cash for this expensive little baby, and all I do is sit in traffic jams. Drive in circles. Island's only forty miles long and thirty miles wide."

As the retractable top opened and glorious Hawaiian sunshine saturated the driver's side of the Beamer, the answer to his question appeared in the flesh—a blonde in a spaghetti-strap yellow sundress in a Chrysler Sebring convertible.

The poor damsel in distress!

Stuck in line on the left shoulder of the road, crawling at a snail's pace even slower than Pete's lane. Her blond hair danced in the breeze off her tanned shoulders. And as her left hand clasped the steering wheel at the twelve o'clock position, the noticeable absence of a ring!

"My, my!" Pete let up on the brakes and rolled even with the Sebring.

She glanced in his direction, and their eyes locked in a millisecond of an electrifying instant. She flashed a magnetic smile.

"Now I remember why I bought this car." He shot her a teasing salute and returned the smile. "Request permission to come aboard?"

"What?" She mouthed the single word in a smiling, bashful fashion, raising her left eyebrow in a curious manner and sporting a look of pleasure about the coincidence that had brought their convertibles side by side in a traffic jam made in heaven.

"Me Clark! You Christie!" he shouted.

She laughed. "I love that old movie."

"You liked *Vacation*? Me too!"

She giggled and, with a swift movement of her hand, pushed a lock of blond hair out of her face. "I loved it!"

"Now me like traffic jams!"

"You're bad!" She smiled.

And then . . . his iPhone rang.

COMSUBPAC. The admiral's office.

Pete swiped his thumb across the iPhone. "Commander Miranda."

"Sir, this is Master Chief Kelly at SUBPAC."

"How can I help you, Master Chief?"

"Sorry to bother you, sir, but the admiral wants you here five minutes early."

Pete looked down at the digital clock. *1350 hours.* Then he glanced over at the Beamer's navigation screen: *3.8 miles to SUBPAC HQ. ETA 10 minutes.*

So much for trading phone numbers with the red-hot soccer mom.

"Gotta get around this traffic." Pete hit his turn signal, blew a kiss to the blonde, and turned right on Moanalua Loop, heading south toward Pearl Harbor. If he could get lucky with some green lights . . .

A few minutes later he sped past the entrance to the USS *Arizona* Memorial, over the causeway bridge, and was bearing right onto Arizona

Road. With the sparkling waters of the harbor in front, Pete stopped at the main gate of the naval base.

As he fiddled for his military identification card, a US Marine, decked in an enlisted dress blue "Charlie" uniform, stood waiting for him.

"Afternoon, Commander."

"Afternoon, Corporal." Pete found the card and flashed it at the corporal.

"Have a nice day, sir." The Marine waved Pete through the gate.

Pete checked the clock on the dash. "Five minutes late!" He banged his fist into the dashboard as his phone rang again.

COMSUBPAC.

Pete picked up the phone. "Commander Miranda."

"The admiral wants to know where you are, sir," the force master chief said.

"In the parking lot, Master Chief."

"Aye, sir. I'll tell the admiral."

Pete turned the Beamer into the first spot for visitors.

Without taking time to raise the top, he popped out of the driver's side, donned his cover, and jogged up the front walkway leading to SUBPAC headquarters. Two petty officers in white jumper uniforms were standing under a blue-and-white sign proclaiming:

HEADQUARTERS
UNITED STATES SUBMARINE FORCE
PACIFIC FLEET

They shot salutes as he raced up the steps to the front door. Pete returned the salutes as a sailor opened the large glass door. Inside the entryway, a model of a *Los Angeles*–class attack submarine sat on a pedestal, cordoned off by a red-velvet-covered rope.

"Commander Miranda!" Lieutenant Commander Frank Carber, one of the admiral's flag aides, greeted Pete in the entryway. "Admiral's waiting for you, sir."

"I'll bet."

"Follow me, please, sir."

"With pleasure, Frank."

Pete fell into line behind the flag aide, making a beeline to the admiral's suite. The aide turned left and stepped through a door past two Marines who came to attention as Pete passed. The large reception area of the admiral's office featured dark blue carpet that gave off the smell of having been recently cleaned. A half dozen sailors—yeoman clerical types—sat at terminal screens, seemingly oblivious to Pete's arrival.

"This way, sir." The flag aide pivoted right, then opened the door leading to the inner sanctum of the admiral's office.

Rear Admiral Chuck D. "Bulldog" Elyea, a pugnacious bulldog of an officer wearing his short-sleeved khaki uniform with two silver stars pinned to each collar, sat back in his chair, his arms folded across his belly. His chief of staff, Captain Lee Teague, stood behind him, mimicking the arms-crossed gesture of his boss. Their silent scowls seemed perfectly synchronized in a symmetry of angry visual lines.

Pete stepped in front of the admiral's desk and came to attention. "Commander Miranda reporting as ordered, sir."

The stare, scowl, and crossed arms lingered. Classic Elyea. The silent treatment as a psychological weapon.

Ten seconds passed. Then, finally . . .

"Pete, I had the master chief call and tell you to report five minutes early, and"—Elyea examined his wristwatch, fixing his stare on it—"and rather than arriving five minutes early, you're five minutes late from the originally scheduled time."

"Sorry, sir. I had a traffic issue."

"What was her name?"

"Didn't have time to find out. Sorry, sir."

"Pete, tell me this. Do you remember Captain Francis S. Low, United States Navy?"

"Yes, sir. Of course, sir."

The admiral steepled his fingers together. "Tell me, who was Captain Low?"

Every sub commander in the Navy knew the name of Captain Francis S. Low. Pete knew this and so did the admiral. But obviously, the admiral wanted to drive home some point.

"Sir, in January of 1942, Captain Francis S. Low, the sub commander on the staff of Admiral Ernest J. King, devised the plan to attack Tokyo in retaliation for the Japanese attack on Pearl Harbor by using

Army two-engine medium bombers launched from an aircraft carrier. Lieutenant Colonel James 'Jimmy' Doolittle executed the mission. The rest is history, sir."

The admiral scratched his chin. "You saw the movie *Pearl Harbor*, didn't you?"

"Sir, yes, sir."

"You remember that scene when FDR called Admiral King and Captain Low into the Oval Office while looking for a plan to retaliate against Japan?"

"Yes, sir, Admiral, I seem to remember that scene."

"Remember what FDR said in that scene?"

"Well, sir," Pete said, "I vaguely remember FDR telling Captain Low that he liked sub commanders."

"And what else do you remember?"

"That the president was pleased that Captain Low devised the strategic bombing plan against Tokyo."

"No!" Elyea slammed his desk. "What did FDR say *after* he told Captain Low that he liked sub commanders?"

Pete shook his head. "I'm sorry, sir. It's been awhile since I saw the movie."

Elyea swigged his coffee, then set the mug down on his desk. "Roosevelt looked at Captain Low and said something like, 'I like sub commanders. They don't have time for bull. And neither do I.' Do you remember that, Commander?"

"I remember something like that."

"Good," Elyea said. "Let me put it this way. I like sub commanders too. But I don't like sub commanders who are late."

"My apologies, sir."

"It's like FDR said in that movie, I don't have time for bull. Have you got that, Commander?"

"Yes, sir. Understood, sir."

"Very well. At ease, Pete."

"Thank you, sir."

"Lucky for you you're the best *LA*-class sub commander I've got. But don't think you can get prima donna treatment."

"Of course not, sir. But thank you, sir."

"Forget it. Listen, Pete. I know you're considering retirement. But your country needs you. And I'm not trying to sound like a detailer with a juicy assignment, but I do have an offer you can't refuse."

Pete chuckled.

"Did I say something funny, Commander?"

"My apologies, sir. But the last time I got an offer I couldn't refuse, I wound up commanding a sub in the Black Sea and nearly started a war between the US and Russia."

The admiral leaned back in his chair. "Have a seat, Pete."

"Thank you, sir." Pete sat in a wingback chair in front of the admiral's desk.

"You acquitted yourself splendidly in the Black Sea and deserved the Presidential Commendation that you received."

"I am humbled, sir."

"But"—Elyea lifted his index finger in the air—"but in fairness, Pete, you volunteered for the Black Sea mission. Every crew member, from the skipper down, and that includes you, was warned of the dangers."

Pete nodded. "True, Admiral. We knew we might not return. And we wouldn't have, but for the grace of God."

"Well, with what I'm about to tell you, you'll think God is about to reward you for your near-death experience in the Black Sea."

"You have piqued my curiosity, sir. It's hard to figure out what might be a more lush assignment than Hawaii."

"Suppose I told you we were going to give you a chance to go home."

"Go home? To Dallas, sir? With respect, I didn't know we had any sub bases in Dallas."

"You're correct, Pete." A look of satisfaction crossed the admiral's face. "But they sure can get a sub into port in Valparaiso."

"Valparaiso?" Pete thought about that for a second. "As in Chile?"

"You didn't think I was talking about Indiana, did you?"

"No, sir. Unless for some reason the president wants an *LA*-class boat on the Great Lakes."

"Well, I don't think the president is interested in the Great Lakes. But he is interested in selling a *Los Angeles*–class boat to the Chilean Navy."

"Oh really?"

"Yes. Our relations with Chile have been superb over the years.

But Chile's relationships with both Venezuela and Argentina are rocky. Chile needs to modernize her sub fleet. So when we announced that we were mothballing the USS *Corpus Christi*, we got a call from the Chilean Navy about purchasing her."

"Hmm. I'm starting to get the picture."

"Good. The Chileans need someone to teach them how to operate this baby. And not only are you my best sub commander but you happen to be the only sub commander in the Navy with a father born and raised in Santiago."

Pete's father, Marvin Miranda, born to a prominent Chilean family, had come as a freshman to Cal-Berkeley all those years ago and met a gorgeous daughter of Connecticut aristocracy, the talented and magnetic Judith Kriete.

Judy would steal Marvin's heart, and his love for the redhead ensured that America would become his new home. His became the classic American success story—an immigrant-turned-American making his name and grasping hold of the American dream.

Marvin and Judy had two boys. Their second son, Peter, had earned an NROTC scholarship at the University of Texas, where he first developed an interest in submarines.

If Pete's life were a painting, that painting would be a satisfying tapestry of blur and motion. Still, that tapestry lacked one meaningful scene. Pete had missed out on his father's Chilean heritage. Yes, they had visited Santiago when the children were young, but as his memories faded, his longing to reconnect—to family, to cousins, to the other half of his heritage—had grown stronger.

"Pete. Still with me?"

"Sorry, sir. Just thinking."

"Well? How does this proposition strike you?"

"I'm interested, sir. How would this work? Would I be on loan to the Chilean Navy?"

"Yes. We would fly you to Santiago, along with a skeleton crew of US Navy *LA*-class submariners. You would meet the crew of the *Corpus Christi* in Valparaiso. The Chileans are renaming the *Corpus Christi* the CS *Miro*, by the way. The *Corpus Christi*'s crew would disembark and you would then train the new Chilean crew on the nuances of submarine warfare, American style."

The notion of an all-expenses-paid trip to Chile, doing what he loved, with a chance to explore a side of his family separated from him by time and distance, sounded intriguing. The Navy had already rewarded him with a final shore tour in Hawaii as payback for his heroism in the Black Sea affair. After Hawaii, he had planned on putting in his retirement papers and returning to Dallas, where he had already bought a swanky retirement condo.

But maybe the call of Dallas and his dream of taking over the family sign business—a multimillion-dollar enterprise started by his brother, John, in a garage—and then running for Congress . . . maybe all that could wait for a while.

"Out of curiosity, Admiral, how long would this assignment last?"

"Six months to a year, Pete. After that, if you want to retire and return to Texas, fine. But if you stay in, you'd be up for captain in the middle of your tour, and I'll personally make a call to the head of the review board and do everything in my power to see that you're picked up."

"Captain Miranda." Pete felt himself grin. "That has a nice ring, doesn't it?"

"Yes, it does," the admiral said. "Which is why you should delay this sign-business idea of yours for another few years. Pete, you'd look good with a silver eagle pinned on that collar of yours. And if you could learn to leave the women alone and make it to meetings on time, maybe even a star one day." The admiral chuckled.

"Okay." Pete laughed. "You've persuaded me, sir. A short-term extension sounds good."

"Great! There's a C-5 leaving out of Hickam tomorrow at 1300, headed to Santiago. We've already booked that C-5 for you, Pete."

"Aye, sir."

CHAPTER 2

Cerro Castillo
president's summer palace
Viña del Mar
sixty miles northwest of Santiago, Chile

The black Rolls-Royce slowed, approaching the swooping circular driveway fronting the stucco-and-tile mansion overlooking the Pacific. At ten-foot intervals along the broad curve, soldiers of the Republic of Chile stood guard, resplendent in dress uniforms, chest medals glistening in the late-afternoon sun, popping to attention and saluting as the limousine rolled to a stop.

A few dignitaries and military officers were gathered at the front of the mansion, waiting in a light Pacific breeze.

A Chilean naval officer stepped forward and opened the back door, and an announcement boomed over a loudspeaker, first in English, then in Spanish. The announcement echoed across the palace grounds: "The foreign secretary of the United Kingdom of Great Britain and Northern Ireland, the Right Honourable John Gosling."

Foreign Secretary Gosling stepped from the motorcar with a smile and wave and received enthusiastic applause. As the applause continued, he extended his hand to the gray-haired gentleman who approached him.

"Welcome to Cerro Castillo, Mister Secretary," the smiling Chilean said, his perfect English spiced with a slight Spanish accent.

"A pleasure to be here, Chancellor Rivera," Gosling responded in

Spanish. "What a picturesque setting. This palace is lovelier than the photographs can show."

The Chilean grinned. "I see that your Spanish is better than my English, Mister Secretary."

"Oh, I wouldn't say that." Gosling put his hand on Rivera's back. "I'm glad that our nations share a mutual respect for the other's history, culture, and language."

"And we shall forge an even stronger and more powerful future," Rivera said, again in English.

The Chilean Navy band began a slow, melodic strain of "God Save the King." Gosling placed his hand over his heart and turned toward the music with a swelling sense of pride as the Chilean honor guard hoisted the Union Jack into the pleasant afternoon breeze beside the flag of Chile.

Then, in stark contrast to the melodic strains of "God Save the King," a brassy, snappy trumpet fanfare introduced the national anthem of the Republic of Chile. The fanfare itself sounded almost like a German military march. But when the people began to sing, hands over their hearts and, for many, tears of pride moistening their eyes, the anthem reminded Secretary Gosling of France's march-like "La Marseillaise." As the Chilean anthem played on, Gosling's mind drifted to the day's agenda—hammering out details of the new treaty between the two countries for signatures at the summit between Prime Minister David Mulvaney and the president of Chile, Óscar Mendoza, at this very location tomorrow morning.

Today's meeting remained a closely guarded secret, with tomorrow's meeting between the prime minister and the president even more clandestine.

The code name for the project, "Black Ice," was known only by those in the highest echelons of power in London and Santiago. The treaty sanctioning it would provide a renewed economic lifeline for Britain, regenerating her relevance as a world power for years to come.

The band finished playing the last strains of the Chilean national anthem. Foreign Minister Rivera dropped his hand and turned to Gosling. "Are you ready to get to work, my friend?"

"I am most anxious to start, my dear chancellor."

"Come with me," the Chilean said. "The draft documents are on the balcony. There, overlooking the Pacific, we can soak in a Chilean sunset, the two of us, and hammer out the details outside the presence of the young bureaucrats. And after that we shall celebrate with the finest Chilean champagne from the valley."

"What a wonderful suggestion."

"Very well," Rivera said. He turned toward the main entrance of the mansion, his hand on Gosling's back to direct him through the large double doors. Chilean officers, adorned in the colorful regalia of the dress uniform of the Chilean Army, snapped to attention and shot salutes as the foreign ministers walked into an open receiving area with white marble floors and gold statues and busts.

Large swirling staircases rose majestically. They stepped down onto the gray-and-white marble floor of the great room, with leather sofas, wingback chairs, mahogany furniture, and marble sculptures, the apparent handiwork of Chilean sculptors and artists.

The back wall of the great room, made of pure glass, stretched a hundred feet wide and twenty-five feet high, providing a spectacular view of the sparkling blue waters of the Pacific. The two men stood there, looking out at the colorful panorama.

"General Pinochet loved this place." Rivera spoke with a tinge of reverence in his voice. "He loved this view."

"That is understandable. This sight is beyond marvelous."

"We shall always be grateful for what your government did for General Pinochet during the last years of his life. Allowing his return to Chile, rather than extradition to Spain."

Gosling wasn't sure how to answer. General Augusto Pinochet remained a highly controversial figure in Chile, even years after his death. Either he was revered or despised. Conservatives loved him for eradicating communism from Chile. Socialists hated him because he had used force when he attacked the presidential palace in Santiago to remove the Marxist government of Salvador Allende.

When former Prime Minister Margaret Thatcher and former US president George H. W. Bush later intervened on Pinochet's behalf after Spain tried arresting him on an international arrest warrant, the British government returned him to Chile, refusing to hand him over to Spain.

Thus, the Spanish-British-Chilean feud lived on, even beyond the end of the twentieth century.

"Prime Minister Thatcher held a debt of gratitude to the general for his cooperation and assistance in our war with Argentina over the Falklands," Gosling said.

Rivera smiled. "Let us then continue the spirit of cooperation begun by Lady Thatcher and General Pinochet and get down to business."

"Yes, let's," Gosling said.

"Step out on the veranda with me, my friend."

A Chilean steward, wearing a white jacket and black dress pants, opened two doors leading outside to the veranda. Gosling looked out at the Pacific.

Two padded chairs sat opposite each other at a white wrought-iron table. A leather notebook displaying the Union Jack and the Chilean flag sat on the table.

"A draft of the treaty is in the dossier. This is the product of the task force of attorneys from each of our departments. I hope you will find it to your satisfaction."

"I look forward to it, Chancellor."

Gosling sat down, opened the binder, and began to read.

SANTIAGO ACCORDS
ENTERED INTO BETWEEN
THE UNITED KINGDOM OF GREAT BRITAIN AND NORTHERN IRELAND
AND THE REPUBLIC OF CHILE

WHEREAS, the United Kingdom of Great Britain and Northern Ireland [hereinafter "Great Britain"] and the Republic of Chile [hereinafter "Chile"] have had a rich history of cooperation and mutual respect and warm international relations with one another; AND

WHEREAS, Great Britain and Chile are also two of seven states maintaining a territorial claim on eight territories in Antarctica; AND

WHEREAS, Great Britain and Chile also maintain overlapping geographic claims on the portion of Antarctica commonly known as the "Antarctic Peninsula"; AND

WHEREAS, certain areas on the Antarctic Peninsula where there are overlapping claims between Great Britain and Chile also involve overlapping claims from the Republic of Argentina; AND

WHEREAS, in light of the discovery of natural oil reserves by British geo-petro-engineers, the parties, previously described under the code name "Black Ice," Great Britain and Chile, wish to cooperate and resolve any and all territorial disputes between them on the Antarctic subcontinent; AND

WHEREAS, both nations desire to construct an infrastructure to drill for strategic petroleum on Antarctic lands claimed by them both and claimed by the Republic of Argentina; AND

WHEREAS, Great Britain and Chile were both original signatories of the Antarctic Treaty executed on December 1, 1959, and entered into force on June 23, 1961; AND

WHEREAS, Great Britain and Chile both lay claim to certain overlapping claims known as the British Antarctic Territory, whose main research base is at Rothera, with such territory as set forth below:

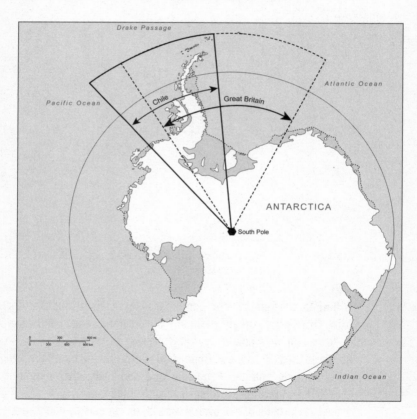

AND
WHEREAS, Chile lays claim to certain areas along the Antarctic Peninsula known as the Chilean Antarctic Territory, which overlaps the British claims, with the Chilean Antarctic Territory shown upon the map as set forth below:

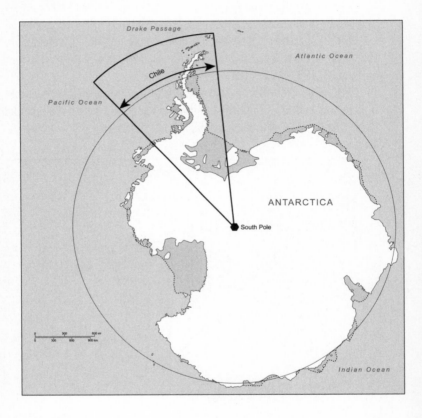

AND
WHEREAS, the Republic of Argentina also lays claim to such territory;

NOW, THEREFORE, Great Britain and Chile hereby agree to and covenant to become mutual enforcers of the following provisions:

Article 1. Great Britain and Chile shall jointly administer all disputed territories along the Antarctic Peninsula, and shall recognize the right of the other to operate within such previously disputed lands.

Article 2. Those disputed, overlapping lands claimed by both Great

Britain and Chile shall hereby forever be designated by both nations as the "Joint Anglo-Chilean Antarctic Territory."

Article 3. Great Britain and Chile shall assert superior claims within the Joint Anglo-Chilean Antarctic Territory over other nations attempting to make claims within that territory.

Article 4. Great Britain shall provide the principal military defence for the Joint Anglo-Chilean Antarctic Territory and shall assume military command of any military defence provided for the Territory, with Chile assisting in the defence under the lead of Great Britain.

Article 5. Great Britain, working through British Petroleum or any other oil exploration companies as designated by His Majesty's Government, shall assume the role of leadership in the drilling and exploration of crude oil within the Joint Anglo-Chilean Antarctic Territory, with Chile providing logistical assistance.

Article 6. Chile, working with technical advisers and with financial assistance from Great Britain, shall allow the construction of refineries upon its sovereign territory in Southern Chile and at other locations throughout Chile, as may be applicable, for the refining of crude oil from the Joint Anglo-Chilean Antarctic Territory.

Article 7. Chile shall permit the construction of updated facilities at its ports upon its sovereign territory in Southern Chile and at other locations throughout Chile for the worldwide shipment of crude oil from the Joint Anglo-Chilean Antarctic Territory.

Article 8. Great Britain and Chile shall become financial partners in the crude oil production operations within the Joint Anglo-Chilean Antarctic Territory, and shall divide profits from crude oil extracted as a part of this endeavor.

Article 9. Great Britain shall assist Chile financially in the construction of pipelines throughout Chile for the movement and sale of crude oil throughout South America and the Americas, and Great Britain and Chile shall engage in diplomatic efforts with other nations, such as Peru, Bolivia, Mexico, the United States, Canada, and various other nations throughout the Americas, to realize the construction of a Pan-American pipeline, originating in Chile, with its principal line running north along the Pacific Coast of the Americas into Central America and North America.

Article 10. Upon execution of this treaty, Great Britain and Chile do hereby establish an organization for mutual cultural and economic cooperation and goodwill to be known as the ANGLO-CHILEAN PETROLEUM ALLIANCE, with political headquarters located in London, and with business headquarters located in Santiago, and with an organizational purpose to extract and sell refined oil upon the world markets for the mutual financial benefit of both nations.

Article 11. For security purposes, the present arrangement, and all references to the "Black Ice" project, shall be held TOP SECRET until such time as announced publicly by joint agreement of both Great Britain and the Republic of Chile.

For the Republic of Chile:

For the United Kingdom of Great Britain and Northern Ireland:

_____

_____

Hon. Óscar Mendoza
President of the Republic

Hon. David Mulvaney
Prime Minister

_____

_____

Hon. Arturo Rivera
Foreign Minister
of the Republic

Hon. John Gosling
Foreign Secretary

Foreign Secretary Gosling closed the leather notebook. He took a satisfying sip of orange juice from a glass on a silver tray that had been placed on the table.

"Chancellor Rivera, I believe that our respective bosses shall be pleased with this collective effort, which, in my judgment, represents everything that we had agreed upon."

The Chilean smiled. "I am glad that you are pleased, Mister Secretary. And in anticipation of the arrival of the president and the prime minister tomorrow, I invite you to join me in a toast to our two countries with a bottle of our finest Chilean champagne."

"A splendid idea," Gosling said. "I would be more than happy to drink to that."

Rivera snapped his fingers and a porter emerged holding a silver tray with two glasses of champagne. He placed it on the table before the two men.

Rivera raised his glass high and declared, "To Chile and Britain, to the Black Ice project, and to an alliance of a thousand years!"

"Hear, hear." Gosling raised his glass. "To our countries, to the Black Ice project, and to an alliance of a thousand years."

CHAPTER 3

Belgrano II base camp
Argentine outpost
Antarctica

twenty-four hours later

On Antarctica's rocky and frigid coast, home to Argentina's Belgrano II base camp, the sun never rose for two weeks in midwinter, around June 21. Six months later, around Christmastime, the sun never set for two weeks during the Antarctic summer.

The skies seemed to switch rapidly from days with long hours of sunlight, each day getting shorter, until months later darkness filled each day, as if a shade had been pulled down. Then with the same rapid change, the blackness of night diminished until there again was no night. No darkness. The sun stayed with them for a whole two weeks.

None of this was lost on Lieutenant Fernando Sosa, who had arrived at base camp in the darkness of August. But now that the first week of September had arrived, he remained astonished and amazed at the rapid lengthening of the days.

As winter turned to spring at the bottom of the world, the long hours of perpetual darkness had given way to a hazy low-hanging sun.

The surveillance equipment air-dropped weeks ago by the C-130 under cover of darkness had been assembled in a high-security facility northwest of Moscow. It featured some of the most sophisticated components in the world. The listening devices and high-speed translators, powered by miniature super-computers that translated English into perfect Spanish, could circumvent the world's most powerful security codes and smash sophisticated firewalls.

In a world of high-stakes nuclear proliferation, burgeoning mega-debt, radical terror, and vicious international fighting for increasingly scarce resources, it paid to have friends.

And in this case, it paid to have mutual friends.

For the equipment, highly secretive and yet undiscovered by the Western powers, had made its way from Russia to this remote Argentinean base camp, courtesy of a common friend.

Lieutenant Fernando Sosa, described by his superiors as one of the brightest young intelligence officers in Argentina, knew about the geopolitical relationships forged between Argentina, Venezuela, and Russia. Britain and Chile had never enjoyed any prolonged harmonious relations with Argentina. And that Anglo-Chilean alliance of the last hundred years remained a pesky thorn for his country.

Hugo Chávez, in 2005, had referred to the growing alliance between Argentina and Venezuela as "a Caracas–Buenos Aires axis." Chávez threw billions in Venezuelan oil money at Argentina, buying up her bonds and retiring her debt with the International Monetary Fund.

Having bailed out Argentina, saving it from financial destruction, Chávez had forged a leftist alliance on the South American continent to counteract right-wing governments like Chile and capitalist forces from the north and from Western Europe.

Chávez's dalliance with the Russians had paid off for Venezuela. And Sosa knew that vicariously the dalliance had paid off for Argentina as well.

Before coming to Antarctica, Sosa trained for six months in an obscure facility outside Buenos Aires that was heavily guarded by crack Argentine troops. Each morning, Sosa and five other Argentine intelligence officers entered the compound through a gate from the north as a team of Russian intelligence officers entered through another gate from the east.

The Russian instructors trained the Argentineans on the operation of the top secret surveillance equipment, made available to Argentina through a mutual alliance with Venezuela.

Sosa and his fellow Argentinean officers were selected based on their scores on a battery of aptitude tests and on their proficiency in English. They knew that they were training for an elite top secret mission at some undisclosed location somewhere in the world. But where?

At the conclusion of the six-month course, Lieutenant Fernando Sosa scored highest on all final examinations, both written and practical, and aced the psychological testing, all administered by the Russians.

Sosa graduated first in his class. And with that achievement, he ended up here, at the bottom of the world. His mission—to keep tabs on Argentina's two most hated adversaries, Britain and Chile, both of which had increased their radio communications in recent weeks and had increased flights in and out of Antarctica.

Of course, all the training, all the sophisticated equipment, and all the top secret status surrounding this mission were not without a cost. There was a quid pro quo. Sosa understood from the beginning that intelligence gathered by the sophisticated equipment would be shared with their Venezuelan and Russian allies.

The spotlight shone on him from many fronts, his work critically important to his commander here at base camp, the head of Argentine intelligence, the president of Argentina, even the presidents of Venezuela and Russia.

No, they might not know his name, but he felt their eyes on him even from half a world away as he monitored the equipment. Sosa punched four buttons on the control panel to widen the frequency band and expand his monitoring range.

It was the middle of September. Dawn lasted for two hours, and then the sun rose and hung low in the northern sky for three hours. That was followed by two hours of twilight, followed by seventeen hours of darkness before the process started again.

For two weeks, since the first of the month, when the dawn hours had started returning to the base camp, Sosa had noticed a difference in performance in the Russian equipment.

In the earliest hours between starlight and dawn, enemy radio signals could be intercepted without much interference. But as soon as the gray light of dawn returned to the Antarctic skies, the Russian surveillance equipment became less effective. Interceptions were more staticky. The voices of the British, who up to this point had said nothing of significance, tended to fade in and out during these haunting dawn hours when the skies went from a dark starry firmament, lightened into an opaque gray on the northern horizon, and then gave way to the beautiful starry firmament again. Around the first week of August, the brief gray of dawn appeared each day between one and three in the afternoon.

Before the static of the predawn started, Sosa had noted two British voices using the phrase "Black Ice."

That sounded odd. He scribbled notes. One Brit used the phrase "Black Ice project." Another said, or seemed to say, "Operation Black Ice." Then the conversation vanished in the static.

Sosa glanced at the wall clock—2:45 p.m. Another fifteen minutes until the dawn subsided and the night appeared again. He hoped the Brits would still be talking about this "Black Ice project," whatever that was.

He adjusted a volume-control button and changed the frequency to get a better gauge on message traffic between the Chilean and British base camps. Nothing.

Out the window, he saw four scientists moving about with flashlights in the snow, attaching wire to a communications antenna. The gray sky faded, and darkness returned. Stars began appearing.

Local time, 2:48 p.m.

If today proved to be like the last three days, he could expect communications to be crystal clear again.

Sosa wondered whether the equipment would work at all during periods of sunlight, especially in December and January, when the sun would be out all day long. The Russians had warned of atmospheric interference that could occur at this time of day as a result of the variance of radio wavelengths at dusk and dawn, the hours between night and day, or, as now, the brief dawn that separated the night from the night.

Sosa glanced at the clock again—2:55 p.m.

Outside, the starry canopy blanketed base camp, and radio traffic from the British station gradually became intelligible again.

Sosa turned the volume up another notch.

His eyes widened.

Had he heard that right?

Communication between the British and Chileans was in English, and Sosa understood every word.

But had he heard that right?

He rewound the recording and replayed it.

"Capitán. Sir. I think you need to hear this."

Antarctica
near British Camp Churchill

one week later

Swiftly they moved across the ice.

They wore white weather gear, from the thermal hoods covering their heads to the heels of their snow boots.

Even their rifles were white. And so were their rockets and mortars and shortwave communications equipment.

They blended into the snowscape, and from a distance, even in a light snowfall, they were practically invisible.

They spoke not a word, communicating only by hand. Yet their minds meshed as a steel-willed, highly trained fighting unit poised to destroy whoever, or whatever, lay in their path.

In the frozen wasteland of Russian Siberia where they had trained with their Russian allies, they had learned to move in frigid conditions that were foreign to their native tropical homeland along the southern Caribbean. In Siberia, in the polar regions near the Arctic Circle, they had become accustomed to the most frigid weather on the planet.

Freezing headwinds they had battled for the last hour had subsided. To take advantage of calmer conditions, they quickened their step to double-time.

Behind them, in the distance, howling gales formed a deep, haunting whistle, feigning the sound of a freight train from miles down the track. But here—in a place farther from civilization than any other place on earth—there were no trains. No railroad tracks, no roads, no major airports.

If a spot on earth resembled the outer planets of the solar system, the planets farthest from the sun, if a setting mimicked the landscape of Neptune or Pluto, that spot was Antarctica.

The rocks.

The ice.

The wind and snow.

This wasteland would seem to be God forsaken.

But God had not forsaken this place. For a thousand feet below their boots and under the thick layers of ice and snow, God had created something that could not be found on any other planet in the solar system.

Oceans of oil.

They marched on as the icy surface yielded to a snowy mix, and their boots crunched in the snow.

The snow started falling again, and soon became thick and heavy. When the south wind whipped into it, stinging ice from the ground and skies blew into their faces. They preferred these conditions. For under the cover of freezing gray clouds, the blizzard conditions allowed them to approach undetected.

There were twenty-five men. They would fight to advance the cause of socialism and to defend the tenets of the Bolivarian Revolution. They were commando units of the National Army of the Bolivarian Republic of Venezuela.

Their leader raised his hand and they stopped.

A hundred yards downrange, at the edge of their envelope of visibility, a narrow opening appeared in the curtain of falling snow. It appeared for a second, then disappeared behind another gust of snow. But when the wind shifted, they again saw the flag with the dark blue background that bore the red diagonal cross of Saint Patrick superimposed on the white diagonal cross of Saint Andrew and, superimposed over that, the red vertical cross of Saint George.

The Union Jack!

Base camp!

Lieutenant Javier Ortiz, second in command, stood still and allowed the goose bumps to crawl down his spine. If only Hugo Rafael Chávez were here for this moment.

For if Chávez was the father of Bolivarianism, Ortiz and his armed comrades were its sons. From the depths of an unimaginable deep freeze, they would launch the Bolivarian Revolution beyond the crystal warm waters of the Caribbean to every crevice on the face of the earth.

"Ready your weapons!" The field commander of the squadron, Major Placido Diaz, broke the silence.

Ortiz reached down, unzipped a side pouch, and extracted a thirty-round aluminum magazine. He popped the magazine into his assault rifle, then worked the slide, bringing the first bullet into the chamber.

It was time.

CHAPTER 4

British base camp
Camp Churchill
Antarctica

S till having connection problems, Leftenant?"

"Must be the storm," Leftenant Austin Rivers, SBS, Royal Navy, said. He edged the mouse over the Reload icon and clicked again.

Loading . . .

Buffering . . .

"I thought you Special Forces chaps were exempt from computer problems, unlike the rest of us poor commoners." The Royal Marine, Captain Timothy Dunn, a Scotsman, stood over Rivers' shoulder. Dunn wore his green Marine pullover sweater and sipped hot tea.

"Unfortunately, the computers they give us don't work as well as the rifles and rockets and knives. I had a chance last year to cross the pond and train in that exchange program with the Navy SEALs," Rivers said. "We Brits invented Special Forces, but the Americans get all the equipment that works. If I had known I would wind up in this frozen hellhole . . ." He lost his thought. "At least Skype works across the pond between London and Virginia Beach."

"Budget cuts," the Marine said. "Labour's members of Parliament are wasting money on socialist programs. Where's Lady Thatcher when you need her?"

"At this point I'd take Meryl Streep playing Lady Thatcher," Rivers said.

"I hear Miss Streep was a looker in her day," the captain said. "Word on the street is that SBS officers have a thing for blondes."

Rivers did not respond. He clicked Reload again.

London was three hours ahead of them. Rivers checked his watch. Soon Meg would put Little Aussie to bed. His time frame for chatting was slipping away unless this blasted computer experienced a quick resurrection from the frozen annals of galactic cyber-obscurity.

"Besides," the Marine continued, "who knew that British Petroleum would stumble on this top secret discovery?"

"You sure the discovery is still top secret?" Rivers quipped.

"Certainly," the captain said. "Downing Street needs chaps like you and me, highly trained assassins, to guard the booty on behalf of British multinationals before the cat escapes the bag."

Rivers snorted. His computer problems worsened, his screen resembling an electronic snowstorm. "Well, you can bet your bottom line, Captain, that if this were an American discovery, the American Navy would send more than two special-ops guys to babysit a bunch of egg-headed engineers."

"Cheer up, ole boy," the captain said. "The discovery occurred just last week. More SBS officers and more Royal Marines are on the way. The way I look at it"—another sip of tea—"you and I . . . we're pioneers on the ground in the tradition of Robert Falcon Scott."

"The Norwegians beat Scott to the South Pole."

"True," Dunn said. "But nobody remembers that part of the story. Besides, the Norwegians are hardly a problem anymore. And besides"— he set the teacup on the table beside the computer screen—"perhaps some of the tax revenue from the discovery will allow the government to purchase a computer that works so you can Skype with your son."

"Perhaps," Rivers said. "We shall see."

CHAPTER 5

Magnolia Flats
Kensington District
West London

7:00 p.m. local time

Meg Alexander had always wanted to live in Kensington. And with her modest salary from her job at the downtown London brokerage house where she worked as a secretary, combined with the child support she received from Austin, she could enjoy a comfortable, though not extravagant, life with her son in a small but cozy London flat.

Robert Austin Rivers Jr., affectionately known as "Aussie" or sometimes "Little Aussie," was the four-year-old love of Meg's life.

Their journey began five years ago at Boleyn Tavern Pub in central London.

From the moment the lad's father tapped her on the shoulder and asked to buy her a drink, electricity would sizzle late into the night. She should have declined his offer.

But she could not resist a man in a naval uniform. That weakness, combined with the once-in-a-lifetime opportunity to spend an evening with an SBS officer, the Royal Navy's equivalent to the US Navy SEALs, fulfilled the ultimate romantic fantasy for a woman attracted to Navy men.

The strapping warrior had disappeared from her bedroom before the sun rose the next morning. When she heard nothing from him for five days . . . and then a week . . . which turned into a month, her initial disappointment changed from heartbreak to a raging fury.

She had allowed herself to become a conquest in a long litany of conquests.

Two weeks later, these words from her physician ignited yet another wild swing in her emotional state.

"Congratulations, Miss Alexander. I am pleased to report that you are expecting."

Whether she kept the baby or not, he would never know. Why should he? The worthless pig undoubtedly had impregnated dozens of attractive young blondes.

"You cannot carry this baby," her girlfriend told her. "The expenses and the burden will mean you will have no life."

The Abortion Act in Britain allowed her to terminate the pregnancy within twenty-four weeks.

At three that same afternoon, nearly five years ago, on a rare sun-drenched day in London, Shelley had dropped her off on the sidewalk in front of the abortion clinic. "Wait here while I park the car. But I'll be with you through the whole procedure. It'll be a piece of cake. We'll hop through the pubs by this weekend," her friend had said with a smile.

In that moment, Meg counted her blessings. What wonderful friends she had.

As Shelley drove off to park the motorcar, a soft voice came from over her shoulder. "God loves you, my sister." Meg turned around, her back to the street. The elderly nun's black habit flowed to the sidewalk, almost swallowing her. Her beatific smile accentuated her eyes, which were blue as the noonday sky. Even her wrinkles seemed to glow. "And God loves that wee little one you are carrying too."

Her accent was more Irish than English. "Would ya mind if I give ya this?"

"Not at all, Sister." Meg reached down and took the pamphlet from the woman's veined hands. She opened it.

The color photograph stopped her. Entitled "Baby Samuel Reaching Out of the Womb," the photograph showed a twenty-one-week-old baby boy reaching his hand out of the womb and grabbing hold of the finger of the surgeon who was operating on him. "For more information, go to http://thornwalker.com/babyhand/babyhand.html."

"Oh, dear God!" She looked up. But the nun had disappeared, as if she had vanished from the planet.

"Are you ready to go in?" She turned and saw Shelley approaching along the sidewalk sporting a cheery smile and anxious eyes. "What's wrong, Meg?"

"I cannot go through with this." Meg's eyes darted about, searching for the mysterious nun who had vanished in the thin air of the sunny London afternoon.

"What happened to you?" Shelley tried to persuade her to go through with the abortion. But the photograph of the baby and the strange nun who had so mysteriously appeared and then vanished had changed everything.

Eight months later, after Aussie was born, she still had heard not a word from the roaming dog since that one-night stand that followed their encounter at the pub.

Then she experienced another surprising change of heart. Aussie had a father, even if he would never see him. The boy had a right to know. So did the father.

A friend's husband serving in the Royal Navy helped make the contact with the SBS officer named Austin Rivers, reputedly attached to a NATO unit in the Persian Gulf or the Middle East. No one knew for certain. Two days later, the phone rang. The international operator announced a call from Bahrain.

"I should have called," he said. He sounded sheepish. What he didn't say was that he wanted no committed relationship with any woman.

His coolness hurt. Even after all these months. Even after her seething anger at him had faded.

But as their conversation turned to their son, a softness came over his voice. He requested photographs. She scanned half a dozen and sent them by e-mail that night.

The next day, another international call came from Bahrain. The photos, he said, were identical to his baby pictures. He promised immediate support and requested wiring instructions, even before she could broach the subject. The next day, he wired fifteen hundred pounds into her account at Barclay's.

When he called the following day to confirm her receipt of the wire transfer, he asked her permission to start a relationship with the boy.

There would be logistical challenges, he pointed out. His military duties would take him away for long periods of time. But modern technology made the world smaller, and his desire to do right by Aussie began to soften the hatred she felt.

He became a face on the computer screen to their infant son, and by the time Aussie could walk, he looked forward to—sometimes, anyway—the face on the computer screen that would call his name and make silly noises and do anything it took to evoke a coo or a smile.

Meg found it amusing—watching this macho he-man of a warrior morph into a clown, cooing and whistling at Aussie on the Skype screen.

On the few occasions when he was in Britain, when he requested to see Aussie, she consented. The boy needed a father even if the father was far away and never around.

And now he was off to Antarctica. What an odd assignment. Why would a Special Forces commando be dispatched to the desolate ice scape of the South Pole? He never explained why. For that matter, he never explained anything.

Meg checked her watch. Fifteen minutes late. "Aussie, time for bed."

When she stood up from the small desk holding her laptop computer, she heard the familiar sound of the electronic ringtone of Skype. She checked the screen.

Austin Rivers calling . . . Accept . . . Decline.

She moved the cursor over the Accept button, clicked it, and his ruggedly handsome face with a broad smile appeared on the screen.

"Sorry I'm late. The weather is bloody harsh."

The screen went blank.

"Austin, can you hear me?"

He reappeared, his image frozen on the screen . . . then another flash.

"Are you there?" The screen unfroze. "I can see you," she said.

"We're having horrible blizzard conditions. It's affecting everything. Computers. Internet. A mess."

"I see you." The sight of his face still melted her like that first night in the pub. This infuriated her.

"I see you too. You look fantastic."

She stared at the grinning dog-of-a-hunk-of-a-man. As bad as she wanted to curse him out, that would do no good. "It's Aussie's bedtime.

But I can keep him up a bit longer. I wake him up early to drop him at day care on my way to work."

"Thank you, my dear," he said. "I won't be long. Just five minutes."

"Okay, give me a second." She got up and turned away. A second later, crackling and exploding sounds erupted from the computer. She turned around. Austin was gone. Only a blank wall on the screen.

"Hit the deck! Hit the deck!" More sounds from the computer. "We're under attack! Grab your rifles!" She didn't recognize that voice.

"Fire! Fire! Fire!" Voices mixed together.

"I see them! I see them! Take the ones on the left. I've got the three on the right!"

"Oh my—"

Smoke filled the image on the screen.

"Austin! Austin!" she screamed. The screen went black. "Austin!"

CHAPTER 6

Bar El Nochebuena
General Salvo 125
Región Providencia
Santiago, Chile

From a wrought-iron chair and table on the outdoor patio of the Bar El Nochebuena, the springtime afternoon sights and sounds and colors of Santiago's upper-crust Región Providencia, as if enhanced by the effects of the vintage pinot noir, were the perfect tonic for his much-needed respite from the sea.

Whenever he was ashore, Pete was a people watcher. And the vibrant scene along the sidewalk on General Salvo beat the heck out of the sight of 110 guys on a *Los Angeles*–class submarine.

When he took the first sip of the second glass, the view became outstanding.

Her beige sundress, hemmed a couple of inches above the knee, provided a nice visual contrast against her dark-complexioned tan. Her wavy brunette hair fell just to her shoulders. And when the breeze lit into her hair and blew some strands of it from the back of her neck over the front of her shoulder, he took a hearty second gulp of the wine. Suddenly he had forgotten his irresistible penchant for blondes.

"Peter!" The sound of his name from another female took his eyes from the brunette.

"Isabel!" He pushed up from the table.

Another brunette. A wide grin on her face. She walked up to him, opened her arms, hugged him, and gave him a kiss on the cheek. "It has been too long since you have been to Chile, Peter!"

"It's been way too long, my sweet cousin." He gazed down at her face. "Thanks for speaking English. My Spanish has gotten rusty."

"*¡No hay problema, mi primo!*" She gave him an affectionate pinch on the cheek.

"Very cute," he said. "How's Uncle Alberto?"

"Alberto's fine." She kept smiling. "He can't wait to see his favorite nephew. And how is Uncle Marvin?"

"Still in Dallas with your Aunt Judy. He's piddling around the house putting up all sorts of electronic gadgets and doing consulting work, although he's supposed to be retired. He works and travels a lot for a retired guy. Does a great job of carving Aunt Judy's Angus beef on the holidays."

That brought a twinkle to Isabel's eye. "I saw him last year when he came to Santiago for a visit. Uncle Marvin will never retire. Oh, pardon me," she said. "Maria, this is my cousin. Commander Pete Miranda, United States Navy." Isabel nodded to her left. As she said this, suddenly the leggy brunette in the beige sundress cropped above the knees was standing by his table.

The brunette spoke, accelerating his pulse. "Navy, huh?" She raised an eyebrow and extended her hand. "Hi. I'm Maria Vasquez."

"Pete Miranda." He took her hand. Instant electricity. "A pleasure, ma'am."

"Maria is my best friend," Isabel said. "She's visiting from Valparaiso. I invited her to have a drink with us if that's okay."

"Any friend of my favorite cousin is a friend of mine," Pete said. "Please. Sit down." He turned and saw the waiter lingering near another table. "Manuel. *Más vino, por favor.*"

"*Si, señor. Enseguida,*" the waiter said.

"Your Spanish isn't so rusty." The hot-looking brunette waited for Pete to get a chair for her and then sat next to him at the round table.

"I wouldn't have to say much more to embarrass myself," Pete said.

"My cousin is too modest," Isabel said. "When Uncle Marvin went to school in the US at Cal-Berkeley all those years ago, he got distracted by this hot redhead, who turned out to be my Aunt Judy. They were the perfect international couple. A red-blooded Chilean macho-man, with a penchant for business and engineering, who spoke little English when he got to America, and a beautiful New England prep girl with an uncanny God-given ability for art. My favorite cousins, Pete and John, grew up in North Carolina and Texas, so we got to visit the US, but not enough. Only on special occasions."

"Special occasions?" Maria nodded and said "*gracias*" as the waiter brought her wine. "And what special occasion brings you to Santiago, Peter?"

"Pete." That's when he saw it. On her calf. The small butterfly tattoo was green, yellow, and orange.

"Excuse me?"

"You can call me anything you want," Pete said. "But my friends call me Pete."

"Suppose I throw a little Spanglish at you?" The brunette winked at him, then took a first sip. "I could call you Pedro and order my wine in English."

"She's funny, Cousin Isabel." Pete glanced at Maria. "Where did you find her?"

"I thought you two might hit it off." Isabel smiled. "Anyway, the lady asked you a question."

Pete smiled and looked back at Maria. "First, you can speak to me in Spanish or any other language you choose to use, just as long as you speak to me. Second, you can call me Pedro or anything else you want to call me, just as long as you call."

"He's even smoother than you said, Isabel. But he still did not answer my question."

"You have him so mesmerized, he's forgotten the question." Isabel chuckled.

"I am insulted, my cousin. A sub commander is trained to keep track of multiple targets at once."

"Targets!" Maria laughed. "That's how you view women?"

"Let me backtrack," Pete said. "My cousin is *not* a target."

"Peter Charles Miranda," Isabel scoffed.

"Pedro Carlos Miranda!" Maria said.

"Okay. Okay. Just a little fun-filled play on words." A sip of red wine. "The lady asked why I am in Chile." He looked at Maria. "To answer your question, I am here on a military assignment."

"Military assignment?" The flirtatious look on Maria's face became a contorted twist.

"You don't like the military?" Pete asked.

Isabel spoke up. "What is the old saying in English? Opposites attract?"

"Oh really?" Pete said. "She's not one of those Allende-Bachalet disciples, is she?"

"What's your problem with Allende and Bachalet?" Maria asked.

"Other than the fact that they're socialists who stole private property, and other than the fact that Allende stole land from my great-grandfather, I have no problem with them at all. So what's your problem with the military?"

A fiery glare from Maria. "Other than the fact that the governments of the earth waste trillions on guns and weapons and airplanes and ships rather than spend money to eradicate poverty, I have no problem with the international military-industrial complex."

"You know," Pete said, "I met a violinist back at the hotel. He's available for hire if that would help."

"Children, children," Isabel said. "Why don't we enjoy our wine and change the subject."

Pete didn't respond.

Neither did Maria, at least at first. Then she said, "So, Pete, Isabel tells me your mom is a fabulous landscape artist."

"Yes, she's wonderful. She paints Chilean landscapes. My favorite is an oil painting of Cape Horn that she gave me." His cell phone rang. *US Embassy Santiago.*

"Pardon me, ladies." He stepped away from the table, moving out of earshot. "This is Commander Miranda."

"Commander, this is Captain McKinley, the naval attaché at our embassy here in Santiago."

"Good afternoon, Captain. How may I serve you, sir?"

"Commander, sorry to cut your leave short, but something's come up. The Chileans have asked that you report to Valparaiso tomorrow at 0700 to begin working with the crew of the *Miro*. Report to the embassy ASAP and I'll brief you."

"How soon do you need me, Captain?"

"Within the hour."

Pete checked his watch. "Aye, Captain. Just gotta close out my tab and get moving."

"Very well. Get here as soon as you can, Pete."

"Aye, sir."

Pocketing his phone, Pete returned to the table. "Ladies, my apologies. I am very much enjoying your company. But duty calls. They've ordered me to report before I'd anticipated." He locked eyes with Maria. Had he seen disappointment on her face? Probably his imagination.

"Where are they going to have you working while you're in Chile?" Maria asked. "Or is this a closely guarded state secret?"

"I can't say what I'll be doing. But I can say I'll be home ported in Valparaiso."

"Valparaiso?"

"Yes. Chile's largest naval base. I start tomorrow morning."

"I live in Valparaiso. You will love it. But be forewarned. You know that Allende grew up in Valparaiso?"

"So did Pinochet, if I recall."

"Hmm." She allowed a soft smile. "You haven't forgotten your father's homeland, have you?"

"Despite my deceiving accent, my father taught me well." His heartbeat accelerated. Should he? Or shouldn't he? "Well then. Since you're going to be in Valparaiso, and since I'll be there when I'm not at sea, maybe we should continue this discussion there."

Cousin Isabel looked down and smiled.

Maria batted those big brown eyes. "Are you asking me out, Commander Miranda?"

"Maybe." He smiled. "Or maybe I'm looking for an opportunity to deprogram a hopeless idealistic damsel in distress who's been brainwashed by the socialists."

"Oh? Maybe it's the right-wing Yankee military guy who needs deprogramming."

"Texans aren't Yankees," he shot back. "But if I'm going to save you from socialism and, on top of that, teach you about the Mason-Dixon Line in the United States, I'm gonna need your number. What do you say?"

"What do you think, Isabel?" Maria said. "Should I trust your cousin with my number?" A suppressed grin. "Is he dangerous?"

Isabel laughed. "Let me put it this way. If I catch wind that he is ungentlemanly in the slightest bit, I'll tell his mother. He'll have Aunt Judy to deal with, and you and I won't have to worry about killing him."

Pete laughed. "My cousin knows my mother still has my best interests at heart, which means I must always behave myself."

Maria smiled. "Okay. As long as we know Aunt Judy will be there to keep your cousin Pedro in line"—she pulled out a business card—"although I may be placing my life in his hands." She began writing on the card. "Perhaps I could make an exception against my better instincts in this case, since your cousin seems to need to be indoctrinated some more." She handed the card to Pete. "Here you are, Commander Miranda. Use this wisely."

"I look forward to my indoctrination."

CHAPTER 7

Operations center
British Embassy
Avda. El Bosque Norte 0125
Las Condes
Santiago, Chile

The British Embassy in Santiago, located at the corner of Avenue El Bosque Norte and Don Carlos Avenue in the Las Condes commune of Santiago province, sat draped in the shadows of the breathtaking snowcapped Andes mountain range. Las Condes became home to many elite political leaders of Chile, including former presidents Michelle Bachalet, Salvador Allende, and Augusto Pinochet, and remained an upscale residential section to high-income families and the country's economic elite.

Long before the establishment of the embassy, the warm ties between Britain and Chile dated all the way back to the Chilean War of Independence that ended in 1826. Their common enemy—Spain.

The British hated the Spanish.

So did the Chileans.

Spain wanted to maintain her colonial dominance over Chile. The Chileans wanted independence.

Spain also wanted to be the dominant colonial power in the world. So did Britain.

The British fleet defeated the Spanish and French fleets in the decisive Battle of Trafalgar in 1805, and the bad blood between the countries festered.

Argentina, a former Spanish colony, emerged as a common enemy of both Britain and Chile because of her ties to Spain. When Argentina attacked the Falkland Islands, 156 years after the Chilean revolution, the common anti-Spanish heritage of the two nations led to Chilean support of the British in the Falklands War.

In keeping with the British-Chilean military alliance, Royal Navy Commander John Gordon, of the prestigious and elite SBS, had arrived at his new station as a military and political officer at the British Embassy in Santiago.

Yet Chile, despite her ties with Britain, was not a typical destination assignment for Special Forces commandos like Commander Gordon.

But these were not ordinary times.

The discovery by British petro-engineers of vast reservoirs of crude below the icy surfaces in Antarctica sent Downing Street scrambling to shore up military security to protect the British Antarctic stations. Most members of the Royal Navy's elite SBS forces were being deployed to various parts of the world in the war on terror—to places like Pakistan, Afghanistan, Israel, Egypt, and on ships cruising the Mediterranean and the Persian Gulf.

The massive discovery had British petro-engineers believing that the nation first staking claim to it could become the richest in the world. For Britain, that meant not only a return to international relevance not known since before World War I but a return to economic and military superpower status.

And so the secret military objective, code named "Black Ice," would shore up defenses in a desolate spot of ice not far from the South Pole on an isolated and oft-forgotten continent.

Commander Gordon, operating from the British Embassy in Santiago, would monitor and command the military buildup surrounding "Camp Churchill," which remained in its infancy stage.

Fifteen hundred miles to the south of Santiago, at the southernmost tip of South America, Chile had allowed Britain to use its Puerto Williams naval base as a staging area to move forces into Antarctica to reinforce Camp Churchill.

Gordon glanced up at the map of Chile and wished he had more time.

Puerto Williams was a few miles north of Cape Horn. And from Cape Horn, five hundred miles of the raging waters of Drake Passage separated the tip of South America from the South Shetland Islands along the coast of Antarctica.

Gordon looked up at the map of the bottom of the world.

The map reinforced the importance of Chile as a British ally. Just 500 miles separated Chile from Antarctica, in contrast with the 3,800 miles separating Antarctica from Cape Agulhas, the southernmost point in Africa, and the 4,000 miles from Antarctica to Wilson's Promontory, the southernmost tip of Australia.

This short distance gave Britain and Chile a strategic advantage in reaching Antarctica over the other powers of the world with the exception of Argentina, whose southern tip was nearly as close to Antarctica as Chile's.

The discovery of oil, which had occurred on Antarctic tundra claimed by both nations, gave Chile and Britain a chance to cooperate in a win-win that could again make Britain the most dominant nation in Europe and Chile a South American superpower.

But one problem remained.

Argentina.

For if Antarctica geographically resembled a pie, then Chile, Britain, and Argentina claimed overlapping slices of that pie. But that piece of the pie was not large enough to be sliced three ways.

For practical purposes, His Majesty's government had seen fit to bring its allies in Santiago in on the discovery.

The first officer on the ground, Leftenant Austin Rivers, under Gordon's direct immediate command and one of the finest SBS officers in the Royal Navy, was a warrior's warrior. But he was one man.

Commander Gordon needed more ground forces—and fast. So far, the darkness in Antarctica had been Britain's ally. But with darkness peeling back each day and giving way to more sunlight, soon the discovery would be visible to observation planes and satellites.

Commander Gordon, as he sipped his afternoon tea while battling knots in the pit of his stomach, perused communiqués from SBS commanders in Afghanistan and Kuwait.

Special Forces Command would not pull the SBS squadron from Afghanistan until reinforcements arrived in full strength in Kabul. That could take up to a week or even more. A few commandos might fly down early. But with the spring season coming on and the rapid pace at which the days were getting longer, this was a race against the clock.

Gordon needed to get enough Special Forces on-site to avoid sabotage by Argentina, Venezuela, or anyone else who might become greedy enough to set sights on the booty.

Now he could only wait. Perhaps he would venture out for some grub. Gordon checked his watch. "Captain Jefferies, you've got the con. I'm going to step out for some fresh air."

"Aye, sir," the Royal Marine officer said.

"I should be back around seventeen hundred."

"Enjoy your break, sir. We'll keep things chugging along until you return."

Gordon stepped out of the basement, where military operations had temporarily been established, and climbed the staircase leading to the main floor of the embassy.

Scattered nearby were a number of restaurants and bars along El Bosque Norte. Gordon stepped onto the sidewalk in front of the embassy when his cell phone rang. Caller ID revealed the caller: *British Embassy Santiago*. "Commander Gordon speaking."

"Sir, Captain Jefferies here. I apologize for interrupting your dinner hour, but we have an urgent matter."

"What is it, Jefferies?"

"Sir, we've received a FLASH message from Camp Churchill." A pause. "They are under attack."

"Under attack? By who?"

"Unable to determine at this time, sir. Their message broke up, incomplete."

"Open a channel to London, Captain. I'll be right there."

CHAPTER 8

Bar El Nochebuena
General Salvo 125
Región Providencia
Santiago, Chile

The sun dipped lower in the afternoon sky but was not yet ready to surrender to the western horizon.

Maria loved this time of day at this time of year. For now, in the middle of October, the sun set close to eight in Santiago, casting orangish horizontal sun rays with an idyllic glow on the outdoor balcony. A few patrons lingered still. The sun and the light breeze rolling down from the Andes created an atmosphere of late-day relaxation.

Maria stirred her margarita with her straw and let her heart and mind swish with the drink. She brought the drink to her lips for a refreshing swallow. *Aaah*. The swig down her throat left a warm trail. A refreshing gust cascading down from the snowcapped Andes gave her a burst of inner confidence.

Isabel had not returned from the ladies' room. And so far, the conversation had remained focused on shopping and the Santiago nightlife. She had avoided any hint that she had felt an instant chemistry or electricity with Isabel's conservative and boneheaded but charming and good-looking cousin.

Should she broach the subject? Surely a casual reference disguised as an offhanded remark might seem natural without Isabel getting too suspicious. Plus, it might elicit some additional information to satisfy what had become a growing curiosity for the last hour or so.

"Juan-Carlos?"

"Yes, *señorita?*"

"One more, please."

"*Si, señorita.* And your friend?"

"I don't know. She's in the *baño*. You can ask her when she returns."

"Certainly, *señorita.*"

The bartender stepped over to the bar.

Maria let her mind wander. What would it be like to be part of the Miranda family? To be related, even by marriage, to her best friend? Even after all these years, it amazed her that she and Isabel had not only remained friends but remained so close. They could not have been more different.

Yes, they both enjoyed the finer things of life. Shopping. Movies. Travel. Vacations. Books. But they remained political opposites. A socialist and a conservative. Some called them the political odd couple.

She decided that yes, she would broach the subject of Isabel's rugged half-Texan, half-Chilean good-looking stud of a cousin. She looked up and saw Isabel strolling across the patio, bearing a wide smile. "I thought you got lost in the powder room."

"I'm sorry," Isabel said. "I bumped into this cute guy I met at work." She pulled up a chair and sat. "You know how that can be."

"Oh yes, do I ever," Maria confessed.

"Welcome back, *señorita.*" Juan-Carlos walked up with the margarita.

"You ordered another one?" Isabel asked.

"Trying to muster my courage."

"Would you care for another, *señorita?*" Juan-Carlos directed his question to Isabel.

"Oh, go ahead, Isabel," Maria said. "I'm paying."

"Are you paying for the cab too?"

"Absolutely," Maria said. "Bring her another one, Juan-Carlos."

"*Si, señorita.*"

"Drink up, Sister Isabel. Maybe you'll get the courage to go back over there and ask the cute guy from work to join us."

Isabel laughed. "And speaking of cute guys, I note that you've been suspiciously silent on the topic since my cousin had to leave."

Maria gulped.

"What's this?" Isabel pressed. "Do I detect blushing from my socialist-liberal friend? Perhaps a tinge of speechlessness?"

"Your margarita, *señorita*."

"How did you do that so fast, Juan-Carlos?"

"I cannot take credit," he said. "I took the liberty of ordering yours when *Señorita* Maria ordered hers."

"You're amazing, Juan-Carlos," Isabel said.

"My pleasure, *señorita*."

"And you!" Isabel took a sip and directed her brown eyes at Maria. "You are still blushing."

"Well"—Maria pulled herself to her fullest height—"I don't know what you're talking about."

"Lying communist scumbag!" Isabel declared.

"Aah! Promoted from socialist to communist?"

"I've promoted you to scumbag!"

They stared at each other, and then Maria burst out laughing, and Isabel joined her.

"You do know me, don't you?" Maria chuckled.

"Yes, I know you. Now tell the truth. I touched a nerve, didn't I?"

They sat back and giggled.

"Okay, okay," Maria said. "I confess. I didn't want to come out and say I think your cousin is hot! I mean, a girl has to keep some things to herself. Doesn't she?"

"Not from her best friend!"

"Ordinarily I'd agree," Maria said, "but when the dirty little secret is that the best friend's first cousin makes a girl's heart flutter . . . I mean, even you've got to admit that could make for an awkward conversation."

"Why do you think I brought you here? I had a sneaky feeling, knowing the two of you, that a little sparked political discussion might ignite a few other sparks. You know. The magnetic-type sparks."

Maria smiled and held up her glass. "To magnetic sparks."

Isabel clanged her glass against Maria's. "To wildly magnetic and mutual sparks!"

"I'll drink to that. So, what do you think? You know your cousin better than I do. Do you think any of those sparks might have been mutual?"

"Well, put it this way, Peter plays a cool hand and shows a good poker face—as I suppose a good sub commander should. But in this case, I have a feeling that maybe—"

Beeping came from inside Maria's purse.

"Saved by the bell." Isabel smiled and concentrated on her margarita.

"Hang on a second." Maria uncovered her phone. "Oh . . . that's odd . . ." Her heart thumped.

"It's him, isn't it?" Isabel grinned.

"I don't know. Just a number. What should I do?"

"Answer it. Find out!"

She punched the Accept button.

"Hello."

"Maria?"

"Yes."

"Pete Miranda."

"Oh, hi, Pete." *Please don't let him suspect I'm about to faint.*

"I told you if you gave me your number, I just might use it."

She fanned her face. "Well . . . uh . . . I'm glad you did."

"Anyway, I enjoyed meeting you."

"It was nice meeting you too."

"I know this is short notice, but you said you're from Valparaiso, right?"

"That's right."

"Uh . . . I've got to drive down there, and I hoped you might like to ride with me. I could use the company, and I'll take you straight to your apartment and promise to be good."

"Aah . . ." What to say, what to say. "Today?"

"If you can't, I understand."

"Aah. What time?"

"Could you be ready in an hour?"

Maria looked at her watch. This was beyond crazy. But delightfully exciting. "Aah . . . sure. Pick me up at Isabel's in an hour."

Isabel's eyes widened.

"Great. We'll have fun. See you then."

"Okay. Bye."

The line cut.

"What?" Isabel put down her drink.

"He wants me to ride down to Valparaiso with him."

"Really? When?"

"Now."

Isabel squealed with delight. "My cousin. The swashbuckling naval officer! I knew it!"

This was all a blur. What to do?

"Juan-Carlos." Isabel raised her hand to summon the waiter.

"Si, senorita?"

"The check, please. My friend has a hot date in an hour, and we must hurry."

"Si, senorita. With pleasure."

CHAPTER 9

Magnolia Flats
Kensington District
West London

Her stomach felt like a cold, wet towel twisting into a tight knot. Her legs were limp as spaghetti, her forehead clammy cool. A perspiration line beaded under her hairline. Meg wanted to vomit.

Four times she tried to reestablish communication with Austin through Skype.

Nothing.

The calls self-terminated after two rings.

What should she do? Who should she call?

Shelley.

She punched Shelley's number.

Three rings. Voice mail.

"Shelley. It's Meg. Call me. Something's wrong. I was on Skype with Austin and someone attacked his duty station. Maybe terrorists. I don't know. Please call." She hung up.

Who to call? Who could help? The constable. She conducted a quick Google search and checked the results: Kensington Police Station: 72 Earls Court Rd, Kensington, London W8 6EQ T: 03001231212.

As she dialed the number, another call came through.

Shelley.

Thank God. "Shelley! Did you get my message?"

"Yes. You sound awful. What happened, Meg?"

"Austin and I were on Skype. He called like he does before Aussie's bedtime. I was going to get Aussie, and all of a sudden I hear what sounds like gunshots and there's smoke and . . . hang on"—she reached over for a tissue to dab her eyes—"and he was gone."

"Okay, listen. Get hold of yourself, Meg. There must be an explanation. Perhaps a drill or something. You know these military types. Always practicing with their guns."

"No, you don't understand," Meg said. "I heard them say they were under attack before the transmission dropped. I heard Austin giving firing instructions, maybe to the Royal Marine who is down there with him. This could not have been a drill. There aren't soldiers or sailors down there. Austin and the Marine are on some sort of guard duty. That's all I know."

"Oh. Let's think." A pause. "We should report this to the authorities."

"I was dialing the constable's office when you called," Meg said.

"I don't think the constable could help. This is a military matter. Although I suppose it couldn't hurt to alert the constable."

"Maybe. But who in the military? The Royal Navy?"

"I think the Defence Ministry. They're over the Royal Navy and the Royal Army. They should know what to do. Why don't you Google their number and call them, and I'll call the Kensington police. Then I'm coming over."

"You are so good. I love you."

She sat down at the computer and typed in a search for the Royal Defence Ministry. She punched in the number and held the iPhone to her ear.

Two rings.

"Ministry of Defence. Commander Haith speaking."

"Yes. This is Meg Alexander in Kensington. I'd like to report what I think is a terrorist attack against British forces."

"Did I understand you to say a terrorist attack against His Majesty's military forces?"

"Yes, Commander. That is what I said."

"And where did this attack take place?"

"Antarctica. The attack took place in Antarctica."

CHAPTER 10

British base camp
Camp Churchill
Antarctica

E verybody stay down!" Rivers said.

Staying low to avoid the direct line of fire from outside, he edged close to the shot-out window of the geodesic dome, which served as base camp headquarters for the British contingency.

On the floor of the dome, eight British petro-engineers lay face-down, their hands covering the backs of their heads.

Four enemy commandos were sprawled out on the floor, each with at least one bullet in the head. The four had blown open the front door with a grenade and charged into the dome.

But once inside, their fate had turned unlucky. Rivers picked off three of them, and his Royal Marine colleague, Captain Dunn, shot the fourth.

The unexpected lick of fire that he and Dunn had poured on the four chaps had deterred the other invaders, at least for a while. But Rivers suspected they were surrounded and greatly outnumbered.

"Captain Dunn, stay low. See if you can check their identification."

"Yes, sir."

Rivers peeked out the corner of the window, then ducked back down. Riflemen were taking their positions outside the dome. It looked to be an Alamo-type situation unfolding out on the tundra. Not even

Davey Crockett and Jim Bowie could hold up being outgunned ten to one. Rivers figured whoever these chaps were, they spoke the same language that Santa Anna had spoken all those years ago.

"Spanish ID cards, Leftenant," Dunn said. "Trying to make out their origin."

"Attention! You! Inside the dome!" The voice boomed over a megaphone in a rich Spanish accent.

"Stay back," Rivers said. "Be ready to fire, Captain Dunn."

"Yes, sir."

"You are surrounded by special forces of the Bolivarian Republic of Venezuela. You are outnumbered. Come out and surrender. Lay down your weapons and you will be granted clemency."

"Venezuela," Rivers said. "I should have known."

"Your situation is hopeless. There are more than fifty of us. You are surrounded."

Cold blasts of air blew in through the shot-out windows. Rivers crouched with his rifle low and just to the right of the bay window. Dunn crouched on the opposite side.

"Dunn. Slip around to the back and have a look. Let's make sure this chap is not blowing smoke."

"Yes, sir."

Rivers took account of his situation. Could they hold out until reinforcements arrived? He had weapons in the dome, but only two Special Forces commandos, including himself. The ten petro-engineers still lying facedown could potentially handle a rifle. But giving a rifle to untrained civilians, especially British civilians having grown up where firearms are banned, could prove disastrous. One was a Royal Army veteran. But the rest? Small, scrawny men. Engineers. Eggheads.

Two looked up at him, fear in their eyes. Macho he-men they were not. Arming them could prove disastrous. A wild shot. They could get hurt.

"Leftenant," Dunn said, "the chap is not exaggerating. We're surrounded. Armed men all around the back."

"I suspected that," Rivers said.

"Attention! You! Inside the dome! You have five minutes to surrender! If you do not, you will be killed!"

Westminster Bridge
crossing the River Thames
London

The black Jaguar XJ X308 rolled over the Westminster Bridge going north. The waters of the River Thames sported a grayish hue. Raindrops pelted the surface of the river. Off to the left, the gothic tower of Big Ben and the Palace of Westminster with the Houses of Parliament loomed as dual watchmen over the great river and the great city.

The sleek motorcar rolled from the green archway bridge onto the north shore, passing Big Ben, and turned right onto Whitehall, heading east, the street paralleling the river.

The Jaguar slowed, then stopped on Whitehall. The passenger sitting in the backseat waved at the few gawkers standing on the sidewalk under umbrellas.

As the Jaguar slowly moved forward again, London constables and His Majesty's security officers rolled back the black iron double gates, affording access to the street beyond. Armed riflemen of the Royal Marines flanked the constables, stepping between the Jaguar and the members of the public who were braving the rain—in the right place at the right time to catch a glimpse of the VIP.

The Jaguar turned left off of Whitehall onto another small street that resembled a concrete alleyway sandwiched between two large stone buildings.

On the building to the left, at the corner of Whitehall and the alley, a small inconspicuous sign identified the alleyway:

Downing Street SW1
City of Westminster

As the motorcar moved onto Downing Street, the passenger glanced back. The constables were securing the iron gates. The pedestrians gathered outside, shielded by umbrellas, were looking in and pointing. Word spread quickly along the street about activity at the gate, but most caught only a glimpse of the Jaguar's taillights.

Half a block down the alley, the Jaguar pulled over to the right and stopped in front of a large three-story brick building.

The building was unimpressive. The bricks on the facade were painted a dull chimney black. A tall-hatted constable stood guard next to the black door in the middle of the building. On the door, painted in white, was the number "10." There was no doorknob.

This incredibly plain-looking building resembled an upper-grade warehouse. Yet this brick monstrosity in the middle of a two-block gated alleyway was the second most famous residence in all of Britain, surpassed only by Buckingham Palace.

For 10 Downing Street, referred to by the British simply as "Number 10," served as headquarters of His Majesty's government and as the official residence and office of the First Lord of the Treasury, an office held by the prime minister.

A constable holding an umbrella opened the back door of the Jaguar. "Good afternoon, Prime Minister."

"Good afternoon, Charles," Prime Minister David Mulvaney said.

"Umbrella, sir?"

"No, thank you, Charles. It's not raining that bad."

"Very well, sir," the constable said as the newly elected British prime minister stepped out of the sleek armored vehicle and onto the cobblestone street into the light drizzle.

The prime minister walked swiftly to the famous black door as flashes of camera and strobe lights erupted outside the iron gates at both ends of Downing from tourists and members of the press with telephoto lenses trying to capture a photographic glimpse for the morning's papers and the many blog sites.

Mulvaney threw a smiling wave in both directions and stepped onto the single white stone step leading to the modest brick front.

"Welcome home, sir," the constable guarding the famous door said. Another constable opened the door from the inside.

"Good to be home, gentlemen," Mulvaney said as he walked in. He removed his jacket and handed it to a cloakman. Another "Welcome home, Prime Minister" from a voice he recognized all too well, the voice of his chief of staff. The right honourable Edward Willingham had served as lord mayor of Cardiff before Mulvaney tapped him for the prestigious position of principal adviser to the prime minister.

"How was Brussels and the EU summit, sir?" Willingham, in his classic white button-down shirt and red bowtie, approached in a quick-step across the black-and-white checkered marble floor in the entryway.

"Too bloody long, Edward," Mulvaney quipped. "These EU types are bound and determined to drag Britain into their little German-run kingdom. I look forward to my brandy after putting up with two full days of Chancellor Schmidt."

"Yes, well, I'm sorry to bother you on your return, but we've got a hot item on the front burner, Prime Minister."

"A hot item?" The two men walked in lockstep past the base of the grand staircase. "What is so urgent?"

"Sir, we've gotten an urgent message from Camp Churchill."

"Camp Churchill? In the Antarctic?"

They turned left, passed two Corinthian columns, and walked into the cabinet room.

A steward in a tuxedo said, "Brandy, sir?"

"Yes," Mulvaney said. "And bring one for Mister Willingham as well."

"Yes, sir." The steward nodded and left the room.

"Don't tell me, Edward, that the Black Ice project has leaked out beyond us and the Chileans."

"Worse than that, Prime Minister. Our contingent at Camp Churchill has been attacked."

After knocking on the door, the steward returned with a full bottle of cognac and two crystal glasses three-quarters full.

"Thank you," Mulvaney said. "Set the tray on the table. That will be all, George."

"Yes, sir."

Mulvaney waited until the steward left the cabinet room and closed the door. "Are you telling me our base camp has been attacked? A military attack?"

"Yes, sir," Willingham said. "That appears to be the case."

The prime minister sat on the edge of the conference table. "What happened? Who? Casualties?"

"It's not clear at this point, Prime Minister. Our military attaché at our Santiago embassy received a FLASH message from base camp. They appeared to be under attack by ground forces. Then they lost all transmissions. That's all we know."

"That's it?" Mulvaney said. "Someone attacked the station by ground, and we've lost communication? And we don't know who?"

"That's all we have, sir, except for one other piece of information."

"Let's hear it, Edward."

"A woman here in London, a young secretary named Meg Alexander, called the Defence Ministry earlier today. She said she was having a Skype conversation with an SBS officer assigned to Camp Churchill. Then he disappeared. Must have ducked down. She heard gunshots, heard them say they were under attack. Saw smoke in the room. Then they lost connection."

Mulvaney took a swig of cognac. "This Miss . . . Abernathy—"

"Alexander, sir."

"Alexander . . . is here in London, Skyping one of our SBS officers, and he's in Antarctica, and they are talking live at the time of the attack?"

"Yes, Prime Minister. That is our understanding."

"And how credible is this Miss Alexander?"

"Good question, Prime Minister. Her story corroborates the broken message that our embassy in Santiago received from Camp Churchill. And the Royal Navy confirms that the SBS officer, a Leftenant Austin Rivers, pays child support to the lady for their son."

"And this Miss Alexander gave us no clue about who these attackers were?"

"No, Prime Minister. She said she heard gunshots. Someone yelled they were under attack. Someone then yelled, 'Fire!' She heard Rivers giving instructions for the Royal Marine to take the one on the left, and that he . . . the SBS officer . . . would take the ones on the right. After that, she said smoke appeared on the screen and then it all went black."

"Any indication whether Miss Alexander knew the purpose of her boyfriend's mission?"

The chief of staff took a swig of cognac. "No, we don't believe so. Miss Alexander knew only his location. She was distraught that her son's father was in danger."

"Hmm. That's understandable." Mulvaney had been in office less than a month when he received a top secret report on the discovery of oil reserves—massive reserves—in the Antarctic by British Petroleum petro-engineers. Not even the king knew. Yet. "We must identify the attackers, ensure that our people are safe, and retake Camp Churchill."

"Agreed, sir."

"Don't we have two flotillas of Royal Marines and a contingent of SBS forces en route?"

"Correct, Prime Minister," Willingham said. "Both the chief of the defence staff and the defence minister are on their way to Number 10 to brief you on the military situation and discuss our options."

Mulvaney crossed his arms, turned, and gazed up at a full-length oil painting of Lady Margaret Thatcher that hung on the wall of the cabinet room. How would the Iron Lady respond to this? What would Sir Winston do? He turned around. "You know, Edward, it's far too early in this administration to be confronted by an international crisis of this magnitude."

"I suppose that's true, sir. On the other hand, Sir Winston not only faced an international crisis early in his ministry but he inherited one."

Mulvaney nodded. "Yes, of course, Edward. You always have a way of putting things in perspective. That's why I appointed you to this position."

"Thank you, sir."

"I must inform His Majesty. It would be a disaster for him to learn of this from the press."

"Yes, sir."

"Edward, notify Buckingham Palace to be on standby. Please have them inform His Majesty that his prime minister wishes to pay him a courtesy call later this evening, after our briefing from the defence minister and the chief of the defence staff."

"By all means, Prime Minister."

CHAPTER 11

Geodesic dome
British base camp
Camp Churchill
Antarctica

You have one minute to surrender or we will open fire."

"Somehow, I don't think this chap is fooling around," Dunn said.

"Neither do I, Captain," Rivers said. "Neither do I."

"If we commence firing, we can pick a few off and even out the numbers."

"That's tempting. Bring the odds down from ten-to-one to five-to-one."

"I'm game if you are, sir," Dunn said.

"Leftenant, I can handle a gun," one of the engineers said.

"Leftenant, please," another chimed in. "My wife and two daughters. They're in Southampton. Please. I . . ."

"I have a wife and children. My son needs me," an engineer said.

Another said, "There's no point in being rash about this. Perhaps we could negotiate a temporary solution."

"All right! Let me think!" Rivers snapped.

"Inside the dome! You have thirty seconds!"

"Captain Dunn, while I'd like to pick off every one of those savages, we cannot sacrifice civilians." He glanced at Dunn. "So here's our plan. One by one, whoever wants to leave, you will put your hands on your head and walk outside. Walk straight to the enemy and make sure you keep your hands up.

"Jones." He looked at the engineer who had mentioned his wife and two daughters in Southampton. "You will go first. After I call out to these savages, I want you to get up, hands over your head, and walk out."

"Yes, Leftenant."

"Gaylord. You mentioned your wife and children. You'll be second."

"Yes, sir."

"Be ready, Jones."

"I'm ready."

"To the commander of the Bolivarian special forces unit!" Rivers yelled out the shattered window. "This is the military commander of the British Scientific Research Unit here at Camp Churchill. Hold your fire. We will exit the facility one by one."

Silence.

"To the military commander of the British Scientific Research Unit. You are now in the custody of the Army of the Bolivarian Republic of Venezuela. Send the prisoners out one by one. Your hands are to remain high above your heads."

"Okay, men. Put on your winter gear. Jones, you're first. Stand up, hands over your head, and walk out. Gaylord. You're next."

"Yes, Leftenant," Jones said.

"Hold your fire! We're coming out," Rivers yelled as Jones hurriedly donned his winter gear. "Okay, Jones. Remember. I've got you covered. Keep your hands high, walk slowly. Nothing provocative."

Jones walked out slowly. Rivers aimed his rifle out the broken window, his mind on his son. He wondered if he would ever see Little Aussie again.

CHAPTER 12

British base camp
Camp Churchill
Antarctica

S ome were on the ground, lying in the snow, their rifles aimed at the dome.

Some were perched behind two storage tanks and several large rocks.

Lieutenant Javier Ortiz, second in command of the Venezuelan-Bolivarian Special Forces commandos, had taken cover behind a sandbag berm straight out in front of the dome.

He trained his rifle on the front door, resting his finger on the trigger.

These Brits may have promised to surrender, but Ortiz had never met a Brit he could trust. Plus, the preliminary intelligence intercepted from Belgrano Base indicated that some Special Forces commandos, most likely SBS, were already in position and were awaiting reinforcements. This explained why they had lost four of their best men. He had been against storming the dome.

Major Placido Diaz's stupid and suicidal order had proven disastrous. "Our first wave will burst in and surprise them before they have had a chance to react," Diaz had argued. "We will capture them using the element of surprise without firing a shot."

The plan had not set well with Ortiz, knowing that SBS officers might be on the premises. Ortiz had favored surrounding the dome and then demanding the surrender of the British.

But Major Diaz would hear none of it. "If we delay, they will dig in and wait for reinforcements. Time and surprise are of the essence."

At one level, Diaz's argument made sense. But surprising an SBS officer could prove risky. Like stepping on a rattlesnake.

And the four men at the tip of the spear had run into a buzz saw.

Ortiz adjusted his rifle and took a deep breath. Tensions were hair-trigger high.

Movement inside the dome.

A figure stepped out into the snow. A Brit, his hands high over his head, walked forward slowly. Two steps. Three. Four. "Don't shoot!" the man cried out, shuffling forward through the snow.

Ortiz drew a hard bead right on the center of the Brit's chest. One false move . . .

"Okay, get him!" Major Diaz shouted.

Two soldiers walked to the prisoner. The sergeant kept his rifle trained on the prisoner while the corporal handcuffed him and led him behind the perimeter where one of the men held him at gunpoint.

Several seconds passed.

A second Brit emerged from the dome. This one too stepped out with his hands up. He walked with a nervous gait, sort of twitching as he walked. Something seemed odd.

Shots rang out!

A smoke burst rose from Major Diaz's rifle.

The Brit stumbled, then fell to the ground, blood oozing into the snow.

Another shot cracked the air!

"Aaaah!" Major Diaz dropped his rifle. He held his hand over his heart, turned his face up to the skies and screamed, then dropped into the snow.

"Hold your fire!" Ortiz barked in both English and Spanish. "Hold your fire! Check the major!"

Two soldiers rushed over and bent over their fallen commander. Ortiz watched as they checked the neck for a pulse.

"Lieutenant, the major is dead! A bullet through the heart!"

Ortiz made a quick sign of the cross.

"This is the commander of the Venezuelan forces surrounding your dome. Cease fire! Cease fire!"

Silence.

Then a voice, in British-accented English. "You're the ones who opened fire on an innocent civilian, you bloody liar! You fire on us again and someone else out there will wind up with a bullet in his heart. You might take me out, but I guarantee this. I'll take out ten of your guys first. So if you want a bloody shootout, bring it on."

Ortiz trained his rifle back on the dome, knowing that he faced a highly skilled sniper as an opponent.

Geodesic dome
British base camp
Camp Churchill
Antarctica

Impressive shooting, Leftenant," Captain Timothy Dunn said.

"That's what he gets for shooting Gaylord. They're lucky I didn't take out more than one, which I could have done. I knew we couldn't trust 'em."

"Why did they fire?" one of the engineers asked.

"Who knows," Rivers said. "They got trigger-happy."

"Give us those rifles, Leftenant," another engineer said.

"Leftenant, Gaylord is moving!" Dunn said. "He's alive."

Rivers peeked out the corner of the window. Gaylord was still down. Blood oozed from his chest, forming a reddish circle in the snow. But his hands were moving and so were his feet. Barely.

"You're right," Rivers said. "We must get him back inside. Dunn, you cover me. I'm going out for him."

"Leftenant. Please."

Rivers looked at Dunn. "You want to leave him out there, Captain Dunn?"

"No, sir. That's not what I'm saying. I agree we need to get him, sir. But you should let me get him. It's far too dangerous to risk sending you out, sir."

"Dangerous?" Rivers snarled. "Dunn, I'm a bloody SBS officer! You think I'm concerned about danger?"

"That's not what I meant, sir. You have a son. I'm single. Your son needs his father."

Rivers did not respond.

"Also, sir, I hate to admit it, but you are a much better shot than I am. I couldn't have put that bullet through that guy's heart without a lucky shot. The Royal Marines Rifle Academy is good, but it's not that good. It makes more sense to have you cover me. If something goes wrong, you're going to take out more of them than I could. You in here provides maximum protection for the rest of us and gives us the best chance to survive this, which is in keeping with our mission of protecting civilians."

Captain Dunn waited. They all knew that Rivers' marksmanship gave them their best defensive asset.

"Very well, Dunn. But before you go out, I'm going to warn those Venezuelans, tell them what we're going to do."

"Fair enough, sir."

CHAPTER 13

British base camp
Camp Churchill
Antarctica

What are your orders, Lieutenant?" Staff Sergeant Jiménez, the senior enlisted man in the unit, looked at Ortiz. Jiménez had been in the Army since Ortiz was a baby. "Do we commence fire?"

Lieutenant Javier Ortiz felt the sudden and unexpected pressure of command. The stares of his men drilled him from every direction. The men needed an order. He hoped whatever he ordered would not be as stupid as the course chosen by his predecessor, who then got trigger-happy. Ortiz had always looked forward to becoming a field commander, but he never envisioned that his first taste of command would come like this.

He could order an all-out assault on the dome. This might be the best approach, militarily. His attack force had overwhelming numbers. But . . . if that British SBS sniper picked off enough of his commandos, one by one, that numerical advantage would be neutralized. The Brits' incentive to surrender would be gone.

"Lieutenant?" Jiménez again. "Your orders, sir?"

"Now hear this!" The voice from inside the geodesic dome. "This is the commander of the British military contingent here at Camp Churchill. You promised us a safe and orderly surrender. We kept our end of the bargain. But you shot an unarmed civilian in cold blood. Why should we trust you again?"

Ortiz's thoughts swirled in a blur. He could simply lay siege to the dome and starve the enemy out over time. But British reinforcements were on the way. He knew that. He couldn't wait. Too risky. "This is the commander of the Venezuelan ground forces. The shooting of the British civilian was accidental. A medic on our team can transport your civilian to a local base camp for medical treatment. But time is running out. You must evacuate the dome. If you do not, we will attack. Your excellent marksmanship will not save you. You will be killed."

Geodesic dome
British base camp
Camp Churchill
Antarctica

He has a point, Leftenant," Captain Dunn said. "Even if we drag Gaylord back in here, we have no way of providing medical treatment until our reinforcements arrive and get these bloody chaps off our backs."

Rivers peeked out the window again at Gaylord. His hands and feet were still moving a little, thank God. But without blood transfusions, Gaylord would never make it.

Rivers thought of Gaylord's wife, Jenna. He spoke glowingly of her. And his two kids—Rivers could not remember their names—but kids need their fathers.

That triggered thoughts of Little Aussie. If only they had had a chance to Skype one last time before the attack. Then his mind raced to Meg.

He dismissed that thought.

A warrior cannot be tied down by a woman. Too many distractions. Too much moodiness. Too much relationship talk.

He should fire on the spineless Venezuelan lapdogs, one on fifty if he had to. And he would if it weren't for the fact that he was responsible for British civilians.

"You! Commander of the Venezuelans! Why should I trust you?"

A second passed.

"I am Lieutenant Javier Ortiz. You have my word as an officer!"

Rivers exchanged glances with Dunn.

"A lieutenant?" Rivers shouted. "In charge of a commando unit for a mission of this importance?"

"You shot and killed the major, our commanding officer. Now I am in command."

Rivers gripped his rifle. "I still do not trust you."

British base camp
Camp Churchill
Antarctica

Of course you do not trust me," Ortiz muttered under his breath. "If I were you, I would not trust me either."

What now? The priest said that God would give wisdom to all who asked. "God, tell me what to do." He muttered the prayer out of ear-shot of all except the Almighty. His men might consider it a sign of weakness if they heard him praying, even such a short prayer in a time of crisis.

"To the British military commander. I am Lieutenant Javier Ortiz, acting commander of the Venezuelan unit that has you surrounded. I repeat, you must evacuate the dome and surrender immediately.

"As a gesture of good faith, I will step forward, out in the open, without my weapon, and with my hands over my head. I will send two of my men to pull your injured man back behind our lines to safety.

"Then you are to resume the surrender process, one by one. I will remain out front, unarmed, in your view, the entire time. We will take your men as prisoners. They will be treated humanely.

"If we renege on our promises, you can shoot me. But if you shoot me, for any reason, my next in command will launch an all-out assault and we will kill you all." Ortiz felt his heart pounding. "What is your response?"

Geodesic dome
British base camp
Camp Churchill
Antarctica

What do you think, Captain Dunn?"

"I don't know what to think of it, Leftenant."

"Under the circumstances, it sounds reasonable enough," Rivers said.

"But how do we know he's not bluffing, sir? Suppose it's a ploy to get us to surrender, and then they gun us down once we've been corralled together?"

"Captain Dunn, we don't know. It could be a bluff or a measure of good faith. But here's what we do know. Poor Gaylord will die if we don't get him some help. And fast."

Dunn nodded.

Austin called out the window, "You! Lieutenant Ortiz! This is the commander of the British military contingent. I accept your proposal for surrender. You will slowly walk out with your hands up to a position halfway between your lines and the dome. You will keep your hands up.

"Then you will have two of your men evacuate the British citizen you gunned down.

"Once I am satisfied that our wounded comrade has been taken to safety, then we shall resume the surrender process. If, however, I sniff even the slightest scent of betrayal on your word as an officer, any strange movement, anything the slightest bit provocative, if any of my men are fired upon or not treated in accordance with the Geneva Accords, I will put a NATO .223 round right through the middle of your nose. And if someone takes a potshot at me and is lucky enough to get me, there are men in this dome with rifles ready to gun you all down."

Several seconds passed.

"To the British commander! Your men will be treated humanely and in accordance with the Geneva protocol on the treatment of prisoners of war. I am coming out with my hands up."

Rivers took a deep breath and looked through the scope of his rifle. Venezuelan commandos had taken cover in the snow, their helmets visible and their rifles aimed at the dome.

He saw movement behind one of the sandbag berms. Then a pair of white gloves came up over the sandbag followed by a white battle helmet as the man stood up. He wore full white camouflage battle gear.

"I am Lieutenant Ortiz!" the man said. "I am coming forward."

Ortiz took one step forward. Then another. Rivers kept the crosshairs right between the man's eyes.

Ushuaia Naval Air Station
Ushuaia
Tierra del Fuego Province
southern tip of Argentina

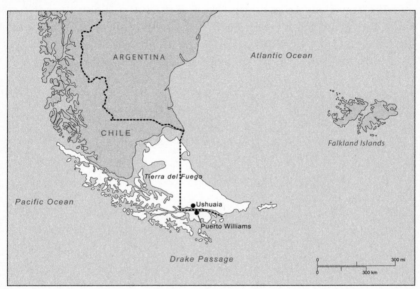

At the southern tip of South America, Captain José Montes peered through his binoculars at the two large jets approaching from the north.

More than thirty years had passed since the Malvinas War. Gomez, now the Argentine naval officer commanding the Ushuaia Naval Air Station—Comando de Aviación Naval Argentina (COAN)—had lost two uncles in that war. He hated all things British. "The only good Brit is a dead Brit," he frequently reminded himself.

He always thought that the Malvinas might provide his opportunity for revenge. He never considered that the opportunity to strike would come in Antarctica.

This time the military landscape had changed. Britain was stronger back in 1982, he thought, under that crazy witch of a female warmonger Prime Minister Margaret Thatcher. But this time when the two nations returned to war, Argentina would not be alone against Britain. If it took ganging up on Britain to defeat Britain, so be it.

Revenge would come soon.

The first plane, a gray four-engine C-130 military cargo plane, swooped low over the runway before beginning its final approach for landing.

The flag painted on the plane's fuselage had three horizontal stripes of color—a yellow stripe on the top, a dark blue stripe in the middle, and a dark red stripe stretched across the bottom. Painted in black on the plane were the words *Aviación Militar Bolivariana Venezolana.*

Montes looked up at the map of South America and studied it.

"El eje sudamericano"
THE SOUTH AMERICAN AXIS

Venezuela in the far north, with Caracas sitting on the Caribbean Sea, is a continent away from Argentina, dominating most of the southern V of South America. Only a narrow string-bean parcel of land west of the Andes belonged to Chile.

Montes drew an imaginary line straight south from Caracas connecting Venezuela in the north with Argentina in the south. High-level commanders within Argentina's military, he knew, were already referring to the new Argentina-Venezuela military alliance as the "South American Axis."

Out on the tarmac, Venezuelan troops were pouring out of the first C-130. Argentinean naval officers, under Montes' command, directed the Venezuelans into one of four helicopters for the flight south over Drake Passage. Their orders—reinforce the attack force at Camp Churchill.

The first Argentinean Navy transport chopper carrying twenty Venezuelan commandos lifted off the tarmac and headed south. As the chopper became little more than a dot on the horizon, the second C-130 touched down on the runway. This plane too bore the markings of the Bolivarian Venezuelan Air Force.

Once again, naval officers and enlisted personnel under Montes' command directed the crack troops from the Venezuelan cargo plane to the other Argentinean helicopters.

As Montes watched the action through his binoculars, he could barely contain his excitement over thoughts about his new assignment.

Ordinarily, assignment of a naval officer from one shore facility to another shore facility would be unappealing. Naval officers were eager to return to sea. But Montes could not say no to this assignment.

A rendezvous with destiny came once in a lifetime. The sea could wait.

10 Downing Street
official residence of prime minister
London

P rime Minister David Mulvaney surveyed the group assembled around the long wooden conference table in the historic cabinet room. When the meeting concluded, his duty would be to brief the king.

And he would first have to inform the king that without His Majesty's knowledge, His Majesty's government had forged a secret international alliance that might have led the kingdom into a perilous military conflict. Camp Churchill was in the hands of an unknown enemy.

The prime minister wished that Queen Elizabeth were still alive. She had experienced war, going back to her childhood when the Nazis bombed London in World War II. She had reigned over every British conflict for over half a century—the Falklands, Iraq, and Afghanistan.

Queen Elizabeth, with her stoic and accepting demeanor, might have been predictable.

With King Charles, one never knew. Yes, Charles possessed his mother's classic British stiff-upper-lip nature, the product of great generations gone by. Yet Charles proved more opinionated than his mother. Sometimes more hands-on, more vocal.

The fact that, under the British Constitutional Monarchy, the king had no official power did not diminish the prime minister's anxiety about the meeting with His Majesty. The king remained as king. And the British monarch had always been the essence of Great Britain in the form of human flesh.

"Very well, gentlemen," Mulvaney said, "since there appears to have been some sort of military action against our installation at Camp Churchill, I'd like to hear from the chief of the defence staff first, and then anyone else can chime in. We'll see if we can agree on an immediate course of action." Mulvaney looked at the white-haired gentleman sitting to his left. "Sir Edmond?"

"Thank you, Prime Minister." Sir Edmond McCutchenson, the highest civilian adviser to the prime minister on military affairs, said, "As you have heard, sir, it appears that we have had a surprise military attack at Camp Churchill in Antarctica." Sir Edmond spoke in a bantam rooster authoritative pitch with a staccato-like cadence that had characterized the speaking style of his great-grandfather, the revered British military legend Field Marshall Viscount Bernard Montgomery, of Alamein.

"Now then," he continued, "there are two immediate questions (a) who did this? And (b) how shall we respond?" McCutchenson turned to one of the military assistants he had brought with him. "Captain Morton, please initiate the electronic map of Antarctica to better demonstrate our position for the prime minister."

"Yes, sir." The senior naval officer typed in a command on a laptop. A second later, a map of Antarctica appeared on each of four large screens positioned around the room.

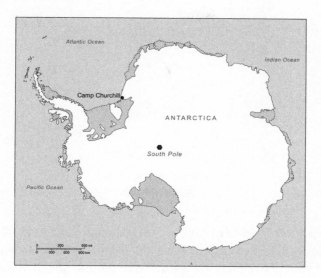

ANTARCTICA
CAMP CHURCHILL
BRITISH OIL DISCOVERY

"Gentlemen. Prime Minister. There you see Antarctica." Sir Edmond tapped a pointer at the screen. "This relatively uninhabited, frozen continent at the bottom of the world is 50 percent larger than the United States and more than fifty times the size of Britain. Antarctica is the fifth largest continent on earth. Larger than Australia and the European subcontinent. During winter, with the ice freezing out many miles from shore, the Antarctic area nearly doubles.

"Now, despite the mammoth size, the human population is scarce. There are no permanent residents on Antarctica. The population fluctuates from a maximum of about four thousand inhabitants in the summer to less than one thousand in the winter.

"We have a full map with all the stations around the continent to put all this in proportion. Captain Morton. Full screen shot, please."

"Yes, sir."

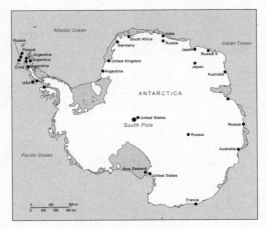

RESEARCH STATIONS
ANTARCTICA

"As you see, there are various research stations dotted all around the continent. Twelve nations have a presence there. But the nations with the most active presence are Chile, Argentina, the UK, followed by the US and Russia.

"Now I direct your attention to the Antarctic Peninsula in the upper left of the map. Captain, pull up that image of the Antarctic Peninsula."

"Yes, sir."

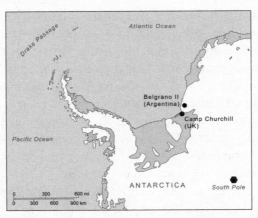

CAMP CHURCHILL (UK) AND BELGRANO II BASE CAMP (ARGENTINA)

"Thank you, Captain," Sir Edmond snapped. "What we're seeing in this image is a view of the Antarctic Peninsula. The dark area of water to the north of the tip of the peninsula is Drake Passage, the treacherous waterway at the bottom of South America that connects the Atlantic with the Pacific. Captain, next screen, please."

"Yes, sir."

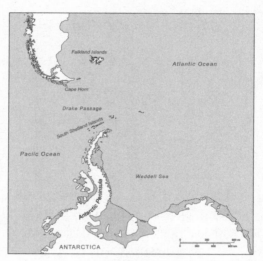

CAPE HORN
DRAKE PASSAGE AND ANTARCTIC PENINSULA

"Ah, yes. Here we are! I thought we had this shot in our presentation," the defence chief said. "Here we see the strategic locations at the bottom of the world that are relevant for purposes of our discussion today. Now we can see Drake Passage separating the northern tip of the Antarctic Peninsula from the southern tip of South America, which is Cape Horn in Chile. The distance across is approximately five hundred miles. This sometimes stormy and treacherous body of water separates Cape Horn from the South Shetland Islands at the tip of the Antarctic Peninsula.

"I believe we have an even closer view of Drake Passage. Captain? Would you display that, please?"

"Yes, sir."

CAPE HORN USHUAIA NAVAL AIR STATION
USHUAIA, TIERRA DEL FUEGO PROVINCE
(ARGENTINA)

"Here we see the close proximity of the various positions. Cape Horn is here, at the southernmost tip of South America. North of that is Ushuaia, where Argentina has a naval base and air station.

"Note how close Ushuaia is to the Chilean border. We expect any military aggression from Argentina into Antarctica to be staged from Ushuaia."

"Excuse me, Sir Edmond," the prime minister said. "Are you suggesting that Argentina is involved in the attack on our position at Camp Churchill?"

The defence chief toyed with his pointer and nodded. "Yes, Prime Minister. That is exactly what I am suggesting. And if Captain Morton here will bring us back to the screen highlighting the position of the Argentine research stations, I will further underscore this point. Captain?"

"Yes, sir," the naval aide said.

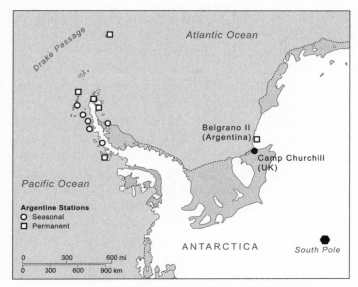

ARGENTINE RESEARCH STATIONS ANTARTICA

Sir Edmond tapped the map with his pointer. "This close-up shows all of the Argentine research stations on the peninsula. The ones shown in white are their seasonal stations that are open only in the summer months. The ones in red are permanent stations that are open year-round. Now bear in mind that we're only highlighting the presence of the Argentine bases on this map.

"But it is here, on the Antarctic Peninsula, that most countries have their research stations. This peninsula hosts most of the human activity on the continent."

Sir Edmond looked at an assistant. "Captain, water, please?"

"Yes, sir."

"Thank you." The defence chief took a sip and set his glass on the conference table.

"Now I direct your attention to the right of the peninsula. This flattened and depressed area not far from the coast is where we have established our base at Camp Churchill. This is the heart of the Black Ice project. It is here that our petro-engineers have discovered what may turn out to be the largest crude oil discovery in the history of human civilization." He tapped the screen on Camp Churchill. "Plans are to begin massive drilling operations and to construct a refinery not far from this area.

"Now then, turning our attention to the right of Camp Churchill, to this position right here"—he tapped again—"the Argentine base known as Belgrano II. This is Argentina's principal year-round base camp located outside the Antarctic Peninsula.

"Our monitoring has found an increase in flights buzzing the area, presumably from Ushuaia, and we have intercepted an increase in electronic traffic. In a word, gentlemen, we believe, based on an analysis of our intelligence, that Argentina has been conducting electronic surveillance out of Belgrano II directed at Camp Churchill. Most likely, they intercepted some message traffic from Camp Churchill and discovered our Black Ice activities.

"Given our contentious history with Argentina over the Falklands, we view them as suspect number one, and we would not be at all surprised to learn that their special forces attacked our encampment."

"Hear! Hear!" exclaimed Admiral Sir Mark Ellington, the first sea lord, the British designation for the highest-ranking officer in the Royal Navy. "And if I may remind you, Prime Minister, that in August of 2012, some thirty years after our glorious victory in the Falklands, the legislature of Buenos Aires province voted to prohibit vessels sailing under the British flag from 'mooring, loading, or carrying out logistical operations' in any of its ports."

The first sea lord continued, "This law, Prime Minister, is designed to hinder British ships involved in oil exploration while navigating waters belonging to the Falklands. It is another in a series of provocations since the Falklands War."

"All right," the prime minister said, "I can buy into naming Argentina as suspect number one. But two questions: First, how do we verify that in fact we're fighting Argentina? And two, what are our military options?"

"Good questions, Prime Minister," Sir Edmond said. "One option regarding intelligence would be to request the strategic cooperation of the Americans."

"The Americans?"

"Yes, Prime Minister. Despite massive cuts to NASA during the Obama Administration, when they suspended their manned space program, their satellite network remains the most sophisticated in the world. Their high-level intelligence satellites, with cameras that can photograph the eye of a needle, would provide an effective intelligence tool. They also might be persuaded to loan some of their predator drones, which could be launched from Puerto Williams in Chile. However, if they were willing to help, my guess is they would prefer more of a low-key approach, at least at first."

"Hmm." The prime minister thought for a second. "That would require letting the Americans in on our discovery of oil sooner than we had planned."

Foreign Secretary Gosling nodded. "True, Prime Minister. But we were going to inform them eventually anyway. I do not anticipate any problem from President Surber, who is a big proponent of drilling. And this discovery will lessen America's dependence on OPEC."

"Good point," the prime minister said. "Secretary Gosling, make plans to request American military assistance through back channels for intelligence support."

"Yes, Prime Minister."

"I want specific military plans for a counteroffensive. We must remove these invaders as soon as possible if we're going to be in a position to commence drilling operations."

"Certainly, Prime Minister." Sir Edmond nodded. "Captain Morton. Back to the close-up of the Arctic Peninsula region."

"Yes, sir."

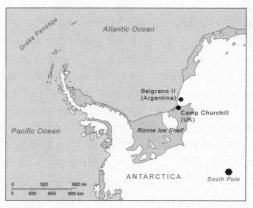

CAMP CHURCHILL (UK) AND BELGRANO II BASE CAMP (ARGENTINA)
RONNE ICE SHELF

"The arrows show the relative positions of both the Belgrano II Argentine camp, over to the right, and Camp Churchill, west of Belgrano. We believe the attack on Camp Churchill originated from Belgrano.

"The Ronne Ice Shelf is this circular depressed area to the west of Camp Churchill. This is actually a large bay that is frozen year-round, but it swells and diminishes between winter and summer. Our discovery of oil, and hence our encampment at Camp Churchill, is on the eastern shore of the Ronne Ice Shelf and west of the Argentine Belgrano II. So it isn't just our past level of acrimony with Argentina that makes them suspect number one. It is the close proximity of Camp Churchill to the Belgrano II."

"Let's get on to proposed military strategy," the prime minister said.

"Yes, Prime Minister," Sir Edmond said. "I shall turn this part of the presentation over to the first sea lord, Admiral Sir Mark Ellington."

"Thank you, Sir Edmond." The robust admiral stood up and accepted the pointer from the defence chief. "As you recall, gentlemen, when Argentina invaded our Falkland Islands in 1982, Prime Minister Thatcher assembled a naval task force headed by our carriers HMS *Hermes* and HMS *Invincible* to sail from bases in the UK and Gibraltar to launch air, sea, and amphibious assaults on both the Falklands and the South Georgia Islands as we replanted the Union Jack in the face of the invaders."

"Hear, hear!" someone said.

"Well, our strategy in repelling Argentina once again will be based on the overall strategy used in the Falklands War, spearheaded by the aircraft carrier HMS *Queen Elizabeth*, alongside our amphibious assault ship HMS *Ocean* and supplemented by the supply ship RFA *Black Rover* and the freighter M/S *Thor Liberty*. The *Thor Liberty* is transporting drilling equipment owned by British Petroleum, along with additional petro- and mechanical engineers to build the initial drilling facilities around Camp Churchill. The submarine HMS *Astute* is already in the area.

"HMS *Ocean* is transporting cargo and assault helicopters, along with three companies of Royal Marines. We are rounding up additional SBS forces from Afghanistan and Somalia, but we're spread thin in light of the budget crisis we're facing."

Prime Minister Mulvaney said, "Do we have sufficient firepower to defeat the invaders?"

The first sea lord said, "Considering the air power from our brand-new carrier, HMS *Queen Elizabeth*, yes, we do, sir. We will have enough for the initial strike. But we will need reinforcements as soon as possible. We are anticipating the same kind of reinforcement for the enemy forces already there."

Mulvaney scratched his chin. "Do we have a map showing our proposed staging area?"

"Yes, Prime Minister," the admiral said. "Captain Morton, bring up the screen showing the naval assault staging area."

"Yes, Admiral."

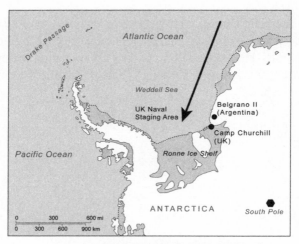

PROPOSED UK NAVAL STAGING AREA
(HMS *QUEEN ELIZABETH* TASK FORCE)

"The basic naval staging area is this body of water known as the Weddell Sea. Part of the challenge we face in sailing into these waters is not only defending against possible Argentine air assaults but also in dodging icebergs, which, as we learned from the sinking of the *Titanic* more than a hundred years ago, can spell disaster for even the largest of ships.

"But the plan is to steam in as close as possible toward the ice shelf, then launch jet and helicopter assaults as necessary to recapture Camp Churchill. I am pleased to report that the five-ship task force had set sail before news of this attack came out. Questions, sir?"

"Yes, Admiral," the prime minister said. "Your comments about ice in the Weddell Sea concern me. How serious is the threat to our task force?"

"Of grave concern, Prime Minister. The waters around the Antarctic continent are charted, but errant icebergs do exist there, so safe navigation in these conditions is not a given. Icebergs can be difficult to detect."

The prime minister stroked his chin. "The thought of losing even one of our ships in treacherous waters, especially our carrier, is disconcerting."

"I can assure you, Prime Minister," the first sea lord said, "that our captains will do everything in their power to ensure the safety of His Majesty's fleet."

"Well then. We Britons have never run from danger. And, speaking of duty, I declare this meeting adjourned. I must venture to Buckingham Palace to inform His Majesty that not only are we facing the prospect of war with Argentina but also His Majesty's flagship runs the risk of being sunk by an iceberg."

CHAPTER 14

Geodesic dome
British base camp
Camp Churchill
Antarctica

O kay, Anderson. It's your turn," Rivers said.

Williams Anderson, the wiry, somewhat reclusive thirty-two-year-old engineer from Cardiff, was lying on the deck, face still down, with his hands covering his head. His hands began shaking, but he did not move.

"Anderson, did you hear me?"

"I heard you, Leftenant . . . It's . . ." His voice trembled and morphed into sobbing.

Captain Dunn, still crouched low with his rifle on the other side of the window, shook his head but didn't say anything.

"Dunn, keep your rifle trained on the Venezuelan leftenant."

"Yes, sir."

Rivers thought of how the great American general George S. Patton, ole "Blood and Guts," had slapped a crying coward in a hospital tent in Italy and ordered the trembling fellow to the front lines. He even considered a Patton-like slap to shock Anderson, but then reminded himself that the poor fellow was a civilian, not a soldier.

"Anderson. My good man. Everything will be all right." Rivers took an uncomfortable stab at the psychologist-comforter role. "These Bolivarian chaps have been true to their word. You're the last civilian out. Captain

Dunn and I have our rifles trained on that Venezuelan leftenant. And he knows we will shoot his brains out if anyone tries to harm you."

"You. Inside the dome! What is the delay? Either come out or we open fire."

More sobbing. "I want my family! Please. I just want to go home."

Austin glanced at Dunn, who again shook his head.

"Anderson! Either you get up and move or I will shoot you myself."

Anderson removed his hands from his head and started pushing up off the deck. "I apologize, Leftenant," he said through sobs.

"Don't worry, Mister Anderson," Rivers said. "Just do as the others did. Hands high over your head. Walk forward and make no jerking gestures."

"Our patience is running out! You appear to have reneged on your promise for an orderly surrender."

"We have not reneged on our promise!" Rivers called out. "One of our men suffers health issues. He's coming out." He looked at Anderson. "Ready, Mister Anderson?"

"I think so, Leftenant."

"All right. Go ahead. Hands up."

"Yes, sir." Anderson shuffled to the door. The image of his body with hands up formed a silhouette against the bright white of the snow and ice outside. Finally, Anderson stepped out into the snow.

Austin watched him from the window, his hands up, trembling with fear, shuffling forward, step after step after step.

"Dunn. Cover Anderson. I need to try something."

"Yes, sir."

Rivers propped his rifle against the window and started crawling, low, across the deck. "How's he doing?"

"He's halfway across, sir. Still shaking and taking his sweet time."

Austin pushed aside the leg of one of the dead Venezuelan commandos sprawled on the floor.

He checked the base radio. As he suspected, it had been riddled with bullets in the initial cross fire.

He reached the base of the computer and pulled up just enough to see that the Skype call had been disconnected.

"Hurry up, gentlemen! This is taking too long!" The command came from outside.

In the upper left of the Skype screen, a photograph of Meg, smiling magnetically. Just to her right on the screen, an oblong green button with the words *Video Call*.

Austin reached up, moved the cursor over the *Video Call* button, and clicked.

A second later, he heard the distinctive elongated electronic *beep* . . . *beep* . . . sound, signifying an active Skype call.

"Are you making a Skype call, Leftenant?"

"Giving it a shot, Dunn."

Magnolia Flats
Kensington District
West London

8:30 p.m. local time

Meg Alexander sat on the sofa stroking Little Aussie's hair, trying to calm him down.

She had wrapped him in a blanket and watched as he closed his eyes. Finally.

The *rap-rap-rap* on the door knocker brought Aussie up off the pillow.

"I'll be back, sweetness. Lie back down." She tucked the pillow under his head and walked to the door.

"Shelley!"

The friends hugged as tears streaked down Meg's cheeks. "Thank God you're here."

"I wouldn't be anywhere else."

"Aussie is dozing in and out, but all the excitement has kept him on edge. Come in. I have tea and scones."

Shelley stepped into the small entryway of the flat, and Meg closed the door.

"Let me fetch you something to drink," Meg said.

"I suppose I might take a spot of something. Anything stronger than tea?"

"I have a French chardonnay." She wiped her eyes. "An expensive brand, wonderfully delicious."

"Perfect," Shelley said.

Meg stepped into the kitchen and reached up to the small wine rack above the coolbox. The rack held three bottles, and she pulled out the one in the middle.

As she set the bottle on the counter, the electronic ringtone of Skype poured in from the living room.

"Mommy! Daddy!" Aussie shouted.

Meg rushed into the living room. A message blinked on the computer screen:

Austin Rivers calling . . . Accept . . . Decline.

"Thank God!" She rushed over and tried to move the cursor over the Accept button, but her hands were shaking so much that she couldn't position the curser.

Little Aussie pointed at the blinking picture of Austin on the screen and shouted, "Daddy! Daddy!"

"Shelley, please help!"

Shelley took the cursor from her hand and moved the arrow over the Accept button and clicked it.

A second later, an image of an empty room appeared. No sign of the handsome face with the cleft chin that had captured Meg's heart.

"Meggie? Are you there?"

"Austin!" His voice sent her heart racing. "Where are you?"

"Meggie, listen carefully. We are under attack by Venezuelan commandos. I don't have long. Do you have your iPhone?"

"Yes . . . yes . . . Oh! I can't find it!"

"Daddy! Daddy!"

"Aussie! Please!"

"Here, take my phone!"

"Who was that?" Austin asked.

"Shelley. She just gave me her iPhone."

"Okay. Does your iPhone have a video record feature?"

"Yes," Shelley said. "Meg, go take care of Aussie."

"Okay," Meg said.

"Now turn on the video. I want to record a message for the Ministry of Defence."

"Yes." Shelley fidgeted with her phone as Meg sat with her arms around Aussie. "Okay! Okay! It's recording. I'm aiming it at the screen."

"I want Daddy!"

"Aussie! *Shhhhhh!*"

"This is Leftenant Austin Rivers, SBS, Royal Navy. I am senior military officer at Camp Churchill in Antarctica. We are under attack by Venezuelan Special Forces commandos. We are surrounded by fifty to sixty riflemen. Gunfire has been exchanged—"

"Leftenant, they have Anderson, sir. It's me and you. What shall we do?"

"Evacuate, Dunn. Same drill. Leave your rifle here. Hands over your head. But move slowly. Buy all the time you can."

"Yes, sir."

Austin continued, "We're surrounded by fifty to sixty Venezuelan commandos . . . versus two British military officers and ten British civilians, all petro-engineers. One civilian, Mister Walter Gaylord, has been shot. His abdominal wound appears serious. He is in the custody of the enemy. Five known enemy casualties. All shot dead by me and Captain Timothy Dunn, Royal Marines.

"Although it goes against every fiber of my being, for the sake of the civilians with whose safety I have been charged, I have ordered the surrender of all personnel at Camp Churchill. Continued resistance, given the overwhelming numbers of the enemy, would mean certain death to British civilians. As I speak to you, I am the remaining Briton still inside the geodesic dome here at Camp Churchill."

"Austin!" Meg said.

"Cognizant of my duty to protect British civilians, I have concluded that my duty is best served to also surrender myself, to attempt to give those civilians the best protection to the best of my abilities under the circumstances of captivity."

"It is time to complete the surrender process!" This voice, in what sounded like a Spanish accent, could be heard off in the distance.

"I must go. Keep us in your prayers, and God save the King!"

London

10:15 p.m. local time

The black bulletproof Jaguar carrying the prime minister of the United Kingdom turned right out of the back entrance to Downing Street and drove along the east side of historic St. James's Park, then made a left turn onto The Mall for the straight shot up to Buckingham Palace, all less than a mile from the prime minister's residence.

London police had closed both Horse Guards Road and The Mall to all traffic for the passage of the prime minister's Jaguar and the eight armed police motorcycles accompanying it for the short drive.

The broad boulevard, colored a reddish tint to resemble a royal red carpet leading up to the palace, was flanked on both sides with dozens of spotlighted Union Jacks.

The prime minister never tired of this sight. For unlike many of the nations of Western Europe, content to abandon their national currencies for a singular Eurodollar, Britain, for the most part, wanted no part of being a mere state in a United States of Europe.

The nation of Churchill, Thatcher, Elizabeth the First, Cromwell, and Lord Nelson remained nationalistic, determined that the Union Jack would never fly subservient to the globalist flag of the European Union or the even more globalist banner of the United Nations. At least the Conservative Party embraced British nationalism.

After passing St. James's Palace off to the right, the Jaguar rolled along Queen Victoria Memorial Gardens near the entrance to the palace grounds, then slowed as it approached the brightly lit Queen Victoria Gate. Guards jumped to attention with snappy salutes as the prime minister's motorcar drove onto the palace grounds.

The prime minister's personal phone rang. Mulvaney looked at the screen: *Chief of Defence Staff.*

He punched the answer button. "Prime Minister here."

"My apologies, sir. But there is late-breaking information that you need to know before your briefing with His Majesty."

"Well, you caught me in the nick of time. What is it, Sir Edmond?"

"Sir, the girl . . . the secretary who dated the SBS officer assigned to Camp Churchill . . . got another Skype message from the leftenant. Rivers said the attackers are Venezuelan."

"Venezuelan? What about our theory that Argentina is behind this?"

"We cannot rule them out. But Leftenant Rivers, the SBS officer, reports that the attackers are Venezuelan commandos."

"Venezuela. I find that shocking. That they would attack us."

"Yes, sir, Prime Minister."

"It's all about the oil. And Chile."

"Yes, the oil. An OPEC member hostile to Western interests. Venezuela does not want Chile to become an oil-exporting superpower.

This would undermine Venezuela's economic and political slice of the pie in South America."

"They don't like us and they don't like the US. Even before Chávez . . . How many attackers? Any idea?"

"Leftenant Rivers estimated fifty to sixty in the initial wave against a handful of civilians and only two military officers. Gunfire has been exchanged. Five attackers are dead. One British civilian has been shot. His condition appears to be critical. For the protection of the remaining civilians, Leftenant Rivers is surrendering to the Venezuelans, hoping they comply with the Geneva Accords and treat them humanely."

"If our officer has reported that they were attacked by Venezuelan commandos, I'm sure the king will want to know why we still suspect Argentina."

"Argentina and Venezuela formed a strong alliance, going back to 2005 when Hugo Chávez used Venezuelan oil money to bail out Argentina's national debt. And Argentina maintains a stronger presence in Antarctica than Venezuela. Remember, sir, Argentina's General Belgrano II base camp is only a few miles from Camp Churchill, on the Churchill Reservoir. There is now little doubt that Argentina intercepted electronic transmissions and shared that information with the Venezuelans."

The prime minister said, "Very well. Let me recap. We now know that Venezuelan ground forces attacked our encampment on the Churchill Reservoir, and our intelligence leads us to believe that Argentina is in cahoots with them. Is that right?"

"Yes, Prime Minister. That's an accurate assessment."

"Thank you, Sir Edmond."

"Good luck with the king."

Oval Office
the White House
Washington, DC

5:18 p.m. local time

A t this time of day, in the later part of the afternoon, with tinges of a gorgeous autumn in the air in North America, the president of the

United States, between appointments and telephone calls, found solitude in whirling his chair around, away from his desk, and gazing from the Oval Office out onto the South Lawn.

In some ways, President Douglas Surber missed the simpler times when he could venture into the crisp autumn afternoon, inhale the cool, intoxicating air, and revel in the orange and yellow and red leaves. Even as Mack Williams' vice president, he could walk out into the backyard at the Naval Observatory, the official residence of the vice president of the United States, and enjoy a few minutes of the changing seasons without anybody noticing. In the fall, he could even pull off an occasional drive down the George Washington Parkway, from Spout Run to Mount Vernon, along the Potomac.

All that changed when Surber replaced his former boss, President Mack Williams, as commander in chief. He marveled at the stark difference between the presidency and the vice presidency, like the difference between night and day.

The presidency's high visibility kept him imprisoned in the Oval Office. In moments such as this, the closest he could get to the crispness of the autumn air came when he could steal time for a gaze out the window.

The sudden shrill of the intercom buzz brought Surber around to face the interior of the Oval Office. He punched the intercom on his large mahogany desk.

"Yes, Gayle."

"Mister President." The voice of longtime presidential secretary Gayle Staff. "The secretary of defense and the chairman of the joint chiefs are here."

"Send them in, Gayle."

"Yes, sir."

"Charlie." The president nodded at a member of his security detail, the Secret Service officer guarding the main interior door of the Oval Office. The officer turned and opened the door.

Surber stood as the two men walked into the Oval Office—one in a gray suit and with the almond-complexioned skin of a Latino and the other a middle-aged Caucasian wearing the blue service dress uniform of a four-star admiral.

"Mister Secretary. Admiral Jones. Please be seated."

"Thank you, Mister President," Secretary of Defense Irwin Lopez said.

"So why this visit by the top brain trust of the United States military on such short notice?"

The two men settled into the chairs in front of the presidential desk.

"Mister President," the secretary of defense said, "we've intercepted some information about a brewing military situation involving two of our allies and a couple of our adversaries that does not yet involve United States military forces. It wouldn't surprise me, sir, if you got a call from the British prime minister within the next few hours."

"From Prime Minister Mulvaney? Tell me what's cooking, gentlemen."

"With permission, I'll defer to Admiral Jones for the details."

"By all means." Surber nodded. "Admiral?"

"Thank you, Mister President," Admiral Roscoe Jones, the chairman of the joint chiefs, said. "Sir, within the last few months, our ground radar positions on the Antarctic Peninsula began noticing an increase in air traffic out of Tierra del Fuego, the southernmost land mass in Argentina that borders Drake Passage to the Antarctic Peninsula.

"Based on these reports, which appeared to identify military flights doing round trips from Tierra del Fuego to one of Argentina's bases down there, a base called General Belgrano II, we became curious about these flights.

"So we repositioned our Air Force SIGINT—our signals intelligence satellites—to orbit overhead, and we began intercepting transmissions between the Brits and the Chileans on one side, and the Argentineans and Venezuelans on the other side. Here's the bottom line, sir. The Brits have discovered massive oil reserves in Antarctica. And because Chile is so close, and Britain needs a close land base, Britain and Chile came up with a secret plan to drill for the oil and share it."

"Where? In Antarctica?"

"Yes, sir."

"I can just imagine what some of these global-warming, carbon-taxing, eco-Nazis are gonna do with this news when it gets out. The environmental wackos won't like it. They'll go ballistic. They'll try occupying the British Embassy. Do some kind of candlelight vigil."

"Yes, sir," Secretary Lopez said.

"I didn't mean to cut you off, Admiral Jones," Surber said. "What military situation is brewing there?"

"Sir, it appears Argentina shared this information with Venezuela, and Venezuela launched an attack against one British position in Antarctica. We believe Argentina is in on it."

"Son of a—" Surber caught himself. "What kind of attack?"

"Small commando raid. Fifty to sixty Special Forces infantry types. Looks like the Brits are surrendering, but my guess is they'll strike back."

"So to make sure I've got this straight, you're saying Venezuela attacked Britain. Not the other way around."

The intercom on the president's desk buzzed. "Yes, Gayle."

"Sir, the secretary of state has arrived."

"Send him in."

Once again, the Secret Service agent opened the door.

"Mister Secretary. Glad you could join us," the president said.

"My apologies," Secretary of State Bobby Mauney said. "Bad traffic coming over from Foggy Bottom."

"Have a seat, Bobby."

"Thank you, sir."

"You are aware, I take it, of the situation that Secretary Lopez and Admiral Jones are briefing me on?"

"Yes, sir, I am."

"So I take it the Brits don't know that we know about it, and nobody else in the world knows."

"That's correct, sir."

"So here's my question," Surber said. "Secretary Mauney, should we contact the Brits and offer our assistance?"

"I recommend against that, sir. It would be embarrassing to admit to our closest allies that we've been conducting electronic monitoring of them without their knowledge. My guess, Mister President, is that we will hear from the Brits soon enough."

"And when we do, what do we expect them to say?"

The secretary of state said, "That may depend in part, Mister President, on how far this escalates. But looking back at the last British war in that part of the world, Prime Minister Thatcher asked President Reagan to be on standby with naval support. Reagan secretly offered Britain use of the USS *Iwo Jima* if either one of the UK's carriers were sunk. My guess is that we might see a similar type of request, coupled with a request for access to our intelligence."

"But at some point, won't we need to be proactive?" Surber asked. "No one needs a war in South America. Besides, I can see Venezuela trying to get help from the Russians. Especially if the Brits start beating up on 'em."

"Sir," Secretary Mauney said, "we think the Russians may already be involved."

"What?" Surber whipped off his glasses. "Secretary Lopez? Admiral Jones?"

Admiral Jones nodded. "Mister President, our satellites have intercepted transmissions coming out of the Belgrano II base camp that are Russian in origin."

"What kind of signals?"

"Sophisticated jamming and eavesdropping transmissions, sir. Stuff that nobody could pick up except for us and the Israelis."

"Hmm. So there had to be communication between Russia and Argentina for this equipment to wind up at an Argentinean research station on Antarctica."

"Precisely, Mister President," Secretary Lopez said. "I think the link is a three-party axis involving Russia, Venezuela, and Argentina. Think about it. Sophisticated Russian spy equipment at an Argentinean research station near a British outpost, and that outpost winds up getting attacked by Venezuelan commandos."

"I agree with that assessment, Mister President," Secretary Mauney said.

"Concur," Admiral Jones said.

"Well then." The president leaned back and crossed his arms over his middle. "We probably know more at this point than the Brits. And they're the ones who have been attacked."

"A fair assessment, Mister President," Secretary Mauney said.

"What's our naval strength in the area?" the president asked. "And how can we provide assistance to Britain and Chile, if the time comes, without jumping too far head over heels into this?"

"Admiral?" Secretary Lopez nodded at the chairman of the joint chiefs.

"As you know, Mister President, the southern tip of South America has not been, historically, the hottest of international hotspots. We have the smallest concentration of forces there. In fact, SOUTHCOM, which would command any military conflict in South America, is the only operational command we have that isn't headquartered on a military base."

"SOUTHCOM is headquartered in Miami."

"That's right, Mister President. And most of our military ops south of the border since the Mexican War in 1848 have been limited to Grenada in 1983 and Panama in 1989. We've been involved in some covert operations in Nicaragua and Colombia, but we have no military bases south of Guantanamo Bay in Cuba. So in situations like this, where we're talking faraway places with no bases, we're thinking the Navy and the Marines.

"Now keep in mind, sir, that Chile has purchased one of our older *Los Angeles*–class submarines, and we've sent one of our sub skippers down to Chile to train them on how to use it. That submarine, which is now in Valparaiso, could be available to assist. Chile has a small but strategic naval facility at Puerto Williams, not far from Cape Horn at the southern tip of South America. So all these things might be options, sir, depending on how things unfold."

"Okay," Surber said. "All this is good to keep in mind. But right now, we don't have a dog in this fight. Let's sit for a few hours and see how things unfold."

"Yes, sir."

"And where are our carriers?"

"USS *Ronald Reagan* is conducting ops off Baja California off the northwestern coast of Mexico. *Reagan* is our closest operational carrier."

"Turn the *Reagan* to the south. Let's get her off the southern coast of Chile just in case."

"Yes, sir, Mister President."

"Secretary Lopez, Secretary Mauney, let's have another update in the next couple of hours."

"Yes, sir, Mister President."

CHAPTER 15

Isabel Miranda's flat
Santiago

All I can tell you, Pete, is that we've got intel that's top secret and we need you to report to the Chilean naval station at Valpo by seven in the morning. I'm sorry to cut your leave short, but we need you to whip that Chilean crew into shape and be prepared to take her to sea in less than a week. Chilean military forces could be engaged in combat soon. If that happens, then that sub, frankly, will instantly become Chile's most formidable military asset."

With those words, Captain Joe McKinley, the United States naval attaché at the American Embassy in Santiago, had reneged on the Navy's promise of a few more days of leave for Pete to explore his father's native country.

Pete Miranda had been a naval officer for too long to believe that promises of leave could be considered sacrosanct. Duty always loomed. Explosions and flare-ups in international hotspots around the globe paid no respect to the leave schedules of American officers.

From the captain's somewhat cryptic set of instructions, it sounded like Pete might deploy on a combat mission with a Chilean crew. He hoped not. Training a foreign crew on the intricacies of a sophisticated nuclear attack submarine would provide enough challenges. But to train that crew and then take them into combat on such short notice might be suicidal. At least six months of training would be necessary to get a new crew, especially a foreign crew, combat worthy. The Chilean

Navy's officers were sharp and its enlisted members were reliable. Still, the time frame specified by Captain McKinley in that phone call seemed impossible.

No point in speculating. He would report to Valparaiso and execute whatever duties were required of him. If he had to take a greenhorn Chilean crew into battle against some unknown enemy, so be it. He had stared down death before. He could do so again if he had to.

He had declined McKinley's offer of a helicopter ride from Santiago to Valparaiso and instead rented a Mercedes convertible. He pulled up in front of his first cousin's home, a modest Santiago flat, and parked the Mercedes. He opened the top and cut the engine.

This was crazy. His heart pounded like when he was preparing for combat. In fact, not even combat affected him like this. Combat produced an adrenaline rush. This involved accelerated heart palpitations.

Isabel's front door opened. His cousin walked outside.

Maria followed her sporting fashionable designer sunglasses and dressed in designer blue jeans, a loosely fitted white top, and fashionable black boots. She slung her chic-looking purse over her shoulder and, with an eyebrow-raising bounce in her step, balanced a garment bag in one hand and a dress bag in the other.

Wow.

"Here, let me help you!" Pete opened the door and walked quickly toward her. "I'll take those." He relieved Maria of the two bags and caught a whiff of her intoxicating perfume.

"Nice car."

"Well, if you're going to keep me awake all the way to Valparaiso, the least I could do is give you a ride in style. Bags in the trunk or in the back?"

"The back is fine."

"You got it." He laid the dress bag on the backseat and put the canvas bag on the floor. "Here, let me get the door." He opened her door, catching another whiff of her perfume as she slid onto the seat. *What is that?* Whatever it was, it was intoxicating.

"Pete!"

"Yes, ma'am." He turned. Isabel stood there, playfully wagging her finger at him.

"Remember. If you don't take care of my friend, I will personally report you to Aunt Judy."

"Yes, ma'am." He gave Isabel a playful salute, kissed her on the cheek, then hopped behind the wheel and cranked the car.

"Ready?" He looked at Maria.

"I'm ready."

"Let's do this." He pressed down on the accelerator, and the Mercedes rolled forward.

What had he gotten himself into?

Dock F
Mar Del Plata naval base
Argentina

5:30 p.m. local time

Mar Del Plata, a city of 600,000 some 250 miles south of Buenos Aires on the Atlantic coast, is Argentina's seventh-largest city and the country's largest beach resort.

The city gained international recognition by hosting the 2008 Davis Cup finals, to the extent that professional tennis still held much international popularity in the early twenty-first century.

A lesser-known fact is Mar Del Plata's status as home port to the small submarine force of the Argentine Navy. The Navy's three submarines, all built in Germany, include one older Type 209 diesel-electric boat built in the 1970s and two highly modernized TR-1700 *Santa Cruz*–class boats, which were the largest submarines built in Germany after World War II and are among the fastest diesel-electric boats in the world.

Selection for command of a *Santa Cruz*–class boat marked the ultimate achievement for a submarine officer in Argentina's Navy.

Two weeks ago, after Commander Carlos Almeyda received a call from fleet headquarters announcing his dismissal as executive officer of the ARA *Santa Cruz*, he had prepared for his assignment to a desk job at fleet headquarters at Puerto Belgrano. A Puerto Belgrano shore assignment represented the final stepping-stone before command at sea.

But things change.

The telephone call at 7:00 p.m. the night before his departure to Puerto Belgrano caught him off guard. Capitán de Navió Claudio Simeone, the commander of the Submarine Service Branch of the Argentine Navy, was on the line.

"Commander Almeyda, we have a change in your orders."

"Yes, Capitán?"

"I know we promised to send you to headquarters, but we are sending you back to sea."

The call had stunned Almeyda. "A naval officer is born for the sea, *mi* capitán. I am honored to return to the *Santa Cruz* as second in command to Commander Gomez for as long as my country needs me there, sir."

"Commander Gomez is a good man and a great officer. And he speaks highly of you," the capitán had said. "In fact, we are taking this action based on his recommendation."

"I do not understand, sir," Almeyda had said.

"We are not sending you back to the *Santa Cruz*. There has been an unexpected change in personnel assignments. The commander slated to take over as commanding officer of the *Santa Cruz*'s sister sub, the ARA *San Juan*, has suffered a stroke. The admiral has ordered you to report to the ARA *San Juan* tomorrow morning as the new commanding officer."

At first, the capitán's words failed to register.

"Commander? Are you up to this task?" the capitán had asked after Carlos' extended silence.

Then it hit him. He would be in command of one of the Navy's newest submarines. "I am ready, *mi* capitán. Please express my appreciation to the admiral for his confidence in me. Tell him that I accept this assignment with a solemn devotion to duty, and that he will not be disappointed."

"Very well, Commander. I am sure the admiral will be pleased by your reaction."

The harbor tug had pushed the *San Juan* away from Pier F. Standing at the top of the conning tower, under the bright Argentine sun, Commander Almeyda reflected on the incredible events that had placed him here, so quickly, in command of the ARA *San Juan*. With his XO and chief of the boat joining him, the time had come to take the *San Juan* to sea. The *San Juan* was not going to sea alone. Her sister sub, the ARA *Santa Cruz*, had just launched from Pier F and had a five-minute head start on the *San Juan*.

"All ahead one-quarter."

"All ahead one-quarter. Aye, sir."

The *San Juan* glided forward, slicing the calm waters as it headed toward the Atlantic. Off to starboard, dozens of well-wishers, friends, and family members gathered on Pier F waved at the departing sub.

Down below, twenty-six crew members were already at their duty stations, responding to whatever commands Almeyda issued.

The surrealistic feeling of power surged through his body. Many wise philosophers had written on the subject of power. Power is the ultimate aphrodisiac. Power corrupts, and absolute power corrupts absolutely.

Dressed in his summer white captain's uniform and feeling a sudden sharp dose of patriotic fervor for Argentina, Almeyda turned and shot a salute to the waving crowd across the water. The Argentinean Navy band, its silver trumpets and trombones glistening in the late-afternoon sunshine, broke into "Don't Cry for Me, Argentina."

Orange rays of sunlight caught the light blue flag of Argentina flapping in the breeze over the waving crowd.

The navigation tug fired a loud horn blast, a final salute as the sub headed to sea.

Almeyda felt overwhelmed with a sudden sense of emotion. He could not let his men see their capitán with tears in his eyes.

He dropped his salute, tried to wipe his eyes, and then brought up his binoculars. Out ahead a quarter mile, the *Santa Cruz*, under the command of his mentor and good friend Commander Alberto Gomez, cut a course to the south, toward the open ocean.

If duty called, they would be prepared to deliver the most lethal one-two punch the Argentinean Navy had to offer. What a privilege to command the *San Juan* on a joint mission with the *Santa Cruz*. Gomez had not only been Almeyda's commanding officer aboard the *Santa Cruz* but, more than that, he had become like a brother. Gomez had personally trained and prepared him for this day.

Their destination—the waters around the Malvinas Islands, the islands claimed by the Brits, who called them the Falklands.

Argentina expected British ships to pass through these waters on their way to reinforce and resupply the Anglo-Chilean effort to drill for Antarctic oil.

Almeyda glanced at the navigation charts that he had brought up to the conning tower.

NAVIGATION CHART
MAR DEL PLATA TO WATERS OFF MALVINAS
MALVINAS ISLANDS

British ships steaming to Antarctica would pass by the Malvinas and, most likely, stop in the Malvinas for replenishment. The British still claimed to own the Malvinas and in 1982 sent twenty-eight thousand men in a naval task force against Argentina to preserve Britain's last vestige of colonialism off the Argentine coast.

Now a new generation of warriors manned the Navy of Argentina. Argentina would again fight Britain, but this time it would be supported by Venezuela and perhaps even Russia.

Any British ship passing near the Malvinas would do so at its own risk.

Almeyda looked up from the charts. ARA *Santa Cruz* had vanished, submerged in the waters of the Atlantic.

ARA *San Juan*'s moment had come.

Almeyda gave the command. "Chief of the boat! Batten down the hatches. Seal all compartments. Prepare to dive!"

"Prepare to dive! Aye, sir! All hands, prepare to dive!"

Chilean Ruta 68
Curacaví Valley
between Santiago and Valparaiso

6:00 p.m. local time

The hilly and sometimes mountainous drive westward out of Santiago along Chilean Highway Ruta 68 descended into the Curacaví Valley and bypassed the small city of Curacaví.

The late-afternoon sun cresting between the hills warmed his face. And this time of year, in October, as the days grew longer and warmer, the great Chilean climate in the Curacaví Valley reminded Pete of the weather in Sicily and Malta and other Mediterranean ports that he had visited often during his tour as a naval officer.

Yes, this two-hour drive through the countryside from the capital to the coast was what the doctor ordered . . . well, almost anyway.

Perhaps his car guest was what the doctor ordered.

Why couldn't he shake her from his mind? The hot little beige sundress? Now the extraordinary jeans and boots?

On the first leg of the drive, she had been less chatty than she was back at the bar. Maybe the cat held her tongue. Perhaps the alligator had clamped hold of his. Perhaps an odd case of mutual nervousness had gripped them. Maybe he should have brought Isabel along to facilitate conversation.

He glanced over at her hair blowing in the wind.

Have mercy! Eyes on the road, Pete!

"Having fun?" he asked.

"Lots of fun." She tilted her head and pushed her hair back. "This is nice and relaxing. Thanks for inviting me."

"My pleasure."

As he rounded another curve, the warm afternoon breeze whipping into the convertible, he felt angry in a way at the bubbly champagne-like feeling in his chest brought on by thoughts of this beautiful, but somewhat mysterious, Maria Vasquez.

"So what's with you and my cousin?"

"What do you mean?"

"You're so different. At least politically. But you're best buds."

Maria paused. "To be honest, our friendship has survived because of Isabel."

"Really?" At least she was talking. "How so?"

"I stopped attending church years ago. Isabel remained faithful. She kept telling me that Christ loves me and wants me back in the fold, and I should be honored to be named for the mother of Christ."

"I agree with my cousin." Pete smiled. "What else? I want to hear more."

"Hah! Isabel challenges my socialist views and even makes me wonder sometimes why I espouse socialism." She pushed her hair back again. It drove him crazy every time she did that. "She says with my love for designer skirts and blouses and spiffy heels and purses I dress and live like a capitalist, and I claim to be a socialist not only because I think it's chic but because the dim-witted stars in Hollywood are that way."

Pete laughed. This girl had a nice self-deprecating sense of humor. "Well? Any progress?"

"Oh, I don't know." Maria chuckled. "I respond with a quote from

Marx or Allende. Sometimes I quote Obama about redistributing wealth. She laughs at me and we change the subject."

"I knew there was a reason I love my cousin so much," Pete said.

That was a nice exchange. But the conversation again receded, as if yielding to the wind and the scenery and the setting sun.

Shake it off, Pete! There's work to do! No time for a woman.

They rounded another curve. The landscape flattened out and the road straightened. A sign for a roadside exit appeared for Ambrosio O'Higgins / Curacaví.

Another curve brought fields of yellow flowers in the valley around Route 68, sending his mind back to Maria.

That beige sundress. Those legs. That smile. The butterfly tattoo.

The Mercedes sped past the Curacaví, leaving it in the rearview mirror.

"So . . ." She paused.

Good. Maybe she wanted to talk again.

"Can I ask you a question?"

"Sure. Anything."

Silence. She turned toward him. "So . . . are you seeing anybody?"

"What the—" Pete swerved left as a silver Jeep sped by on his right.

"Whoa," she said in a startled voice. "Relationships scare you that much?"

"No. I mean yes." He glanced at the Jeep that nearly clocked them. "I mean no." A deep exhale.

"So is that an answer to my first question or my second? Or maybe a mixed answer to both questions?"

"Maybe to all of the above!" He forced a grin.

Did the question show interest? Of course it did. That was good. Wasn't it? But then again, she had broached the *R* word. Superman had his kryptonite. Pete Miranda had the topic of relationships. "Aah . . . the answer to the first question is no. To the second question . . . some say I suffer from relationship-a-phobia."

That brought a velvety-smooth chuckle from a voice that he could listen to all day. "Relationship-a-phobia! That's funny! What's the Spanish for that? Anyway, your cousin already warned me. But I had to ask."

Green Drawing Room
Buckingham Palace
London

10:35 p.m. local time

The cathedral ceiling of the grand room rose thirty feet above the floor. Its walls, covered in a rich greenish wallpaper, served as a backdrop for life-sized oil paintings of past British monarchs all framed with black backgrounds and ornate golden frames. Interspersed on the walls between the paintings were long larger-than-life mirrors with gold frames.

A massive cylindrical crystal chandelier hung from the ceiling on a long chain. Classical music, strains of Rachmaninoff, filled every corner of the room, but at a volume sufficiently subdued to allow for conversation.

The royal red carpet had gold embroidery throughout, and the curtains matched the red of the carpet.

Off to the side in a corner, in front of a white marble fireplace with a great gold-framed mirror, two chairs covered in green velvet with gilt legs sat catty-corner to one another. A small table for tea sat between the chairs.

Buckingham Palace referred to it as the "Green Drawing Room," and tonight marked Prime Minister Mulvaney's second visit. For tonight would mark only his second meeting with the new British monarch, King Charles Philip Arthur George of the House of Windsor, known by his subjects as King Charles the Third. David Mulvaney served the king as prime minister and would carry out his duties to the Crown. Although the monarch technically wielded no actual political power over the kingdom anymore, under the British Constitution, the monarch had the right to be apprised of the affairs of state and to give advice on such matters.

Over the years, Queen Elizabeth II had met with more prime ministers than any other monarch in the history of the Crown. Elizabeth established the tradition of meetings with her PMs on Thursdays. Though her sovereignty remained titular, her breadth of experience gave her the viewpoint of a statesman that many of the British PMs had come to value and rely on. Elizabeth understood the importance of showing the face of a united Britain to the world, one in which the government and the Crown remained in lockstep.

But Elizabeth's death brought new uncertainty over the relationship between the government and the monarchy.

With large sections of the British public clamoring for Charles to abdicate the Crown to the wildly popular Prince William, and with Charles already a senior citizen when he ascended to the throne, some crown watchers speculated that Charles would make a larger splash by asserting himself in public affairs more than his mother, Elizabeth.

Mulvaney checked his pocket watch, mindful that he was waiting for the king and not the other way around.

The piped-in classical music stopped. Regal silence pervaded the room. Two large doors opened, and a tall servant in a black tuxedo stepped in.

"Prime Minister. The king."

Mulvaney stood. King Charles, dressed in a gray wool suit and red tie, with the suit matching the monarch's graying hair, walked into the room.

"Good evening, Prime Minister." The king sported a grin that looked half forced.

"Your Majesty." Mulvaney bowed in reverent submission and waited for Charles to extend his hand.

"Please be seated, David." Charles pointed to one of the green velvet chairs.

"Thank you, sire."

The king sat first. The prime minister followed. "You realize, Prime Minister, that too many of these late-night meetings shall get me in trouble with Queen Camilla."

"My apologies to Queen Camilla and to Your Majesty for the lateness of the hour, but there is an urgent military situation unfolding, and I need to brief His Majesty before the press grabs hold of it."

That brought a driving stare from Charles, then an angry contortion on his face. The king crossed his legs and put his hands in his lap. "A military situation, you say?"

"Yes, sire. A military situation unfolding at the bottom of the world. I regret to inform you that British civilians, mostly petro-engineers who were defenseless except for two Special Forces officers who were on-site to offer protection in advance of the arrival of additional Special Forces personnel, have been attacked by Venezuelan commandos and been taken as prisoners. We believe that the Argentine is complicit in the operation."

"The Argentine," Charles mumbled.

"Yes, Your Majesty."

"Why am I not surprised?" the king said. "You know my brother, Prince Andrew, flew helicopters in the British naval task force sent to the South Atlantic in 1982 when the Argentine invaded the Falklands."

"Yes, Your Majesty. I am familiar with Prince Andrew's distinguished record of military service."

"What details do I need to know, and what will we do about it?"

Mulvaney explained the situation, and when he finished, Charles just stared at him, deploying the royal silent treatment as a rather effective weapon.

"Prime Minister, in the future, if the government concocts grandiose plans for lofty alliances with other nations, either economic or military, please inform the Crown on a timelier basis, not waiting until the last second when the nation is engaged in a military standoff that could send us into war."

The prime minister nodded. He had not told the king sooner because of the top secret nature of the operation. How could he explain that omission? Be truthful? That the government did not trust even Buckingham Palace to maintain secrecy?

"My apologies, Your Majesty. The Crown should have been informed. Rest assured that this will not happen again."

"Apology accepted," Charles said. "Know this, Prime Minister. As was the case with my mother, Queen Elizabeth, and my grandfather, King George, even if we express private disagreement with governmental policy, the Crown shall remain in public lockstep with the government for the sake of British unity to the world."

"Thank you, Your Majesty."

"But as you know," Charles continued, "our Constitution grants the Crown the absolute right to advise the government, and there is one bit of advice that I shall dispense, which you may accept or reject."

"Yes, sire?"

"Since the beginning of the twentieth century, Britain has had one great, dependable, and steady ally. The United States. And I would advise you to make President Surber aware of this situation, request the assistance of the Americans, and accept whatever help they may provide."

"Thank you, Your Majesty. I can assure you that the government plans to do that."

Charles forced another contrived smile. "I believe we are adjourned." The king stood and the prime minister followed suit.

"Thank you for your time this evening, sire." The prime minister bowed.

"Good-bye, Prime Minster."

"Good-bye, Your Majesty."

Approaching Maria Vasquez's flat
337 Avenue de Tomás Ramos
Valparaiso, Chile

The sun set in Valparaiso, the colorful Chilean seaport, just as the Mercedes reached the outer limits of the city. Maria had turned her head toward him, resting against the bucket seat, and closed her eyes. She had napped for the last fifteen minutes, and he had stolen more than a few glances, especially at the red light at the last intersection.

Perhaps she'd fallen asleep because she had too much red wine.

Perhaps she found him boring.

Maybe it was good that she felt comfortable enough to take a nap on their first trip together.

Then again, maybe she considered this their final trip together.

Who knew?

At least he'd avoided more talk of the dreaded *R* word. Why did they all want to talk about that? Then again, she really didn't ask him about *wanting* to have a relationship—only if he was seeing anyone. But her second question had in fact incorporated the *R* word when she asked if relationships scared him. What scared him most was that her use of the *R* word did not scare him as much as when others had used the *R* word.

If only she had stuck to the first question.

"Approaching 337 Avenue de Tomás Ramos, on right," the voice on the GPS announced.

He pulled the Mercedes to the curb.

What now?

He nudged her on the shoulder. "Wake up, sleeping beauty."

She looked up and brushed a strand of hair off her face. "This place looks familiar. I'm impressed."

"Don't be." He shut off the engine. "I set the GPS to speak English."

That brought an irresistible giggle.

"Anyway, let me get your bags and walk you to the door."

She smiled. "That would be nice."

He got out and opened her door, helped her step out, and then got her bags. She looked even more gorgeous with moonlight caressing her face.

Now what? "Shall we?"

"Sure," she said. "Right this way."

They walked up the sidewalk to the front stoop of her apartment, a quaint-looking place from what little he could see of it. Not that his attention was on the apartment. He watched her turn the key and crack open the front door. Then she turned and looked at him. "Thank you for the ride."

"Thank you for riding with me."

Awkward silence. "I hope I didn't take you away from my cousin too soon."

"I think she was ready to kick me out."

"Well . . ."

They stood awkwardly looking at each other, not knowing what to say.

He wanted to kiss her. How would she react? Not now.

"Can I ask you a question, Maria?"

"Sure."

Should he ask? Or not?

"Aah . . . are you seeing anybody?"

Her smile beamed. "No. But if you call me again, I'd love to show you the city."

He nodded. "Great idea."

She reached up, kissed him on the cheek, stepped in the apartment, and closed the door.

CHAPTER 16

On a broad snowy patch, corralled in a human circle like an American football team gathered to call their next play, they stood and stared at one another.

And if they had been an American football team, Austin Rivers was their quarterback and Timothy Dunn was their star receiver. The rest made up a ragtag group of third-string walk-ons, thrust prematurely into prime time. Their eyes displayed fear.

Surrounding them in a larger circle, Venezuelan commandos aimed rifles at them, keeping watch over this makeshift stockade of prisoners.

All of them, including Dunn, looked to Rivers, their eyes pleading for answers. But Leftenant Austin Rivers, SBS, Royal Navy, had no answers. At least they were all in the circle, except for the wounded Gaylord.

The commandos had dragged Gaylord, along with the body of the Venezuelan major whom Austin had shot, inside the geodesic dome, turning it into a makeshift hospital and morgue.

Four Venezuelans, including Lieutenant Ortiz, were inside the dome. This concerned Rivers, as Ortiz appeared calm and coolheaded in command. Ortiz's orchestration of the surrender, by making himself vulnerable as a target, proved gutsy. Rivers could have killed Ortiz. But Ortiz kept his word as an officer, and so had Rivers.

Rivers had seen enough of Ortiz to believe he could trust him to the degree that one could trust an enemy in combat. He could not say the same for the ragtag group of trigger-happy hoodlums with loaded rifles surrounding his men.

Rivers had never felt fear. In fact, he always relished the excitement of his daring lifestyle—staring death in the face—dodging bullets, disarming explosives, being forced to kill an opponent before that opponent killed him. He had gunned down the Venezuelan major in retaliation for shooting Gaylord, an unarmed civilian holding his arms up in surrender.

But with the assault on Camp Churchill, a strange fear had crept up on him. Not of dying. But now Rivers could not shake his thoughts of Little Aussie. The boy needed a strong father figure. What if he did not survive?

This question he had never considered until today. Until today, his self-defined model of fatherhood involved sending money to Meg, occasionally showing up in London for sporadic playtime, then whooshing off to some other bloody adventure, leaving Meg behind to do all the dirty work and to perform the heavy-lifting role of parent.

He intended to one day take time to play cricket with Aussie, perhaps teach him the intricacies of soccer or coach his rugby team. And one day he would teach Little Aussie horsemanship, inspire him to attend the Royal Military Academy at Sandhurst. Or better yet, even the Britannia Royal Naval College at Dartmouth, following the educational pedigree of the king himself, alongside the king's father, Prince Philip, and the king's brother, Prince Andrew.

All these dreams could be best achieved by the boy under the guidance and firm hand of a strong father.

Watching Gaylord take a bullet reminded Rivers that he too remained one bullet away from all his hopes for Aussie vanishing forever.

Meg was a good lady. Attractive. Smart. She gave birth to Aussie and raised him well. She deserved better. Still, a boy needs a father.

His own father had commanded a corvette in the Royal Navy. Although Captain Rivers remained at sea for most of Austin's youth, at least he found time for the boy during his times ashore.

Austin hoped for more time together after his father's retirement. They had planned on making up for lost time by doing many things together as a grown-up father-and-son tandem. They would fish the

Thames. Maybe hunt quail in Scotland. But almost as soon as Captain Rivers retired, Austin entered the Britannia Royal Naval College at Dartmouth, on the banks of the River Dart. There Austin's own military duties intensified with his selection into the prestigious Special Boat Service. The old man strutted about, proud as a peacock, when he learned of Austin's selection into the Special Forces.

But that's where the relationship ended.

Only two short months after Austin began his academy service—two months and two days to be exact—came the diagnosis. Pancreatic cancer. Had they caught it earlier, there would have been hope. But with delays in Britain's disastrous socialized medicine system, three months passed before Captain Rivers saw a doctor. By then, the cancer had spread. Nothing could be done.

Standing in full-dress uniform on a drizzly, chilly Tuesday afternoon in a small cemetery near Wimbledon, Austin watched in sadness and anger as an honor guard from the Royal Navy removed the Union Jack from his father's coffin, then folded it and presented it to his mother.

All these years later, reflecting on the event, Austin never understood if the source of his anger was at his father for not being there, or at Britain's socialized medical system for not treating his father in time to save him, or at God for not allowing him enough time with his dad. All Austin knew was that he felt cheated. Cheated of the time lost with his dad, both as a boy and as an adult.

So when he found out that he had a son, he began supporting Aussie beyond the minimal standards required by law.

But after watching Gaylord be mowed down by a bullet—Gaylord the family man who, moments before being shot, had talked of his wife and children—Austin pondered anew the responsibilities of fatherhood, and yes, even his responsibilities to Meg, his boy's mother.

Should he marry her? Like his mother, who had been a splendid officer's wife, Meg would make remarkable arm-candy at social events of the Royal Navy's officer corps. His father often advocated the importance of a polished and beautiful woman as a key to advancement up the ranks of the British military. Meg, with her flowing blond hair and shapely legs and magnetic eyes, met the attractive-officer-wife test—and more. She could be an asset to him. Yet he felt guilty for thinking of her as some trophy.

And would it not be better for Aussie if his parents were married? But that thought scared him more than the idea of taking a bullet.

Perhaps she would not have him. He met her for a one-night stand, shamefully took advantage of her and impregnated her, then dumped her. And he was bloody lucky that she was the only woman he had gotten pregnant . . . at least the only one of whom he was aware.

But if he ever returned to the UK, he would engage in some serious soul-searching.

"Excuse me, Leftenant?"

Rivers looked over at Andrew Bach, a small Welshman from Cardiff. Bach had a look of grave concern.

"Yes, Mister Bach. What is it?"

"Just thinking about Gaylord, Leftenant."

"We're all thinking about Gaylord, Mister Bach. But unfortunately, there's nothing we can do for him.

"Well, with respect, Leftenant, I beg to differ."

"You have a plan to rescue Gaylord and get him medical assistance?"

Bach looked down and seemed a wee bit embarrassed. "Well, yes, sir. In one sense, I do have such a plan."

Austin glanced at Captain Dunn. "Very well, Mister Bach. But I must warn you. It might be best to leave military strategy to the professionals, just as we leave the petro and drilling issues to you engineers."

"Well, Leftenant, I was a-wondering if I might say a prayer for poor Gaylord and his family. He looked bad, and I'm afraid he might not make it otherwise."

A cold wind swept in. Men held their arms up over their faces to shield their eyes. When the wind died down, Rivers wiped his eyes to regain clear vision. All eyes were again on him, awaiting an answer to Bach's question.

"Well, Mister Bach, I've never been a praying man, but if you wish to lead the group in a few words of supplication to the Almighty on behalf of Gaylord, as long as you might be willing to put in a little additional request on behalf of my little boy back in London, I suppose a little prayer could not harm anything."

The icy wind whipped up again, and the graying Welshman looked up and smiled. "What is your son's name, Leftenant?"

"Austin. His mother named him after me. We call him Little Aussie."

"And what is his mum's name?"

"Meg. Meg Alexander."

"Thank you," Bach said. "Let us bow and petition the Lord on behalf of those in need of prayer."

Austin bowed, and he felt Bach's hand rest on his shoulder.

"Almighty Father," the Welshman began, "maker of heaven and earth, and Father of our Lord Jesus Christ, born of a virgin, who died for our sins, rose from the grave, who ascended into heaven, and who is coming again to judge the quick and the dead, we raise our prayers to you on behalf of those of our friends in peril.

"First, for our friend Walter Gaylord, a good friend who loves his family, who is loved by his wife, Mary, and his daughters, Caroline and Elizabeth, and who is fighting for his life, we ask for your help. Be with him. Strengthen and heal him so that he will survive this bullet in his body and bring him back to Britain alive.

"And for our brave friend and leader, Leftenant Austin Rivers"— Bach squeezed Austin's shoulder—"we pray for his precious wee one, Little Aussie, and for Aussie's mum, Meg Alexander. Guard over them. Keep them safe, and guard over the leftenant and keep him safe too. Grant him wisdom and divine guidance to protect us, and deliver us all from the hands of our enemies. For it is in the incomparable name of your Son that I pray, the One who was, and who is, and who is to come. Amen."

The wind died down again just as Bach finished praying. A peaceful silence hovered over the snowy landscape.

British base camp
Camp Churchill
Antarctica

How is he?"

Inside the captured British dome, Lieutenant Javier Ortiz watched two of his medics down on the floor on their knees attending to the wounded British civilian.

"He's delirious, Lieutenant," one of the medics said.

"He needs morphine," the other said.

"That might polish him off," the first warned. "Plus, we may need that morphine for our own men before this is over."

"True," the other medic said.

"If the chopper doesn't get here soon, he's done."

"Agreed."

"He is losing blood from the entry wound in his chest. Pass that bandage."

"Here."

The man's shirt had been removed, and his rib cage looked bone white. The bullet had hit the middle of his ribs on the right and probably had penetrated his lung.

The man's face was contorted. His forehead was beaded with sweat.

When the medics applied compresses to the wound, the man responded with a bloodcurdling scream.

More screams. "Caroline! Daddy loves you! Elizabeth! Aaahhhhh! I'll miss you!" Delirious cries morphed into a sobbing and then heaving.

Javier Ortiz could barely watch. He uttered a silent prayer and made the sign of the cross over the dying man.

British base camp
Camp Churchill
Antarctica

Rivers looked around, searching for a weakness in the enemy lines. If he had his gun, he could take out half of them.

Bach still had his head bowed and appeared to be praying in silence.

Did God answer prayers? Rivers had not seen many answered from firsthand experience. Then again, he hadn't uttered many from firsthand experience.

Time was his only ally. If he waited long enough, the enemy would make a mistake, and with a bit of luck, he could exploit that mistake.

Of course, given the frigid weather, time could become an enemy.

If he could only hold off until SBS reinforcements arrived.

A distant roar sounded off on the horizon out to the left.

"Choppers!" One of his men pointed to the horizon. There were two of them, inbound straight toward the camp at a thousand feet off the deck.

The Venezuelan guards outside the dome turned and pointed at the sky.

If ever there were a time to strike, the time was now. If only someone besides Dunn could fire a rifle. Of course, if those choppers were British, transporting British special forces, it would prove a long afternoon for the Venezuelans.

Men from inside the dome poured out, including Lieutenant Ortiz.

The choppers flew in closer, and from this distance, they resembled Royal Navy Sea King MK2 choppers, the type that transported SBS squadrons.

Perhaps an answer to Bach's prayer!

When the choppers flew closer, he saw that they were Sea Kings! His men waved like ground troops watching a fighter jet doing a flyover before bombing an enemy encampment.

With a loud, almost deafening roar, the first chopper passed low overhead. The light blue flag painted on the side had a white horizontal stripe down the middle. The middle of the white horizontal stripe featured a yellow sun.

"Argentina," Rivers said. "I should have known! No way could these Bolivarian chaps pull this off on their own." He cursed under his breath.

The two choppers slowed to a hover over the base camp, two hundred yards apart. One broke off and flew about a hundred yards off to the left. The chopper that broke away began a slow descent, and as it did, its downdraft blew a snow cloud up from the ground. The snow draft hid the chopper from sight even after it touched down.

The second chopper began descending a couple of hundred yards to the right, its rotors also storming up a cyclone of snow.

As the snow began to settle back down to the ground, the passenger bay door slid open. Armed troops, with white winter protective gear, began pouring out of the first chopper. Twenty-five troops moved single file from the helicopter. Small Venezuelan flags were sewn on the shoulders of their jackets. More troops piled out from the other helicopter and converged on the base camp.

Argentinean choppers transporting Bolivarian Special Forces. Obviously a joint operation, Rivers decided.

The first officer to step from the chopper jogged straight toward

Lieutenant Ortiz. Ortiz shot the first salute, meaning the officer from the helicopter outranked Ortiz.

Rivers tried a quick head count. Another fifty troops had been added to those already on the ground.

The first wave of enemy reinforcements had arrived.

Despite the roar of the helicopter engines, Rivers saw that an animated conversation had erupted in Spanish between Ortiz and the officer he had saluted. After a while, the senior officer began giving hand signals. Two of his troops ran over to him. He said something to them, and they sprinted back to the first helicopter.

Ortiz looked over toward the group of British prisoners and pointed straight at Rivers just as the two men who had rushed to the chopper came back out carrying a stretcher. The men jogged over to Ortiz and the senior officer, spoke a few words, and then Ortiz led the entire group into the dome.

"What do you make of it, Leftenant?" Captain Dunn said.

"Hope they're going in for Gaylord. And it appears they're serious about digging in here. This will be a bloodbath before it's over."

"Looks like you're right, sir," Dunn said. "I wish I could be on the first British reinforcement wave to run these rats out of the kitchen."

"Hmm. You might get your wish. And if you do, I hope I'm in that first wave with you."

The door of the dome opened. The two soldiers who had run for the stretcher emerged carrying the stretcher with a body on it.

Rivers craned his neck for a better view.

"Leftenant. It's Gaylord."

All eyes in the British contingent focused on the stretcher as the Venezuelan soldiers lifted Gaylord toward the second helicopter.

"I think he's dead, Leftenant," Dunn said.

"I can't see. Is he moving?" Rivers said.

"It doesn't look like it," Dunn said.

"Don't give up the faith," Bach said. "Our God is faithful."

"God might be faithful, Mister Bach, but he might have to be faithful enough to raise someone from the dead."

"He can do that too, Leftenant," Bach countered. "He did it with Lazarus and he did it with his own Son."

The commandos lifted Gaylord into the chopper as Lieutenant Ortiz and the other officer began walking straight toward Rivers.

"Leftenant, I think I saw Gaylord moving as they put him in the chopper," Dunn said.

But Rivers had not noticed. His eyes were fixed on the two officers who stepped through the line of armed guards and walked right up to him.

Rivers shot a salute to his captors.

"Lieutenant," Ortiz said in English, "this is Major Crespo. He is relieving me of command."

"Major." Rivers nodded.

The officer nodded back.

"The major does not speak English well," Ortiz said.

"And I regret that my Spanish isn't all that extraordinary either," Rivers said.

"Leftenant," Ortiz said, "you and your men will soon be evacuated. We expect your cooperation."

"Where are you taking us, Lieutenant?"

"To an undisclosed location. But rest assured that your men will be treated humanely in accordance with the Geneva Accords."

"Lieutenant Ortiz, you do understand, do you not, that most of these men are civilians. They are not combatants. As such, I would argue that they cannot be held hostage under international law and should be released to the British Embassy in Caracas or put on a civilian airliner back to London."

"Leftenant, as I said, your men will be humanely treated. As to when or how they are released, I cannot say. That decision is for someone above both of our pay grades."

Rivers nodded. Ortiz had given the correct answers. And if it weren't for the fact that he would gladly put a bullet between the man's eyes— and between the eyes of every Venezuelan soldier on the ground if he had a chance—he respected Ortiz's professionalism as a soldier.

Behind Ortiz, Venezuelan soldiers carried the other bodies into the helicopter.

"One last question?"

"One more. But make it quick."

"Gaylord. The British civilian they shot. How is he?"

Ortiz grimaced as the second helicopter, the chopper that would transport Gaylord, began revving its engines. The deafening *chop-chop-chop* of the rotors drowned out speech. The helicopter lifted off, blowing another snow cloud as it did. It climbed a couple of hundred feet, hovered for a second in a stationary position, then turned in a path right over the Brits and headed out in the direction of the sun.

"Your man is alive, but barely. We will get him medical care. But it would not surprise me if he does not survive the flight."

The news felt like a punch in the gut. "Thank you for the information."

"Certainly," Ortiz said. "Now please get your men into single file and lead them over to the other helicopter. Immediately."

Rivers turned to Dunn. "Captain Dunn. Round up the gentlemen. It looks like we're going out for a nice little flight."

"Yes, sir."

Belgrano II base camp
Argentine outpost
Antarctica

Welcome to Belgrano II, Capitán." The lieutenant colonel stood at attention by his desk in the geodesic dome that served as headquarters of the base camp and snapped the sharpest of salutes, which, in and of itself, sent a chill down the spine of Navy Capitán José Montes, Commando de Aviación Naval Argentina. "We know of your confident and effective leadership at Ushuaia Naval Air Station, and we are honored to have you take command here at Belgrano II. I will consider it an honor to serve as your executive officer."

Pleased at his initial reception, Montes returned the salute, allowing the lieutenant colonel to drop his. "Stand at ease, Lieutenant Colonel Sanchez."

"*Gracias, mi* capitán."

When taking command of a new duty station, especially when removing an officer like Sanchez who had been in command of that duty station, no doubt could remain about who would be in charge.

"I hear that you have served the Republic well as base camp commander in the months leading up to this day, Colonel," Montes said.

"*Gracias, mi* capitán. It is my life's desire to serve Argentina."

"Excellent. And you will continue to serve Argentina, *mi* colonel. But to do that effectively, I have found that it is always an excellent idea for a commander and his assistant to have a chat to ensure that a mutual understanding is reached from the beginning. Don't you agree?"

"Of course, *mi* capitán."

"The first issue always is establishment of a command headquarters." Montes looked around the makeshift office. "I take it that this dome has served as headquarters for the entire base camp?"

"Yes, this is headquarters, sir."

"Hmph." Montes grunted. "I suppose it is adequate. No reason to make a military headquarters ornate."

"No, sir."

"Adequate. Utilitarian. Efficient."

"Thank you, sir. This was our goal from the beginning."

"Yes, I see."

Montes glanced around once more. "And this is your desk?"

"Yes, sir."

"The desk of the base commander?"

"Yes, Capitán. As you said, it is non-spectacular, but functional and efficient."

A brief pause.

"Then here is my first order. As the new base commander, I am ordering you to come out from behind that desk and to stand in front of the desk facing it, standing at attention until a further order from me."

"Sir?"

"I sense hesitancy on your part, Colonel. Do you not understand my order?"

"No, sir. I understand, sir."

"Then execute my order."

"Yes, sir."

Sanchez walked out from behind the desk, pivoted to the left, and then turned back toward the desk and stopped. He came to attention, facing the desk.

Montes crossed his arms and stared at Sanchez. Then he walked behind the desk to the chair that Sanchez had been sitting in and sat down.

He steepled his fingers under his chin and stared up at his second in command for a few more moments. "At ease, Lieutenant Colonel Sanchez."

Sanchez transitioned from his posture of strict attention to a more relaxed "at ease" position.

"Now, do not think that I will become an unreasonable leader. I will not always issue such picayune orders. However, as when God once ordered Abraham to sacrifice his own son to test his loyalty, I wanted to judge your reaction to an order which you might not personally care for."

"I understand, sir."

"You are now my second in command, and from this point on, there is but one base commander. This is not a command by committee. Do you understand?"

"I understand, *mi* capitán."

"Excellent. I am delighted that we have an understanding." Montes eyed the colonel. Perhaps he could be trusted. Perhaps not. "Tell you what, Sanchez. Now that we've gotten the preliminaries out of the way, pull up a chair and have a seat."

"Thank you, sir."

Sanchez stepped across the room to fetch a chair and, as he sat down, Montes plopped his boots up on the desk, aiming the soles of his boots at Sanchez.

Montes reached into his shirt pocket for a hand-rolled Cuban cigar. "You wouldn't have a light, would you, Colonel?"

"Yes, sir." Sanchez pulled out a lighter and struck it.

Montes leaned over the desk and met Sanchez halfway, drawing a satisfying drag of smoke into his mouth. He sat down and exhaled in the direction of his second in command. "Thank you, Colonel. By the way, I have another. Reserved for this very occasion. I would be honored if you would share it with me." He handed the cigar across the desk to Sanchez.

"Thank you, Capitán." Sanchez lit the cigar.

Montes said, "Because of these recent international events, with Britain and Chile working together in a sinister plot to revive British imperialism and steal oil from Antarctica, Argentina must stop this aggressive power play."

"Yes, sir."

"I realize you were selected for command of this post because of your background as a scientist. But now our mission shifts from research to military. As you know, our first military mission will be to establish a military prison. So tell me"—another drag on the cigar—"what initial steps have been made for receipt of the British prisoners?"

"Capitán, in anticipation of the arrival of the prisoners, I ordered two domes set aside for containment of prisoners. We have also requested shipment of barbed wire to be dropped by air to be rigged around the domes for additional security."

Montes studied his inferior. He seemed subservient enough. But his superiors were correct to order a change in command. Especially under these circumstances.

"Excellent, Colonel. But understand this. Our role can be best facilitated not only by maintaining order among the prisoners but also by the extraction of intelligence. As this initial wave of British prisoners comes in, we must establish order quickly. And then I want to know everything that the British pigs know and when they knew it. Don't you agree?"

"Yes, of course, sir."

"You know, my subspecialty is naval intelligence. Specifically, the extraction of intelligence from enemy insurgents."

"Yes, *mi* capitán, I know of your background in this area."

"Good. You have done your homework. My work in advanced interrogation techniques is renowned. It is the principal reason why I have been selected for this important post at this time in our nation's history. And I am willing to serve as your mentor in this most important area if you are anxious to learn and willing to listen."

Sanchez nodded. "I am honored to serve as your protégé in this way, sir."

"Very well. When are the first British POWs due?"

Sanchez glanced at his watch. "In less than one hour, Capitán."

Montes leaned back and folded his hands across his belly. He relished the idea of leading the interrogation and sinking his teeth into some of these British dogs still trying to hang on to the last vestiges of imperialistic notions that faded two centuries ago. He would personally conduct these interrogations for his uncles, Arturo and Juan, who lost their lives to these scum in the War for the Malvinas.

"You know, Colonel, some say you can judge a man by the kind of woman he is able to acquire. Do you agree with that?"

Sanchez looked perplexed. "Well, *mi* capitán . . . I—"

"But you know," Montes said before Sanchez could finish, "I find that to be only partially true."

"Yes, Capitán."

"Do you know what I think?"

"I am afraid that I do not, sir."

"Well, I think the definition of manhood, and the test of an officer, starts with his woman, who should be a good conversationalist and able to move gracefully in social circles and within military, diplomatic, and government circles. Her conversation should be graceful, with an ability to chat about meaningless social pleasantries. But she should avoid excessive talking and should learn to shut up on cue if the officer gives her the signal that it is time to shut up."

Sanchez nodded. "Of course, sir."

"Her appearance should be pleasant. Not with supermodel magnetism, but sufficiently attractive that senior officers considering her husband's promotion will have positive impressions." He paused, waiting for a response.

"Of course, sir."

"She should also be lively in her dress, sporting a variety of colors, and should always be seen in public wearing either a dress or a skirt. No shorter than knee length or even slightly below, and her legs are by far one of her most important features. Pants and pantsuits out in public are a social faux pas. She must always remember her place as the wife of an officer. Do you not agree?"

"Completely, sir."

"My first wife failed in these qualifications. She became an impediment to my career. The problem was her mouth. She would not shut up. She kept shoving her political opinions on the wives of senior officers and would not shut up when I gave her the signal.

"Word came to me that she grated upon the nerves of the admiral's wife. So do you know what I did?"

"No, sir."

"I divorced her. Then I petitioned the church for an annulment. And then I replaced her with a younger model." Montes leaned back and allowed himself a satisfying laugh. "Like stealing candy from a baby. I purchased a few ads on one of those Internet dating sites and they lined up, competing to become the wife of a Navy capitán!"

"Sounds like an efficient means of dealing with the problem, Capitán."

"Efficient? Hah! That's one way of putting it. And an officer's wife is only one way of judging the man. There are more important methods. Do you have any idea what these might be?"

"I must confess, *mi* capitán, you have piqued my curiosity."

Montes rocked in the chair a few times, satisfied that he had stumped his newfound subordinate. "Tell me, Colonel. What sidearm do you carry?"

"Nine-millimeter Glock, sir."

"May I see it?"

Sanchez seemed to hesitate. "Certainly, sir." He pulled his gun from his holster and slid it across the desk.

Montes picked up the Glock. He held it up to the overhead light. "You know, Colonel, that the final and most important outward gauge of the measure of a man is what kind of firearm he carries. This tells a lot. Take the great American general George S. Patton. Do you know what sidearm he carried?"

"A Colt .45 as I recall."

"Not bad," Montes said. "I see you have a grasp of military history."

"Thank you, sir."

"Throughout his military career, General George S. Patton Jr. fired many different handguns. However, Patton preferred a .45 caliber Colt Model 1873 single-action Army revolver with a four-inch barrel.

"Patton acquired the pistol in 1916 while serving with General Pershing in the Pancho Villa Expedition in Mexico. This was no ordinary Colt. It was silver-plated, and Patton had it fitted with ivory grips carved with the initials *GSP*.

"One of the greatest generals in history used a single-action revolver. He cocked the hammer each time he fired a shot. Now what does that say about Patton? A double-action revolver or a pistol would have allowed him to shoot faster."

Sanchez sported a quizzical look. "I suppose with the single-action revolver, a weapon that would not allow him to get off as many shots, he must have been confident that his first shot would find its target."

"Precisely, Colonel!" Montes said. "You are a quick study! What do you suppose your nine-millimeter says about you?"

"I never thought about it," Sanchez said.

Montes worked the slide on the pistol, chambering a bullet into firing position. "There's nothing wrong with the Glock. It's a fine pistol. It fires fifteen shots in short order. But you know my criticism of it?"

"No, sir."

"Not imaginative. Nothing distinctive. Everybody has one. As your woman should be the subject of conversation, so should your firearm. As for me, like General Patton, I prefer a revolver"—pause—".357 Magnum." He laid the Glock on his desk and extracted his revolver. "This baby comes with a seven-inch barrel and is manufactured by Taurus in neighboring Brazil. I love a long-barreled revolver, Colonel. So authoritative." He brought the barrel to his lips and kissed it. "And do you know what is most distinctive about this baby, Colonel?"

"I apologize, Capitán."

Montes popped the swing-out cylinder and spun it, then passed it to Sanchez. "Count the rounds."

Sanchez counted. "Seven rounds instead of six."

"Precisely. And seven is the number of perfection, which gives it a level of distinction."

"Absolutely, Capitán."

"Now tell me, Colonel." Montes held up both weapons—the Glock in his left hand and the long-barreled Taurus revolver in his right, pointing both weapons toward the ceiling. "Which of these would be more intimidating pointed at the skull of an uncooperative British prisoner?"

Sanchez looked from one weapon to the other. "In sheer appearance, the revolver appears more intimidating. Partly, I suppose, because the barrel is so long."

"Good observation!" Montes kissed the revolver again and slid the Glock back across the desk to the colonel.

"Soon we shall see what these Brits are made of. I predict they will wet their pants. And if we must waste a bullet or two to underscore a point, then so be it."

CHAPTER 17

Magnolia Flats
Kensington District
West London

11:15 p.m. local time

Meg Alexander stood in her kitchen and sipped a French merlot. Her hands shook and her wine sloshed in her glass. Her stomach felt like a twisted wet rag.

Shelley had gone into the bedroom to check on Aussie. The evening's events had riled the boy so much that, for a while, Meg thought he would not sleep at all. For a solid hour he kept crying, "I want Daddy," until he simply cried himself into exhaustion.

Another sip of wine.

Shelley stepped out of Aussie's bedroom, closing the door behind her. "He's asleep. Finally."

"Thank God," Meg said. "Care for a glass?"

"That would be lovely."

"Michelle, we need to talk." She poured a splash of wine in Shelley's glass.

"It's not often that you call me Michelle."

"I know." She pushed the glass across the counter. "Shelley's an affectionate nickname. I use Michelle when I want to get your attention on something serious."

"I know. And I like it. Bob would call me that before . . ." Her voice trailed off.

Meg ignored the comment. Shelley's breakup with Bob had sent her into a depression that required counseling and even medication.

"I'm sorry."

"It's okay. I'm beyond that. Please, I rather like that nickname. It reminds me of the good times with him."

Meg smiled. "May I ask a favor?"

"Anything." Shelley sipped her wine.

"I need to go to Chile. I want to be as close to Austin as possible. You probably think I'm crazy. There's no commitment between us and no real hope. But there is Aussie. I need to be there for him, just in case . . . I don't even know. I have some holiday time coming. Listen to me. I don't even know if Chile requires a visa."

Shelley took her hand. "If you're asking me to keep Aussie while you go to Chile, or wherever, I'd be delighted. But on one condition."

"And what might that be?"

"Two conditions."

"I'm listening."

"First, promise to be careful and stay out of harm's way. Aussie needs you to be safe, and I do too."

"I promise." She smiled. "What else?"

"Promise to call or Skype every day. Otherwise I shall be nervous beyond my ability to function."

Meg held her arms out and they hugged. "I promise."

"You'd better. I love you, and Aussie needs you. And one day"—she pulled her face back as tears streamed down her cheeks—"one day I have this feeling that Austin will need you too." She wiped her eyes. "You'll see."

Belgrano II base camp
Argentine outpost
Antarctica

Capitán Montes, standing with his arms crossed, his new second in command, Lieutenant Colonel Sanchez, at his side, watched as the helicopter from the British base camp feathered down for a landing.

"Company! Surround that chopper!" A company of Argentine soldiers swarmed the helicopter that contained the British prisoners.

The roar of helicopter engines gave way to the sound of whirling blades, and then whirling blades gave way to the haunting sound of the wind howling over the snowscape. Montes waited for the snow cloud to settle back down to the icy surface.

"Sergeant" the Capitán yelled. "Bring the limey pigs out here and put them in a group in front of me."

"Yes, Capitán!" The sergeant hustled over to the helicopter as crew members rushed to open the back cargo door of the chopper. "Out! Hands up! Single file!"

Montes watched as the first British pig stepped from the helicopter. Followed by another. And then another. They were a pathetic-looking bunch, like a bunch of pale ghosts lining up in front of the gray chopper.

Montes' hatred boiled as they piled out one by one. "This is for you, my uncles, and for you, my mother," he whispered under his breath as the sergeant got the Brits in line at gunpoint.

"The prisoners are in line, Capitán!" the sergeant yelled from over near the chopper.

"Very well, Sergeant! March them in this direction and stop them when I order you to do so!"

"*Sí*, Capitán!" The sergeant pivoted around. "You heard the capitán! Move! Eyes ahead! Do not look to the left or right. Move! Move!"

Five armed soldiers surrounded the British prisoners as they began shuffling slowly in the snow, walking toward Montes and Sanchez. Their heads hung low, except for two, whose heads remained high in an apparent air of defiance.

"A pathetic-looking bunch, isn't it, Colonel?"

"Pathetic indeed, Capitán," Sanchez said.

"Looks like a couple of bantam roosters will need to be taught a quick lesson."

"Yes, sir."

"That's far enough, Sergeant."

"Yes, sir," the sergeant said. "Halt!" he yelled in accented English and held his hands up in the international *halt* gesture, and his men trained their rifles on the prisoners.

The Brits came to a stop in the snow and stood silently, lined one behind the other. Montes conducted a head count. There were twelve. "Follow me, Colonel," Montes said.

"*Si*, Capitán."

Montes and Sanchez walked along the line, then stopped. They stood there in their white protective snow gear, breath steaming from their mouths in the cold, not saying a word.

"Turn them this way, Sergeant!"

"*Si*, Capitán."

"Right face!" The sergeant snapped the command in English.

Two of the Brits, the ones with defiant looks on their faces, pivoted to the right on cue. The others shuffled about, seemingly confused by the order.

"It appears we have two military men among this ragtag bunch," Montes said.

"Move!" The sergeant walked along the line, manually turning shoulders the right way. Soon the scruffy bunch was all turned and facing Montes and Sanchez.

Montes had hoped for more than twelve prisoners. But the number was not as important as the information he would extract.

These prisoners were at ground zero of the British operation. Their knowledge and access to top secret materials would prove valuable to the war effort and would grab the attention of the top command in Buenos Aires.

He eyed them contemptuously. The information extracted from these British pigs would guarantee his promotion to admiral!

"Welcome to Belgrano II Base. From this day forward, if you hope to leave here alive, you are no longer a subject of the king of England. From now on, you are the property of the Republic of Argentina!"

He looked up and down the line of men. Judging their faces. Waiting for some response. Any response. Nothing but twelve stone faces.

He slowly walked down the line, determined to get into every one of their faces.

"I am Capitán Montes of the Navy of the Argentine Republic. Your country's meddling in this part of the world is not appreciated and has not been forgotten. Britain's despicable colonialism is despised by the world. And your imperialist actions in the Malvinas have been neither forgotten nor forgiven.

"While the Argentinean people are among the most peace loving in the world, when our interests are threatened, we become the most vicious warriors on the planet!

"If you think we're still living in 1982, when Britain claimed to have won the battle of the Malvinas, think again. Today Argentina is superior, and we shall, along with our allies, display our might for the world to see. You men have two choices. Either cooperate or die! Am I making myself clear?"

No response.

"Not going to answer? Then we shall begin with some obedience lessons. Down on your knees!"

"Don't move, men!" one of the prisoners said.

Montes and Sanchez exchanged glances. "Oh, I see!" Montes shouted. "Going to play this way, are we? Well then. It's time you had a dose of who you are dealing with! Sergeant!"

"*Si*, Capitán."

"Mobilize the firing squad! Get me twelve riflemen. One for each of these white-skinned fogheads!"

"*Si*, Capitán."

"We will see how stiff-upper-lipped you imperialists are with a FARA 83 assault rifle aimed down your lousy throat!"

Belgrano II base camp
Argentine outpost
Antarctica

Rivers stood, biting his lip, staring into the barrel of the Argentinean assault rifle. Two more riflemen scurried across the snow, headed to the last two positions so that the firing squad would have one rifleman per target.

The only other military man in the group, Captain Tim Dunn, stood unflappable in the Antarctic breeze.

Williams Anderson, the one who shook so much in fear that Rivers worried his furtive movements might get him shot, had started shaking again.

"Calm down, Anderson," Rivers whispered. "Have a stiff upper lip, man. You're British."

"I'm trying, sir."

"Don't call me sir, Anderson. I'm military. You're civilian. You're not in the chain of command."

"Yes, sir." Anderson's voice kept shaking.

Rivers watched as the last two riflemen moved into place. As the principal protector of his civilian countrymen, he realized the situation placed him in an awkward predicament. He could not act on his instincts. The issue of life or death for his countrymen might depend on whether he could read the mind-set of this large he-man of a warden, this Capitán Montes.

If Montes was an out-of-control British-hating ideologue, this could become a bloody massacre. With that thought, his mind switched to Aussie and Meg. He even considered blurting out a private prayer, except that he did not pray, didn't really know how, and did not have time to pray. Not now. He had to be aware. No distractions.

The notion of Montes as a British-hater remained all too real. Decades later, legions of Argentineans still despised the fact that British forces under the bold leadership of Lady Margaret Thatcher had placed an embarrassing butt-whipping on Argentina.

If Montes was more a hater than a professional officer, then within minutes, streams of British blood would be running in the white snow beneath their boots. But if Montes was more of a professional officer, then maybe they had a fighting chance.

The British had what Montes wanted—information. Classified information extracted and relayed to Buenos Aires could make Montes a military hero—at least in his own mind.

SBS training in counterterrorism and POW techniques taught Rivers a valuable and possibly life-saving message. Montes could not extract information from them if they were all dead.

That did not mean that Montes would not kill some of them to make a point with the others. But the worst thing that any of them could do would be to show weakness. Rule number one of POW survival: Weakness in the face of the enemy was the quickest path to death.

That didn't mean that one should engage in stupid bravado, which could also be a recipe for getting shot between the eyes. But one should avoid blinking at the first sign of danger.

"Firing squad! Atten-hut!" The twelve-member execution squad snapped to rigid attention, bringing their guns down to their sides. "Firing squad! Ready! Take aim!"

Magnolia Flats
Kensington District
West London

11:35 p.m. local time

Thank God." Meg Alexander stared at the computer screen. Her wineglass sat on the table beside the keyboard, half empty.

"What is it, Meg?" Shelley, looking exhausted, got up off the sofa and walked over to her.

"I'm on the British Embassy site in Santiago. According to this, I am not required to get a visa for Chile unless I'm planning to stay ninety days."

"That's wonderful news. That means you only need your passport. Is your passport valid?"

"Yes, thank God."

"Excellent. Then it's settled. All you have to do is purchase your tickets. I could take you to Heathrow in the morning."

"Sometimes you can get a better fare out of Gatwick," Meg said.

"Yes, of course," Shelley said.

"Either way, I'm sure the price will be exorbitant at the last second like this. Let's see. What's the British Airways website?"

"Try ba.com."

"How could I forget?" She typed in the BA website, and as it popped up, her stomach felt suddenly twisted. "Something isn't right."

"Problems with the website?"

"No. It's Austin. I can't explain it. I . . ." She remained lost in her thoughts, sensing the presence of lurking danger. Her anxiety sharpened into a sudden dagger.

She had not grown up as a Christian. But her unexpected transformation came with the birth of Aussie—and to think that she had nearly killed him by an abortionist's knife.

Aussie became the gift of life that brought a transformation of her soul. She loved him as she had never loved anyone. For weeks after his birth, she had nightmares that she had gone through with the abortion.

She would wake up sweating, thankful that Aussie was safely asleep in the next room, thankful to God for his life. In fact, she convinced herself that the elderly nun with the Irish accent outside the abortion clinic who had given her the photo of the tiny hand reaching out of the womb was no nun at all, but an angel sent from God as a messenger to save her soul from condemnation.

Oftentimes, as she pondered it all in the first few weeks after Aussie's birth, she would visit the website thornwalker.com and marvel at the picture of the fetal hand reaching from the womb and grabbing the finger of the doctor operating on him.

She started reading the New Testament for the first time and found herself strangely drawn to the gospel of John and to an age-old exchange between Jesus and Nicodemus that she at first did not understand. *"You must be born again."* The words of the ancient text somehow spoke to her heart!

Baby Samuel had been born. Little Aussie had been born.

"Lord, whatever that means, I wish to be born again," she had said aloud in a manner intended as a prayer, after having read that verse from the great gospel at least a hundred times. After she uttered those words, a strange warmth had come over her. She felt flooded with an inexplicable warmth that felt like love. She could not see him, but she sensed the presence of Christ himself, somehow celestially wrapping his arms around her. She began crying and could not stop.

From that point on, she possessed a strange sense about things, and at this moment, a premonition cascaded over her and fear took hold.

"I'm sorry, Shelley," Meg said. "I know you don't believe in this, but I feel the need to pray for Austin."

"Whatever floats your boat. It won't offend me." She put her hand on Meg's shoulder.

Meg bowed her head. "Lord, I don't know what's going on other than what we have already seen. But I know that my heart feels troubled. Please protect Austin from harm. In Jesus' name. Amen."

"Do you feel better?"

"Not yet," Meg said.

"Well, let's hope this Jesus of yours can answer prayers."

"He can," Meg said. "If only he will."

CHAPTER 18

Belgrano II base camp
Argentine outpost
Antarctica

With his hands clasped behind his back, Montes strolled up and down the line behind the firing squad like a ruffle-feathered peacock. "We shall discover how stupid, or how smart, some of you are.

"If any of you hope to leave here without having your dirty colonialist blood spilled all over the ice and snow, then what you must first understand is that cooperation with me is not optional." He stopped at the end of the line and eyed them all.

"Down on your knees, you British scum!"

"Nobody move!" Rivers snapped.

Montes stared at him. "I see! A renegade. And with a military background, I presume. Very well, we can shoot all of you." He turned to the firing squad. "Firing squad! Ready . . . aim . . ."

"Wait! Please!" Williams Anderson blurted out. "I want to live. I will get on my knees if you don't shoot. Please!"

"Anderson, shut up and remain standing," Rivers said.

But Anderson, his voice shaking, dropped to his knees. "I apologize, Leftenant. But"—his voice trembled as he began to weep—"I want to see my family."

"Well now." The ruffle-feathered peacock smiled. "It seems we have one sane Brit in the bunch." The capitán walked toward Anderson and looked down at him. Anderson remained on his knees, trembling, his face down, looking at the snow. "Look up at me, Brit!" Montes commanded.

Anderson brought his face up. Tears streamed from his face and dropped into the snow.

"What's your name, Brit?"

"Anderson. Mister Williams Anderson, sir."

"Repeat that, please."

"Anderson. Mister Williams Anderson, sir."

"Did you say Williams—with an *s*—as opposed to William—without an *s*?"

Anderson wiped tears from his eyes. His hands shook as he wiped his gloves across his face. "Yes, sir."

"Williams with an *s*?" Montes asked. "Are there two of you, Mister Williams Anderson?"

This question brought snickers from the firing squad.

"Well, Mister Williams with an *s* Anderson. I assume you are in command of this ragtag mission. No?"

"No . . . I . . ."

"Not in charge? Well you know, do you not, that I possess the power to place you in charge of this entire ragtag group of losers."

"I . . . I . . ."

"Well, clearly, since you are obviously the most intelligent among this bunch, since you are the only one to obey my commands, I hereby declare you to be in command of this group."

Anderson did not respond but stayed on his knees. Weeping. Shaking.

"This should be reason for celebration. Is this not reason for celebration, Mister Williams Anderson?"

Still no response.

"Aah. Well, the first thing we must do is assign a new military position to the new commander of the British. Therefore, I hereby declare you, from here on, to be known as Commander Williams Anderson. So what do you say to that, Commander Williams Anderson?"

Anderson looked up at him.

"Nothing to say? I should think that you would wish to express at least a modicum of appreciation before your men. Show some of that unflappable British leadership and resolve, Commander Anderson!"

"Thank you, sir," Anderson said sheepishly.

"This promotion is to commander—notice I did not promote you to capitán. In every navy in the world of which I am aware, while a commander has considerable responsibility, a commander is always outranked by the capitán. And on this base, there can be only one capitán. And that would be me. Do you not agree, Commander Williams Anderson?"

"Yes, of course, Capitán."

"Yes, of course," Montes mimicked Anderson. "Well then. Now that you have accepted your promotion to commander of the British brigade, I think the celebration should begin. What else can we do to prolong the festivities?"

Montes went silent. Anderson had stuck himself in the middle of this by opening his mouth and cooperating against specific instructions from Rivers.

"Aah, yes." Montes wagged a finger. "I've another idea. Since you British seem so obsessed with the fairy-tale idea of knights and princes and dukes and duchesses, I think we should have a knighting ceremony. Ha-ha!" He looked at the Argentinean troops surrounding him. "Does anyone have a sword by any chance?"

The Argentineans shook their heads.

"No swords? Well, we shall make do by improvising. You! Sergeant Ginoble!"

"Yes, Capitán."

"Bring me your rifle!"

"Yes, Capitán." The solider stepped over and handed Montes his rifle.

"Since Commander Williams—with an *s*—Anderson, the commander of the British in Antarctica, is already on his knees, where all good knights begin their knighthoods before their lords and masters, and where all British citizens should be in the presence of their Argentinean masters, this ceremony should be simple."

Montes took the rifle and laid the barrel on Anderson's shoulder and declared, "As senior military commander of all Argentinean forces stationed on the continent of Antarctica, and as most high lord and master over all British forces and civilians subjugated to the great power of the Argentine Republic in Antarctica, it is my honor and great personal privilege to hereby declare you, Commander Sir Williams—with an *s*—Anderson, Knight of the Royal Order of the Argentine and local commander of all British forces in the Argentine, yet loyally obedient to all lawful orders directed at you by officers of the Argentine Republic!"

Montes stood back and snapped, "Sergeant, take the rifle."

"*Si*, Capitán."

Montes crossed his arms. "What is this? Tears streaming from the eyes of the Knight of the Royal Order of the Argentine? How could this be, Sir Williams with an *s*?"

"I . . . I . . ."

"Say no more, Sir Williams," Montes sneered. "I understand these tears of yours. Why, to realize a lifetime dream of assuming command of men—why, I could see that could become emotional. But more than that, to be bestowed the highest order, the Knight of the Royal Order of the Argentine, to become allied in a sense with the greatest nation on the face of the earth, why, it's enough to bring even the strongest of men to an emotional abyss of gratitude."

"I . . . please . . ."

"Do you know what we need, Sir Williams, to lighten up the mood around here?" He crossed his arms and looked at Anderson.

No answer.

"I'm waiting for an answer, Sir Williams."

"I don't know, sir."

"What we need is a celebration. Don't you think so, Commander Sir Williams?"

Anderson nodded. "Yes, sir."

"Yes, of course you agree. Now we are getting somewhere. How could we celebrate the promotion of Sir Williams to commander and his ascension to knighthood? Anyone have any suggestions? Firing squad? Any suggestions?"

No answer.

"What about you British pond scum? Any suggestions on how you wish to celebrate the promotion of your hero? Perhaps there is some British celebratory custom of which I am unaware."

Rivers could offer to trade places with Anderson. But that would make matters worse and put the others in mortal danger. Anderson made the mistake of showing weakness in the face of a captor.

"No suggestions? Well then, I have an idea or two. Sir Williams!"

"Yes, sir." Anderson's voice quaked like a Geiger counter.

"Tell me, Sir Williams, do you like to dance?"

"I've never been one to dance, sir."

"Then I think it's time that you learned. A knight must be schooled in all the proper social graces. Why, what if you were invited to a black-tie affair at Buckingham Palace? You would wish to be skilled in the fine art of ballroom dancing. And what better place to learn than the frozen tundra of the Antarctic. This will be in keeping with the longstanding British tradition of experimenting with exciting endeavors in foreign places. Prince Harry in Las Vegas. Now Sir Williams dancing on the Antarctic tundra. I suppose it's a British thing. Ha-ha-ha!"

Montes pulled out his pistol and unleashed another belly laugh as he fired into the snow inches from Anderson.

Anderson jumped up, and Montes fired another shot at his feet. "Dance, Sir Williams, dance!" He laughed, and the air cracked with two more shots.

Anderson jumped and hopped, trying to avoid a shot to the foot.

"Somebody get a cell phone and film this so we can put this on the Internet!" Montes shouted. "Colonel Sanchez, you film it."

"*Si*, Capitán." The colonel pulled out a cell phone as Montes fired two more shots at Anderson's feet and then bent over laughing.

"That's enough! Stop it!" Rivers could no longer contain himself.

"What is this?" Montes stared at Rivers. "A party pooper in our midst?" He reloaded the revolver. "Perhaps you wish to dance with Sir Williams?" He pointed his gun and fired three shots at Rivers' feet.

The shots hit the snow inches from where Rivers stood. But Rivers stood like a rock and did not flinch. Instead, he bore a steely glare at Montes.

"I see you are not as much fun as Sir Williams," Montes snapped, then turned and shot two more bullets in the ground at Anderson's feet.

Anderson jumped and danced around again. "Please! Please!" he cried.

Montes doubled over laughing. "Okay. Okay. Enough dancing, Sir Williams!" He stood and reholstered his pistol. "Anderson, you can take a break from the dancing." He turned to the lieutenant colonel standing beside him. "Did you get a video of that, Colonel Sanchez?"

"*Si, mi* capitán."

"Let me see it!"

The colonel held up his cell phone, showing the video, and Montes responded with delight, laughing and guffawing as Anderson got up off his knees.

"There is good news, Sir Williams," Montes announced. "My second in command has captured riveting footage of your command performance for all posterity! Soon you will be an international star!"

Anderson did not respond. More tears rolled down his cheeks.

"Now, now. Do not cry, Sir Williams! There is one other thing that I need you to do before you and your men go to your cell."

Anderson stood there, unresponsive.

"Do you not wish to know of your assignment, Sir Williams?"

Anderson looked up and then down, and then looked over at Rivers, making eye contact with eyes full of fear. He looked back at Montes. "Yes, sir. I suppose, sir."

"Excellent," Montes said. "Here is your first command." He held out his revolver, which looked like a long-barreled .357 Magnum.

The revolver glistened in the dim sun as Montes reloaded it, then holstered it. This time he spoke in a lower, sterner voice, a dark and stark contrast to the strident mocking tone that he had used when making Anderson dance around the bullets fired at his feet. "Order your men to their knees."

Magnolia Flats
Kensington District
West London

11:55 p.m. local time

S till fighting nervousness, Meg ran down the list she had thrown together. "Toiletries. Check. Pantyhose. Check. Razors. Check. Toothpaste. Oh, darn it." She stepped into the WC, grabbed the last tube of toothpaste, and placed it in her travel bag.

She folded a pair of designer jeans and placed them on the top of her suitcase and proceeded through her checklist. Passport—check. One-way ticket from Heathrow to Santiago via São Paulo/Guarulhos International

Airport in Brazil—after a hit of nearly five thousand pounds to her Visa card—check.

With Shelley's help, she had rushed to plan this trip, and in four hours she would be on a British Airways jet for the first leg of the twenty-hour flight to Santiago.

Her mind flooded with thoughts, her heart swirled with emotion—flying off to find a man she loved and yet hated who did not love her, and even if she found him, how could she help? Why go?

The answers eluded her. Yet with tears streaming down her cheeks, she would obey an overwhelming compulsion within her soul and she would go. Somehow, some way, when she got to Chile, she would trust the One who saved Little Aussie's life on what to do and where to go and what to say.

A knock on her bedroom door. "Meg, the taxicab is here."

Those words ignited another emotional wave.

Aussie had finally fallen asleep. She had resolved to slip out and let him sleep.

Shelley would take him to school tomorrow and explain to him that his mommy would be back in a few days. "Aunt Shelley," as he called her, would take him to the zoo, take him to Horseguards Park, and even take him for a cruise down the Thames on the London Showboat.

"Please. Could you tell the cabbie I'll be right there? I want to look in on Aussie."

"Certainly."

She pushed open the door to his bedroom. Tiptoeing across the carpet, in the soft glow of the light from the hallway, she saw he was still sleeping. She wanted to wake him to say good-bye, but her maternal instincts told her otherwise.

She got on her knees and put her arm around him. She kissed him on his forehead and silently prayed. She stood and tiptoed out of the room.

"Mommy?" he called as she stepped into the hallway.

"Yes, Aussie?"

"Are you going to find Daddy?"

She stepped back into the small bedroom and kneeled beside him and hugged and kissed him again. "How did you know that, Aussie?"

"I heard you and Aunt Shelley talking."

"Yes, sweetie, I will try to find your father. But you will have lots of fun with Aunt Shelley, and Mommy will be back soon." She kissed his head.

"Mommy?"

"Yes, sweetie."

"When you find Daddy, will you tell him I love him?"

Her tears flowed like a river. "Of course I will."

"I'll miss you, Mommy."

"Mommy's going to miss you too, Aussie."

"I love you, Mommy."

"I love you, baby."

She kissed and hugged him a final time, then rushed out of the room.

She had to leave before she changed her mind.

Belgrano II base camp
Argentine outpost
Antarctica

Did you hear me, Sir Williams?" Montes snapped. "I told you to order your men to their knees."

"I . . . yes, I heard you."

"Well? What is your delay?"

Anderson hesitated. "I'm sorry. I don't think I can do that."

"What did you say?"

"I'm sorry, sir. I don't think I can do that."

"Did you say you don't think you can obey my order?"

This time Anderson did not respond.

"Not going to obey me, Sir Williams?"

Still no response.

"Perhaps you need to dance a bit more, Sir Williams!" Montes pulled his revolver out again.

The first shot struck the snow to the left of Anderson's foot.

"Please!" Anderson pleaded.

The second shot struck him between the eyes and blew the back of his head off. The force of the shot from the front knocked Anderson back, and his body sprawled faceup in the snow. Anderson's mouth froze open, and his left eyeball protruded like a large white marble. Blood gushed from the bullet hole, from the eye socket, and brains and blood spread out from the back of his head.

Three men started heaving. One down toward the end of the line, Rivers could not tell which one, bent over and vomited. And although the sight of death and gore did not shock Rivers, as he had seen such sights many times before, in Afghanistan and Africa, he felt himself seething. Montes had better hope he did not find himself one-on-one with Rivers.

In the wind-filled moment, full of whistling howls, no words were spoken. In this surrealistic moment of death, the Argentineans stared at the body. And even the murderer, Capitán Montes, by allowing a spontaneous moment of silence, seemed to stop to pay a strange tribute to the dead.

A whispering came from the British line. "The Lord is my shepherd, I shall not want. He maketh me to lie down in green pastures. He leadeth me beside still waters. He restoreth my soul."

Bach's voice. Reciting something. Perhaps a prayer. Perhaps something from the Bible. Austin wasn't sure.

"He leadeth me into the paths of righteousness for his name's sake. He restoreth my soul."

"Squad leader!" Montes yelled over the top of Bach's prayer.

"*Sí*, Capitán!"

"Lead the prisoners to their quarters!"

"*Sí*, Capitán!"

"Yea, though I walk through the valley of the shadow of death, I will fear no evil. For thou art with me."

"You heard the capitán!" the squad commander screamed. "Left face!" Soldiers moved into the line and turned the British to their left. "Forward march! Move! Move! Move!"

They stepped forward, trudging across the snow, but not in any semblance of military precision.

Captain Dunn walked at the head of the line. Rivers followed behind him. Bach, the self-anointed group chaplain, followed Rivers, still muttering that same prayer verse or whatever from the Bible.

"Okay, drag the body out of the way and get the blood out of the snow!" Montes barked instructions as the group walked across an open space toward a white geodesic dome, the door guarded by two soldiers. Other armed guards, half a dozen altogether, stood guard around the perimeter.

One of the guards opened the door and pointed inside. Dunn stepped in first, followed by Rivers. The dome, typical for this part of the world, housed a large open space in the middle with a few adjoining rooms. It had only one WC, a condition inadequate for ten men.

Dunn walked over to Rivers, and they stood together as the others formed a semicircle inside. There had been twelve of them. And now, with Anderson dead and Gaylord possibly dead, ten remained.

Rivers felt conflicted in his role, which felt like half SBS officer and half babysitter. He had not trained for this in Special Forces school. He was a trained killer. Not a babysitter. If these chaps had any military instincts at all . . .

"Dunn?"

"Yes, sir?"

"I don't know how I'm going to do it, but before we leave this place, I am going to kill that Montes chap."

CHAPTER 19

Control room
ARA San Juan
South Atlantic Ocean
50 miles southeast of the Malvinas (Falkland) Islands
depth 100 feet

8:00 a.m. local time

The German-built ARA *San Juan*, identical in design to her sister boat, the ARA *Santa Cruz*, measured 216 feet in length, carried a crew of twenty-nine, and was powered by diesel engines and electric motors.

By contrast, the more powerful *Los Angeles*–class nuclear attack submarines, the workhorse attack submarine of the US Navy, measured 366 feet in length, 150 feet longer than the Argentine boats, and carried 110 crew members.

Pitted one-on-one against an American submarine, either the *Santa Cruz* or the *San Juan* would be at a significant disadvantage. But against any other ship in the world, including against a powerful American supercarrier, they were a powerful one-two punch for the Argentine Navy.

With six torpedo tubes in her bow, the *San Juan* packed a deadly strike, carrying a total of twenty-two torpedoes and another thirty-nine mines.

In command of the *San Juan*, one hundred feet below the surface of the chilly waters of the South Atlantic and fifty miles southeast of the Malvinas Islands, known by the British as the Falkland Islands, Commander Carlos Almeyda sipped black coffee and surveyed the flurry of activity in the control room. Ten miles off to his north, submerged at one hundred feet, the *San Juan*'s sister boat also lay in wait.

Like wolves stalking their prey, the two Argentinean submarines had reached their patrol area. Their mission—to attack any British ships sailing to Antarctica to reinforce the British-Chilean oil exploration efforts.

Britain had always been a sea power, and Britain would carry out her attempted power grab for Antarctic oil by the sea lanes, just as she had done in her embarrassing defeat of Argentina in 1982, delivered by the Royal Navy and Royal Marines.

Now, on this submarine and from this control room, with an unfathomable weight of responsibility placed upon him, Carlos Almeyda and his men waited as a first line of defense in dangerous waters against the same enemy that had defeated his country before. Before history would again repeat itself, these men would sacrifice their lives if necessary.

"Sonar Officer. Report."

"Still nothing, Capitán," the sonar officer said. "Except a couple of whales moaning in the distance. Other than that, only the gurgling sounds of the sea."

"Only the gurgling sounds of the sea?" Carlos sipped his coffee and smiled. "You have a poetic way with words, Lieutenant Fernandez. You should write a book when you retire from the Navy."

"Thank you, sir," Fernandez said. "I minored in Spanish literature and would love to do that one day."

"I think you should," Almeyda said. "But before you trouble yourself with such a laborious undertaking, I want you to continue to focus on those . . . what did you say? . . . ah, yes . . . focus your attention on those gurgling sounds of the sea. And when you hear something other than a couple of frolicking whales, something sounding like a British warship, notify me immediately."

"*Si*, Capitán. With pleasure."

Bridge
M/S Thor Liberty
British Registry cargo ship
South Atlantic Ocean
50 miles east of the Falkland Islands
course 180 degrees

8:10 a.m. local time

From the bridge of the freighter *Thor Liberty*, Captain Bob Hudson looked out over the cold, gray waters of the South Atlantic.

With her storage compartments loaded down with tons of petro-drilling equipment destined for the frozen Antarctic tundra, the *Thor Liberty* sailed in the center of a four-ship flotilla bound for the turbulent waters of Drake Passage between Cape Horn and the Antarctic Peninsula.

Off to the left, sailing in front of the rising sun, the gray assault ship HMS *Ocean*, carrying more than eighteen helicopters and eighty-three Royal Marines, cut a course parallel to *Thor Liberty.*

To the right, the British ship RFA *Black Rover* cut the same course, sailing under the Royal Fleet Auxiliary, a division of the Royal Navy.

Black Rover: the civilian-manned naval vessel that supplied the Royal Navy with fuel and ammunition, and also transported a contingency of another two hundred Royal Marines to supplement those on board HMS *Ocean.*

Out front of HMS *Ocean*, RFA *Black Rover*, and M/S *Thor Liberty*, the powerful new flagship of the British fleet, the HMS *Queen Elizabeth*, plowed through the waters, leading the British flotilla. The brand-new supercarrier gave Britain the most powerful warship in the world, with the exception of the American supercarriers.

Somewhere out there, under the cold Atlantic waters, the nuclear attack sub HMS *Astute* patrolled nearby, packing tons of additional firepower in defense of the carrier and in support of the mission.

The five-ship Royal Navy task force, including the *Astute*, would be the first to resupply and support the British expedition of Antarctica.

All his life, Bob Hudson had wished for nothing other than a life in the Royal Navy. His father and grandfather were Royal Navy sea captains.

And his father sailed with the naval task force that had emancipated the Falklands in 1982.

Bob, hoping to follow in his father's footsteps, had enrolled at the Royal Naval College at Dartmouth.

There he excelled, and he fell in love with the great natural beauty of Devon County. But the beautiful countryside in southeastern England was not all that he fell in love with.

Her name was Shelley.

Her shiny black hair, which she would push flirtatiously across her forehead, glistened in the afternoon sunshine. Her dauntingly blue eyes and her pencil-thin waist would remain in his dreams years later.

On their boat trips down the River Dart, when they snacked on a picnic basket full of champagne and olives on the grassy riverbank, he discovered for the first time the feeling of love.

They discussed marriage and Navy life, and she had made clear her desire to become an officer's wife.

This budding relationship had seemed perfect in every respect. For it would take a rare and special lady to put up with a naval officer and to maintain a stable and lovely home and to care for children while the officer would literally spend years at sea over the course of a career.

On a Saturday afternoon boating picnic trip during his final year at the academy, they had pulled the boat up to a private grassy area along the shoreline, and after two glasses of champagne, he asked her to marry him.

She accepted immediately.

They spent the rest of the afternoon on the grassy bank celebrating and sipping champagne.

The next Saturday, after a week of exciting wedding planning, she sat dutifully in the stands of the athletic fields, watching his rugby league match. Though he often played the position of a winger, as he had one of the fastest foot speeds on the team, on this day he shifted to fullback because of an injured teammate.

Their opponents from Sandhurst, the Royal Military Academy team, were out for blood against Bob's Dartmouth team. Nothing like a feud between Army and Navy to get the juices flowing.

Bob had dropped out of the defensive line to cover the rear from kicks and runners breaking the line. He converged on the Sandhurst runner advancing with the ball when a collision blindsided him.

He saw a flash of stars and then fell face-first to the grass. Sometime later, he woke up to the blinding lights of the Naval College sick bay, battling knife-like pain in his kneecap and his head. He blacked out again, then woke up later at Dartmouth Hospital on the South Embankment, swarmed by nurses from the National Health Service. Bob recovered from the severe concussion. But the ligament and cartilage damage would have lifelong consequences.

The Royal Navy frowned on such injuries and rejected his application for a commission.

Unfortunately, the injury led to more than the loss of his naval officer's commission. Within a few weeks, Shelley grew strangely cool. Shelley wanted to be an officer's wife. Bob Hudson would never be an officer in His Majesty's Navy. Within weeks, she terminated their relationship.

With Shelley gone, Bob had to refocus. Though he could no longer join the Royal Navy, he still hoped to go to sea.

At the end of World War I, King George V bestowed the title of Merchant Navy on the British merchant shipping fleets following their valiant service supporting the war. When a friend referred Bob to the offices of Thorco Shipping in London and helped him arrange an interview, he secured a job as a navigator on board the freighter *Thorco Africa*.

He would later serve on a number of Thorco ships, including the *Thorco Attraction*, the *Thorco Asia*, the *Atlantic Zeus*, and the *Thor Sapphire*.

Thorco paid well but required long periods—sometimes months—at sea. Yet the sea helped him keep his mind off of her, for the sea became a jealous mistress.

Three months ago, Bob had gotten a call from Thorco's vice president in charge of personnel assignment.

He would never forget the question. "Bob, are you ready to assume command?"

For a mariner, whether military or civilian, this would become one of those frozen-in-time moments—the moment he was offered command at sea.

Due to an early retirement, an opening had come up aboard the freighter *Thor Liberty* to become the ship's master, and Bob's stellar service as first officer on the M/S *Thor Sapphire* made him the company's leading choice to take command. The job was his—if he wanted it.

Bob accepted the job and reported to *Thor Liberty*'s home port at the city of Douglas, on the Isle of Man, a British island in the Irish Sea between Ireland and England.

There he learned that the ship's first mission under his command involved the Royal Navy. *Thor Liberty* would sail in a four-ship flotilla along with HMS *Queen Elizabeth*, HMS *Ocean*, and RFA *Black Rover* on a top secret mission to the Antarctic region.

While HMS *Queen Elizabeth* would pack most of the firepower with her air wing of brand-new F-35 attack jets, and HMS *Ocean* would bring additional firepower, including helicopters and Royal Marines, *Thor Liberty* would transport munitions and petro-drilling equipment owned by British Petroleum. Also on board *Thor Liberty*, a team of petro- and mechanical engineers who would be transported by helicopters to the drop site.

Black Rover's mission would be to replenish the other ships and transport several platoons of Royal Marines to supplement the group on board HMS *Ocean*.

This mission provided a level of excitement for Bob. Aside from the thrill of being selected to carry out a mission in service to the Crown, which fulfilled his sense of patriotism, Bob delighted in the fact that several of his classmates from the Royal Naval College were stationed on board both HMS *Queen Elizabeth* and HMS *Ocean*. This provided a personal sense of satisfaction. Unlike his milestone achievement, few of his classmates from Dartmouth had yet to achieve anything even close to what he had achieved—command at sea.

This thought brought a smile to his face.

And so did another thought.

What would she think? Last he had heard, she had moved to London. And still had not married.

After all these years, he still kept her photo in his wallet. He never knew why he kept it, but only that he could never rid himself of it.

Oh well. It was jolly academic at this point.

He took another sip of hot tea and looked out at the choppy waters of the South Atlantic.

In a few hours, when they entered the waters of the Drake Passage, the swells would go from choppy to menacing.

"Navigator! Updated course status."

"Holding at one-eight-zero degrees, Captain."

"Very well. Steady as she goes, Mister Smithwick."

"Aye, Captain."

Control room
ARA San Juan
South Atlantic Ocean
50 miles east of the Malvinas (Falkland) Islands
depth 100 feet

8:30 a.m. local time

E ven before Lieutenant Julio Fernandez became a physics major at the University of Buenos Aires, specializing in the physics of sound acoustics, he developed an insatiable fascination with submarines. This fascination grew when, as a teenager, he had become a fan of American submarine movies. *Run Silent, Run Deep*. *The Hunt for Red October*. *Crimson Tide*.

His native Argentina had only three submarines in its fleet. Four others scheduled to be built were scrapped because of costs. Fernandez had considered moving to the United States to join the US Navy.

But when his scores in acoustical physics were among the highest registered at UBA, he received a call from an Argentinean Navy recruiter.

And now, here he sat at the sonar station as the sonar officer on the most important mission for the Argentine Navy in a generation.

In the subdued lighting of the *San Juan*'s control room, with myriad yellow, green, and red lights flashing all around him, Fernandez adjusted his headset and closed his eyes.

One of the basic principles in acoustic physics is that the speed of sound in water travels five times faster than the speed of sound in air.

The sound of gushing water rushed across his headset. Again, more gurgling interrupted by the singing of humpback whales. No, not a humpback. Different whales produce different sounds. That was more of a long drawn-out note. The sound of the large deep-water blue whale.

How ironic that a single whale, in the right water conditions, could be heard from hundreds of miles away, but the sounds of something powerful and man-made, like the sounds of an aircraft carrier, depended on being in the right place at the right time.

Being an effective sonar man required not only a keen understanding of acoustical physics—combined with a God-given gift of extraordinary hearing—but also extraordinary patience.

The British were out there.

Somewhere.

He knew it.

He would combine all the resources at his disposal—including great patience—to find them.

Fernandez closed his eyes and enjoyed the harmonic sounds of the sea.

Bridge
HMS Queen Elizabeth
South Atlantic Ocean
50 miles east of the Falkland Islands
course 180 degrees

8:55 a.m. local time

From the bridge of the brand-new British supercarrier *Queen Elizabeth*, Captain Edwin Jones-Landry looked down over the gray flight deck and out toward the bow.

Four American-built F-35A Lightning attack jets, ultra-sophisticated stealth fighter bombers built by Lockheed-Martin and carrying twenty-four million lines of software data in each plane, were chained down on the forward flight deck, ready to be armed and moved to the ship's catapult on a moment's notice.

Three times the size of HMS *Illustrious*, the British carrier that led the successful assault against the Falklands in 1982 and previously the largest carrier in the Royal Navy, the great new flagship of the British fleet, with forty aircraft and a crew of over seven hundred, plowed steadily through the gray rolling waters of the South Atlantic, leading a small flotilla nearing the earth's southern subpolar region.

The carrier's fighter wing would get one of her biggest tests early on—to support Royal Marines dispatched from HMS *Ocean* in an effort to retake British territory at Camp Churchill. And after that, to protect and support construction of the joint British-Chilean refinery on Antarctica.

Jones-Landry had received one of the supreme appointments in the Royal Navy with his selection for command of the *Queen Elizabeth*, the pride of Britain and the flagship of the entire fleet.

Even King Charles had attended the change-of-command ceremony.

Now Britain would reap the dividends of her investment.

"Navigator. Current position."

"Fifty-three degrees, one-four-four south latitude, fifty-seven degrees, two-three-eight west longitude. Course one-eight-zero degrees. Approximately fifty miles from the Falkland Islands, sir."

"Display our position on the screen and report, Leftenant."

"Aye, Captain."

Computer screens on the bridge lit up with an electronic map showing the course and current location of the British task force.

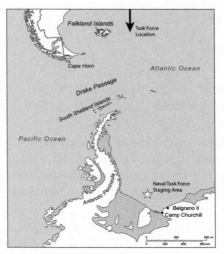

FALKLANDS ANTARCTIC PENINSULA STAGING AREA FOR NAVAL ASSAULT

"The arrow on the left points to the position of the Falklands, Captain. We are at the tip of the white arrow, which marks the current position of the Royal Navy task force. As you can see, sir, we're currently passing to the east of the islands. Fifty miles to our west is the capital of the Falkland Islands, Port Stanley.

"We are on a course of one-eight-zero degrees, due south, headed toward the naval staging area, marked by the star on the map. We will launch our assault to recapture Camp Churchill from this staging area.

"Current speed is twenty knots, slow enough so that the other ships in the flotilla can keep up."

"Very well. Thank you, Leftenant," Jones-Landry said. "Helmsman. Steady as she goes."

"Steady as she goes. Aye, Captain."

Bridge
M/S **Thor Liberty**
British Registry cargo ship
South Atlantic Ocean
50 miles east of the Falkland Islands
course 180 degrees

9:00 a.m. local time

Captain Bob Hudson, like so many mariners living most of their lives on the sea, enjoyed tinkering with shortwave radios. While the Internet had become increasingly common at sea, it sometimes proved unreliable and slow.

But the far-reaching grasp of shortwave radio was never slow.

Years before his promotion to captain, Hudson purchased a little Grundig G3 shortwave receiver that he carried on cruises. During downtimes, Bob enjoyed going out on deck and tuning around the bands to see what he could hear.

Once, when crossing the Pacific, just north of the equator, the little shortwave radio picked up radio station KH6BB, operated by the USS *Missouri* Amateur Radio Club on board the USS *Missouri*, permanently anchored in Pearl Harbor. Bob, at that time the navigator on board the

Thorco Asia, upon his arrival in Hong Kong had mailed the station a reception report, hoping they got a kick out of being heard in a location hundreds of miles south of Hawaii.

He later got a postcard signed by six volunteers running the radio room on the *Missouri*, thanking him for the greeting. That postcard got him hooked on shortwave.

The little Grundig shortwave turned out to be a better radio than expected. It featured a synchronous detection for AM use, which reduced fading, making it easier to tune in single sideband. Not only could the radio receive AM broadcast, but it also received FM stereo and Aircraft Band and could pick up most of the standard shortwave bands available at the touch of a button.

Sometimes at night, when on the seas half a world away from home, he would go out on deck and search for the comforting sounds of the BBC. On nights when the atmospheric and temperature conditions aligned ever so properly, and when the Grundig caught the reassuring voices from back home, Bob thought of her—of what might have been.

This morning Captain Hudson brought the radio on the bridge with him, and with *Thor Liberty* sailing behind the HMS *Queen Elizabeth* and between the HMS *Ocean* and the RFA *Black Rover*, he decided to give it a whirl. He powered the thing up, then hit the AM scanner.

The green light raced across the diode from left to right, searching. A few seconds later the light locked onto a signal.

Bob reached down and turned up the volume. He heard a male voice, distinctively British in accent.

"Good morning, Port Stanley. Broadcasting live from John Street in downtown Stanley, this is F-I-R-S, the Falkland Islands Radio Service. Looks like another chilly and overcast morning in the Falklands. Temperature at Port Stanley Airport is currently holding firm at fifty-two degrees. Ocean watchers reporting calm seas at Surf Bay, Rookery Bay, and Gypsy Cove. Meteorologists do expect this marine cloud cover to burn back when the sun climbs a tad higher in the sky around midmorning."

"Captain! Captain!"

The ship's radar/sonar officer rushed onto the bridge with a look of ghastly panic etched on his face.

"What is it, Mister Johnson?" Bob turned down the volume on the shortwave.

"Captain, a few moments ago we picked up on passive sonar what sounded like a submarine!"

Nothing else like the word *submarine* could strike fear in the heart of the captain of a surface vessel. Bob's mind raced. "HMS *Astute* is in the area. Are you sure that's not what you picked up?"

"We can't say for sure. We had a fix on it for a few seconds. But it sounded like a diesel-electric boat. The *Astute* is nuclear."

Bob released a worried exhale. "Are you sure, Mister Johnson?"

"Mister Adams heard it too, Captain. Whatever it was, it disappeared. But we both thought it sounded like a diesel-electric boat."

Bob wiped his forehead. "Very well. Communications Officer, open a secure channel to HMS *Queen Elizabeth*. Get Captain Jones-Landry on the line."

"Aye, Captain."

Bridge
HMS Queen Elizabeth
South Atlantic Ocean
50 miles east of the Falkland Islands
course 180 degrees

9:05 a.m. local time

Are you certain it was diesel-electric?" Captain Edwin Jones-Landry, in command of HMS *Queen Elizabeth,* put the question to his sonar officer.

Jones-Landry wanted to know because the British and American navies operated only nuclear-powered submarines.

A diesel-electric submarine would be operated by a nation other than the US or the UK.

And while a diesel-electric boat could not stay submerged as long as a nuclear boat, nor could it move as silently or as swiftly through the water, a diesel-electric submarine, positioned in the wrong place at the wrong time, could pack a deadly punch—even against a supercarrier.

"We heard it for five seconds, Captain. We're running the digital recording against the sound database in our acoustic computers to try to verify what we heard."

"Very well," Jones-Landry said. "Alert me the second the acoustical analysis is available."

"Yes, Captain."

"Bridge! Radio Room!"

"Radio. Bridge. Go ahead."

"Captain. We've gotten a call from Captain Hudson on the *Thor Liberty*. Sir, the freighter also picked up a brief signal on passive sonar that they think might be a diesel-electric submarine. They tracked the sound for five seconds, and then it disappeared."

"Very well." Jones-Landry had in his gut the sudden feeling that the dynamics of the operation had just changed. "Radio. Contact Captain Hudson. Tell him we heard it too. Tell him we're running the digital recording through our acoustical computers to try to verify the source."

"Aye, Captain," the radio officer said.

"Radio. Contact the captains of HMS *Ocean*, HMS *Astute*, and RFA *Black Rover*. Inquire about whether they heard anything on their passive sonar."

"Aye, Captain."

Standing at the bridge, still overlooking the flight deck of Britain's most treasured naval asset, Jones-Landry pulled his binoculars to his eyes and scanned the gray waters out in front of the ship, looking, desperately, for the sign of a periscope.

Of course, visually spotting a periscope, even if one were out there, would be like finding a needle in a haystack. But even still . . .

"What do you make of the situation, Captain?"

The captain looked at his trusted executive officer, Commander Donald Parrott. "I don't know, XO. But I do not have a good feeling."

"Do you think one of the Argentinean submarines could have penetrated our screen?"

"Possibly," Jones-Landry said. "Either they have penetrated our screen or we've sailed right over the top of them."

"Or perhaps we heard an electronic anomaly."

"Let's hope so, XO. Somehow I am not so optimistic."

"Bridge. Radio."

"Radio. Go ahead."

"Sir, the captains of the *Ocean*, *Black Rover*, and *Astute* report no sonar contact. They've heard nothing, sir!"

"Thank you, Leftenant." A temporary sigh of relief.

"Well, sir," Commander Parrott said, "there's room for some optimism."

"Perhaps," Captain Jones-Landry said. "Perhaps we heard an electronic anomaly between us and *Thor Liberty*."

"That sounds like a plausible theory, sir."

"Perhaps. But not so plausible that my stomach has stopped feeling like a frying pan full of scrambled eggs."

"I understand, Captain. Perhaps the sonar officers can shed some extra light on the matter."

"Let us hope," Jones-Landry said. "Petty Officer!"

"Yes, Captain."

"Would you please fetch a spot of tea for the XO and me?"

"Right away, sir," the eager young sailor said.

Jones-Landry pondered the situation. What if there were Argentinean submarines in the area? Or another nationality? The Russians operated a slew of older diesel-electric boats. Russian subs had a history of tagging along behind NATO battle groups.

But no Russian sub had ever fired on a NATO ship.

But if the sub were Argentinean . . .

"XO. I have this sneaky feeling that we will be at battle stations sooner than we had hoped for."

"Bridge. Sonar."

"Sonar. Bridge. Go ahead," Jones-Landry said.

"Sir, acoustics computers have completed their analysis of the sound recorded from passive sonar."

"Let's hear it, Leftenant."

"Captain, computers confirm a 97.5 percent possibility that what we heard is a diesel-electric submarine."

Jones-Landry looked over at Commander Parrott. "We've got a sub, XO." He turned to the sonar officer. "Very well, Leftenant. What does the computer show on range and classification?"

"Captain, because of the short duration of the recording, and also because of the relatively poor quality, the mathematical certainty drops from that point."

"Let's hear it."

"Yes, sir. Based on the quality of the recording, we estimate range to target to be anywhere between four to twenty-five miles. There is a 50 percent probability that the submarine is Argentinean in origin, possibly *Santa Cruz*–class. There is a 45 percent probability that the submarine is Russian in origin, possibly *Kilo*-class."

"Very well," Jones-Landry said. "Bridge. Radio."

"Radio. Go ahead, Captain."

"Notify London. FLASH message. Be advised sonar has detected an unidentified submarine in the area, believed to be hostile, most probably diesel-electric Argentinean or Russian origin. Acoustic computers show 50 percent probability that the sub is Argentinean *Santa Cruz*–class and 45 percent probability that she is Russian *Kilo*-class. Request instruction on rules of engagement."

"Bridge. Radio. Aye, Captain. Transmitting FLASH message."

"Very well." He turned to Commander Parrott. "XO. Sound general quarters. Take the ship to battle stations. Notify the air wing commander. Let's get four Merlins airborne and get sonobuoys in the water. Then I want two F-35 Lightnings in the air. Armed with antisubmarine torpedoes. Notify HMS *Ocean* and HMS *Astute*. HMS *Queen Elizabeth* is at general quarters. Let's get moving."

"Aye, Captain," the XO said. "Mister Rogers. Sound general quarters. Open the 1-MC."

"Sounding general quarters!" Bells sounded all over the great ship. Down on the flight deck, up in the bridge, all over the ship, seven hundred sailors scrambled to their stations.

"Aye, XO. The 1-MC is open."

"Now hear this! This is the executive officer. General quarters! General quarters! All hands to battle stations! Sonar has confirmed the presence of an unidentified submarine, possibly hostile, in the area! ASW Squadron One. Prepare to scramble!"

The HMS *Queen Elizabeth* maintained her course as alarm bells sounded general quarters all over the ship. Captain Landry-Jones brought his binoculars to his eyes and surveyed the scene down on the flight deck.

"All hands, except for essential personnel, clear the flight deck. Stand by for flight operations!" the air wing commander's voice boomed over the ship's 1-MC.

Four gray Royal Navy Merlin Mk1 helicopters sat on the flight deck, and flight crews had already scrambled to them in a mad rush.

The Merlin in recent years had become the Royal Navy's workhorse helicopter. The birds carried sophisticated sonobuoys to drop in the water at various points to establish a defensive perimeter miles from the ship. The Merlins would fan out and drop dozens of electronic buoys in the water, which would broadcast sonar signals spanning a larger area of ocean, covering hundreds of square miles.

If the diesel-electric boat was still out there, hopefully the choppers could set a protective net and trap it. Hopefully they weren't too late. A ship captain's worst nightmare would come if a sub slipped in undetected, close enough for a point-blank shot.

For even against a supercarrier, the powerful giant of all warships, a well-placed torpedo could kill like a stone in David's slingshot.

Down below, the first of the large Merlins, its prop a whirling blur, lifted off the deck. The chopper rose up, hovered ten feet over the deck, dipped its nose, and then flew out to the east, climbing to five hundred feet over the water, flying out toward the port horizon.

A minute later, all four Merlins were airborne, with each one flying out in a different direction—to the north, south, east, and west—to drop the buoys that would set up the safety perimeter.

"All hands! Stand by for Lightning launch!"

Jones-Landry walked over to view the stern of the ship where the first F-35 Lightning sat in takeoff position.

The F-35's main Pratt & Whitney F135 jet engine roared. The single-seat attack jet shook, then rolled forward, and with increasingly rapid acceleration shot off the end of the carrier's flight deck, then nosed up and shot into the sky, peeling off to the left of the carrier's path.

Thirty seconds later, the second jet swooshed off the end of the flight deck and began its climb into the morning sky, peeling off in a direction opposite the first.

The jets carried additional security and firepower to attack the sub in the event of discovery.

Jones-Landry toyed with his chin. "We shall wait for instructions from London on the rules of engagement in this situation. But you can rest assured that I shall not leave this ship in a defenseless position."

CHAPTER 20

Prime Minister David Mulvaney, finishing a luncheon speech to the alumni of the London School of Economics, abruptly cut short his remarks, waved good-bye, and rushed off the podium without shaking hands. His chief of staff, Edward Willingham, had handed him a note at the lectern that an emergency meeting of the national security staff was commencing at Number 10 on a possible threat to the British flotilla and the HMS *Queen Elizabeth*.

They rushed him to his waiting Jaguar and by 1:25 p.m., with Willingham at his side, he stepped quickly into the historic Cabinet Room. A grim-faced quartet consisting of Foreign Secretary Gosling, Defence Chief McCutchenson, McCutchenson's aide Captain Morton, and First Sea Lord Admiral Ellington greeted him, all standing around the conference table.

"Be seated, gentlemen," Mulvaney said. "Let's get down to business, Sir Edmond." He looked at his senior defence chief. "What's this about a possible threat to our flotilla and to our carrier?"

Sir Edmond adjusted his glasses. "Sir, less than thirty minutes ago, as the task force passed to the east of the Falkland Islands on a course due south to the staging area, passive sonar on two of the four surface ships picked up what sounded like a submarine. Acoustics computers on board *Queen Elizabeth* have confirmed a diesel-electric submarine in the area, probably either Argentinean or Russian. We cannot say with greater certainty because the recording was neither long enough nor of sufficient quality for a better match."

Mulvaney slid on his reading glasses. "So we basically have a coin toss about whether we're dealing with Russia or Argentina."

"True, Prime Minister," Sir Edmond said. "Surely the Russians will have an interest in keeping an eye on our new supercarrier. But our proximity to the Falklands makes me believe that Argentina may be the culprit. At any rate, sir, the commander of the *Queen Elizabeth*, Captain Edwin Jones-Landry, has requested instructions on setting the rules of engagement for this situation."

The prime minister leaned back and crossed his arms. "So what are you gentlemen suggesting?"

The men looked at one another, then Foreign Secretary John Gosling spoke up.

"As His Majesty's principal diplomat, serving at your pleasure, Prime Minister, it is my duty to address the potential diplomatic problems of attacking the submarine. Obviously, if she is Russian, we run the risk of a wider diplomatic and military confrontation than if she belongs to Argentina. Bear in mind, Prime Minister, that there is freedom of navigation on the high seas. If the sub is Russian, she has every right to be submerged on the high seas. The issue is whether her presence is a threat to our flotilla. If we attack the sub, and if she's Russian, we could find ourselves facing a spectrum of responses ranging from condemnation to all-out war. And obviously, sir, a war with Russia, or even an international confrontation with the Russians short of war, would mean graver consequences than a blowup with Argentina."

Mulvaney uncrossed his arms and leaned forward. "And what would be the position of the Foreign Office should I order an attack and the submarine happens to be Argentinean?"

"Naturally, Prime Minister, the Foreign Office is interested in solving all conflicts through diplomacy. But in this case, if it can be proven that the submarine is Argentinean in origin, then we could claim legal justification for attacking it, based on the intelligence we have received linking Argentina to the attack on our Camp Churchill."

"So if I can summarize your position, Foreign Minister, the Foreign Office would oppose an attack on a Russian submarine, but could legally defend an attack on an Argentinean submarine?"

"Prime Minister, we hope that diplomacy prevails. But recognizing that British forces will engage in military action to recapture Camp Churchill, our role will be to present a legal defence and justification for those actions before the United Nations and in other international forums. It will be up to you, sir, but we will have a greater challenge both diplomatically and from a public-relations standpoint if we attack a Russian submarine."

The prime minister nodded. "Sir Edmond? Admiral Ellington? What do my military commanders say?"

"Admiral?" Sir Edmond said. "Why don't you take this one?"

"Certainly, sir," the first sea lord said. "Prime Minister, our recommendation is rooted in part on comments made by the foreign minister. Our naval task force is headed for a military showdown in the next day or so in Antarctica. With the attack against Camp Churchill, military action on the part of our forces is imminent.

"Even though we did not get the best recording for a definite identification of the sub, there is a 5 percent higher chance that this is an Argentinean sub as opposed to a Russian sub. The sonar picked up the sub off the coast of the Falkland Islands, which in our opinion elevates the chances that it is Argentinean. So if we mistakenly attack a Russian submarine, we have a good-faith defence based on the data that we have.

"But more importantly, Prime Minister, and this is crucial"—the first sea lord wagged his finger—"with a submarine in that close, even within twenty-five miles, our brand-new flagship could be in danger. If it is Argentinean, given the fact that Argentinean forces may have attacked our facility at Camp Churchill, we fear that they could take the first shot. Even a point-blank shot." Admiral Ellington stopped and looked straight at the prime minister. "A single well-placed torpedo, fired from close range, could sink our carrier. And that, sir, could be a monumental disaster for Britain."

The prime minister allowed that warning to set in. Then Mulvaney spoke up. "So are you recommending, Admiral Ellington, Sir Edmond, that I should issue an order to sink this submarine?"

The defence chief responded, "Yes, Prime Minister, this is exactly what we are recommending. Helicopters from the *Queen Elizabeth* are already dropping sonobuoys in the water in a two-hundred-square-mile radius around the carrier.

"If we discover that submarine anywhere within that sector, then we recommend that you formulate the rules of engagement to allow us to attack it and sink it. Under the circumstances, we cannot afford the risk of allowing the submarine to get off a first shot."

Mulvaney leaned back and scratched his chin. "Very well, Sir Edmond. Set the rules of engagement. If we discover that submarine anywhere within that two-hundred-square-mile sector, then our forces are to attack it and sink it."

"Yes, Prime Minister."

Bridge
HMS **Queen Elizabeth**
South Atlantic Ocean
50 miles east of the Falkland Islands
course 180 degrees

9:30 a.m. local time

Bridge! Radio!"

"Radio. Go ahead," Captain Edwin Jones-Landry said.

"Captain. We've received a FLASH message from London with rules-of-engagement orders."

"Let's hear it, Leftenant."

"Sir, our orders are to track and locate the unidentified submarine. If that submarine is located within a two-hundred-mile radius of HMS *Queen Elizabeth*, our orders are to attack it and sink it."

"Who signed the order, Leftenant?"

"Captain, Prime Minister Mulvaney signed the order."

Jones-Landry and Parrott exchanged glances.

"Very well," Jones-Landry said. "Transmit the order to all aircraft and to HMS *Ocean*. Prepare to attack and sink enemy submarine if located within two-hundred-mile radius of HMS *Queen Elizabeth*.

Pier 3
Armada de Chile
Valparaiso naval facility
Valparaiso, Chile

10:00 a.m. local time

Under the morning Pacific sunshine and cool western breezes, they stepped through the black iron gate onto the concrete pier.

Their arrival garnered immediate attention from the young sailors, officers, and Chilean Marines, who snapped to attention at the flag officer's surprise appearance.

The admiral spoke fluent English, with his Spanish accent barely detectable. Most Chilean naval officers had a strong multilingual capacity, often with English, German, or Russian as the second language. This trait Pete admired and wished that the US Navy required the same multilingual discipline among its officer corps.

Admiral Carlos Delapaz of the Chilean Navy returned the salutes of the gawking young sailors and continued his tour. "The Chilean Navy, or the *Armada de Chile*, as we call it in Spanish, consists of twenty-five thousand sailors and officers, along with five thousand Marines. We currently operate sixty-six surface ships, and twenty-one of those are based right here in Valparaiso."

Pete looked out over the harbor's blue waters and inhaled the salty Pacific air. Nothing like returning to the hustle and bustle of a navy base, even a foreign naval base, for reinvigorating the soul. "Your facilities are impressive, Admiral Delapaz. This base is active and vibrant. As I drove down into the city yesterday and looked down on the harbor, I realized that this reminds me of our naval facilities in San Diego."

"Interesting that you would say that, Commander," Delapaz said. "On my visits to your facilities in San Diego, which I have visited on official military business, I have always observed the remarkable similarity between San Diego and Valparaiso. Similar climate. Similar mild ocean breezes. A beautiful natural harbor, graceful palm trees, and teeming with activity."

Pete smiled. Valparaiso would be a nice final duty station to relax in while training the Chilean Navy. "I couldn't have described it better myself, Admiral."

"Of course, our fleet is smaller than the US Navy's fleet at San Diego. Here we have no carriers, and our four older diesel-electric subs are home ported at Talcahuano, which is 365 miles to the south."

"And as I recall," Pete said, "you are currently operating two French-built *Scorpène*-class boats and two German Type 209s?"

"I see you have done your homework, Commander." Delapaz smiled.

"I'm a sub commander, Admiral. I take pride in knowing the fleets of other navies."

"Which is why you are perfect for this assignment, Peter," Delapaz said. "With our purchase of the USS *Corpus Christi*, soon to be the CS *Miro*, the fleet of your father's homeland will possess the most powerful naval weapon in all of South America."

"It is my honor to participate in this historic transition, Admiral."

Delapaz smiled like a proud grandfather. "Let's walk down the pier and take a look at her. Shall we?"

"With pleasure, sir," Pete said. They walked down the long pier, past two amphibious assault ships, CS *Acquiles* and CS *Rancagua*. Sailors scampered up and down catwalks to the ships. As Pete and Delapaz cleared the *Rancagua*'s fantail, down on the left, at the end of the pier, the sleek, familiar black design of the *Los Angeles*–class submarine came into view.

Typically in port, a US warship flies two primary flags, one on the bow mast and one on the stern mast. The one on the bow is known as the Jack, while the flag on the stern is known as the Ensign and is the warship's national flag. The Jack on a US warship is comprised of the blue field of fifty stars typically seen on the US national flag.

In this case, the United States Jack fluttered in the breeze atop the bow mast of the nuclear submarine formerly known as USS *Corpus Christi* in her life and service to the United States Navy. But from the stern, two national flags flew—the Stars and Stripes of the United States flew alongside the Lone Star flag of Chile, which closely resembles the Lone Star flag of Texas. The sub, for the time being, still had painted in white on her black conning tower the *Los Angeles*–class designator number 705.

Above the designator number, painted in white on a long red stripe resembling a red yardstick, was the official US Navy name for the sub: USS *City of Corpus Christi*.

Four armed Chilean Marines who were guarding the sub snapped to attention and shot salutes as Delapaz came into view.

"At ease, gentlemen." Delapaz turned to Pete as the guards returned to parade rest. "Obviously, we still have some work to do to complete the transition. We will repaint her today with her new hull number— SSN 30—and then tomorrow we officially rechristen her as CS *Miro*. The American ambassador will be on hand for the transition ceremony, and I would consider it a personal honor, Commander, if you would accompany me as my guest. Service dress blues, of course."

"It would be my honor, Admiral."

"Good," Delapaz said. "After the christening ceremony, you will get the first opportunity to meet our replacement crew at 1300 hours tomorrow afternoon." The admiral checked his watch. "I had hoped that Commander Romero, the new commander of the *Miro*, would be here today so that you could brief him on procedures. Commander Romero has skippered our diesel-electric boats and is a nuclear engineer. He is the ideal candidate to command our first nuclear boat. Unfortunately, he's detained at Puerto Williams, our naval base down at the tip of the continent near Cape Horn."

Pete had heard that things were heating up in the Antarctic region but resisted any temptation to comment so as not to signal what he had learned through secret American intelligence channels. "I'll look forward to meeting Commander Romero and working with him, and I'm going to make sure that the inaugural Chilean crew of CS *Miro* will be the most professionally trained submarine crew in the world, sir."

The admiral smiled. "I like your enthusiasm, Pete. If you wish to take some more personal time today to get yourself moved in, or to deal with correspondence or whatever, please do so. I'm headed back to my office. I have some work to do in preparing for the transition ceremony. Enjoy your day, Pete."

"Thank you, Admiral. If it's all right with you, I think I'll stay here and do a quick check of the sub to make sure she's ready to go tomorrow."

"As you wish, Commander. Be at my office at 0800 hours tomorrow in service dress blue uniform. You can accompany me and my party to the transition ceremony."

"Yes, sir, Admiral." Pete stepped back and rendered a sharp salute.

Admiral Delapaz returned the salute, then pivoted and headed back down the pier.

Pete walked in the opposite direction, inspecting the submarine tethered to the pier by eight large ropes tied down to steel cleats.

He waited for the admiral to walk farther down the pier and then pulled out his smartphone and headed toward the end of the pier, away from the Marines guarding the submarine.

He had faced death in combat, been attacked by Russian naval forces in an international incident in the Black Sea, and faced an international criminal trial in which a conviction could have meant life in prison or possibly even execution. But Pete Miranda had never felt such chest-pounding anxiety at the mere thought of making a telephone call.

She'd just spent two hours in his car last night. He found her number in his phone contacts. She suggested that he call. Why not? "Let's do this." He punched the call option for Maria Vasquez.

The first ring.

The second ring.

His heart beat even faster.

The third ring.

Sweat beaded on his palms.

Voice mail.

"¡Hola. Habla María. Por favor deje su nombre y su número de teléfono, y le devolveré su llamada. Por favor hable despacio. Tengo ganas de hablar con usted."

She had changed the message on her voice mail. Interesting. Should he leave a message? Pete had never cared for leaving messages. He hung up, stuck his phone in his pocket, and waited for his pulse to decelerate. Even on her voice mail, her velvety voice was as electrifying in Spanish as it was in English.

He tried.

Maybe it wasn't meant to be.

Oh well.

Anyway, he was about to begin a major military assignment that would occupy the next few days.

Maybe this wasn't the right time.

Time to inspect the sub to make sure she was shipshape.

Pete walked back toward the sub, and as he stepped over to the catwalk that separated the pier from the deck, there was a buzzing in his pocket.

He returned the Chilean Marine's salute and retrieved his phone.

Maria Vasquez calling . . .

He pivoted around and headed back onto the pier to answer the call. "Hey, you! What's up?" He walked quickly back away from the Marine guards.

"This is Maria. How are you?"

"I'm doing fine." In reality, Pete felt exceptionally fine. Giddy in fact. "What are you up to this morning?"

"Running errands. I'm getting ready to paint my sunroom. How about you? I enjoyed my ride down last night. What are you doing?"

"I've been down at the Navy base. The view is beautiful. It's like San Diego."

"Yes, it is beautiful, isn't it?"

"Yes, it is."

No response.

Awkward silence.

"Anyway, I thought I would be occupied all day. But I've just learned that I have the rest of the day off and . . ."

"You were going to ask me out?"

He smiled. "Well . . . yes. That's exactly what I had in mind."

"Great! I would love that! When and where?"

"When? As soon as possible. Maybe we could meet for lunch and hang out a bit this afternoon?"

"I'd love that. Where did you have in mind?"

"Well . . . do you know any good places near the waterfront?"

"As a matter of fact, my favorite place is a quaint café called La Concepción. It's got a great view of the ships. It's on the south waterfront away from the naval station."

"Sounds perfect," he said. "What time did you have in mind?"

"Oh, gosh, I need to go change into something suitable. How about two hours?"

"Sounds great," he said, battling a runaway imagination triggered by her comment that she would *change into something suitable*. "Okay, I'll see you in two hours."

"I look forward to it."

Control room
Argentinean submarine ARA Santa Cruz
South Atlantic Ocean
depth 100 feet

10:35 a.m. local time

Navigator. Report position. Range to target," Commander Alberto Gomez said.

The navigator on the ARA *Santa Cruz*, Lieutenant Albert Gonzales, said, "Aye, Capitán. Course one-eight-zero degrees. Depth one hundred feet. Speed eighteen knots. Range to target, ten thousand yards. The *San Juan* is eight thousand yards off our starboard."

"Very well," Gomez said. "Steady as she goes. Let's stay in the carrier's wake and pray that she doesn't catch wind that we're here."

"Steady as she goes. Aye, Capitán."

ARA *Santa Cruz* trailed the carrier ten thousand yards to her stern, the equivalent of 5.7 miles, barely within range of the sub's twenty-two Mark 37 torpedoes.

Gomez wanted to get in closer . . . close enough for a point-blank shot, but not so close to avoid slipping away undetected after launching that shot. This was a tight balancing act.

At this distance, the torp might lock on any of the four ships in the British flotilla if it locked on any ships at all.

To get the shot he wanted against the British flagship, Gomez needed to close that distance in half, to five thousand yards. He needed to get in closer, into the carrier's wake. That meant *Santa Cruz* needed to cover some ocean to close the distance.

In a flat-out race across the oceans, the American nuclear supercarriers at full speed could outrun any submarine in the world. Though the Brits had never revealed the *Queen Elizabeth*'s full capabilities, most intelligence reports speculated that she could match the American supercarriers in speed, meaning that in an open-ocean sprint, the *Santa Cruz* would get left in her wake.

But in this case, with the carrier slowing her speed for the slower ships in the British flotilla behind her, opportunity knocked.

The element of surprise was the key to submarine warfare. Any sudden increase in speed increased the danger that the sub might be heard on passive sonar. Pursuing the carrier from behind gave the sub the best opportunity to avoid detection because the ship's engines and propellers created a wash that muffled sounds.

"Helmsman. All ahead two-thirds."

"All ahead two-thirds. Aye, Capitán."

Royal Navy Merlin Mk1 helicopter
ASW Naval Squadron 814
South Atlantic Ocean
10 miles south of HMS Queen Elizabeth

10:49 a.m. local time

The Royal Navy Merlin helicopter settled into a hover at five hundred feet above the ocean's surface. Commander Chris Stacks, lead pilot and squadron commander, pulled back on the stick and spoke into his headset, piping his instructions throughout the cockpit.

"Chief Welton. On my command, prepare to begin dropping sonobuoys in the water."

"Aye, Skipper. Preparing to drop sonobuoys on your order, sir."

Stacks pushed down on the collective pitch control, and the chopper began to slowly descend. The pilot kept his eyes on the electronic altimeter and the aircraft feathered down closer to the water.

450 feet . . .

400 feet . . .

The sonobuoys would be dropped from the helicopter aircraft in canisters and would deploy upon water impact. An inflatable float with a radio transmitter would remain on the surface for electronic communication with the chopper, while hydrophone sensors and stabilizing equipment would descend below the surface to a selected depth. The buoys would then relay acoustic information from their hydrophones via radio to operators on board the chopper, which would be relayed back to the *Queen Elizabeth*.

Like all sonar equipment, the sonobuoys fell into two categories, active or passive.

Passive sonobuoys emit nothing into the water. These instruments listen, waiting for sound waves from a ship's power plant or propeller or even door closings and other noises from ships or submarines. The advantage to passive sonar is that the enemy does not know you are listening.

Active sonobuoys emit sound energy into the water and listen for the returning echo before transmitting usually range and bearing information via UHF/VHF radio to a receiving ship or aircraft. The sound energy comes across as loud, nearly deafening *pings*.

With the powerful pinging signals slicing through the water, active sonobuoys can track down an enemy sub with more speed and precision, but it also alerts the enemy of the attacker's presence.

Active sonar, in a word, removes all semblance of surprise.

In this case, with instructions to quickly find and destroy the enemy submarine, the Merlins would be dropping active sonobuoys into the chilly waters of the South Atlantic.

250 feet . . .

200 feet . . .

"Chief. Prepare to drop sonobuoys."

"Aye, Skipper. Preparing to drop sonobuoys."

150 feet . . .

100 feet . . .

Stacks stabilized the collective pitch control, and the Merlin leveled out at 50 feet above the water, close enough that the chopper's powerful rotors kicked up a whirling circle in the water below.

"Drop sonobuoy!"

"Dropping sonobuoy! Aye, sir."

Stacks rotated the chopper on an axis and glimpsed the long metal cylinder splashing into the water below.

The cylinder disappeared below the surface, and two seconds later it popped back up onto the surface, corralled by the flotation raft that had deployed upon impact.

"Sir! Sonobuoy one has deployed and is successfully broadcasting!"

"Very well," Stacks said. "Stand by for active sonar broadcast on my command."

Stacks pushed down on the cyclic. The chopper moved forward in the air on a course of one-eight-zero degrees, and when he had covered one thousand yards, he pulled the chopper into another hover and dropped another sonobuoy. Rotating the chopper in the air again, he flew out another thousand yards to a spot that would make the third spot in a triangle. There the chopper dropped a third sonobuoy into the water.

The process was called triangulation, whereby helicopters dropped a net of floating sonobuoys in the water, in floating triangular positions, over large spaces of water in an effort to locate by sonar anything that might be submerged under those positions.

"Good show, sir," Leftenant Drew Jordan, the helicopter's copilot, said.

"So far, so good," Commander Stacks replied. "Now let's spread the net, drop a dozen more of these puppies, and then light them up and see what's down there."

Control room
Argentinean submarine ARA Santa Cruz
South Atlantic Ocean
depth 100 feet

11:15 a.m. local time

H elmsman. Speed and distance to target."

"Speed twenty-one knots. Range to target, nine thousand yards, Capitán."

"Very well," Gomez said. "Still another half an hour before we start getting into comfortable range for a good shot."

"Should we go ahead and prepare torpedoes, Capitán?"

"Good suggestion, XO. Prep torps one and three."

"Prep torps one and three. Aye, sir."

Alberto Gomez checked his watch. A powerful air of electricity had permeated the control room. Fact was, every sub commander for generations had trained for a moment such as this, but history had called few to be in the right place at the right time.

"XO."

"Aye, Capitán."

"Open the 1-MC."

"Aye, Capitán."

The executive officer flipped two switches, then handed the microphone to Gomez. "The 1-MC is open, sir."

"*Gracias*, XO," Gomez said. He took the microphone. "Now hear this. This is the capitán speaking." Gomez paused. "As you know, we are the lead sub in this mission, and ARA *San Juan* is our backup.

"Shortly before we sailed, I attended afternoon mass in Buenos Aires. That afternoon, the priest read something from the Bible. He said—and I quote—'many are called, but few are chosen.'"

Gomez paused, absorbing the significance of the moment. Goose bumps crawled up his arms and up his neck.

"Men. Be ready. Be vigilant. Soon we will begin the attack that will change history, the most important military operation in the history of Argentina. Many have been called, but we have been chosen. That is all."

Gomez handed the microphone back to the XO.

"Navigator. Range to target."

"Range to target eight thousand seven hundred yards, sir."

"Very well. Steady as she goes."

"Steady as she goes, aye, sir."

An electric silence again permeated the bridge as the sub closed in on the *Queen Elizabeth*. Gomez thought of his wife, Louisa, and his teenage sons, Juan and Pedro.

Juan had just turned thirteen, and Pedro would turn sixteen next week. Unfortunately, Alberto would be at sea for Pedro's birthday, so they had gone to mass as a family before his deployment. Then, as an early birthday present, Pedro got to pick where they went to dinner. Pedro chose his favorite restaurant, Café Torntoni, where they had enjoyed quesadillas and soft drinks and celebrated an early surprise birthday party. Louisa had arranged for six of his best friends to meet them at the restaurant.

Both boys had proclaimed their desire to follow their father in the Navy. They were young at the time and could change their minds. But still, he could hope.

He smiled at the memories of their last supper together and wondered when they would be together again.

The first *ping* hit the sub hard, sloshing Gomez's coffee.

"Sonobuoys in the water, sir!"

"Emergency dive! Go to six hundred seventy-five feet! XO, alert the crew!"

"Aye, Capitán!" The XO picked up the microphone as the sub's bow started dropping. "All hands! Emergency dive! Emergency dive! Sonobuoys in the water! Brace yourselves!"

Gomez braced against the periscope housing as his sub angled down forty-five degrees and the depth meter began dropping.

Depth 150 feet . . .

Depth 175 feet . . .

The second *ping* rocked the ship as she crossed the 200-foot threshold.

Depth 250 feet . . .

Gomez felt sweat bead on his forehead as the sub continued to dive.

He had executed the emergency dive to lower depths to make it more difficult for the sonar to pick up on the sub and also to make it more difficult for depth charges and torpedoes to find the sub if they were attacked.

Unfortunately, the *Santa Cruz*, for all its versatility, did not have the same diving capability as the more powerful American boats. The American nuclear boats could safely dive to a test depth of 1,600 feet and a crush depth of 2,400 feet. The *Santa Cruz* could dive to a test depth of only 700 feet with a crush depth of 890 feet.

That meant the American boats could hide under twice as much water as the *Santa Cruz* and her sister boat, the *San Juan*.

Now, ominous electronic *pings* that had shocked the boat guaranteed that the *Santa Cruz* had, for the time being anyway, lost her most powerful weapon—the element of surprise.

Gomez's focus had suddenly shifted from a surprise attack on the British carrier to saving his sub and saving his men.

Gomez would dive his boat as deep as he could safely dive, to just above his test depth of 700 feet, and hope and pray that temperature inversions in the water would provide a protective cover against the British sonar.

The capitán made a sign of the cross and glued his eyes to the sub's electronic depth gauge.

Depth 300 feet . . .

Depth 325 feet . . .

Depth 350 feet . . .

Royal Navy Merlin Mk1 helicopter
ASW Naval Squadron 814
South Atlantic Ocean
9 miles south of HMS Queen Elizabeth

11:25 a.m. local time

Commander! We have active sonar contact!" Sonarman Chief Philip Welton, Merlin's flight crew chief, announced. "Two confirmed *pings*! She's diving, sir. Last reported depth 250 feet and dropping, sir."

"What bloody luck!" Commander Chris Stacks said. "Do we have a make?"

"Diesel-electric. Acoustic computers reporting ARA *Santa Cruz–*class, sir."

"Very well! Drop three depth charges. Calibrate to detonate at 500, 600, and 700 feet. Then I want two torps in the water. Move! Move!"

"Aye, sir! Preparing to drop depth charges."

"Leftenant Jordan. Notify the *Queen Elizabeth*. Advise that we have sonar contact with enemy sub and that we're attacking. Request additional F-35A air cover. Let's send this underwater canoe from the banana republic to the bottom of the sea!"

"Aye, aye, Skipper!"

Control room
Argentinean submarine ARA Santa Cruz
South Atlantic Ocean
depth 600 feet

11:29 a.m. local time

Silence pervaded the control room as the sub continued her dive. Commander Gomez kept his eyes on the depth gauge.

Depth 550 feet . . .

Depth 600 feet . . .

The sub's angle leveled out as she approached her target depth.

Depth 650 feet . . .

"We've reached our target depth, Capitán, 650 feet," the helmsman said.

"Very well," Gomez said. "All engines stop!"

"All engines stop! Aye, sir."

Silence.

Only the dim hum of sophisticated electrical equipment.

Perhaps the active sonar was an intimidation tactic. Perhaps the British were intent on knocking the submarine off the carrier's trail. If so, they had succeeded.

Gomez looked around the control room. Men nervously looked up at the ceiling, as if they had X-ray vision to pierce through the layers of steel, through the dark water, and then up to the sky to see what was there.

The compulsion to look up was instinctive. For somewhere up there lurked mortal danger. And nothing could be done except wait, move quietly, and hope the waters hid them from the enemy.

Even Gomez found himself staring up . . . waiting.

"No more *pings*, Capitán." The executive officer broke silence. "Perhaps they have moved on to another sector of the sea."

"Perhaps," Gomez said. "But somehow, my gut tells me that we have not escaped danger. Not yet."

The sudden explosion shook the sub, sending the capitán's heart into overdrive.

"Depth charges in the water, sir!"

"Too close!" Gomez said. "Sonar, how close?"

"Two hundred yards above us, sir."

"You can be sure that's not the only one they'll drop," Gomez said.

"I agree," the XO said.

"XO, secure damage reports," Gomez said.

"Securing damage reports. Aye, sir."

"Helmsman, maintain battery power. Set new course for zero-nine-zero degrees."

"Aye, sir. Setting new course for zero-nine-zero degrees."

Gomez wiped sweat from his forehead as the submarine began a slow turn from due south to due east. The course change would take them off the trail of the new British supercarrier.

"Damage reports are in, Capitán," the executive officer said. "All systems functioning and operational. No confirmed damage."

"Thank God," Gomez said.

"Capitán," the helmsman said, "we have completed our course change. Course now bearing zero-nine-zero degrees. Speed fourteen knots, sir. Maintaining battery power."

"Very well," Gomez said. "Steady as she goes."

"Steady as she goes. Aye, sir."

The second explosion felt like a collision with a Mack truck, rocking the sub so hard that men fell to the deck as alarms sounded in the control room. Gomez kept his balance by grabbing the periscope housing, but the XO and the navigator were sprawled on the deck.

"Everybody okay?" Gomez said.

"They're calibrating the explosions for varying depths," the navigator said.

"Damage reports," Gomez said.

A third explosion sent powerful shock waves through the sub, setting off more alarms. A second later the control room went black.

"Jesus, help us."

"Somebody grab a flashlight!"

"What's going on?"

The control room lights flashed on and off twice and then flashed on again.

"Do we have damage reports?" Gomez pressed.

"We temporarily lost electrical power, but all systems are now recovered, sir. The alarms sounding are collision alarms. That blast was so close that the sensors picked it up as a collision."

"All right. Turn the alarms off and let's get moving. Navigator! Change course! Go to zero-four-five degrees!"

"Changing course to zero-four-five degrees. Aye, sir!"

"Capitán! We have a torpedo in the water! One thousand yards and closing!"

"Probably a British Spearfish!" Gomez cursed. "Engineering! All ahead full!"

"All ahead full. Aye, sir!"

"Navigator! Keep me posted on that torp."

"Aye, Capitán! Incoming torpedo at nine hundred yards and closing!"

"Engineering! Get those blasted engines up! Now!"

"Working on it, sir."

"Incoming torpedo now at eight hundred fifty yards! Still closing!"

"Engines reengaged, Capitán!"

"All ahead full!"

"All ahead full! Aye, sir!"

Gomez felt the submarine lunge forward as the boat's engines reengaged.

"Incoming torpedo at seven hundred fifty yards! We're picking up the *ping* from the torp's nose, Capitán."

"Weapons Officer, prepare to fire two stern torpedoes on my command. Let's see if we can shake it off our path."

"Aye, sir. Preparing to fire two stern torps at your command."

"Mister Ramirez!" he yelled at the sub's helmsman. "Listen to me carefully."

"I'm listening, sir."

"You know we cannot outrun that torpedo, and if we maintain our current course, they'll blow us out of the water."

"Yes, sir."

"When I order those two rear torps shot, you are to dive another fifty feet and turn fifteen degrees. Got that?"

"Aye, Capitán."

"If we get a lucky shot, we take that fish out. But if the stern torpedoes miss, we launch countermeasures to throw it off. The only way we can survive this is an emergency dive and turn and release flares prior to torpedo impact."

"Understand, Capitán."

"Incoming torpedo now five hundred yards! We're still picking up the *ping* from the torp's nose, Capitán."

"Launch stern torpedoes!"

"Launching stern torpedoes! Aye, sir!"

"Mister Ramirez! Dive the boat! Turn! Turn!"

"Diving the boat! Turning! Aye, Capitán!"

Santa Cruz's nose dipped and twisted.

Gomez grabbed the periscope casing to maintain his balance as the sub dived. A second later, the violent explosion rocked the sub, knocking Gomez off his feet.

The blast set off the collision alarm, but this time the power stayed on in the control room.

"Capitán! We intercepted the British torpedo!"

"Praise God!" Gomez got up off the deck. "Everybody okay? XO, get me an updated damage report."

The executive officer picked up the microphone. "This is the XO, all stations. Report damage."

"Control Room. Radar. All systems functional. No damage reported."

"Control Room. Weapons. All functional. No damages, sir."

"Control Room. Radio. All systems functional. No damages."

"Control Room. Fire Control. No damages, sir."

"Control Room. Engineering. We've got a problem, sir."

Gomez looked at his XO, who looked back before proceeding. "What problem, Engineering?"

"Sir, we've got a leak in the interior hull, starboard aft. That explosion cracked the hull."

"Give me that." Gomez took the microphone from the XO. "Chief, this is the capitán! How bad is it?"

"Not good, sir. We are trying to get pumps on it, and I think we can neutralize it somewhat, but it's gushing in pretty fast. If we can keep the pumps running without any power interruptions, and if we do not get hit again, Capitán, we might contain it. Otherwise, I do not know."

"Push it hard, Chief. Get that pump going."

"Yes, Capitán."

"XO, go down there and have a look. Bring me back a report."

"Aye, sir."

Gomez took four deep breaths. The XO stepped out of the control room. Another close hit could be debilitating.

"Capitán. Now maintaining course zero-seven-five degrees. Speed is eight knots."

Gomez started making the sign of the cross. But he stopped midstream to avoid sending any message of panic to the crew. "Very well. Steady as she goes."

"Steady as she goes. Aye, sir."

"Sonar. We hear anything else out there?"

"Not yet, Capitán."

"Good. Let's hope it stays that way."

Gomez sat down in the captain's chair.

Only the near-silent hum of the ship's battery-powered electric engines could be heard. Gomez checked his watch. If they survived another thirty minutes at this depth without another British attack, they could reengage the fight.

He wished in that moment that he could make a trip to a confessional. His sin? It happened at his son's birthday. He had allowed his eyes to linger too long on the waitress on more than one occasion as she had walked back and forth from the table. Pure unadulterated lust overcame him that day. He hoped his wife had not noticed. "Control Room. Engineering." Gomez recognized the XO's voice on the intercom.

"Engineering. Control Room. Go ahead, XO."

"Capitán. Could you please pick up the telephone?"

"Stand by." Gomez picked up the inter-ship telephone, taking the XO off the loudspeaker. "What is it, XO?"

"Sir, the situation down here is worse than the chief said."

"Explain."

"We've got cold seawater pouring in, sir. They've got these pumps running, and the pumps are barely keeping up with the infusion. In my judgment, we're going to need to surface as soon as possible and return to port for repairs."

"How soon do you think we need to surface?"

"I think we are okay for another ten to twelve hours, as long as our pumps keep working, and as long as the leak isn't further breached. We need four or five more sailors down here, Capitán."

"Go ahead," Gomez said, "select five additional men to work the pumps, then return to the control room."

CHAPTER 21

Apartment of Maria Vasquez
337 Avenue de Tomás Ramos
Valparaiso, Chile

11:30 a.m. local time

Maria scurried about the sunlit apartment, her eyes dancing back and forth between her closet and her digital clock.

Her heart pounded as if she had finished a hundred-meter dash.

She held the yellow sundress up to the skylights in her ceiling. A perfect cut that fell just above the knee. But too early in the season for yellow?

She wore beige yesterday, and he seemed to like that, judging by the glint she thought she noticed in his eyes. She wasn't sure if he liked the jeans.

In two more weeks, the yellow dress would be fine, would it not?

What would a macho American submarine commander be most attracted to?

Still holding the yellow dress against the light, she glanced at the clock again. If she didn't get a move on, she would be late.

Fashionably late, even by a few minutes, was always best for a lady.

It was not too early for the yellow, she decided, then changed her mind. She wore light yesterday. Show him some contrast. Men liked contrast. She held up the short black cocktail dress.

Surely he would like this. Too bad he wouldn't get to see it. Not yet, anyway.

Wrong occasion. Maybe some other time.

Next she held up a little red silky top. "This is perfect with that little black skirt and black heels." She allowed a smile to cross her face. She slipped her right arm through the blouse, and then her left, and then began to button the front. She stepped into the little skirt and pulled it up and buttoned it. The hemline fell two inches above the knee.

A snug fit, but not too tight.

Perfect.

Absolutely perfect.

Or was it? Why did she feel like an idiot schoolgirl?

"Think, Maria."

She reached into the drawer and retrieved the Clive Christian No. 1 perfume that she had ordered from Neiman-Marcus in New York. There. A faint scent under her neck should do.

She looked in the mirror at her hair. Yesterday it had bounced lightly on her shoulders, which hopefully he liked.

She reached into her jewelry box and picked up the beaded pearl ponytail holder that she had bought at Flabella Department Store in Santiago. Quickly she pulled her hair back, secured it with the ponytail holder, and took another look.

Perfect. A classic ponytail, not overdone, calling attention to her face, the blouse, the little skirt, and her legs. The black heels rounded out her appearance.

"Gosh, I've got to go." And she headed out the door.

Control room
Argentinean submarine ARA Santa Cruz
South Atlantic Ocean
depth 700 feet

11:39 a.m. local time

Gomez checked the chronometer on the bulkhead. Ten minutes had passed since that last explosion. Perhaps the danger had passed.

Gomez needed to surface the sub. Then, if they could blow out enough water, his men might be able to weld a patch over the leak that would hold long enough to limp into port.

But surfacing the sub anytime soon meant certain suicide.

Gomez reasoned that the sonobuoys had been dropped by British helicopters, most likely from the British aircraft carrier or possibly from the amphibious assault ship HMS *Ocean*. The choppers were most likely still patrolling the area. If Gomez surfaced, he would likely be spotted on the open water and sunk immediately.

With the British task force steaming due south, Gomez opted for another course change, this time due north to rapidly increase the distance between the sub and the task force.

"What do you think, Capitán?" the XO asked.

Gomez did some quick calculations in his head. "If they are steaming south at eighteen knots, and we are steaming north at eight knots, that means after one hour, we will have achieved a separation of twenty-six knots from them, a distance of thirty miles.

"If we surface at that point, we are still within the range of their aircraft. If our pumps hold up and we can make it another two to three hours, opening up a sixty- to ninety-mile separation, even though we would remain in range of their aircraft, I think we are safer. I doubt they will be looking that far north from their ships. Why should they? We pose no effective or immediate danger to them at that point."

"More coffee, sir?" A petty officer offered to refill Gomez's mug.

"Thank you, Petty Officer." Gomez looked at the XO. "Your thoughts, Commander?"

"I agree, sir. Plus, if we can make it another sixty to one hundred miles to the north, we are within radio range of other Argentinean naval and air forces and will be able to request assistance."

Gomez took a sip of coffee. "Good points, XO. Not only that, but we will be in radio range of the Argentinean mainland."

Beep-beep-beep-beep . . .

"Capitán! Torpedo in the water! Range, one thousand yards and closing!"

"God help us," Gomez said. "XO, sound general quarters!"

"Sounding general quarters! Aye, Capitán!"

"Helmsman! All ahead full!"

"All ahead full!"

"WEPS! Prep two more stern torpedoes. Now! Prepare to fire on my order."

"Aye, Capitán! Prepping torps!"

"XO. Open the 1-MC."

"The 1-MC is open, sir." He handed the microphone to Gomez.

"Now hear this. This is the commanding officer. We have another torpedo in the water headed our way. We are going to attempt to intercept this torpedo, like we did the last one, by firing two stern torpedoes at it. We are going to try to intercept it farther away from the sub to avoid an explosion. If we miss, prepare for impact. That is all."

"Incoming torpedo now at eight hundred fifty yards! Still closing!"

"Very well! All ahead full!"

"All ahead full! Aye, sir!"

Once again, Gomez felt the submarine lunge forward under full power.

"Incoming torpedo at seven hundred fifty yards! We're picking up the *ping* from the torp's nose."

"Weapons Officer, prepare to fire two stern torpedoes on my command. Let's see if we can shake it off our path."

"Aye, sir. Preparing to fire two stern torps at your command."

"Stay ready, Mister Ramirez."

"Aye, Capitán!"

"Weapons Officer! Fire stern torps!"

"Firing stern torps. Aye, sir."

The sub seemed to jump once . . . then twice as compressed air helped shoot the two stern torpedoes away from the *Santa Cruz*.

"Incoming torpedo now at seven hundred yards!

"Incoming torpedo at six hundred fifty yards!

"First torpedo missed intercept, Capitán!"

"Dear Jesus, no."

"Incoming torpedo now at six hundred yards!"

"Incoming torpedo at five hundred fifty yards!"

"Come on, baby! Intercept!" Gomez blurted.

"Incoming torpedo now at five hundred yards!"

"Second torpedo missed intercept, sir!"

"XO. Warn the crew! Brace for impact."

"Aye, Capitán!" The executive officer took the 1-MC. "This is the executive officer! Interceptor torps have missed. Brace for impact! Brace for impact!"

"Incoming torpedo at four hundred fifty yards!"

"Are you ready, Mister Ramirez?"

"Ready, Capitán!"

"Incoming torpedo at four hundred yards!"

"We will launch countermeasures at inside two hundred yards, then break in another emergency dive at one hundred yards. That's a tight time frame. I need you to be on your game. Are you ready?"

"Ready, sir."

Torpedo countermeasures involve launching a drum-like device filled with compressed air. The compressed air is released in the water in the form of tiny bubbles. This serves two functions: To passive sonar, it sounds like propeller cavitation from a fast-running submarine. To active sonar in the torpedo's nose, the spinning metallic barrel looks like a big fat target. After launching a countermeasure, standard evasive tactics call for the escaping submarine to make radical changes in course, speed, and depth.

"Incoming torpedo now at four hundred yards!

"Incoming torpedo at three hundred fifty yards!

"Torpedo two hundred fifty yards and closing!"

"Be ready!"

"Torpedo two hundred yards!"

"Release countermeasures!"

"Release countermeasures! Aye, sir!"

A slight bump, as spinning drums with compressed air spun into the water.

"One hundred fifty yards and closing!"

"Dive! Dive!"

Santa Cruz dropped quickly through the water, like a roller coaster dropping from the first peak of the track.

The ferocious explosion shook the sub like a powerful, angry jackhammer. The collision alarm blared all over the submarine. Lights in the control room blinked. Then went black. Then back on again. Then darkness again.

"Grab a flashlight!" the command master chief yelled through the dark.

"I've got it! I've got it!"

A narrow bright flashlight beam shot across the control room.

"We've lost power!" someone yelled.

"Hit the auxiliary battery!" Gomez screamed.

"I got it, sir!"

A second later the control room lit up again, with lights half as bright as before. The sub had switched to emergency battery power, drawing juice from batteries with no external generators.

"Somebody kill the collision alarm," Gomez said.

"I've got it, sir."

The executive officer pulled the switch, deactivating the collision alarm.

A lonely, dark silence permeated the control room.

Was this the end? No time to dwell on that thought. Gomez picked up the microphone, silently praying that someone would answer at the other end. "Engineering."

Static.

"Engineering. Can you hear me?"

"We hear you, Capitán!"

"What's the status with our engines?"

"Power plant is down, sir. Engines inoperable. We are working to try and restore power. Unfortunately, we've got a ton more water gushing in down here, sir, making our working conditions difficult."

"All right, get on it," Gomez said. "We've got to get main propulsion restored."

"We are trying, sir. But with so much water flowing in here . . ."

Gomez exchanged glances with the XO. "Doesn't sound good, XO. Go down and check it out and bring me a report."

"Aye, sir."

Restaurant La Concepción
Papudo 541
Valparaiso, Chile

11:53 a.m. local time

Pete spun the silver Mercedes convertible around the corner onto Papudo Street and slowed down.

The small street featured a cobblestone alleyway look that resembled old streets in Colonial Williamsburg. The feel and architecture were classic Neoretroism, reflecting the cozy juxtaposition of small unique buildings in close and intimate proximity, as roughly defined by the great American international developer Jeffory D. Blackard, a Texan.

"Approaching Papudo 541, on right," the female voice announced on the GPS in English.

Pete looked over and saw the quaint facade of La Concepción, a small white stucco two-story restaurant sandwiched between two other buildings. The restaurant had two windows at street level, trimmed in navy blue, with navy blue shutters bracketing the windows in sharp contrast to the white stucco. A natural wooden-colored archway curved over the front door.

Pete wheeled the Mercedes into a space almost right in front of the door.

Still in his service dress blue uniform, Pete donned his cover and stepped onto the sidewalk and headed for the restaurant. Inside, the host stood there smiling in a white dinner jacket and black trousers.

Pete decided to try his Spanish. *"Disculpe, señor. ¿Tiene usted una reservación a nombre de Miranda o de Vásquez?"*

"Ah. Commander Miranda," the host replied in perfect English. "Yes, sir. We do have reservations for you. Miss Vasquez called. She is a loyal regular. We have been expecting you. Right this way, sir."

"Thank you."

They walked through the restaurant and then into a small sunroom off to the left. "This is our sunroom dining patio. Miss Vasquez requested it. It is her favorite. No one else has reserved it. I think you will enjoy the privacy."

"Thank you." Pete sat down. How many men had Maria Vasquez met in this intimate little restaurant?

The square table, covered with a white tablecloth, featured flowers in the center. Maybe daisies? Maybe dandelions? All flowers looked the same except red roses, which were the only flowers he could swear under oath to recognize.

Oh well. Whatever. At least she agreed to meet him. Besides, the view provided a wonderful panorama of the blue waters of the harbor.

"Hello, Peter."

The velvety smooth voice with the Spanish accent turned his head from the view of the crystal blue bay. And oh, what an improvement the new view turned out to be!

Her ravishing combination of black velvet and silky red rivaled a Brazilian supermodel strolling into the room. As an officer and a gentleman, Pete rose to his feet and noticed her hair pulled back into a classic ponytail, nicely accentuating her smile. And in the light her face seemed to be more beautiful than he remembered. His eyes were too distracted yesterday afternoon by the equally attractive sight of her legs. But now . . .

"Well, hello!" Why did she have to be a socialist-liberal? "You look marvelous."

"Thank you, Commander." Her smile had a tinge of shy embarrassment.

Was that a blush? What happened to the in-your-face socialist?

"You look rather handsome yourself in that uniform."

"Thank you." An awkward moment. "Here, let me get your chair." He stepped over and pulled her chair out and guided her into it.

"Such a gentleman."

One chair sat across from the other, with the flowers in the middle. But in that instant, Pete made a command decision. He moved the chair to a position right beside her, with only the table corner separating them.

"I hope you don't mind."

"Not at all."

"*Señor y señorita*, something to drink?"

Pete looked at her. "Up to you," he said.

"Pinot noire, please, Fernando. My usual."

"And you, sir?" Fernando looked at Pete.

"I'll have what the lady is having."

"Yes, sir."

"So . . . ," he said.

"So . . ." She broke into a giggle. "I must say, this is the first time I have ever had lunch with a conservative American naval officer."

"I hope you won't be disappointed."

"And I hope you won't be disappointed having lunch with a socialist liberal activist."

Pete grinned. "I consider that part a unique challenge." Before he could finish the thought, the waiter returned with a bottle of red wine and, holding the bottle with a white linen napkin, poured a splash into Pete's glass.

Pete took a quick sip. "Perfect."

Fernando filled both glasses quickly. "Would you care to place an order? Perhaps an appetizer?"

Pete looked at her. "Are you hungry?"

"Not particularly. Maybe later."

"Fernando, if you could keep watching our glasses here, I think we might hold off on ordering. That okay with you?" He looked at Maria.

"Sounds great," she said.

"Very well, sir." Fernando nodded. "I shall return a bit later to check on you."

Maria sipped her wine and smiled. "I believe you were saying something about a unique challenge?"

"Ah, yes. You wondered how I felt about having lunch with—I think you described yourself as a socialist activist or something—and I think I said that I consider it a special challenge."

"So you think I am a challenge, do you?"

"Maybe."

She looked at him. "What kind of a challenge, if I might ask."

"What kind of a challenge do you like to be?"

"You are answering a question with a question without answering the question, Commander."

"You know, your English is impeccable." When her leg brushed against his, he lost his concentration.

"You know," she said, "if you're not too hungry, maybe we could polish off this bottle, and then I'd be happy to show you around. And maybe we could grab a little dessert later."

"Sounds good to me," he said.

"Do you like peach pie?"

"Love it."

"I make a ravishing peach pie, I'm told. My apartment is a half mile from here and I have one just baked. Are you interested?"

He looked into her eyes. "Is that an invitation?"

She took a large sip. "I can't eat all that dessert alone."

The sip that he took warmed his throat. "You don't look like you eat dessert at all."

"Thank you, I think, but you didn't answer my question, Commander. Perhaps you are not interested." Her leg brushed against his again, causing him to swallow hard.

"Dessert sounds good to me."

Control room
Argentinean submarine ARA Santa Cruz
South Atlantic Ocean
depth 750 feet

12:03 p.m. local time

Twenty minutes had passed since Gomez sent the XO below to check out the leaks, and still the main propulsion system had not re-engaged. The *Santa Cruz*'s life-support systems were functioning on auxiliary battery power, which provided barely enough energy to keep dim lights on throughout the sub, allowing light for the attempted repair, but not enough power to engage the sub's engines to allow for maneuverability.

The good news? The British had ceased their fire. Gomez silently thanked God because another blow, even nearby, would finish the *Santa Cruz*.

He realized that the *Santa Cruz* might not be able to survive. But he could not allow the crew to sense his doubts. A wave of fear and panic would doom the sub and seal their fate.

With the main propulsion out, the sub had sunk another fifty feet. They were still two hundred feet above the sub's crush depth. But if they kept sinking, even slowly, eventually the sub would implode.

In the dim light provided by the emergency batteries, Gomez picked up the inter-ship telephone. "Engineering. Control Room."

"Control Room. Engineering," the XO said.

"XO, what's going on down there?"

"Sir, the situation is not good. We have not been able to stem the flow of the breach. Still no success with the power plant. The water is obstructing our ability to make repairs. Sir, with respect, you may wish to come down here and have a look."

"I'll be right there, XO." Gomez replaced the microphone. "Mister Ramirez. You have the conn."

"I have the conn. Aye, sir," the helmsman said.

Gomez headed over to the steel ladder and climbed down to the deck below, the berthing area.

The engineering spaces were two decks below that, and as he started down the last leg of his descent, he looked down and saw men working frantically in waist-deep water.

The XO spotted him on the ladder and waded over to help guide him down.

Gomez stepped down into the cold seawater, and when his shoes reached the bottom deck, the sloshing water rose to several inches above his waist.

"The water is gushing in faster by the second, Capitán," the XO said. "The breach is back down toward the stern. It's like a fire hose back there, sir."

"Let's have a look," Gomez said.

"Make way for the capitán," the XO said.

Gomez waded back through the frigid water toward the stern section, following the XO, hoping to get a better assessment. A bubbling and gurgling in the water on the right bulkhead pinpointed the source of the leak, with water rushing in through the hull and inner wall of the sub.

The water continued to rise and now reached Gomez's chest. No need to proceed farther. "XO, order all hands to abandon the lower decks."

The XO looked at him. Their eyes locked, and the clear and unmistakable understanding arose between them.

The XO, in nearly a whisper to keep the men from hearing, said, "We are going to lose the sub, sir."

Gomez nodded. "Let's get these men up to higher ground so they can live a little longer."

"Aye, Capitán." The XO turned around. "But, sir, I suggest that you first get back up to the control room. We are going to need you at the conn for as long as possible, even up to the end."

Gomez nodded. "Very well, XO. Get back up top as soon as you can get these men moved. I'm going to need you at my side."

"Aye, Capitán." The XO shot Gomez a salute, and Gomez at that moment knew that it might be the last salute he would ever receive. With frigid water nearly up to his neck, he returned the salute and then scampered up the ladder, headed up to issue his last orders from the control room.

Down below, the XO executed Gomez's orders. "All hands up the ladder! Up to the berthing decks. Move. Move."

Belgrano II base camp
Antarctica

12:07 p.m. local time

Lieutenant Fernando Sosa sat alone at the communications desk inside the geodesic dome. Since the successful Axis attack on the British facilities at the Churchill base camp, shutting down the British facilities, communications interceptions had gone dark. Only static blared over the loudspeakers.

With Sosa's objective accomplished, there was talk of decorating him when he returned to Buenos Aires for his work in uncovering the British discovery of oil.

The new base commander, Capitán José Montes, had stopped by and announced that he would recommend Sosa for the Order of Military Merit and recommend him for early promotion.

Frankly, the Order of Military Merit sounded overblown for his accomplishments. But if Montes recommended it, how could he argue?

Still, despite the promise of military decoration, the twisted feeling in his stomach had magnified.

It was the British prisoner.

Frankly, Sosa could not shake the image of the British prisoner gunned down in cold blood. A military prison camp required a stern disciplinarian in command. But to shoot a prisoner in cold blood? A civilian prisoner at that? Who, by all accounts, had the noodle spine of a fearful wimp?

Sosa witnessed the whole thing. Montes had clearly gotten the prisoners' attention with the shooting, but Sosa had serious reservations. What if all this came out after the war? What if the United Nations or the United States convened a war crimes tribunal? Surely Montes might be held responsible.

But what if they indicted all the officers who had witnessed the event as coconspirators? Sosa had nothing to do with it.

And even if he, Sosa, were not implicated in a worst-case scenario, how could he live with his conscience, having seen what he had seen? How would he face Father Joseph at confessional?

What did Lieutenant Colonel Sanchez think about Montes? Sanchez was a good man. Sosa respected him as base commander.

"Atten-chun!" the duty sergeant yelled.

Sosa stood and turned as Capitán Montes strutted into the dome.

"Lieutenant Sosa!" Montes snapped.

"Yes, *mi* capitán," Sosa said.

Montes stood there with an almost angry glare. "Put on your jacket and come with me. I will show you the finer points of witness interrogation."

"Yes, sir." Sosa grabbed his winter jacket, put it on, and zipped it up.

"This way." Montes opened the door, and they stepped out onto the frozen snowscape, where two armed soldiers stood with loaded AK-47s. "I have seen your talent, Sosa. You excel at electronic surveillance, but you are one-dimensional. A good intelligence man is multidimensional. Do you understand what I mean?"

"Yes, I believe so, Capitán." Sosa did not understand the direction of Montes' question. But admitting that lack of understanding might ignite the temper of the officer bearing the nickname of "The One."

As a good intelligence officer, Sosa had run his own private background check on Montes and learned that the nickname "The One" came from Montes' reputation as "The One" ego-temper combination unmatched by any man in Argentina. The informal intelligence dossier—prepared by a friend and colleague at intelligence headquarters in Buenos Aires for Sosa's eyes only—had warned, "While the nickname 'The One' is widely used by his subordinates when not in his presence, it remains unclear whether Montes is aware of his moniker. Therefore prudence dictates never using the moniker anywhere within earshot of this officer."

Montes stared at him for a second, as if waiting for Sosa to elaborate. Sosa bit his tongue, for he had recently heard a sermon from Father Joseph from Proverbs on the importance of remaining silent.

"In case you have any questions, Mister Sosa, let me explain," Montes said. "The most crucial elements for any military intelligence operation are (a) interception, which you clearly are a master at, and (b) extraction, and that verdict is out on you.

"Now then"—Montes tramped across the deep snow, joined by four more soldiers—"intercepted intelligence can be from electronic or other means. But the common denominator in the interception of intelligence is this: The enemy does not know the intelligence has been intercepted." Montes stopped in the middle of the base camp, in the circle of eight white geodesic domes. "But in stark contrast, when we are discussing intelligence gathered by extraction, the enemy knows exactly and precisely that the intelligence is being turned over because he is spewing the information out to the interrogator directly. Do you understand?"

"*Si, mi* capitán," Sosa replied.

"Now sometimes it is intelligence we are after, and sometimes it is a confession we are after. Are you familiar with case studies involving extraction confessions?"

Sosa knew of extraction confessions. But beating someone to a pulp until the victim confessed to satisfy the captor's objectives frankly turned his stomach. He hesitated to answer, then decided to. "Yes, I am familiar, for example, with the Vietnamese extracting confessions from American POWs in Vietnam."

Montes' eyes lit up. "An excellent answer! And do you know the value of those American POWs denouncing the war?"

"I suppose that it demoralized other American troops and undermined the war effort," Sosa said.

"Excellent answer!" Montes exclaimed. "You have studied well, Sosa! Extraction confessions do that. They demoralize the enemy while at the same time boost the morale of the home forces. So when the North Vietnamese forced American POWs to denounce America and denounce the war, it served as a valuable gut punch to those hawks supporting the war and as a boost to the antiwar protestors in America. Do you not agree?"

Sosa bit his lip. "An extraction confession serves certain propaganda purposes."

"Yes, of course! Now, while we await more prisoners, we will maximize our time. We will practice our confession interrogation techniques on the foolish British prisoners currently under our command."

Sosa did not respond.

Montes pulled out his long-barreled revolver, holding its silver barrel out under the low-hanging sun. "Care to hold it?" He thrust it over toward Sosa.

"An impressive revolver, sir." Sosa feigned his interest in the weapon. He held it up against the sun, examining it. "Taurus makes a good weapon, sir. South American manufacturer."

Montes reached to take the revolver back. "And what sidearm do you carry, Lieutenant?"

"Standard Glock nine-millimeter, sir."

"What a shame." Montes reholstered the revolver. "You know that a man's sidearm is a direct statement about masculinity?"

Sosa wasn't sure how to respond.

"And did you also know, Lieutenant," Montes said, even before Sosa could answer the previous question, "that a pistol can be used in numerous ways in an extraction interrogation?"

"I was not aware, *mi* capitán."

"In this case, Lieutenant, pay close attention. You will be amazed at the things you can learn.

"Sergeant!" Montes snapped at a soldier accompanying them as they walked to the entrance of the dome housing the prisoners.

"*Sí*, Capitán."

"Round up eight more armed guards. Then send them into the dome to surround the prisoners. Lieutenant Sosa and I will be there shortly. Immediately!"

"*Sí*, Capitán." The guard yelled out orders, and ten armed soldiers quickly entered the dome.

"Follow me." Montes stepped through the entrance to the dome.

"Atten-chun!" the sergeant screamed. "On your feet! Stand at attention for *el* capitán."

The Brits came to their feet, bunched together in the middle of the dome, surrounded by a circle of armed Argentinean soldiers.

Montes folded his arms and began walking in a circle around the prisoners. "As I recall, when we brought you British pigs in on the helicopter, and as you were all standing around out in the courtyard area, I had an interesting conversation with one of the more talented members of this despicable bunch." He pivoted. "Of course, as I recall, that talented fellow had a special propensity as a dancer. What was his name?" A feigned curious pause. "Ah, yes." Index finger held up. A look of contemplation. "Sir Williams, as I recall. Yes. Sir Williams, the dancing Brit!"

Montes bent over, appearing to wheeze, and then broke into a belly laugh. "Sir Williams, Sir Williams, the dancing Brit! Dancing on the snow! A little bitty Brit!" Montes stood, still reveling in his laughing monologue. "But for the stupid British knight, there wasn't much wit! So an Argentine bullet sent him to a snowy, bloody pit!"

He laughed, looking at the prisoners. *What wasted talent!* he thought. He could have won *Dancing with the Stars!* More laughing. "As I recall, at the time that the late dancing Sir Williams lay bleeding in the snow, a priest appeared among us. Hmm?"

The prisoners looked at one another.

"Oh, come! Come! Come! Which of you is the local priest? You know, the one who said, 'The Lord is my shepherd,' or something like that?"

Again, no response.

"What is this? Do we have a priest who is ashamed of the priesthood?"

"I am not ashamed of my Lord." A gaunt-looking runt of a man with a British accent spoke up. "And I am not ashamed of the gospel."

"Yes, I remember you!" Montes bellowed. "You were standing beside Sir Williams Anderson, commander of the subjugated British forces on the continent of Antarctica. Were you not?"

"Aye, sir. That would be me."

"Well then, tell me, Father . . ." Montes hesitated. "You are a priest, are you not?"

"I am no priest," the man said. "Not in the sense you mean."

"What is your name?"

"Bach, sir. My name is Andrew Bach."

"Step forward, Father Andrew Bach! Out in front."

"Aye, sir."

The man stepped out in front of the other prisoners and came to attention.

"Now, Father Bach, do you have an ability to dance like your late colleague, Sir Williams, the tippy-toed tulip?"

"No, sir. I am not much on dancing, sir."

"Well, you should give it a try for us. What do you think, Father Bach?"

"I'm sorry. But I'm not much on dancing, sir."

"What did you say, Father Bach?"

"I said, I am not much on dancing, sir."

"Well, I think you are, Father. I think you should try your hand at it. Right here and now!"

The short man did not flinch. "I am sorry, sir. I cannot dance."

"Knock it off!" one of the prisoners shouted. "Under the Geneva Accords, he is only required to give his name and military identification number."

"Oh?" Montes pulled his revolver from his holster and grabbed it by the long barrel. "Perhaps this will awaken the talent within you!" He swung his arm and smashed the gun in the Brit's face, knocking him to the floor.

Two other prisoners lunged forward toward Montes, but were restrained by six guards. "You won't get away with this!" one of them yelled. This was the same Brit who earlier had cited the Geneva Accords.

"You! What is your name, rank, and branch of service?" Montes snapped. "Since you are so familiar with the Geneva Accords, you will know that I am entitled to your name!"

"Austin Rivers. Leftenant. Royal Navy of the United Kingdom." The prisoner shot a defiant glare at Montes. "That's all you're entitled to, and that's all you are getting."

"We'll see about that, Mister Rivers," Montes said. "I shall deal with you later."

The man who had been knocked on the floor looked up at Sosa. Blood dripped from his mouth.

Montes sneered at the man, then shoved the revolver back into his holster and looked at Sosa. "An example of the great versatility of a long-barreled revolver. Sometimes you do not even fire a shot! And I have not attempted to extract a confession yet. But then again, I do not wish to overwhelm you in the educational process."

He laughed and turned to the man on the floor. "On your feet, Father Bach."

The man stood and then stumbled and fell again.

"Get him up," Montes ordered.

Two guards rushed over and pulled Bach to his feet.

"When I return," Montes said to the group, "I will seek men with courage to stand up and condemn Britain for her illegal and imperialistic attempt to ravage the natural resources of Antarctica. And for those brave enough to tell the truth, there will be food and warmth and new accommodations with more privacy. For those foolish enough to resist me"—he looked around with his piercing black eyes—"remember Sir Williams and Father Bach here when you consider the consequences. That is all."

Montes turned and looked at Sosa. Then he looked back at the British. "The more you cooperate, the better your treatment. If you oppose me, you do so at your own risk."

He stepped back and headed out the door. "Let's go, Lieutenant."

They walked back into the frigid Antarctic air, and as they trudged across the snow from the prisoners' dome to base headquarters, Montes put his hand on Sosa's shoulder. "Tell me, Lieutenant Sosa. You are an intelligence officer. But your specialty is electronic intelligence. Mine is human intelligence. This is one of the many reasons I am in command here. Now one of my duties as commander is to train and make better the officers who are subordinate to me in my chain of command. Which of those worthless Brits do you think might become the most challenging impediment to our mission?"

Sosa thought for a second. Why did this seem like a trick or a test? Why did standing in this man's presence turn his stomach? "Well, sir, it seems that the one who cited the Geneva Accords, the one called Rivers, is their leader."

"Precisely," Montes said. "And tell me this, Lieutenant Sosa, if Rivers is so quick to cite the Geneva Accords, what does this tell us about him?"

"It tells me that he is most likely military, sir. Most likely an officer with an elevated knowledge of the law of war. Perhaps a special forces officer dispatched to guard a group of civilian engineers on a highly sensitive mission."

"Well done, Sosa!" Montes slapped him on the back. "You do have potential, my boy."

"Thank you, sir."

"Step with me into my office."

They walked across the center area, through blustering wind and blowing snow, and stepped into the geodesic dome serving as command headquarters. Montes removed his thermal jacket. "Hang your coat there," he commanded, pointing to a portable coat tree.

"Yes, sir." Sosa complied.

"Sit here, in the chair in front of my desk."

"Yes, sir." Sosa complied again.

Montes kicked his booted feet up on the desk. "Let's let the educational process continue, Lieutenant." He crossed his arms over his belly. "You wouldn't object to that, would you?"

"No, sir."

"Good." Montes pulled out a flask and two glasses and started pouring liquor. He took a swig and pushed the other glass across the desk toward Sosa. "Tell me, Lieutenant, what is the most important maxim that a successful intelligence officer must always follow?"

Another trick question? "Successful intelligence means that one must know thy enemy."

"Very good, Lieutenant!" Montes took a swig of the liquor. "Have a drink, Lieutenant. Tell me if you can identify my libation."

Fernando hesitated, but he had been given an order. He picked up the glass and took a sip. The flow down his esophagus felt smooth and warm. "A fine selection of brandy, *mi* capitán."

"Excellent, Lieutenant. You are two-for-two. Here is a third question, and it is a follow-up to the first question and is somewhat related to the second. Are you ready for the question?"

"I suppose I am ready. But I will not know until the question is asked."

Montes unleashed a sinister-sounding laugh. "Very well. Here we go. If the answer to your first question is that the most basic maxim of good intelligence is 'know thy enemy,' then riddle me this: What is the best way of knowing one's enemy?"

"Ah, *mi* capitán." Sosa set the brandy down. "This goes to the heart of the debate about which intelligence one believes is best. Electronic intelligence versus human intelligence. And as you know, sir, I am an electronic intelligence aficionado."

"Hah!" Montes slapped his hand hard on the desk. "I knew you could not keep up with me. You've missed the point!"

"I . . . I . . ."

"Lieutenant. The answer to the riddle is right before you. It isn't about human versus electronic intelligence." Another shot of brandy. "The best way to know thy enemy is to drink what thy enemy drinks!" He put down the glass and unleashed more laughter at his own brilliance. "Now then, Lieutenant. Who was the greatest British leader of them all?"

"In my opinion, Churchill."

"Yes! Churchill! And what was Churchill's drink of choice?"

"Brandy, as I recall. Cognac."

"Yes! Correct again! Which is exactly what we're drinking." Montes poured more brandy into Sosa's glass, bringing it to the rim. "You see, Lieutenant, when we drink like them, we begin to think like them! Do you understand?"

"Yes, sir."

"And when we think like them, we learn to outmaneuver them. You see, this was our problem in the Malvinas War. Too much swilling red wine. Not enough spots of brandy." Montes held high his glass, as if calling for a toast.

Fernando Sosa clanked his glass with the capitán's, placating the strange sense of exhilaration oozing from Montes.

"Lieutenant, riddle me this. What is the best way to kill a snake?"

"Cut off its head."

"Precisely! There is hope for you, my dear Sosa!"

"Thank you, sir."

"And that's exactly what we're going to do."

"Sir?"

"We are going to cut off the snake's head."

"I do not understand, sir."

"Again? Just when I thought we were on the same page." More brandy. "Who would you say is the head of the snake in the British camp?"

"You are referring to Austin Rivers, sir?" Sosa asked.

"Precisely. And tomorrow at high noon, we're going to publicly execute Rivers, outside, with the other British pigs watching, which will cause them to melt like butter in a microwave. They will then sing like a chorus of frightened canaries, telling us anything we wish to know." A smile of self-satisfaction. "And would you like even more exciting news?"

"Certainly, sir."

"You are chosen to do the honors."

"Sir?"

"I have decided that you, Sosa, will personally carry out the execution."

"Me, sir?"

"Yes. You. You may use my revolver, a big gun for a big man. A single shot to the head will do. But if you wish to waste another shot into the corpse for the dramatic effect of underscoring our seriousness to the British pigs about their cooperation, feel free. Every intelligence officer must develop an insatiable taste for blood. Once you taste it, you will thirst for more and more. You must cut off the head of the snake," Montes said. "Shoot him."

"Cut off the head of the snake."

"Shoot him."

Control room
Argentinean submarine ARA Santa Cruz
South Atlantic Ocean
depth 850 feet

12:17 p.m. local time

Deathly silence took over the control room of the *Santa Cruz*. The auxiliary battery barely provided enough dim light to illuminate monitors and faces. The silence, in the mind of the commanding officer, permeated the somber atmosphere in what felt like a death watch.

Seawater continued pouring into the lower decks. *Santa Cruz* was sinking. They could not stop it.

Gomez eyed the depth meter, now approaching 850 feet. Men stared at one another. Looks of helplessness were frozen on their faces.

"We will be approaching crush depth soon, Capitán," the executive officer said.

"Another hundred and fifty feet." Gomez felt powerless. He could offer no solutions. "Two hundred if we're lucky."

A pause.

"It's been a pleasure serving with you, sir."

"It's been a pleasure serving with you too, XO." Gomez turned and looked at his second in command. "But before we say our final good-byes, we still have a bit more work to do."

"How may I be of service, sir?"

"XO, it is time to launch an emergency rescue buoy. While there is no realistic chance of us being saved at this depth and under these circumstances, we need to record for the high command in Buenos Aires what has happened here. Prepare to launch rescue buoy containing this message."

"Aye, sir." The XO extracted a pen from his pocket and picked up a legal pad. "Preparing to transcribe message at your direction, Capitán."

"Very well. Take this down. From commanding officer, ARA *Santa Cruz*. To National Command Authority, Republic of Argentina; Commanding Admiral of the Navy of the Republic of Argentina; all ships and aircraft in the area. Please be advised that the submarine ARA *Santa Cruz* has been attacked by enemy forces believed to be British utilizing depth charges and torpedoes and has suffered irreparable damage. *Santa Cruz* is taking on water rapidly. We have been unable to restore power. Salvage pumps inoperative. Soon approaching crush depth. Estimated time to crush depth, T-minus thirty minutes. Respectfully, A. Gomez, Commanding Officer."

"Got it, sir."

"Okay, get it transcribed and launch emergency rescue buoy immediately. As you know, XO, we don't have much time."

"Aye, sir."

Gomez watched as the XO stepped over to the message transcription station on the starboard side of the control room. The message, once transcribed, would be logged into the memory banks of the computer of the emergency transmission buoy. The buoy would be launched from the sub and would float 850 feet to the surface.

Once the buoy reached the surface, it would transmit the encrypted message, announcing the fate of the *Santa Cruz*.

In shallow waters—less than one thousand feet in depth—if a sub could come to rest on the bottom without imploding at crush depth, and if water could be kept out of the sub to prevent the crew from drowning, then the buoy could serve as a real chance for a rescue attempt if anyone heard the broadcast beacon in time.

If the bottom was shallow enough, a rescue line would be connected from the submarine to the buoy at the surface on the theory that the line could lead rescuers down to the sub.

But in this sector of the sea, with water depths between one and a half and two miles, the *Santa Cruz* would either flood or implode on her way down long before she ever reached the seabed.

Gomez hoped the auxiliary battery had enough juice to facilitate the launch of the buoy.

"Sir. Transcription complete. Ready to launch buoy."

"Very well. Launch rescue buoy."

"Launching rescue buoy."

A gentle *puff* sound, not nearly as pronounced as launching a torpedo.

"Rescue buoy away, sir."

"Very well."

"Depth approaching nine hundred feet, sir," the helmsman said.

"Very well." Gomez wiped sweat from his forehead and watched the depth meter.

Depth 892 feet . . .

Depth 894 feet . . .

Depth 896 feet . . .

The high-pitched shrieking sound from the bow of the boat turned the heads of every crew member in the control room.

"What was that?" someone said.

The shrieking yielded to a grinding sound. The sound of metal on metal, as water pressure from the increasing depth pushed mightily against the hull of the sub. A thousand times as a boy and as a teenager, Gomez had crushed an empty soda can in his hands. Now the cold water of the Atlantic began crushing the *Santa Cruz*.

Depth 900 feet . . .

Depth 914 feet . . .

More shrieking

More grinding.

"Capitán!" the chief of the boat shouted. "We've got water flooding the berthing spaces below. Those men will drown unless we get them up here in the control room."

"Very well," Gomez said. "Order all hands to the control room. Now!"

Control room
Argentinean submarine ARA San Juan
South Atlantic Ocean
7 miles SSE of last known position of ARA Santa Cruz
depth 200 feet

12:25 p.m. local time

With lights flashing and sonar screens sweeping inside the control room of the ARA *San Juan*, Commander Carlos Almeyda, the rookie commanding officer, could not grasp the queasy feeling that had settled in the bottom of his stomach. As an executive officer aboard the ARA *Santa Cruz*, he had never felt his stomach go queasy.

Not like this.

Could it be the strain of command?

Perhaps a case of the butterflies to mark his first solo combat voyage?

Capitán Gomez had never gotten nervous like this. In two years of serving as Gomez's executive officer aboard the *Santa Cruz*, if Gomez had felt a tinge of nervousness, Almeyda had never witnessed it.

"Sonar Officer. Anything out there?"

"Nothing, Capitán. Passive sonar still revealing the sounds of the sea, sir. Would you like to light it up with an active *ping*?"

"That's a negative," Almeyda said. "Maintain passive sonar."

"Maintain passive sonar. Aye, sir."

"Radio. Prepare to launch communications buoy. Launch on my command."

"Prepare to launch communications buoy. Aye, sir."

Almeyda hoped that launching the communications buoy might allow him to pick up updated instructions transmitted from Buenos Aires.

"Communications buoy is ready for launch, sir."

"Very well. Launch communications buoy."

"Launch communications buoy. Aye, sir."

Control room
Argentinean submarine ARA Santa Cruz
South Atlantic Ocean
depth 950 feet

12:27 p.m. local time

This way! Hurry up!" the chief of the boat yelled.

Men from belowdecks scurried up the black steel ladder into the control room one by one. Their boots and uniform pants were soaked with seawater. For some, the water line had reached their waists. For others, it was all the way to their chests.

"Get a move on. That water's rising fast!"

The long grinding sound of metal on metal took on an eerie sound. Almost like a humpback whale.

"Approaching one thousand feet, sir," the executive officer said.

Gomez eyed the depth meter.

Depth 960 feet . . .

Depth 972 feet . . .

More shrieking.

More grinding.

Their rate of descent had increased. Almost five feet per second. "All hands present and accounted for in the control room, Capitán!"

"Very well, Chief."

Across the control room . . . from a voice full of fear . . . "Hail Mary, full of grace . . ."

Someone else, "Blessed art thou amongst women."

The voice of the helmsman, "Blessed is the fruit of thy womb, Jesus . . ."

"Here comes the water!" The chief of the boat pointed down into the ladder shaft.

Raging water bubbled up into the control room. Sheets of seawater quickly blanketed the deck.

Men packed together like sardines, shoulder to shoulder, waiting. Some prayed. Their voices blended together.

"Help us! God, help us!"

Icy water filled their boots. Then, quickly, up their pant legs.

Depth 1,000 feet . . .

Depth 1,015 feet . . .

"Hang on!"

The water rose above their waists.

Gomez looked over at his executive officer. "Thank you for everything, Pedro," he said. "I wish we could have served longer together."

The XO raised his hands out of the water, and the two men grasped hands as bubbling water rose up to their necks.

"Oh, dear God, no!"

Gomez stood on his tiptoes as the water reached his chin, trying to gasp for the diminishing layer of air over their heads.

"Good-bye, Capitán!" The XO raised his pistol out of the water, put it to his head, and pulled the trigger. Blood gushed into the water, and the XO's body floated beside the capitán.

Only ten inches of air remained between the rising waterline and the ceiling.

Two more pistol shots.

"Madre! Oh, Madre!" The cries of grown men calling for their mothers in the moment before their deaths.

Alberto Gomez treaded cold seawater, struggling to keep his face and nose up in the vanishing pocket of air above him. He thought of Louisa and his boys, Juan and Pedro, who would now be fatherless. They were only thirteen and sixteen. He would never see them again. "God! God! Please take care of Louisa! Please take care of my boys!"

His heart racing, he pushed up desperately, virtually kissing the ceiling as he sucked in all the air he could and went down, under the water.

All the lights flickered, then went out.

Gomez lunged back up again. Another desperate inhale.

Maybe half an inch of air left.

He held his breath underwater and felt men's arms and legs kicking and flailing in desperate panic. A thousand regrets flashed through his mind in an instant.

If only he had taken more time for family.

If only more time for God.

He slowly exhaled, and then the instinct to breathe overtook him. His body screamed for air.

He pushed up again. This time, cold salt water flooded into his throat and lungs.

He coughed under the water and flailed his arms.

Dear Jesus, help me!

Gomez felt his body going limp in the cold water.

Argentine Air Force C-130
South Atlantic Ocean
100 miles east of the Malvinas (Falkland) Islands
altitude 5,000 feet
course 180 degrees

12:57 p.m. local time

Major Juan Alvarez banked the four-engine C-130 aircraft to the left, swinging it around to a course of due south. He looked out through his aviator glasses to his left and saw nothing but grayish-blue water all the way out to the horizon.

In the cockpit seat to his right, his copilot, Lieutenant Miguel Castro, scanned the seas in the opposite direction.

The major ships of the British task force, spearheaded by the super-carrier *Queen Elizabeth*, had already passed to their south. But on the high seas, with RADAR from surface ships sometimes limited by the drop-off of the horizon, visual spotting from aircraft often provided the best intelligence about enemy ships at sea.

"Anything out there, Lieutenant?"

"Negative, sir. Only cold ocean and whitecaps."

"Keep looking. I'm going to bank us back for another loop. If we don't find anything, we'll move the search pattern farther south."

"Yes, sir."

Alvarez turned the yoke to the right, and the plane banked again, this time turning back toward the Malvinas Islands, which the British still insisted on calling the Falklands. One day, and hopefully soon, the phrase "Falkland Islands" would be an obscure footnote in a history book, and the islands would be forever restored to their true Argentine name and heritage.

"Sir. Picking up an automated distress signal."

Alvarez looked over. "What is it, Lieutenant?"

"Just a second, sir. Let me try to narrow the frequency band." Castro fidgeted with the frequency. "Sir. It's an automated distress signal from the *Santa Cruz*'s rescue buoy. Not good, sir. *Santa Cruz* reporting they've been attacked. Sounds like the sub has been lost, sir."

"Dear Jesus, please no."

"Automated message reporting they were attacked by torps and depth charges believed to be British in origin, sir."

Alvarez thought for a second. "If that's true, then we're officially at war with the British."

"Yes, sir," the copilot said.

"Very well. Let's pinpoint the location of that rescue buoy and get a FLASH message to Buenos Aires."

"Yes, sir."

Apartment of Maria Vasquez
337 Avenue de Tomás Ramos
Valparaiso, Chile

1:03 p.m. local time

I hope you can overlook the mess." Maria giggled and took Pete's hand and led him up the brick steps to the small porch at the entrance of the narrow townhouse. The light touch of her hand shot powerful bolts of electricity through his body.

She released his hand and fiddled in her purse, looking for her keys.

He could not avoid staring as the afternoon Pacific breeze swept her ponytail and ruffled her silky red blouse.

Would he be led to the slaughter? Falling in the manner of Sampson and King David? And even more recently, General Petraeus?

Be careful, Peter, a voice in his gut warned him.

"Mess? Right. I'll bet the place is impeccable. Besides, my only concern is that slice of peach pie you promised me."

"Mmm. My peach pie?" She extracted her keys from her purse and smiled radiantly. "That's all you have on your mind, Commander?"

He stared into her sparkling eyes and radiant smile. "I didn't say that was all I was thinking about."

"That's more like it." She held up her key. "Would you like to do the honors?"

He took the key and his heart pounded. The key slid easily into the keyhole, and he turned it and opened the door.

She took him by the arm and escorted him into the foyer.

With light streaming through open skylights in a cathedral ceiling, the small flat presented a spacious, airy feeling. On the light-colored walls, painted white and yellow, there hung bright art—oil paintings and watercolors. Green plants sat in pots in some of the windows.

The stunning vibrant colors reflected her personality and her exciting looks.

But off on a distant wall in a room in the corner, visible through an open door, hung the portrait of Salvador Allende.

The portrait brought a tinge of sickness to his stomach, an internal tug-of-war pulling against the feeling of bubbly ecstasy generated by the touch of Maria Vasquez.

"I love your place," he said. "So airy."

"Would you like a tour?"

I should probably turn around right now. "Sure. Why not?"

"What would you like to see first?"

"It's your place. I'll follow you."

"Hmm. Okay." She took him by the hand. "Let's see. Well, since you said you came here only for the pie . . ."

"That's not what I said."

She smiled. "Maybe I want to see if you like my cooking before I show you anything else."

He smiled back at her. "So show me."

"This way."

The pie sat in the middle of the small wooden table in the kitchen, in the back of the flat.

"Sit here," she said.

He complied.

"Do you like a big piece?"

"Looks great. Sure."

She sliced a wedge and spooned it onto the plate in front of him.

He looked at her, smiled, and forked a small piece of the pie into his mouth and savored the flavor of fresh peach, crust, and brown sugar.

"Well?" An expectant look.

"Delicious."

"You can eat more than that." She spoke in a teasing tone. "Here." She pulled her chair up next to his, took his fork, and speared a larger chunk with more crust and peach. "Open up."

"If you insist." The second piece seemed sweeter than the first. "Mmm. I love that."

"Really?" She touched his forearm.

"Really." Her leg brushed his.

"I hope you like this even better."

She leaned into him, and when their lips met, he understood for the first time the meaning of nuclear fission.

His arm found her back and he pulled her in close to him. Suddenly they were standing, tightly embraced, unable to pull apart. With his back against the wall, they kissed again. Pete had never experienced anything like the warm magnetism of her lips.

"Want to see my bedroom?" The longing look in her eyes revealed her intentions.

"I'm not so sure that's a good idea."

"Oh, come on. Let me give you the rest of the tour." Gently, she caressed the side of his face.

"I'd love to, but I should be leaving now."

She gazed at him with eyes that were hypnotizing. Another long, passionate kiss. Five minutes passed? Ten?

She took him by the hand and began to lead him, slowly, out of the kitchen.

Part of him wanted to follow. The other part knew this was wrong.

The sound of a text message rang on his cell phone.

"Let me check this."

Urgent Message . . . Call SUBPAC . . . Punch Secure Code 9034582*14.

"Give me a second." Pete called the number and punched the secure code, ensuring that anyone trying to eavesdrop would get an earful of electronic scrambled eggs.

"SUBPAC. Captain Teague."

"Sir, Commander Miranda here. I got an urgent message to call."

"Ah, yes, Commander. Hold for Admiral Elyea."

Pete looked at Maria, who sat in a wingback chair and crossed her legs and smiled up at him.

"Pete?" The familiar voice of Rear Admiral Chuck "Bulldog" Elyea. "You there?"

"I'm here, sir."

"Pete, things are heating up in the South Atlantic. Our satellites picked up a distress signal. It appears the Brits have sunk the Argentinean sub *Santa Cruz*."

"You're kidding."

"No, I'm not, Pete. We're listening in to radio traffic between Buenos Aires and an Argentinean C-130 searching the area. Apparently no survivors."

Pete felt his stomach drop. The news of the loss of any submarine, even a foreign submarine, struck fear in the gut of any submariner.

"Sounds like this thing could heat up fast, sir."

"Ya got that right, Commander."

"What's our role?"

"Whatever you're doing, I need you to get back to that *LA*-class boat immediately. The *Corpus Christi* or the *Minnow* or whatever the Chileans are calling it now."

"The *Miro*, sir."

"Right. The *Miro*," Bulldog said. "Listen, Pete. Remember the change-of-command ceremony with the ambassador that's been scheduled for tomorrow?"

"Yes, sir. I've been invited to attend as the guest of Admiral Delapaz."

"Well, scratch that. It ain't happening."

"Sir?"

"Pete, you're taking that sub to sea tomorrow."

"But, sir, I haven't even started training the crew."

"No time for that, and it won't matter. The only Chilean you'll be taking is the new captain. Captain Romero, I think his name is. The rest of the crew is American. Most of the crew members who brought the boat down are still in the country. You won't have a full crew, but you'll have some experienced guys, and you'll have enough of a skeleton crew to get the job done. We've ordered them to report and be ready to get under way at 0600 hours tomorrow. You'll be diving under the name of the CS *Miro*. The world could explode in the Antarctic region, Pete. This is the president's way of helping the Chileans help the British. You can train the Chilean crew when you get back."

Pete looked at Maria, who had a starry gaze in her eyes. "Aye, Admiral. I'm on my way."

"I'm depending on you, Pete. The president's depending on you. You're the best we've got. You can be a knucklehead sometimes, but you're the only sub commander in the fleet that I've got enough confidence in to put in charge of a crew, sight unseen, and carry out any mission we ask you to do."

"Thank you, sir."

"Do us proud."

"Will do, sir."

Pete disconnected the call and put his phone in his pocket.

"You have to leave?" Maria stepped close to him and caressed his shoulder.

"I'm sorry. Duty calls."

"You have to go?"

"Yes."

"Will you take the rest of the peach pie? So you won't forget me?"

He drew her into his arms. "Hang on to that pie. But pie or no pie, there's not a chance I'm going to forget you."

She smiled. "I'm worried about you. Will you be okay?"

"I'm going to sea. I don't know when I'll be back. But when I come back, I'll finish that pie." He kissed her on the cheek and walked out the door.

CHAPTER 22

Control room
Argentinean submarine ARA San Juan
South Atlantic Ocean
15 miles SSE of last known position of ARA Santa Cruz
depth 200 feet

1:25 p.m. local time

In the control room of the submarine ARA *San Juan*, Commander Carlos Almeyda checked his watch. Two hundred feet above and a quarter mile behind the *San Juan*, on the surface of the South Atlantic, the submarine's communications buoy was being towed along at eight knots.

And if anyone saw the buoy, they would see a strange watermelon-shaped ball skimming across the surface of the water, almost like a big floating football. Some might even think they were witnessing something extraterrestrial.

But it wasn't the untrained eye that had Commander Almeyda concerned. To the trained eye—a military helicopter or airplane equipped for antisubmarine warfare or the watch stander on board an enemy destroyer or cruiser—the moving gray watermelon-shaped buoy could amount to a bull's-eye painted on the hull of his submarine.

Already the buoy had floated on the surface nearly an hour—well beyond Almeyda's comfort zone—with no messages received. So Almeyda had run the risk of exposing his boat and his crew and had come up with nothing.

Why no messages? Why no anything?

Had the British fleet passed them by?

Had Capitán Gomez taken the *Santa Cruz* in pursuit of the British carrier? Leaving the *San Juan* alone in this sector of the sea?

The silence from above was deafening.

Silence or no, Almeyda could not risk leaving the communications buoy on the surface any longer.

"Lieutenant, prepare to retrieve communications buoy."

"Prepare to retrieve communications buoy, aye, sir."

"Capitán! We are beginning to receive a transmission from the surface!" the radio officer announced.

"Belay that order, Lieutenant."

"Aye, sir."

Almeyda felt his stomach knotting.

"Sir, message is completed."

"Give it here and get that buoy down!"

"Aye, sir!"

The communications officer ripped the message from the printer and headed to the captain's seat.

"Buoy's down, sir," the XO said.

Almeyda snatched the message from the hands of the radio officer.

FROM: Commander Argentine Naval Submarine Force
TO: Commanding Officer, ARA *San Juan*
PRECEDENCE: FLASH, TOP SECRET
SUBJECT: Attack on ARA *Santa Cruz*, Orders Update

1. Be advised of attack upon ARA *Santa Cruz* by British naval forces.
2. ARA *Santa Cruz* has been declared missing and is believed to have been sunk.
3. Argentine submarine ARA *Salta* is being dispatched to the area to reinforce ARA *San Juan*.
4. ARA *San Juan* is now lead submarine in task force. ARA *San Juan* is ordered to attack British naval task force and then to dive and retreat.
5. British naval task force last located at -54.755062 South Latitude; -57.304688 West Longitude; course 180 degrees.

6. Execute orders to attack and destroy ships of the British fleet, with priority target HMS *Queen Elizabeth*.
7. Execute orders immediately.
8. End of transmission.

"XO, look at this." Almeyda handed the orders to his executive officer.

The XO read the message and made the sign of the cross. "They've sunk the *Santa Cruz*, and they're headed for us."

"Yes, they are, XO. And payback is hell," Almeyda said. "Submerge to 400 feet. Prepare to launch torps. We'll hit them with all we've got."

"Prepare to launch torpedoes. Aye, Capitán."

Royal Navy Merlin Mk1 helicopter
ASW Naval Squadron 814
South Atlantic Ocean
17 miles south of HMS **Queen Elizabeth**
altitude 1,000 feet

1:30 p.m. local time

Are you sure you saw something, Leftenant?" Commander Chris Stacks, at the controls of the Merlin Mk1 helicopter, looked over to the right, out at the sea.

"I'm sure I saw something. Right out there. At least I think I did."

"You think you did?"

"Yes, sir. It looked like a gray flash or something, and then it disappeared."

"Very well, let's go have a look." Eyeing the fuel gauge, Stacks banked the chopper to the right and flew to the area where Jordan thought he saw something.

"Right out there somewhere, sir." Jordan pointed to a large expanse of sea.

Stacks brought the chopper into a stationary hover and looked through his binoculars, scanning the sea. Nothing but whitecaps cresting atop the swells separating the long troughs of gray water.

"What do you think you saw, Jordan?"

"Something in the water. Perhaps a small boat or raft. Perhaps a communications buoy from a submarine."

The pilot scanned some more. Still nothing. "Could it have been a whale cresting the water? Or a porpoise?"

"Possibly, I suppose. But I don't think so."

"Well, we're low on sonobuoys and dangerously low on fuel. We need to get back to the carrier ASAP. So you must be certain that you spotted something before we start dropping more sonobuoys."

"I don't think it was a fish or a mammal. It looked grayish. Maybe made of steel. The sun glanced off it with an orange or yellow reflection."

"Orange or yellow reflection? Are you certain?"

"I think so, sir."

"Sometimes the sun glancing off a whale or a porpoise can create a yellowish orange tint."

"Yes, sir. But I don't think it was a porpoise, sir."

"How long did you have a visual on it?"

"A second," Jordan said. "But I saw something."

"Chief, how many sonobuoys are left?"

"We're down to three, sir. Two passives. One active left."

Stacks thought for a second. He did not have either fuel or sonobuoys to waste on what might have been a reflection of the sun against a wave. On the other hand, if another sub was down there . . . with the carrier headed in this direction . . .

"Okay. Here's our plan," he said, thinking aloud. "Since we have two passive sonobuoys and only one active left, we are going to drop one of the passive sonobuoys in the water and see what we can hear. If Leftenant Jordan did in fact spot a communications buoy, and there is a submarine down there, it cannot be that far from the surface. We should be able to hear something with passive sonar." Stacks looked at his copilot. "Do you agree, Leftenant?"

"Yes. I would think we should be able to hear her engines close to the surface, sir."

"Agreed," Stacks said. "Chief, prepare to drop passive sonobuoy. On my command."

"Preparing to drop sonobuoy. Aye, sir."

Commander Stacks brought the Merlin down to an altitude of two hundred feet, low enough to safely drop the passive sonobuoy into the ocean below, and low enough that the chopper's downdraft stirred up the waves and swells on the surface.

"Sonobuoy's in the water, Skipper," Sonarman Chief Philip Welton announced.

CHAPTER 23

Control room
Argentinean submarine ARA San Juan
South Atlantic Ocean
15 miles SSE of last known position of ARA Santa Cruz
depth 300 feet

1:35 p.m. local time

Depth approaching three hundred feet, Capitán."

"Very well," Commander Almeyda said. "Continue descent to target depth of four hundred feet. Prepare to arm torpedoes."

"Continue descent to four hundred. Prepare to arm torpedoes."

An eerie silence pervaded the control room of the *San Juan* as the depth meter reflected the submarine's fast dive.

310 feet . . .

315 feet . . .

320 feet . . .

"Capitán!" the sonar officer said. "Splash on the surface, sir. Sounds like a sonobuoy."

"I was afraid of that," Almeyda said.

"Should we prepare for evasive maneuvers?" the XO asked.

"No," Almeyda said. "If we do that, they'll definitely hear us. We may or may not get away, but we'll definitely have to dodge torps and depth charges if we get away. Let's stay quiet and hope it's passive sonar. And pray we can get below the thermal layer before they hear us."

Royal Navy Merlin Mk1 helicopter
ASW Naval Squadron 814
South Atlantic Ocean
15 miles south of HMS Queen Elizabeth
altitude 200 feet

1:40 p.m. local time

S onarman Chief Philip Welton sat in the cargo bay of the Merlin with an acoustical headset on.

Commander Stacks, at the controls of the Merlin, checked his fuel gauge. "I need to know if anything's down there, Chief. We can't keep this baby in the air much longer."

"Okay, sir. I'll need a few minutes to analyze the situation, sir."

Stacks examined his watch. "Five minutes max, Chief. Otherwise we'll all be swimming back to the *Queen Elizabeth*."

CHAPTER 24

Control room
Argentinean submarine ARA San Juan
South Atlantic Ocean
15 miles SSE of last known position of ARA Santa Cruz
depth 360 feet

1:43 p.m. local time

When a submarine detects that sonobuoys have been dropped in the water, that ordinarily means one thing—the enemy above is an aircraft. The submarine's main weapon, the torpedo, is a weapon that attacks ships in the water. The torpedo cannot hit an aircraft flying a thousand feet above the surface of the water.

Commander Carlos Almeyda feared he might be facing such a mismatch—one that favors the aircraft. If the aircraft pinpoints the location of the submarine, it becomes a one-way shootout, with the sub rendered totally defenseless.

The submarine's best friend becomes a thick blanket of water below the surface of the ocean called the "thermal layer," or thermocline, in which the ocean temperatures are much colder than the surface water temperature. If a sub can sink below the thermocline, that thermal layer can help hide the sub not only from passive sonar but even from the *pings* of active sonar.

The thermal layer effectively dampens and sometimes blankets sound. The more turbulence in the water generated by rough seas, the greater the protective blanket for the sub trying to evade sonar.

Commander Almeyda knew that the thermocline at this time of year in the southern hemisphere—October, or late spring—could be rather deep. He watched the depth meter and mentally calculated whether he would have enough depth to get under the protective blanket before being picked up by enemy sonar.

Depth 360 feet . . .

Depth 370 feet . . .

Depth 380 feet . . .

"Approaching target depth of 400 feet, sir," the diving officer said.

"I'm not sure that's enough to clip the thermocline based on the water temperature, Lieutenant. Maintain dive. Set new target depth at seven hundred feet."

"Aye, sir. Maintain dive. Set new target depth at seven hundred feet."

Royal Navy Merlin Mk1 helicopter
ASW Naval Squadron 814
South Atlantic Ocean
15 miles south of HMS Queen Elizabeth
altitude 200 feet

1:45 p.m. local time

D espite the somewhat unrealistic demands of the top brass in the Royal Navy, submarine hunting couldn't be likened to popping an English muffin in the microwave. It involved a combination of art and science—and more art than science. To find a submarine lurking below the high seas, one could not merely pop a problem in a computer and wait thirty seconds for a solution. Like a fox hunter waited for his prey to emerge from the woods before taking a shot, patience and a good ear were the hallmarks of a good submarine hunter.

Against this backdrop, Sonarman Chief Philip Welton, Royal Navy, sat in the back of the helicopter at the sonar station and adjusted his acoustic headset. Less than two hours earlier, Welton was hailed as the man who discovered the first enemy submarine. He had listened intently as the torpedoes and depth charges dropped from this helicopter attacked and destroyed the Argentine *Santa Cruz*–class submarine.

The sinking, the first British kill against the enemy in retaliation for the coordinated attack against British civilians in Antarctica, had generated considerable excitement among the ships of the British task force. The commanding officer of the *Queen Elizabeth*, Captain Jones-Landry, had personally called on the secure ship-to-air frequency to congratulate Welton for his work in locating and sinking the enemy submarine.

Now Welton was hunting for another submarine, this time under less-than-ideal circumstances. His pilot stood over him, rushing him and reminding him of their critical fuel situation. All the fuss probably because of a flash of sunlight against a long swell spotted by a young, overly enthusiastic copilot still excited by the electricity of combat.

"Hearing anything, Chief?" Commander Stacks pressed for an answer.

"Hard to say, sir. Lots of sloshing and turbulence."

"We need to know something, Chief. With these headwinds picking up, we're going to burn more fuel to get back to the ship. We need an answer now."

"It often takes some time, Commander. I have nothing so far but ocean slosh."

"Very well. We'll set a course back to the carrier. We have got to refuel."

"Wait a second . . ."

"What is it?"

Welton adjusted his headset. "I thought I heard something."

"What?"

"Give me a second, sir."

"Chief, we don't have a second."

"Please, sir." Welton turned up the volume on the acoustic sensors to maximum. He had heard something. A strange sound. A whine. A faint clang.

Now, nothing. Ocean turbulence again.

"I heard something, sir. Now it's gone. Could've been a whale. Possibly an electronic reverberation. Maybe a submarine fleeing the area or diving. I'm sorry, sir. I could not get enough of a fix for any kind of match. We would need more time."

"Time is something we don't have," Stacks said. "Leftenant Jordan, set course for the *Queen Elizabeth*."

"Aye, sir."

CHAPTER 25

M/S Thor Liberty
British Registry cargo ship
South Atlantic Ocean
60 miles southwest of the Falkland Islands
course 180 degrees

2:10 p.m. local time

Five hours had passed since the sonar officer aboard the *Thor Liberty* had first picked up sounds of the enemy submarine and relayed the message to HMS *Queen Elizabeth*.

Oh, the sweet irony, that a ship captained by one who had aspired to be a Royal Navy officer, having been rejected over a minor sports injury, had detected the enemy submarine even before the naval ships of the flotilla had detected it.

From the bridge of the *Thor Liberty*, Captain Bob Hudson checked the other three surface ships of the flotilla through his binoculars.

HMS *Ocean*, with her eighteen helicopters and eighty-three Royal Marines, still steamed off to the left, though she had opened up a bit more distance off the freighter's port than before. The RFA *Black Rover* had moved another thousand yards off the right, and the flagship *Queen Elizabeth* remained out front, but had opened up a distance of another thousand yards in front of the *Thor Liberty*.

The instructions to spread the ships more in the water, issued by the task force commander aboard the *Queen Elizabeth*, would increase the range of sonar coverage for the possibility of more submarines that might be in the area. Part of the reason that only two ships had detected the first sub may have been noise turbulence from the ships being bunched so tightly together. With all the engines of the flotilla churning in close proximity, the turbulence made it harder to hear anything.

Captain Landry-Jones must have been embarrassed that the only other ship to have heard the submarine besides the *Queen Elizabeth* was the *Thor Liberty*. This brought a smile to Bob Hudson's face.

Bob gave the credit to his superb sonar operator, Mister Brice Johnson, the venerable Scotsman who had spent twenty years in the Royal Navy before retiring and starting a new career at Thorco Shipping. Johnson was better and more experienced than most military sonar operators in the Royal Navy and probably better than those now in the task force vessels.

Johnson's discovery of the submarine was a credit to the *Thor Liberty* and to Bob, personally, as captain.

Yet in a strange sense, the reality of the kill tempered the excitement of the discovery. The eerie groaning death sounds of the submarine on passive sonar as she reached crush depth and imploded under tons of powerful water pressure would haunt Bob for the rest of his life.

How horrible that must have been—to have been trapped in a steel cylinder hundreds of feet below the surface, realizing that there was no hope, that torrents of cold seawater would soon flood the dark steel-encased abyss and fill the lungs of the crewmen.

What a lonely way to die.

Bridge
HMS Queen Elizabeth
South Atlantic Ocean
61 miles southeast of the Falkland Islands
course 180 degrees

2:12 p.m. local time

Captain, we're receiving a distress message from the lead Merlin helicopter out on antisubmarine detail."

"Put it on the loudspeaker, Leftenant," Captain Jones-Landry said. "And give me the microphone."

"Aye, sir."

A brief static over the bridge's loudspeakers.

"Mayday. Mayday. This is the pilot of ASW Chopper Merlin 1. Please be advised that we're perilously low on fuel and may need to ditch. HMS *Queen Elizabeth*, please respond. Over."

"Merlin 1. This is HMS *Queen Elizabeth*. Report your position, your bearing, and your predicament. Over."

"*Queen Elizabeth*. Merlin 1. We are twenty miles out, sir. On course back to the ship. We were delayed because of a possible sub sighting. We took time to investigate but could not verify. We thought we had enough fuel, but headwinds returning to the ship have been extraordinary, and we've burned all reserves. We're flying on fumes, Captain."

"Merlin 1. *Queen Elizabeth*. We're headed your way. We will increase speed to try and close the distance. Hang tight, my friend."

"Thank you, Captain."

"Engineering. Bridge."

"Bridge. Engineering. Go ahead, Captain."

"Leftenant, we've got a chopper going down. Out front of us, due south. I want to close the distance. Give me full power. All engines full."

"All engines full. Aye, Captain."

"XO. On the 1-MC."

"On the 1-MC. Aye, Captain." The executive officer handed Jones-Landry the microphone, which would carry his voice to every crevice of the ship.

"Now hear this. This is the captain speaking. We have received a distress signal from one of our Merlins, operating twenty miles to our south but running out of fuel. We've gone to full power to try to close the distance. Prepare for search-and-rescue operations. Fire crews, prepare the flight deck for a crash landing. I want two additional helicopters launched immediately to spearhead our recovery efforts. All hands to recovery stations! Stand by for recovery efforts. This is the captain."

The carrier's nuclear-powered engines hummed to a higher whining pitch, and the *Queen Elizabeth* lunged forward in the ocean at a speed that would leave the other ships of the task force in her wake.

The others would catch up soon enough, but for the time being Jones-Landry would do everything in his power to save the crew of the British chopper.

"Captain!" the bridge watch officer said.

"What is it, Leftenant?"

"Sir. I see the Merlin. Through the binoculars, sir!"

"Where?"

"Right out there, sir! Inbound! Just above the horizon!"

Jones-Landry brought his binoculars to his eyes. There. The black silhouette of the inbound chopper appeared over the horizon.

"Captain, we have another call from the chopper."

"Put it on the loudspeaker."

"Aye, sir."

"*Queen Elizabeth*. Merlin 1. Sir, we've got you in our sights. But frankly, I don't think we can make it back. The fuel alarm is buzzing."

"Hang in there, Commander. We've got two Merlins headed your way to pull you out of the water if you ditch. We're steaming at maximum speed. Try to squeeze a couple more minutes out of that bird. That's all we need."

"Aye, sir."

Control room
Argentinean submarine ARA San Juan
South Atlantic Ocean
15 miles SSE of last known position of ARA Santa Cruz
depth 300 feet

2:13 p.m. local time

Capitán!" the sonar officer said. "I'm picking up engines on passive sonar . . . multiple targets. Most likely the British task force, sir. They sound close, sir. Range to target, one thousand yards to our north! Sir! They are closing in on our position!"

A surge of adrenaline shot through Almeyda's body. "Go to periscope depth! Prepare to fire all torpedoes on my command. Then prepare to dive on my command!"

"Go to periscope depth! Prepare to fire torpedoes! Then prepare to dive. Aye, sir!"

His heart pounded with a hammering *thump, thump, thump* as the *San Juan* rose toward surface depth. Like a deer hunter in a tree stand, this was a sub commander's dream—to silently wait in the water while unsuspecting prey wanders in for a point-blank shot. Could he have gotten so lucky?

"Sub's at periscope depth, Capitán."

"Very well. Up scope."

"Up scope. Aye, sir."

The sound of a small electric motor hummed throughout the control room as the telescope rose to the surface.

"Scope's up, sir," the watch officer said.

"Very well," Almeyda said. The capitán stepped over to the periscope, grabbed the grips on each side of the periscope column, and peered through the eyepiece.

His first view showed only water and gray-blue sky. Almeyda pivoted a quarter to his right, and when he did, his heart nearly stopped. There, in the middle of the screen, steaming toward them from the north, the wide image of the flattop in the crosshairs! The HMS *Queen Elizabeth* was steaming right at him, like an unsuspecting elephant walking into a safari gun trap.

"Down scope! Prepare to fire torps one through four! Prepare to dive!"

"Down scope! Prepare to fire torps! Aye, Capitán!"

Almeyda glanced around at his men. Tension electrified the control room. The moment of truth had arrived.

"Scope's down, sir!"

"Very well! Fire torp one!"

"Firing torp one, aye, sir!"

"Fire torp two!"

"Firing torp two! Aye, sir!"

"Fire torp three!"

"Firing torp three! Aye, sir!"

"Fire torp four!"

"Firing torp four! Aye, sir!"

"Weapons Officer! Report status!"

"Four torps in the water, Capitán! Torp one, time to impact two minutes, sir!"

"Very well! Emergency dive to seven hundred feet. Then set course at zero-nine-zero degrees, full power. Let's get out of here!"

Bridge
HMS Queen Elizabeth
South Atlantic Ocean
61 miles southwest of the Falkland Islands
course 180 degrees

2:15 p.m. local time

Q*ueen Elizabeth*. Merlin 1. Captain, our engine is sputtering. We aren't going to make it, sir."

"You're only half a mile away, Commander!"

"Can't make it, Captain. We're starting to drop!"

"Initiate auto-rotation, Commander!"

"Not enough altitude, sir!"

"Air ops commander! Notify rescue choppers. They're going down!"

"Aye, sir."

Jones-Landry looked out at the inbound chopper. Even without binoculars, he could clearly see that the Merlin was in trouble. The gray chopper tipped from right to left, then appeared to stall and, in a millisecond, plunged into the ocean.

"All engines stop!" Jones-Landry said.

"All engines stop! Aye, sir!"

As the *Queen Elizabeth* reversed her engines to avoid overrunning the downed chopper, two Merlin helicopters flew in and hovered over the downed chopper. As the Merlins flew into position, the downed chopper rolled over on its side in the water and appeared ready to sink.

Four British frogmen in black thermal diving suits leaped from the hovering helicopters into the sea.

Captain Jones-Landry brought his binoculars to his eyes. Swimmers in the water were cutting strokes toward the sinking helicopter. So far, there were no signs of life around the chopper except the frogmen.

"Captain! Captain! We've got four inbound torpedoes, sir! Time to impact thirty seconds!"

"What the bloody . . . Which direction?"

"Straight off the bow, sir! Time to impact twenty-two seconds!"

"Reengage engines! All ahead full! Right full rudder!"

"All ahead full. Right full rudder!"

"XO, warn the crew! Brace for impact!"

"Aye, Captain. This is the executive officer! Four torpedoes inbound! Brace for impact! Brace for impact!"

"Time to impact eight seconds, Captain!"

As *Queen Elizabeth* began her evasive maneuver turn to the right, the first torpedo struck, rocking the ship with a powerful explosion, knocking Jones-Landry off his feet. A powerful second blast followed the first. And then a third, setting off collision alarms all over the ship.

MV **Thor Liberty**
British Registry cargo ship
South Atlantic Ocean
60 miles southwest of the Falkland Islands
course 180 degrees

2:16 p.m. local time

C aptain!" the radio officer said. "We've received a radio message from the *Queen Elizabeth*, sir! They've been hit by torpedoes! Multiple strikes! They're reporting three strikes to the underside. The situation is critical!"

"What?" Captain Hudson raised his binoculars and looked at the British flagship, a mile out front. *Queen Elizabeth* remained afloat, but billowing black smoke rose from her port side.

"All ahead full! Prepare to pick up survivors."

"All ahead full! Aye, sir!"

"Captain! Torpedoes in the water! Headed our way, sir. Time to impact fifteen seconds!"

"Right full rudder!"

"Right full rudder! Aye, sir!"

"Hang on, gentlemen!" Captain Hudson shouted.

Like a giant ski boat making a sharp turn in the water to pick up a downed skier, *Thor Liberty* banked hard to the right, bringing the deck of the bridge to nearly a forty-five-degree angle in a desperate evasive maneuver to avoid the approaching torpedo. Some men lost their balance in the turn. Bob grabbed a support bar and remained on his feet.

"Time to impact, eight seconds!"

The explosion rocked the ship with a vengeance, knocking computer screens off their positions and onto the deck and knocking Bob off his feet.

"We've been hit!"

Thor Liberty leveled out of her turn.

Bob jumped to his feet and grabbed the 1-MC. "This is the captain! I want damage reports! Now!"

As other men pulled themselves up to their feet, a blaring came over the ship's loudspeaker in the bridge.

"Bridge. Engineering."

"What do you have, Mister Pittenger?" Bob asked.

"Sir, we have massive amounts of seawater pouring in. In my estimation, the situation is unrepairable. If we're able to sustain buoyancy for another thirty minutes, we will be lucky."

Bob took a deep breath. He had to make a quick decision—a correct decision. "Very well, Mister Pittenger. Stand by for further orders."

"Aye, Captain."

Bob looked at his executive officer and saw, for the first time in a long time, fear in another man's eyes. He held the microphone to his face and clicked to the 1-MC. "Now hear this. This is the captain speaking. We have been struck by an enemy torpedo. We have assessed the situation to be irreparable. Prepare to abandon ship."

CHAPTER 26

La Casa Rosada (the Pink House)
presidential palace
Buenos Aires, Argentina

3:15 p.m. local time

The black armored Audi A8, the official state car used to transport the president of the Argentine Republic, drove up Rivadavia Avenue, then turned right onto a heavily guarded driveway and stopped in front of the magnificent neoclassical Pink Mansion, 1830s vintage, the official residence of the president of the republic.

President Donato Suarez had been summoned for an emergency meeting with his top military advisers over the exploding situation in the Antarctic region. Even after three years as president, he could not help but admire the stately majesty of the Argentinean "Pink House," which in his opinion still stood as the most regal executive mansion in the world.

A bodyguard opened the back door of the Audi, and Suarez stepped out into the afternoon sunshine. He looked up with pride at the national flag flying atop the mansion, the light blue horizontal stripes sandwiching the white horizontal stripe blending brilliantly with the azure of the sky and the white puffy clouds dancing over the palace.

Surely God would continue to bless Argentina, for her national flag and the color of her skies were one and the same.

"This way, Mister President," an aide said as a small band of armed presidential security guards whisked him in through the front doors of the Pink House into the checkered-marble-floored Hall of Honor. They walked between the regal interior colonnades and past extravagant oil paintings. The soles of their leather shoes clicked against the marble, echoing like a clackety stampede as they rushed deep into the interior of the building to the presidential office, a large ornate room replete with marble fireplaces and a long conference table surrounded by ten white wingback chairs.

The men who had been sitting in the chairs, the most senior-ranking officers in the Argentinean military, stood as Suarez entered the room.

"Be seated!" the president snapped. "Admiral Blanco. What is our status?"

"Mister President, I regret to inform you, sir, that we have lost the *Santa Cruz.*"

Suarez glanced at the faces of his commanders. "How is this possible?"

The admiral said, "Sir, we suspect a helicopter attack launched from Britain's new supercarrier, the *Queen Elizabeth.*"

Suarez began to seethe. "I issued orders for our fleet to fire if fired upon. Was this carried out?"

"*Si*, Mister President. The sister submarine of the *Santa Cruz*, the ARA *San Juan*, launched an attack against the *Queen Elizabeth*. Sir, we believe we have achieved a strike on the British carrier. But we don't know the extent of the damage."

"A strike on the *Queen Elizabeth*?" Suarez stroked his chin and smiled. His father had served in the Malvinas War and had surrendered to the British. "What are your recommendations, Admiral?"

"Mister President, we expect the British to increase their naval forces in retaliation for our strike on their new prized flagship. The Americans and Chileans may even provide support. We recommend increasing our naval presence in Drake Passage and in the waters surrounding it."

"How much of an increase are you recommending, Admiral?"

"All four of our destroyers. Nine corvettes. Two fast-attack craft. Six patrol boats. Two amphibious transport ships. The submarine ARA *Salta* has already been dispatched to the area to replace the ARA *Santa Cruz.*"

"Admiral, you are talking about sending most of our fleet to Drake Passage."

"Most of our combatant ships, yes, sir. This leaves most of our Atlantic coastline vulnerable, but we feel that the Air Force patrolling the coast can provide more than adequate short-term protection. We hope that with a formidable naval presence, the British will second-guess things and reconsider. Especially with their flagship potentially crippled."

"Where is the Venezuelan firepower? They're supposed to be in this with us."

"The Venezuelans are increasing their naval presence. But not just the Venezuelans. The Russians too, sir, are sending ships into the area."

Suarez thought for a second. Sending that kind of firepower could escalate an already explosive powder keg. On the other hand, Britain defeated Argentina in the Malvinas War because Argentina was outgunned.

"Very well, Admiral. Order the fleet to sail south. Secure Drake Passage and defend the interests of Argentina."

"Yes, Mister President."

10 Downing Street
London

6:30 p.m. local time

C ome in, gentlemen." British Prime Minister David Mulvaney looked up from the report on his desk as the British chief of defence, Sir Edmond McCutchenson, and the Royal Navy's highest-ranking officer, the first sea lord, Admiral Sir Mark Ellington, walked in. By the worried looks on both of their faces, Mulvaney knew that something disastrous must have happened.

"Thank you, Prime Minister," McCutchenson said.

"With the less-than-jolly looks on your faces, I take it that you are not bearing the best of news."

"I regret to inform you that tragedy has struck, Prime Minister."

Mulvaney's stomach knotted. "You aren't going to tell me that something has happened to the *Queen Elizabeth*."

"Sir, two of the ships in our flotilla have been torpedoed." The defence minister looked at the first sea lord.

Admiral Ellington spoke up. "Sir, an enemy submarine torpedoed HMS *Queen Elizabeth*. We suspect the ARA *San Juan* as the attacking sub. Three torpedoes struck the *Queen Elizabeth*. In addition, another torpedo struck the merchant vessel M/S *Thor Liberty*."

The prime minister stood up behind his desk. "Dear God, have mercy on the souls of our sailors."

"Prime Minister," Admiral Ellington said, "we have not yet lost the *Queen Elizabeth*. The situation is perilous, and she is taking on water, but the double hull built by our British ironworkers has bought us more time."

"What are our chances of saving her, Admiral?"

"Sir, we've turned her to the northwest, toward the Falklands. Our best chance of salvaging the ship, frankly, is to beach her in shallow waters near the Falklands. That is the only way we can keep her from sinking. At that point, we could send naval engineers to try to salvage her. However, Prime Minister, this is a race against time. We could lose her before she reaches Port Stanley. Frankly, it will depend on how effectively the ship's bilge pumps can slow the flooding from the gashes torn in the hull by the torpedoes. And it also depends on no more strikes from enemy torpedoes. Frankly, it's a miracle that the *Queen Elizabeth* isn't on the bottom of the Atlantic. To survive three torpedo strikes for this long is beyond remarkable."

Mulvaney nodded. "What about the merchant vessel. The *Thor Liberty*?"

"*Thor Liberty* was a lighter single-hulled freighter. She was transporting drilling equipment and petroleum engineers to support drilling operations at Camp Churchill. Unfortunately, a single torpedo blast took her out instantly."

"Survivors?"

"A handful have been picked up by RFA *Black Rover* and HMS *Ocean*. Many others are missing. The Chileans have offered to set up a refugee camp at their naval station at Cape Horn, on Drake Passage, which is the closest allied base."

"Where does this leave our military mission?" Mulvaney asked.

"Sir, we can still proceed," Sir Edmond said. "We still have plenty of firepower, including helicopters and Royal Marines on HMS *Ocean* and RFA *Black Rover,* to launch an assault and recapture Camp Churchill. But without the carrier's air wing, our military superiority is no longer overwhelming."

Mulvaney folded his arms. "If we can't save the carrier, can we save her air wing? Perhaps fly those planes to a base in southern Chile to reinforce our operations?"

"Good questions, Prime Minister. Because of damage to the ship, and because of water she's taking on, we cannot safely initiate air operations. I recommend sending heavy naval reinforcements into the area."

"Where's that stray submarine?"

"We have choppers in the air from HMS *Ocean* dropping sonobuoys looking for it. But my guess is that she has skedaddled out of the area."

"Attack and run like a coward," Mulvaney said.

"Precisely, sir."

Mulvaney crossed his arms and looked at the portrait of Churchill hanging on the wall. What would Sir Winston do? *We shall fight them on the beaches. We shall fight them in the streets. We shall fight them in the hills. We shall never surrender.*

"Very well, Sir Edmond. Deploy as many ships as necessary to Drake Passage to protect all British interests in the region. Send the entire Royal Navy if you must. We shall do what we must do. This aggression against Britain shall not stand."

Situation Room
the White House
Washington, DC

1:45 p.m. local time

With his trusted chief of staff, Arnie Brubaker, at his side and two Secret Service agents, President Douglas Surber rushed through the double doors of the White House Situation Room, causing the secretary of state, the secretary of defense, the national security adviser, and the chairman of the joint chiefs of staff to all rise to their feet.

"Sit down," Surber ordered, still miffed from being pulled from a Rose Garden ceremony honoring the World Series champion San Diego Padres. "Do y'all know how long it's taken my Padres to finally win a World Series? This better be good. What's up?"

Secretary of Defense Erwin Lopez said, "The situation's blowing up in the South Atlantic, sir. We got a call from Prime Minister Mulvaney. It appears that an Argentinean submarine has torpedoed the HMS *Queen Elizabeth*."

"Say that again?"

"The new British aircraft carrier, HMS *Queen Elizabeth*, has been hit by three torpedoes. It's fifty-fifty whether they can save her. Another British ship, the *Thor Liberty*, a freighter, has been sunk."

Silence. Surber tried to get a perspective on the news. How surrealistic. From a fluffy public relations ceremony to the brink of war within a matter of seconds. A sad commentary on how dangerous the world had become. "What does Prime Minister Mulvaney need?"

"Admiral Jones?" Secretary Lopez deferred to the chairman of the joint chiefs, Admiral Roscoe Jones.

"Mister President, as you recall," Jones said, "we're already loaning our crew to Chile to operate the *Los Angeles*–class submarine that we sold them. Our crew will be taking that to sea under the Chilean flag in support of the British. But with the attack on the British carrier, the situation has escalated. We've intercepted communications that the Argentineans, Venezuelans, and the Russians are building up their naval presence within the next few hours around the tip of South America in the South Pacific, the South Atlantic, and the Drake Passage that runs between them."

"Did you say the Russians?"

"Yes, Mister President," Jones said. "We have information that the cruiser *Varyag*, along with the destroyers *Admiral Panteleyev* and *Marshal Shaposhnikov*, are entering Drake Passage from Russia's Pacific fleet. And from the northern fleet, they've dispatched the battle cruiser *Pyotr Velikiy*. So we have the Russian and Chilean navies pouring in from the Pacific, and now the British, Venezuelan, and Argentine navies pouring in from the Atlantic."

"Hmph." Surber slammed his fist on the table. "The Russians just had to get involved, didn't they?"

Secretary of State Robert Mauney took this one. "Russia, Venezuela, and Argentina want to split up that Antarctic oil, sir."

"So the Russians are tipping the power balance, and the Brits need us to cover their backs. Is that what I'm reading here?"

Secretary Mauney nodded. "The prime minister will be calling you soon, sir. In the meantime, the Brits would appreciate any naval support as a show of force that you could send to the region."

The president sat back and looked around the table. "Where are the carriers?"

Admiral Jones spoke up. "USS *Ronald Reagan* is in the area, off the Chilean coast, as a follow-up to your earlier command. In the Atlantic, USS *Nimitz* is operating off the coast of Brazil and is scheduled for a port stop in Rio this week."

"A port stop in Rio," Surber mumbled. "I'm about to disappoint five thousand red-blooded American sailors."

No response to that comment.

"Very well. Send the *Nimitz* and the *Reagan* and their battle groups to Drake Passage. Issue orders to support our British allies. Secretary Mauney, call an emergency meeting of the UN Security Council. Let's see if we can get ahold of this thing before it blows up even more."

Belgrano II base camp
Antarctica

8:00 p.m. local time

Fernando Sosa, wearing acoustical headphones, sat alone in front of the electronic interception equipment in the surveillance dome and toyed with alternating frequencies. But it wasn't the static in the earphones that had his attention, but rather the static in his stomach.

Sosa was an intelligence officer—not a firing squad captain.

War required killing. He knew that. He understood the necessity of killing an enemy combatant on the battlefield or on the high seas. But killing an unarmed enemy prisoner? As he had been ordered to do?

The Geneva Accords prevented the execution of prisoners of war, and even if war had not been declared, the Accords prevented the execution of enemy combatants.

Ambiguities in the law of warfare allowed for gray areas in interpretation. Al Qaeda detainees at the Guantanamo Bay naval base in Cuba he knew had been subjected to questionable treatment, even torture. The Bush Administration claimed that detainees at GTMO were technically not "prisoners of war" and, therefore, various interrogation techniques prohibited under the Accords were permissible. But aggressive interpretations of acceptable POW treatment could be risky.

Some American liberals had even advocated prosecuting former president George W. Bush and former vice president Dick Cheney for "war crimes." The Bush Administration defended the techniques as having prevented further acts of terror in the US for the next seven years and, later, as the basis for allowing the Obama Administration to hunt down and finally kill Osama bin Laden. And no GTMO detainees were executed short of a trial.

Sosa believed that Montes might face a war crimes tribunal because he shot the poor British civilian, the one they called Williams.

Now Montes had ordered him to carry out the next execution, specifically to kill Austin Rivers. Sosa realized this put him in an unenviable position.

Execute Rivers and risk possible prosecution at a war crimes tribunal, possibly facing the same fate as such notorious characters as Saddam Hussein and *Slobodan Milošević* or . . .

Refuse the order and risk a criminal court martial by the Argentine military and possible imprisonment. Surely he would be stripped of rank—ending his career.

If he carried out the order and later was prosecuted for crimes against humanity, the fact that the order came from a superior officer would be no defense. Yet Rivers was military, not a civilian. Maybe executing Rivers wouldn't be a war crime.

Sosa wiped his hand across his forehead. Something seemed instinctively wrong about killing a defenseless man in cold blood. But Sosa had to admit that Montes did have a point. Eliminating Rivers would simplify the extraction of intelligence from the others.

Fernando looked at the wall clock. 11:59 p.m.

Twelve hours before the execution. Twelve hours to decide. What could he do? It would be a long night.

What to do . . . better to be safe . . . Sosa got up and put on his thermal jacket. It would be better to do this now, before there were any witnesses.

He felt for the pistol in his holster, then took the pistol out and chambered a bullet. Ready to fire. Montes could ridicule the Glock and boast about his seven-round .357 all he wanted. But at point-blank range, the Glock chambered twice as many rounds as Montes' revolver.

He reholstered the Glock and walked over to the small-arms locker. The safety key inserted easily. He turned it counterclockwise. Three more nine-millimeter Glock pistols were positioned side by side in the arms locker. Also in the arms locker were three EXO FailZero suppressors.

The suppressors, or "silencers," were more expensive than the guns themselves, costing about two thousand American dollars. But for killings and assassinations that needed to be accomplished without drawing attention to the fact, the silencers proved invaluable.

Sosa screwed the silencers onto the barrels of all three guns.

Stuffing two pistols in his back belt, he stuck the third inside his jacket. He checked the mirror to make sure the weapons were not visible.

Good. The thick parka hid the outlines of the guns.

He checked the clock on the wall, his heart pounding like a jackhammer.

It was time.

Magnolia Flats
Kensington District
West London

11:00 p.m. local time

Shelley sat on the edge of the prim sofa in the living room and sipped the French merlot that she had started the night before. With Aussie finally asleep in the next room and the lights off, she hoped the merlot would calm her nerves.

But still, after having finished the first full glass, the alcohol had not assuaged her nerves.

Why? Why did her conscience feel so tortured?

Her time with Aussie had ignited a strange sense of irrepressible guilt whenever she gazed at the boy. An invisible knife stabbed her each and every time he called her Auntie Shelley. The pain worsened when, in his own sweet way, he repeated the words that Meg had taught him, "I love you, Aunt Shelley."

The merlot started soothing the nerves in her chest and arms.

She got up, stepped over to the sound system, and flipped on BBC radio. The sounds of the Ulster Orchestra playing Handel filled the room. Aah—nothing like red wine and classical music, in this case Judas Maccabeus, to bring instant relaxation.

She lay back on the sofa and closed her eyes. For a while, her mind drifted somewhere into the recesses between happier days and nagging regret.

The announcer's voice woke her from her slumber. "This is the BBC. We have breaking news from the South Atlantic. A British naval task force, led by the aircraft carrier HMS *Queen Elizabeth*, has been attacked by enemy submarines from the Republic of the Argentine. Information released moments ago from Number 10 indicates that two British ships have been torpedoed, including the HMS *Queen Elizabeth* and the merchant fleet ship M/S *Thor Liberty*. Two other British ships, the Royal Navy ship HMS *Ocean* and the Royal Fleet Auxiliary ship *Black Rover*, were unscathed in the attack.

"Number 10 is reporting that while HMS *Queen Elizabeth* sustained serious damage in the attack, hope remains that she can be saved. *Queen Elizabeth* is sailing for safety in the waters near the Falkland Islands, the British territory claimed by Argentina since the mid-1900s.

"However, Number 10 also reports that the merchant vessel M/S *Thor Liberty*, a British Merchant Marine freighter that was supporting the naval task force, was sunk in the torpedo attack. There are no details about any survivors of the *Thor Liberty*. The ship was commanded by Captain Bob Hudson, an experienced mariner and veteran Merchant Marine captain who joined the British Merchant Marine years ago after a sports injury prevented him from joining the Royal Navy."

"What?" Shelley sat up.

"It is not known whether Captain Hudson or any of his crew survived."

"God! Please, no!"

"The BBC has been told that Prime Minister Mulvaney has briefed King Charles about the situation. Britain has launched a protest with the United Nations, and various sources report that more Royal Navy warships are being dispatched to the area.

"Once again. Breaking news from the South Atlantic . . ."

"Dear God, no! Please!" Shelley buried her face in her hands and began to weep.

**Belgrano II base camp
Antarctica**

8:02 p.m. local time

Fernando Sosa stepped out of the geodesic dome into the open center area of the camp, the space referred to by the Argentine soldiers as the "snowy courtyard." The sun, which still hung low this time of year, hid behind a cloud cover rolling in from the Weddell Sea.

Sosa eyed the landscape. Two guards stood outside the Command Dome, located three domes to the right of the Intelligence Dome. Montes would be inside. Hopefully he would remain in the Command Dome.

Other armed guards bearing Russian-made AK-47 assault rifles milled about in the snow-covered courtyard. Three stood huddled together off to the right, chatting and smoking cigarettes. Two more stood talking at the center of the courtyard, fifty yards away, also smoking, under the flagpole bearing the colors of the Argentine Republic.

Two more guards, one hundred yards across the courtyard, stood guarding the entrance of the geodesic dome housing the prisoners, with two more standing nearby.

With purposeful strides, Sosa marched across the snowy courtyard, past the smoking soldiers under the flagpole, exchanging limp salutes with them, and trudged on without making eye contact.

When he approached the entry of the prisoners' dome, the guards snapped to attention with sharp salutes.

Fernando returned the salute. "Open the door. I am going in for a word with the prisoners."

"Would you like for one of us to accompany you, sir?" the sergeant on the right asked.

"That won't be necessary, Sergeant. I need a *mano-a-mano* with a couple of these Brits, and then things will go a lot more smoothly around here. If I'm not out within thirty minutes, then you can come in and do whatever you need to do. Are we clear?"

"Yes, sir."

Kensington Gardens
Princess Diana Memorial Playground
London

10:00 a.m. local time

In the green surroundings of Kensington Gardens, at the Princess Diana Memorial Playground, Shelley sat on a bench under unusually sunny skies. Donning a pair of shades, she watched Aussie running and squealing with delight.

She had followed the BBC all night and into the early hours of the morning, and still no news of the fate of the man she had once loved but had kicked to the curb over something over which he had no control. So far, the broadcast words had not changed. "No word on the captain of the *Thor Liberty* or of its crew, who are feared to have perished in the cold waters of the South Atlantic."

The words rang in her head all night. No new information on Bob's ship in the morning. The *Thor Liberty* was an irrelevant afterthought in the focus of the news. People were interested in the *Queen Elizabeth*. Not so much the *Thor Liberty*.

But Bob was no afterthought to her. Not even after all these years. If only she had not rebuffed him and they'd gotten married. Perhaps he would have become an accountant or something and he would still be alive.

Then again, nothing would have kept him from the sea. He would still have joined the Merchant Marine.

Or perhaps not. She would never know.

But one thing she now knew after the events of the last eleven hours—her flame for him, though it had flickered over the years, had never died.

Now the waters of the South Atlantic had doused the last of any hopes of that flame reigniting.

Lucky she wore large dark shades to hide the tears cresting over her cheeks. If only she had someone to talk to. Someone who would listen. She reached into her purse and retrieved a hankie and dabbed her cheeks.

"What a lovely boy." The sweet, kind-sounding voice came from over her right shoulder.

Shelley looked up.

The elderly woman wore a black nun's habit. Her hauntingly blue eyes seemed to glow. "Is the boy yours?" The woman's voice projected overpowering love.

"Do I know you, Sister?" Shelley asked.

No response. Only a radiant, peaceful smile with an inexplicable magnetism.

Tears, once again, started flowing down Shelley's cheeks.

"I apologize." Shelley dabbed her eyes again. "No, Sister, the boy isn't mine. I am watching him for my best friend while she is out of the country."

"Our Lord does have a strange sense of humor. Does he not?"

"I'm sorry, Sister. I don't understand."

"It's all right, my daughter." The nun touched Shelley's shoulder. "This is all you need to understand. No matter what storms we are facing, God will lead us through and provide comfort."

Who was this woman? Where was she from? "I feel as if the storms in my life are greater than they have ever been."

"I can sense this, daughter. We all face deep, dark nights of the soul. The past is the past. But God calls us in the present and into the future, and his Son died and rose from the grave to give us hope for the future. Wherever he calls you, whatever voice he uses, make sure you respond and make sure you go. In him there is hope for the future."

"Aunt Shelley! My shoe!" Aussie was sitting on the ground and pointing at his feet.

"It appears that he has lost a shoe." The nun chuckled. "You better attend to him."

"Of course, Sister. I'll be back."

Shelley got up and walked toward Little Aussie. "What's the matter?"

"My shoe!" the boy protested, pointing at his foot.

"Aah. I see. Your shoe came untied. Auntie Shelley will take care of it."

She went down on one knee, kissed the boy on the head, and then slid his left foot back into his shoe and tied it for him. "There! Go play with your friends."

"Thank you, Aunt Shelley!" Aussie gave her a bear hug and ran back over to his playmates.

Shelley dusted the dirt off the knees of her jeans and stood. "Sister?" Shelley walked back over to the bench where the mysterious nun had appeared. Off to the left, a group of women were chatting. "Pardon me, ladies. Did any of you see a nun? She was just here, dressed in black. Did you see where she went?"

The women shook their heads, then returned to their conversation.

Shelley's cell phone rang. She rushed back over to the park bench to fish it out.

Meggie calling . . .

"Meggie!" Shelley exclaimed. "Is it really you?"

"Shelley. I need to ask you something. And if you cannot do this, I will understand."

"Sure. You know you can ask anything of me."

"Well . . ." She hesitated.

"Go ahead and ask, Meg." Shelley looked over toward Aussie. So far so good with the shoe.

"I need you and Aussie here. If I pay for all of your expenses, would you consider coming to Chile and bringing Aussie with you? . . . The authorities here at the British Embassy have been wonderful and are prepared to smooth all travel obstacles on humanitarian grounds because Aussie is Austin's son. I know it's last second . . . and I know . . . Shelley? Are you there? It's okay if you can't do it."

"I'm sorry, I spaced out."

"Are you all right, Shelley?"

"Just thinking about something someone just told me, that's all."

"Do you want to call me back?"

"No. Give me a second."

She looked out in every direction, trying to see the nun. How could she have come and gone so quickly?

Wherever he calls you, whatever voice he uses, make sure you respond and make sure you go. In him there is hope for the future.

"Shelley, are you still there?"

"Yes, I'm here. I'm glad you called. I can't explain it. But something tells me I need to be with you there in Chile as much as you need me there. Yes. Of course I'll come. I'll start making the arrangements. Aussie and I will be on the first flight out of Heathrow. I'll call you as soon as I know the flight number and the time."

"I love you, Shelley."

**Peninsula los Molles
overlooking the Pacific
Valparaiso, Chile**

6:50 a.m. local time

The Peninsula los Molles, the peninsula that had been compared in its shape to the American state of Wisconsin, jutted out into the Pacific to the north and west of the city of Valparaiso.

The peninsula is the natural arm that buffers the inner harbor from winds and the sea in times of rough weather and storms. This jutting landmass makes Valparaiso a splendid natural harbor, keeping the waters around the city's docks and piers calm even on days when the Pacific is not so calm. The peninsula also affords the best view of the bay and of ships entering and exiting the harbor. Despite the magnificent view, Maria rarely drove out here unless an out-of-town visitor came for an overnight stay and she needed a place to show off one of the prime views of the city.

In her handful of visits here, she had never come before seven in the morning. Nor had she been here at any other time in the morning.

But then again, she had never met a man like Peter Miranda—a stubborn, conservative, ruggedly handsome right-wing American who ridiculed her political beliefs but had a powerful ability to make her melt.

Suddenly politics and debates and arguments seemed foolish, all shoveled by his powerful charm onto the ash heap of irrelevancy.

He said he would be heading out to sea this morning, about sevenish.

She wanted to be as close as she could be to catch a glimpse of him, maybe wave a longing good-bye, perhaps even blow him a kiss.

This early in the morning, the air was still over the harbor, the water still glassy. Most boats remained secured in their slips. Off to the right, along the main shoreline of the port, the Valparaiso waterfront had not yet awakened.

She checked her watch.

No sign of the sub.

Sadness flooded her.

Was yesterday their final good-bye?

How foolish she felt, high over a still-sleeping city, waiting for the possibility of a passing glimpse of a submarine captained by a man she barely knew but who had in an inexplicable and incomprehensible way invaded and stolen every crevice of her heart.

She had to get hold of herself. She should leave. That would be best. Besides, she had work to do. Pete Miranda was a passing, crazy fancy. What had she been thinking?

Maria reached into her purse for her keys. As she glanced up from her purse, a movement in the periphery of her vision sent her heart into a frenzy.

There!

The sleek black submarine slipped out from behind a moored passenger ship.

The sub cut a slow course, moving from the inner recesses of the harbor out toward the open sea. Her wake sent long swells rolling across the glassy water in both directions.

The sight of three men on the top of the submarine quickened her heart. Was that Pete looking out over the water? From this distance, she could not say for sure. But in her heart, she knew.

So much for simply driving away, going about her business, forgetting him, chalking him up to a short-term crush.

Her eyes filled with tears, and she began to do something that she had not done in years. As she watched the sub pick up speed, heading out to the open sea, she began to pray.

"God, bring him back. If you are real, please bring him back."

CS Miro
1 mile west of Valparaiso naval facility
Valparaiso, Chile

7:00 a.m. local time

As the sun rose over the peaks of the snowcapped Andes mountain range to the east, the nuclear-powered *Los Angeles*–class attack submarine formerly known as the USS *City of Corpus Christi* and now the CS *Miro* powered to the west into the calm waters of the Pacific.

In command of the *Miro*, at the top of the conning tower, Pete Miranda engaged in his good-luck ritual that he practiced before every dive. First, a lungful of fresh morning air, the last he would get before the sub surfaced again, if she did surface again.

One of the fringe benefits of being a sub commander was that the captain, along with whoever he invited up on the conning tower before a dive, would be the last crew members to see the open skies above the earth.

With his crew at work below him in the black steel hull of the submarine, Pete spent the last few minutes topside with his executive officer, Lieutenant Commander Norman Rodman, and Commander Oscar Romero, the Chilean captain who would assume command of the sub when they returned—if they returned.

Pete had faced death before. He never took this moment before a dive for granted. This could be his final view of land, standing in the conning tower.

From his front pocket he extracted three items—a long Macanudo cigar, a Bic lighter, and a cigar cutter.

"You gentlemen care for a cigar?"

They both shook their heads and appeared to return to their own silent thoughts.

Smoking, even smoking a fine Dominican stogie like a Macanudo, had become politically incorrect over the years.

But Pete could not care less. Political correctness could burn in the depths of hell as far as he was concerned.

He turned around, longing for one final glance of the snowcapped Andes of his father's fatherland.

Was this his last view ever of Chile?

The first drag on the Macanudo sent him into a philosophical mood.

The way his grandmother explained it, we were called to our destiny if we were part of God's "elect."

Pete was a sub commander. He was no theologian. He didn't know what all that meant. But deep down, he believed his grandmother.

Another drag of the cigar.

Why him?

Why now?

The practice of nations loaning officers to the militaries of allied nations dated back to the beginning of the republic. France loaned Lafayette to the American colonies in the Revolutionary War. The father of the US Navy, the Scottish-born John Paul Jones, later accepted a position as an admiral in the Russian Navy in their Black Sea naval wars against the Turks.

In the opening days of World War II, United States Army Air Corps pilots joined their British Royal Air Force comrades in the dark days of 1940, when for three months Nazi bombers tried to bomb Britain into oblivion in what would become known as the Battle of Britain.

Now, sailing into the Pacific as an American officer on loan to Chile, Pete joined the ranks of an elite group of warriors entrusted by America to carry out a military mission not only as a warrior but as an ambassador of America.

So when Admiral Chuck "Bulldog" Elyea told him in Hawaii of this assignment to Chile, Pete had expected to be detailed to a training mission. He had not expected to go to war.

The unexpected surprise of war he could handle.

But the unexpected surprise named Maria Vasquez? She was another matter.

He had seen many women since his divorce . . . women he could handle. But something very different about Maria made her stand out. Something he could not put his finger on.

Would this election that his grandmother spoke of help him with what he had lost in the past? Maybe let someone into his life?

Or was his destiny to die at sea?

Enough ruminating.

He flicked the cigar overboard and checked his watch.

Time to go to work.

"XO, take her down," Pete ordered.

"Take her down. Aye, sir," Commander Rodman picked up the microphone on the bridge. "Control. Bridge." A brief pause. "Sounding."

"Bridge. Control. Sounding one . . . two . . . zero fathoms."

"Lookouts, clear the bridge!" the XO ordered.

"Clear the bridge. Aye, sir." Three orange-jacketed lookouts scrambled down the aluminum ladder to the control room.

"Officer of the deck, prepare to dive!"

Pete descended the ladder and hopped from the last step to the control room floor. "Captain is down."

"Captain is down!" the officer of the deck parroted.

The Chilean officer, Commander Romero, followed Pete to his post.

The clanking and rumbling of shoes on the steel-grate floors echoed throughout the sub as men jogged down metal ladders to get to their stations. Some slid down the handrails to their positions. Red lights flashed on and off. A cacophony of sirens filled the air.

"XO down," Rodman said as his feet hit the deck of the control room.

"XO is down!" the officer of the deck repeated.

"Submerge the ship!" Pete ordered.

"Diving Officer, submerge the ship!" the XO repeated. "Make your depth one-five-zero feet."

"Make my depth one-five-zero feet! Aye, sir!" the diving officer repeated. "Chief of the watch. On the 1-MC!" The diving officer's order boomed over every loudspeaker on the sub.

"Dive!"

"Dive!"

"Dive!"

"Make your depth one-five-zero feet," the diving officer said to the planesman, the young petty officer who sat at the control of the submarine. "Five degrees down bubble."

The planesman pushed the "steering wheel" down.

Miro's nose angled down and slipped under the surface. Geysers of water shot up as rushing seawater flooded the ballast tanks in the forward section of the sub.

Time was of the essence. Pete had to get *Miro* on station and in a position to perform the mission if President Surber ordered it.

"Approaching one-five-zero feet," the diving officer said.

"Very well," Pete said. "Set course for one-eight-zero degrees. All ahead two-thirds."

"One-eight-zero degrees," the OOD parroted, and *Miro* turned on a course due south. "All ahead two-thirds."

"Maneuvering. Conn. All ahead two-thirds."

"All ahead two-thirds."

Miro's engines revved. She sliced through the depths, a silent hunter-killer on a life-or-death mission.

El Libro y la Taza
Santiago, Chile

10:48 a.m. local time

Near her small hotel near the British Embassy, Meg had found warmth and understanding and hospitality at a cozy hole-in-the-wall that felt like a home away from home.

El Libro y la Taza, which in English means The Book and the Cup, was established by an English expatriate years ago, right around the corner from the British Embassy, to satisfy the near-perpetual needs of embassy employees for spots of tea, cheeses, and various scones and light fruits.

Meg wondered why the owner-founder, Mister Johnson, in marketing to a niche British clientele in the midst of Santiago, had chosen the Spanish name instead of its English equivalent. A waiter told her the owner had hoped to lure native Chileans in as customers, and although the small tea pub never took off among the locals, he stubbornly kept the Spanish name. And so El Libro y la Taza had become a small British oasis in the midst of a great South American capital.

The enchanting scent of fresh-baked scones evoked flashes of her favorite London afternoon tea spots.

Meg closed her eyes and allowed her mind to wander to happier and simpler times, to reflect on peaceful respites in the midst of a sea of personal anxiety in a land across the ocean seven thousand miles from home. Soon she would have her son with her, and her best friend too.

The thought of Aussie's face brought a smile to her own.

"Could I bring you anything, miss?" She opened her eyes at the sound of a British accent.

"Another spot, please?"

"Of course, madame," the aging Englishman said.

It was once true that "the sun never sets on British soil." While that great Briticism was no longer true, one truth about the British remained. In all corners of the globe, the British took care of the British.

The waiter stepped away, and Meg battled conflicted feelings. Her heart twisted in a raging turmoil that she could not control. The nightmare had scared her at around four in the morning and had rendered her sleepless for the rest of the dark hours.

The scene on a dreary British day, typically gray, chilly, and somber, had been all too clear. She, Aussie, and Shelley, at RAF Northolt Air Base outside London, stood on the wet tarmac, accompanied by a Navy priest.

Christmas was less than a week away, and as the large green cargo jet landed and began to slowly taxi its way over toward where they were standing, a Royal Navy chorus began a slow, melodic rendition of Austin's favorite Christmas carol, "Drive the Cold Winter Away":

> *All hail to the days that merit more praise*
> *Than all the rest of the year,*
> *And welcome the nights that double delights*
> *As well for the poor as the peer!*
> *Good fortune attend each merry man's friend,*
> *That doth but the best that he may;*
> *Forgetting old wrongs, with carols and songs,*
> *To drive the cold winter away.*

As the Navy chorus finished the first stanza of the carol, the plane stopped only feet from where they stood. A large cargo door opened in the back of the plane, and a ramp extended down to the tarmac.

The Royal Navy band, standing at attention beside the chorus, began a solemn rendition of "God Save the King" as an honor guard of six SBS members in navy blue uniforms slowly walked a casket down the ramp.

They covered the casket with the Union Jack, and a corner of the flag kept flapping in the brisk December breeze.

The honor guard set the casket on the pedestal in front of them, and Meg woke up, heart pounding, tears flowing.

God was preparing her for the inevitable. She knew it.

Austin was going to die.

Aussie would be fatherless.

Meg wanted to cry out and pray to God. Her mind flashed to the kind nun who spoke to her nearly five years ago on the day scheduled for the abortion. What became of her? Perhaps she was an angel from God. She had appeared and just disappeared. If only somehow she were here now.

"Your tea, madame." The waiter returned with a sliver tray with a pot of hot tea, scones, and fruits. "You look tired. So I took the liberty of bringing a few extra munchies, in case you were hungry."

"Thank you, George."

"My pleasure, madame. Is there anything else that I can do for you?"

Meg hesitated. "Do you know of a priest who might be nearby?"

"A priest?" The waiter looked quizzical. "Is everything all right?"

"I don't know. I need someone to pray for me and I thought, who better than a priest?"

The waiter smiled. "I've been told that we don't need a priest to pray for us. That we can pray on our own. All we must do is talk to God and he will listen. About anything. Wherever we are. And he will listen."

"Oh. Yes, I agree. But when it comes to prayer, I believe there's strength in numbers." She looked at him. "Do you believe in answered prayer, George? Have you ever witnessed it with your own eyes?"

"Yes, a few times. Although not always."

"Really? Would you mind telling me?"

"I had lost my job at the local newspaper and needed employment to be able to stay in the country. I prayed for a job. Then one day one of my mates told me about this place, that they were looking for someone. I came in and they hired me immediately."

"Really?"

"Absolutely."

"But you also said that prayers were not always answered."

"Not all mine anyway."

"For instance?" She sipped her tea.

"Well, last year the doctor diagnosed my mum with cancer back in London. As she got sicker, I prayed that God would heal her. But she died at home with my brother."

"I am so sorry, George."

"Thank you. A priest once told me that we have all been appointed a time to die, and if it's our time, it's our time."

Those words hit her like a wet blanket. "Not exactly what I wanted to hear, George. If God answers some prayers and not others, and if we all have a time to die anyway, then why even pray?"

Tall, balding, and midforties looking, George studied her with a raised eyebrow. "Are you worried that someone close to you is going to die?"

"Yes. A sick premonition, actually. The father of my child. He may already be dead, for all I know."

"I am sorry. But the way I look at it, if the chances of answered prayer are at least fifty-fifty, then why not pray? Tell you what. I will personally pray for you and the father of your son. I cannot promise a result, but I can promise to pray. And I will."

"Thank you, George."

"Oh, and one other thing, if I may?"

"Yes. Please."

"A Christian friend once told me something, and I have found this to be true. He said, 'George, no matter what storms we are facing, God will lead us through and provide comfort.'"

Belgrano II base camp
Antarctica

11:50 a.m. local time

The *beep-beep* on Lieutenant Fernando Sosa's watch signaled the time—ten minutes until the scheduled execution of the British prisoner Austin Rivers.

Fernando holstered his Glock and donned the thermal jacket.

The front door of the dome flew open, ushering in a blast of freezing air and swirling ice particles. A wrenching feeling gripped his stomach.

"Are you prepared to carry out your duties, Lieutenant Sosa?" Montes snarled, standing outside the dome.

"Yes, *mi* capitán. I am prepared."

"Excellent," Montes bellowed. "Step into the courtyard and prepare to receive your final instructions."

Sosa stepped out into a light snow. Although the sun remained hidden behind the clouds, he donned a pair of shades to dim the near-blinding effect of all the white.

"Over there, under the flagpole, I have instructed some of our soldiers to erect the execution pole . . . right there."

Montes pointed to a black creosote-soaked post about eight feet high. The post stood as a cruel death pole . . . standing in the midst of the falling and blowing snow, an eerie and ominous contrast centrally visible against the placid white snowscape. The sight of it ignited memories of a homily that Father Joseph had delivered in Buenos Aires a few months earlier, when the priest described Christ being tied to a pole and lashed thirty-nine times before being brought back before Pilate to face news of his final fate.

"Sosa? Did you hear me?"

"My apologies, Capitán. My mind had wandered elsewhere."

"Get your mind in the game, Lieutenant. And NOW!"

"My apologies, sir. It will not happen again."

"Back to protocol," Montes continued. "We shall strap Rivers to the pole. We shall follow all the humanitarian protocols required of a legally acceptable execution. First, we will offer him a cigarette. And then we offer him an opportunity to say a few words. And then we blindfold him.

"The other British prisoners, of course, will stand off to the side, guarded at gunpoint, but with a clear view to witness the event.

"At that point, with Rivers tied to the post, I will ceremoniously hand you the execution instrument, which of course is my personal .357 revolver. As you know, it is an honor to carry out this mission with this glorious weapon."

Montes' eyes morphed into a trance-like state while he described his revolver, as if it were some type of god-object.

"Yes, sir. It will be a high honor to carry this out with your revolver, Capitán."

"Yes, well." Montes' eyes thawed from their trance, as if he had returned from an alternate universe. "I shall hand the revolver to you. You are to pause and to befittingly hold the revolver high up to the heavens for all to see—especially the prisoners.

"Then after that, you are to take aim slowly, and you will fire into the skull of the prisoner. The bullet will explode his skull, killing him instantly. His body will slump. His hands will remain tied behind his back to the execution pole.

"As he slumps, you are to fire two additional shots into the body. Space the second and third shots approximately two seconds apart to maximize drama and psychological leverage with the Brits. This will send the message to cooperate, or they will be shot in the same way. Do you have any questions?"

"No, Capitán. I understand. First shot to the head. Two more shots to the body as he slumps down the execution pole."

Montes unleashed a delighted laugh. "You will make an excellent commander one day, Sosa."

"Thank you, sir."

"Very well." Montes turned and yelled out, "Ruiz, Alonso, Torres, Dominguez! Come! Come here."

Four crack soldiers, members of the execution detail, trudged over through the snow.

"Gentlemen," Montes said, "Lieutenant Sosa and I are going into the prison dome. You will come with us. We are going to order the prisoners out into the courtyard for the execution. The condemned will be tied to the post. You will stand the rest of the prisoners, the witnesses, over there in a straight line. Remember. Only one other appears to be military. So I do not anticipate any problems. But if anyone tries to interfere, you will shoot them on the spot. Is that clear?"

"*Si*, Capitán."

"*Si*, Capitán."

"Very well. Let us proceed." They walked over to the entrance of the prison dome. "Open it," Montes said.

The armed guard on the left opened the door and stepped back.

"Ruiz, Alonso, Torres, Dominguez! The four of you go in first.

Round the prisoners into the middle of the dome and call me when you have finished."

"*Si*, Capitán." The four soldiers walked into the dome. A few minutes later, Ruiz called out, "The prisoners are ready, Capitán."

"Very well. Here is our plan. We will go in and I, as base commander, will inform Austin Rivers of his death sentence. Then we shall solemnly march them into the courtyard for the ceremonies. The cigarette ceremony, the blindfolding, and the last words will be taken care of. Lieutenant Sosa, all you then need to do is take the revolver and carry out the execution."

Sosa nodded.

"Are you ready?"

"Ready, sir."

"Very well," Montes said. "Let's get on with it."

They stepped into the prisoners' dome, Montes leading the way. Sosa noticed a faint yet distinct stench of sewage that he had not smelled yesterday.

The British prisoners were huddled in the center of the room. The four armed guards stood in a semicircle along the periphery of the dome.

Montes stepped forward and waved Sosa to step forward with him.

"Leftenant Austin Rivers! Royal Navy! Front and center!"

Rivers stepped forward and came to attention.

"I regret to inform you, Rivers," Montes said, "that your time has come."

"My time has come?" Rivers quipped. "Ya don't say. Time for what? For some more of this bloody horrible excuse of a porridge meal you've been feeding us?"

"The time has come . . . Rivers . . . for you to die."

"I think you have it bloody wrong, ole boy."

It happened faster than a flash of lightning. Rivers whipped out a pistol and fired before Sosa could blink.

In an incredible whirl of precision, Rivers and one of the other Brits, who also brandished a smoking pistol, had shot the four Argentine soldiers between the eyes.

Rivers had the gun barrel aimed straight at Montes' nose before the Capitán could think about reacting.

"Looks like your shipmates aren't having a jolly good day, ole chap." Rivers grinned and nodded at the bodies of the soldiers sprawled out on the concrete floor, faces covered in blood.

"Where . . . where did you get that pistol? . . . That silencer?" Montes said in little more than a whisper.

"Never underestimate His Majesty's Special Forces," Rivers said. "Captain Dunn, grab the rifles off the bodies. We'll put them to good use. Then cover the door. If anyone comes in, take 'em out with the handgun."

"Yes, sir, Leftenant," Dunn said.

"You shall never get away with this," Montes snapped.

"Perhaps not," Rivers said. "But I shall have a ton of fun at your expense. Hands up! And down on your knees! Both of you." Rivers kept the gun pointed at Montes' head. "Unless you want me to turn your brains into scrambled eggs."

Montes looked at Sosa. "Do as he says."

"Very good," Rivers said.

Sosa and Montes dropped to their knees, hands up.

"Now listen carefully. Unholster your sidearms, put them on the floor, and slide them in this direction. And don't try anything. Unless you want to get into a fast-draw competition with one of His Majesty's SBS officers."

Sosa glanced over at Montes. He hoped Montes would not try something stupid, given the capitán's strange obsession with his revolver. Then Sosa, wasting no time, put his Glock on the concrete floor and slid it toward Rivers.

"Good!" Rivers said. "Now you!"

Montes' face contorted into an angry grimace. His lips trembling with anger, he unholstered the silver revolver, gently placed it on the floor, and then slid it across toward Rivers.

Rivers reached down and picked up the revolver and studied it in the light. "An interesting revolver. My compliments to you, Capitán. But this gun does look somehow familiar. Captain Dunn, does this weapon look familiar to you?"

"Aye, Leftenant," the Scottish Marine said. "A fine weapon indeed. But you are right, sir, she does look familiar."

"Yes, Captain Dunn. One of those fine revolvers that serves a dual purpose. Sort of a dual-purpose weapon, say . . . One purpose might be shooting an unarmed man. A second purpose might be to pistol-whip an unarmed man. Hmm?"

"I think you may be onto something, Leftenant," Dunn said.

"Why don't we solicit the capitán's input on the matter," Rivers said. "After all, he is the proprietor of this weapon."

"A fine idea, sir," Dunn said.

"What say you, Capitán?" Rivers glared at Montes. "Would you agree that this fine weapon has the multifunctional capabilities of fulfilling multiple purposes?"

Montes glared back at Rivers but did not respond.

"Not going to answer, are you?" Rivers said. "Very well then, this is for our Father Bach, as you call him." Rivers smashed the gun against the right side of Montes' face, knocking him to the floor. Blood streamed from Montes' nose and mouth and dripped onto the concrete.

"Please, Leftenant," Bach said. "That isn't necessary. Not on account of me. I know he hit me yesterday, but the Bible says turn the other cheek."

"Oh, I'll turn his other cheek," Rivers said, "and I'll break the bones on that side of the dog's face too."

"Please. No, Leftenant," Bach pleaded.

But Rivers ignored the little man's plea. He reached down, grabbed Montes by the collar, pulled him to his feet, and with a powerful blow, smashed the gun against the other side of his face.

Montes collapsed to the floor again, his nose and his mouth spewing more blood.

"There, Mister Bach. As you suggested. I turned his other cheek. On your feet, dog!" Rivers commanded. "I said, on your feet!"

Montes reacted slowly, appearing to be dazed.

"You." Rivers looked at Sosa. "Help your comrade to his feet."

"Yes, sir," Sosa said. He reached down and lifted Montes under the armpits. Montes staggered but managed to get back on his feet.

"Bach," Rivers said, "since you are the one who asked me to turn the capitán's other cheek, how about checking the WC for some paper. You can wipe the blood off his face before I draw some more from elsewhere."

"Yes, of course, Leftenant."

When the man Montes had sarcastically called Father Bach opened the bathroom door to get tissue paper, the scent of sewage magnified.

Bach walked back out, a wad of paper in one hand, and closed the door. He went to stand by Rivers.

"Clean his face, Bach," Rivers said.

"Of course, Leftenant." Bach stepped over to Montes and began dabbing blood off his face.

In a hushed, almost whispered tone, as if he wanted no one else to hear, Bach spoke to Montes. "I forgive you for what you did to me. And God will forgive you too, if only you will accept him."

Montes did not respond. He just looked away.

"All finished, Leftenant."

"Thank you, Bach, that looks better," Rivers said. "Step aside."

Bach tossed the tissue paper into a wastebasket at the side of the room.

"You know, *el* Capitán," Rivers said, "as Bach started cleaning that bloody mess off your bloody face, I thought of a third functional purpose for that revolver of yours. Yes, how could I forget? This fabulous weapon can be used to magically make an unarmed innocent man dance to the delight of the holder of the weapon. Sort of like you when you made the chap you called Sir Williams dance . . . before you shot him in cold blood. You do remember Sir Williams, don't you, Capitán?"

Again, Montes remained silent, sullen.

"What's wrong, Capitán? Kittycat got your tongue?"

Still no response.

"Don't want to chat? No problem, ole chap. Tell ya what. Rather than give us a speech, how about a little tap dance? Hmm? Kinda like you made Williams dance?"

Montes stood stone-faced.

"Don't feel like a tap dance? That's all right. Too bad. How about a ballet dance then? I've heard all the men in Argentina are into ballet."

"Please, Leftenant," Bach pleaded.

Montes stared at Rivers. Rivers returned the stare.

"Well, all right then. You know, I think your versatile weapon can make a man dance without even wasting a bullet." Holding the gun by the barrel, Rivers smashed it into Montes' groin.

"Aaaaaahhhhhhhhh!" Montes bent over, his knees hitting the floor again.

"How delightful. So fleet afoot." Rivers chuckled. "Too bad Williams couldn't witness that. Captain Dunn. Don't you think Williams would have enjoyed the capitán's exquisite little tap dance?"

"Oh, immensely, sir," Dunn said.

"Now that you have been given a fine British welcome, Mister Monte, it is my duty to inform you that you are in the custody of His Majesty's government. You are going to do what I tell you, or it will be my pleasure to scramble your worthless brain like a pot of breakfast stew. Now . . . call your second in command, and you are going to do everything I tell you."

Rivers pulled Montes up by the collar and stuck the capitán's own revolver against the back of his head. "Listen carefully, Montes. You and I are going to walk to the door, and we're going to open the door, and you are going to order your men to lay down their weapons. Then you are going to call for your second in command and order him to do everything I say. Is that clear?" Rivers jammed the barrel of the revolver hard against Montes' skull.

"Clear," Montes said.

"All right. Gentlemen, don your all-weather gear. We're getting ready to take a trip. Bach, go open the door and stand back, out of the line of fire."

"Yes, Leftenant."

The door swung open, Bach stepped back, and Rivers, literally breathing down the capitán's neck with his revolver against his temple, pushed Montes to the entrance. "Tell 'em, Montes! Now!"

"Lay down your weapons! Hold your fire! Bring Lieutenant Colonel Sanchez here! Now!"

Belgrano II base camp
Antarctica

11:58 a.m. local time

Lieutenant Colonel Ramon Sanchez, former base commander of Belgrano II but demoted to executive officer, sat at his desk in his quarters. His new job involved record-keeping—maintaining troop musters and mission logs and requisitions orders and so forth—all part of the job description of every second in command in every efficient military unit in the world.

Stay in the background—make the commander look good.

Sanchez resented the demotion and resented the humiliating duty, having to remain on the base he had once commanded to work under Montes, a loose-cannon cowboy.

His superiors had informed him that he would be transferred out of Belgrano as soon as a new post opened for him. But until then . . . Frustrated by the delay, he was, at that moment, processing an expedited request for change of orders. He hoped his buddy at Army headquarters in Buenos Aires could work some magic and get him out fast.

Sanchez logged onto the secure line to Buenos Aires and hit the Send button.

There. Finished.

He glanced up at the clock.

Two minutes before the execution. At least Montes had not ordered him to attend. The British prisoner, Rivers, had done nothing to warrant being shot at the stake. Sanchez knew Montes would doctor official records, trumping up justifiable charges to cover his actions, and there were enough British-haters at Army headquarters to look the other way.

Montes would kill Rivers, intimidating the rest of the British, especially the civilians, into saying anything he wanted. Montes would extract sensitive information and be hailed the hero.

Personally, those tactics made Sanchez ill. Perhaps that was why he had been replaced, he thought.

The high command knew what they were getting when they sent Montes to replace him. Montes, known as a ruthless interrogator, would use CIA-like tactics and worse to get the information they wanted. High command wanted all the classified information about the oil reserves the British had found. And no better source existed for that intelligence than the British petro-engineers being held in the prison dome across camp.

War was war, but there had to be a better way than trumping up an excuse to shoot a man execution style.

Three sharp raps on the door.

"Enter!"

"*Mi* colonel. We have a hostage situation unfolding at the prison dome!"

"What? Who?"

"The capitán and Lieutenant Sosa. The British have taken them hostage. The capitán has ordered our troops to stand down and is calling for you now."

"How did this happen?"

"I do not know, sir, but the capitán is calling for you."

"I will be right there."

Belgrano II base camp
Antarctica

11:59 a.m. local time

Captain Dunn. Can you come over here and give me a hand with Capitán Yellowbelly? I need to have a word with the men."

"Aye, Leftenant." Dunn walked over to Montes and stuck his revolver to the back of Montes' head as he stood in the open doorway.

Rivers turned back toward the center of the dome, keeping his gun trained on Sosa. "You people listen up and listen fast. When all this began . . . when they attacked us . . . there were twelve of us. We're down to ten. I need you all to stand up like men and be prepared to kill if necessary. It's either us or them. Are you with me?"

"Yes, Leftenant."

"Edwards, you were Royal Army. Remember how to fire an M-16?"

"Can I fire an M-16? Leftenant, I was Highlanders, 4th Battalion, Royal Scots Regiment. With respect, I can load, unload, and fire an M-16 in my sleep."

"Excellent. I'm depending on you. These rifles we took off these dead soldiers are FARA 83s. Not as good as the M-16, but good enough. Their operation is virtually identical. Thirty-round clip. Action lever on the right. We have four of them. Soon we should have more. Grab one of them, work the action, and get it ready to fire. Then show your mates here how to do the same. You are engineers. You should catch on fast."

"Aye, Leftenant," Edwards said.

"Leftenant," Dunn said, "the second in command is out in the courtyard."

"You"—Rivers nodded at Sosa—"what is your name and rank?" He said it loud enough for Montes to hear. He owed it to Sosa to cover the fact that Sosa had, by saving his life, betrayed the Argentineans.

"Sosa. Fernando. Lieutenant, Army of Argentina."

"Mister Sosa. You will be a human shield like your friend the capitán. Over here. Now." Rivers put his gun to Sosa's head. "We are going to walk slowly outside the door and stand right beside Captain Dunn and the capitán. You know the drill. Make a wrong move and you're a dead man."

"I understand."

Belgrano II base camp
Antarctica

Noon local time

With the snowfall now thickening, Lieutenant Colonel Sanchez walked toward the center of the snowy courtyard and approached the flagpole. A group of Argentinean soldiers quickly surrounded him. Some of the soldiers still had their rifles. Others had laid their rifles down.

"They have the capitán and Lieutenant Sosa." Sergeant Iglesias pointed to the prison dome.

Sanchez looked over through the falling snow and saw four men by the entrance to the dome. The two hostages being held at gunpoint were Montes and Sosa. He could not believe what he saw.

"I am Lieutenant Colonel Ramon Sanchez, the base executive officer. What do you want?"

A few seconds passed. A strong wind whipped into the snow, swirling it around the men. Then, "I am Leftenant Austin Rivers. I am in command of British forces and the British citizens you have unlawfully captured. You have critically wounded one unarmed man and murdered another. We have demands. We expect your full cooperation. If you fail to cooperate, we shall execute your Capitán Montes and Lieutenant Sosa."

Sanchez had been joined by Major Gimenez, the base's third in command. Sanchez and Gimenez exchanged glances. "And what are these demands?" Sanchez shouted.

"Simple. Listen and listen carefully. I want ten snowmobiles, full of gas, and ten pull sleds—"

"We do not have ten snowmobiles," Sanchez said.

"I better not find out you are lying!" Rivers replied.

"I need to hear from the capitán before I agree to anything, Mister Rivers."

Another pause. The snowfall was much thicker. The wind picked up. Visibility, even halfway across the courtyard, proved problematic.

"Give him whatever he asks for. All eight snowmobiles," Montes said. "Anything he requests. That is an order."

"Did you hear that, Lieutenant Colonel Sanchez?" The voice of the British leftenant.

"I heard!" Sanchez shouted.

"Very well. I want all eight snowmobiles with snow sleds chained to the back. Each snowmobile is to be full of gas. I want two gas cans, full of gas, tied down to each snow sled. I want two sets of handcuffs with keys. I want twenty yards of rope and two hunting knives. I want ten FARA-83 assault rifles, fully loaded with thirty rounds in each clip, and for each rifle, two additional clips with thirty rounds. That's ninety rounds per rifle. I want two fully operational GPS devices with solar batteries and polar power pack.

"You are also to provide one hundred MREs, ten thermoses full of water, one portable gas heater, and one all-weather tent to sleep six. Finally, I need one megaphone. Do you have any questions?"

"This fellow does not ask for much, does he?" Major Gimenez said in a low voice.

"He must think I am Papa Noel," Sanchez said.

"What will you do, sir?"

Major Gimenez had asked an excellent question. Frankly, if the only hostage were Montes, Sanchez would be tempted to order his men to launch an assault on the dome, and if Montes was killed in the cross fire, too bad. But Montes was not the only hostage.

Sosa was a fine young officer, one of the brightest and finest the Argentinean military had. He had a beautiful young wife at home. They were still newlyweds, as Sanchez recalled.

"And if I do not comply?" Sanchez yelled across the courtyard.

"That is your choice," came the reply. "We have already killed four of your crack troops. If you choose not to cooperate, we will kill both of our hostages, including your capitán. The choice is yours. My patience is running thin."

"I think he means it," Gimenez said.

"No doubt, Major," Sanchez replied.

"It sounds like they are planning to escape, Colonel."

"An astute observation."

Sanchez yelled again, "I need to hear from the capitán!"

"Hold on!" the Brit shouted.

"Sanchez! This is Capitán Montes! Do as he says! That is an order!"

The situation put Sanchez in a tough position. A sudden, unanticipated hostage crisis. A direct order from his superior, even though a superior he hated.

"That's quite a laundry list you have demanded! I need an hour to get all these materials together."

"That's a negative, Colonel," the Brit said. "You have thirty minutes or we begin executions. And make sure the snowmobiles are running and ready to go as soon as you deliver the supplies."

Sanchez looked at Gimenez. "Major, you're in charge of getting these materials together. Grab some men and get moving."

Gimenez shot Sanchez a salute. "*Si, mi* colonel."

Bridge
HMS Queen Elizabeth
South Atlantic Ocean
approaching Falkland Islands
course 90 degrees

12:04 p.m. local time

The term for the depth of water a ship needs to float without running aground is referred to as the "draft."

For the 920-foot-long HMS *Queen Elizabeth*, her draft rivaled that of the American supercarriers of the Nimitz class—36 feet. This meant that once she entered waters that were shallower than 36 feet, she would be aground, unable to move.

In nearly every case in every navy around the world, a ship's captain would be relieved of his duties for running his ship aground and, in some cases, even court-martialed.

But in this case, Captain Edwin Jones-Landry, Royal Navy, had determined that running the *Queen Elizabeth* aground, given the extensive damage done by enemy torpedoes, would be the only way to prevent her from sinking.

Though the attack had occurred less than one hundred miles from the Falklands, and although at top speeds the *QE* could have reached the waters outside Port Stanley in a few hours, Jones-Landry and his crew had soon discovered that the faster they tried steaming through the water, the faster seawater rushed into the lower compartments of the ship. Full speed or even half speed would have sunk the ship before they had a prayer of reaching shallower waters.

Over the last twenty-four hours, Jones-Landry had discovered, through trial and error, that by slowing the speed and diverting more power to the carrier's bilge pumps, they could slow down the leaking.

Now, with the coast of the Falkland Islands in sight, the flight deck had sunk perilously low to the water. Could they run the ship aground before the ocean swallowed her?

Jones-Landry feared that his ship's fate may follow that of the great World War II British aircraft carrier HMS *Ark Royal*, once the greatest carrier in the British Navy, which also had been torpedoed in the Atlantic by a submarine, a German U-boat.

The *Ark Royal* had survived close to twenty-four hours after the attack, taking on massive amounts of water through the holes in her hull. Her bilge pumps still working, she tried to limp to safety in the harbor at the British base at Gibraltar.

As every carrier captain in the British and American navies knew from their studies of case histories, *Ark Royal* had initially stabilized after the attack, but began to list at a steep angle, finally forcing the captain to abandon ship. She sank thirty-five miles from Gibraltar, her wreckage not discovered for sixty years.

Jones-Landry could not help but wonder. Was history repeating itself? Had he and his crew been in the wrong place at the wrong time?

Like the *Ark Royal*, his ship, the *Queen Elizabeth*, had initially stabilized but was now sinking lower in the water.

Four oceangoing tugs and two helicopters had arrived from the British enclave of Port Stanley, the capital of the Falklands, to accompany the *Queen Elizabeth* to the shoreline.

But all the tugboats and hovering helicopters in the world could not keep the angry seawater from flooding the bowels of his ship.

Jones-Landry brought his binoculars to his eyes and studied the distant shoreline of the low-lying Falkland Islands. What a bloody shame it would be to come this close and still lose the greatest warship Britain had ever built.

Would he be the captain who saved the *Queen Elizabeth* and her crew? Or the last man standing as she sank to the bottom of the sea?

"XO. Give me an updated sounding on depth and distance."

"Stand by, sir," Commander Donald Parrot said. "Sir, water depth is at one hundred feet. Distance to shore just under one mile. Range to draft-depth waters, one-half mile, sir."

"Half a bloody mile, and we can barely move. We're about to go under." Jones-Landry looked down at the bow. Swells started breaking over the flight deck. The situation was beyond critical.

"Engineering. Bridge. I need more out of those bilge pumps."

"Bridge. Engineering. I'm giving her all she's got, Cap'n!"

"Well, give me more, Commander. Have your men get out the buckets and start bailing if you must!"

"Aye, Captain."

Belgrano II base camp
Antarctica

12:10 p.m. local time

Rivers had moved Sosa and Montes back inside and placed them at opposite sides of the prison dome. Four British petro-engineers were aiming rifles, two on Sosa and two on Montes.

Sosa was leaning up against the wall looking down at the gun barrels of two FARA-83s. But it wasn't the gun barrels bothering Sosa so much as the menacing glances that Montes shot across the room at him.

Was he suspicious?

Perhaps.

Rivers had worked Montes over pretty hard with a pistol whipping and then the pistol smash to the groin, but done nothing to Sosa.

Not that Montes hadn't deserved it. Sosa knew it was payback.

But now Sosa almost wished that he'd gotten a punch in the stomach from Rivers . . . something . . . to make the treatment look a little more even-handed.

Or was this nothing more than his imagination? Those menacing looks might just be Montes' anger at having gone from being the man in command to a powerless pawn in a hostage crisis.

But Sosa felt a sick twisting over what he had done. If Montes ever figured out where those guns came from . . . or Sanchez . . . what would they do? They would say he had betrayed his country, that he had rendered assistance to the enemy and put his countrymen in danger.

And there was truth to all that. Four Argentinian soldiers were dead because of him.

But what choice did he have?

Montes had murdered a British civilian and seriously wounded another.

And then to order Sosa to do the same? Out of some sick sense of . . . of what? Some manhood test? Montes had gone way over the line and left Sosa with no good options.

To have gone over Montes' head would have been a huge risk. High command had sent Montes to command Belgrano II and would have sided with Montes. He was sure of that. He could have disobeyed the order. He considered that. But that too would have brought great personal risk, possibly a court-martial or the immediate risk of being shot on some trumped-up charge. He dared not jump the chain of command or disobey the order.

What, then, were his options? None.

And he could not carry out the order.

Yes, war was war, but Sosa could not murder a prisoner in cold blood.

Still, he knew an investigation would follow. Four Argentinean soldiers were dead because of what he had done. They would discover firearms missing from the small-arms locker in the intelligence dome.

Yes, he had given the pistols to Rivers. He just wanted to give Rivers a fighting chance. He could not see him being murdered in cold blood.

Rivers' lightning speed with a pistol was something Sosa had never before witnessed. Now four of his countrymen were dead, but Montes remained alive.

Suicide was the best solution.

He could make a quick movement toward one of the trigger-happy civilians and they would shoot him. He would not be accused of betrayal. He would die in the line of duty, defending his country. That would remove any suspicions that he had rendered aid to the enemy.

That's what he would do.

CHAPTER 27

Control room
Argentinean submarine ARA San Juan
Drake Passage
60 miles east of Cape Horn
depth 300 feet

12:20 p.m. local time

Commander Carlos Almeyda had just read the message to his crew, but for his own satisfaction, he wanted to read it once more before moving on.

FROM: President of the Argentine Republic
TO: Commanding Officer and Crew, ARA *San Juan*
PRECEDENCE: FLASH, TOP SECRET

1. The People of Argentina are grateful, and the undersigned is personally grateful for your brave work in attacking enemy naval forces in
   the South Atlantic near the Malvinas Islands.
2. You have brought pride to your country.
3. Now you are being dispatched to the waters of the Drake Passage to
   oppose more enemy forces set upon colonializing our native region.
4. The eyes of a grateful nation are upon you, and our hearts are with you.
5. With enemy ships pouring into the region, surely your bravery and
   professionalism shall deter their will to fight.

6. Godspeed for safety in battle and a safe return to the Republic.

> With eternal gratitude,
> Donato Suarez
> President of the Republic of Argentina

Almeyda shook his head in disbelief. One month ago he served as executive officer for his friend and mentor, Commander Alberto Gomez. Now, suddenly, he was not only the senior sub commander in the Argentinean Navy but had scored more kills than any other Argentinean sub commander in the twenty-first century! Even the president had recognized him!

All this had happened so quickly. But enough contemplation. Almeyda folded the message and stuck it in his pocket. Intelligence relayed to the sub indicated that British warships had entered Drake Passage from the Pacific and were operating near Cape Horn.

"Navigator, report on our position," Almeyda said.

"Drake Passage, sir. Sixty miles east of Cape Horn. Depth 300 feet. Course two-five-zero degrees."

"Put her on the screen, Lieutenant."

"Aye, sir."

The navigational display popped up on the big screen.

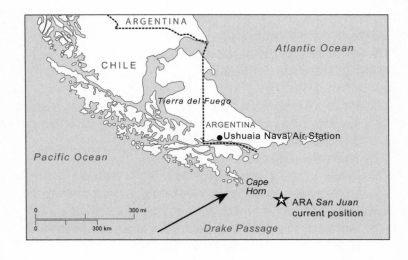

"The star on the right marks our current position, sir. The tip of the arrow to the left marks the last known area of three British frigates operating in the area. These frigates are believed to have entered the area from the Pacific."

"XO. On the 1-MC."

"Aye, Capitán."

"Now hear this. This is the capitán. Be advised that British warships have been reported in the area, surface combatants. We had some excellent hunting yesterday and have either sunk, or at least taken out of commission, the largest and most powerful warship in the British fleet. By neutralizing the *Queen Elizabeth*, we have leveled out the balance of power in the region. You have captured the attention of the nation and even our president.

"But, gentlemen, this war isn't over, and our job isn't done. Be alert. Be ready. And be prepared to go hunting soon. This is the capitán. That is all."

Belgrano II base camp
Antarctica

12:25 p.m. local time

Lieutenant Fernando Sosa looked at the time. If he was going to provoke the British guards, he needed to act now, before Rivers and the rest of the Brits tried to escape camp. Once they escaped, if they escaped, there would be no enemy soldiers to kill him. His legacy, rather than being one of heroically dying in combat, would be that of Argentina's Benedict Arnold.

Rivers had given Colonel Sanchez until 12:30, which meant Fernando had five minutes max to pull this off.

"Are you married?"

What an odd question from out of the blue—from one of the men guarding him with the assault rifle. From the one Montes had called Father Bach.

"Yes, I'm married. Why?"

"I was once married," the man said. "My wife died of cancer at an early age. Cherish her and take care of her."

Bach's words punched him hard in the stomach.

Carolina.

Of course!

He was more worried about his own legacy than protecting his wife. They'd just gotten married. How could he be so selfish?

But if he became Argentina's Benedict Arnold, like everyone else, Carolina would reject him.

Or would she?

She once told him, "You might be only one person in the world, or you might be in another part of the world. But to me, you are the world."

Did she mean that?

Would he still be the world to her if he disgraced Argentina?

Had Montes' planned execution of a prisoner taken place, that would have been the real disgrace to Argentina. But only he and God knew the truth.

This wasn't about him.

This was about duty.

Bach's words reminded him: his duty was to take care of his wife. He had promised this to the priest and before God. Taking action now to provoke his own death would break that vow.

"Mister Bach, would you please tell the leftenant I need to speak with him? It's important."

"Aye. Why not, mate. I'll see if I can get him."

He received another menacing glare from Montes. Now or never. There would be no turning back.

Rivers walked over. "What do you need, mate? I don't have much time."

"May I speak with you in private?"

Montes' eyes were firing darts.

"Step over here."

They moved away from the others. Sosa spoke in a whisper. "Leftenant, the third dome to your right is the communications dome. Take it out before you leave or they will call in reinforcements as soon as you leave. Once they lose all communication, search helicopters will be dispatched to investigate. But if you take it out, you will have a running start. There is a small-arms locker in that dome. I'm asking you to take all the rest of the guns with you . . . if you catch my drift."

Rivers looked at him with a nod and a twinkle in his eye. "I catch your drift, mate."

From outside, the sound of gas-powered engines.

"Leftenant, they're back with the snowmobiles!"

"So I hear," Rivers said.

"The colonel told the truth. There are only eight in the camp," Sosa said.

"Very well," Rivers said. He turned to the capitán. "Montes. Get up! You're useful when you play the role of a human shield." Rivers jerked Montes up by the collar and stuck the .357 at his temple. With gun in one hand and Montes' jacket collar in the other, Rivers shoved Montes toward the door.

Control room
Argentinean submarine ARA San Juan
Drake Passage
20 miles south of Cape Horn
depth 250 feet

12:25 p.m. local time

Capitán! Enemy contact! Multiple screws, sir. Acoustics computer suggests 72 percent probability of British warships. Preliminarily identified as *Daring*-class guided-missile destroyers. I hear two . . . no, three screws, sir! Count that three targets in the water, Skipper!"

"Range, Mister Valera?"

"Range, two thousand yards, sir."

"Very well. Load torps one, two, three, and four."

"Load torps one, two, three, and four. Aye, Capitán."

"Take the boat to periscope depth. Sound general quarters."

"Take boat to periscope depth. Sounding general quarters. Aye, sir."

Belgrano II base camp
Antarctica

12:32 p.m. local time

Holding Montes in front of him as a human shield and jamming the barrel of Montes' revolver against the capitán's temple, Rivers stepped outside of the prisoners' dome into the snowfall.

Eight snowmobiles, their engines all running, were lined up in front of the dome. Each had a pull sled hitched to the back. The weapons and materials were spread out over the sleds behind the snowmobiles.

Because of heavy snows, visibility extended only to the flagpole area in the center of the camp, blinding from view the Argentinean soldiers on the other side.

Perhaps God had sent the weather as a blanket of invisibility at just the right time.

"Captain Dunn!" Rivers shouted over the rumbling of the snow-mobiles. "I need your help."

"Aye, Leftenant."

"Get that megaphone on the back of that sled and grab two pairs of handcuffs."

"Yes, sir." Dunn ventured through the snow to the sled containing a white megaphone. He retrieved it, got two pairs of handcuffs, and brought the megaphone and the cuffs back to Rivers.

"Very well, Capitán Montes. Hands behind your back."

Montes complied.

"Captain Dunn, cuff him."

"With pleasure, sir."

"Edwards!"

"Yes, Leftenant."

"Go out to the sleds and bring back six assault rifles. I want a loaded rifle in every man's hand."

"Aye, sir."

Edwards quickly grabbed six rifles and passed them out, instantly transforming the petro-engineers into a small military platoon.

Rivers turned his attention to Montes. "Listen carefully, *el* Capitán. You are going to take that megaphone right now, and you are going to order all of your men to go into their quarters and close the doors and remain for a minimum of thirty minutes. They are to sequester themselves immediately. No one is to go near the communications dome."

"What are you planning to do?" Montes asked.

Rivers smashed the gun against Montes' nose, knocking him down onto his rump and drawing more blood. "Let's get this straight, Capitán." Rivers peered down at Montes. "When I issue you a command, asking a question is not the most intelligent response." Rivers reached down and pulled Montes out of the snow. "Have I made myself clear?"

"Perfectly."

"Good. Then Captain Dunn will hold the megaphone to your mouth while I hold your gun to your head. Order your men to do as I said. Captain Dunn?"

Dunn held the megaphone to Montes' mouth. Rivers whispered in his ear, "I've always heard these .357 revolvers are more accurate if you cock the hammer rather than just pull the trigger."

Click. "All the better to blow your brains out with if you don't comply by the count of three. One . . . two . . ."

"This is the capitán," Montes said. "To all personnel at Belgrano II base camp. Go immediately to your quarters. Close the doors and remain there for thirty minutes. Evacuate the communications dome. Move immediately. Colonel Sanchez. Acknowledge my order."

Silence.

Only the motorized rumbling of the snowmobiles.

A voice from through the snow. "We acknowledge your order, Capitán. Our men are returning to their quarters."

"Excellent," Rivers said. "Edwards."

"Yes, Leftenant."

"Move quickly. Get a couple of men and cuff Mister Sosa. Tie Sosa and the capitán onto separate sleds. They're going with us. And get the rest of the men on the snowmobiles."

"Yes, sir."

"Captain Dunn. I have an assignment for you."

"Yes, sir."

"I think the dome over there on the right is the communications center. Sophisticated communications and surveillance equipment. Disable everything in there. Fill the communications equipment full of lead. Use the pistols with the silencers. No point in agitating these Argentineans with the sound of grenades. And clean out any arms locker. We'll take the weapons with us. Leave nothing."

"Yes, sir."

"Take a man with you. We'll be ready to move out as soon as you get back. Make it fast."

"Yes, sir. Evans. Come with me." Dunn and Evans rushed over to the communications dome.

"All right, men, let's mount up," Rivers said. He took one of the snow-mobiles in the center of the line as the others climbed onto their seats.

Dunn and Evans emerged from the communications dome, each carrying a canvas bag with rifles sticking out the end.

"No one will be broadcasting out of that place for a while, sir." Dunn secured the guns to the sled behind his snowmobile and then mounted his seat.

"Excellent, Captain Dunn. All right, men! Hit your headlights. Let's ride!"

Rivers gripped the throttle and turned it. The snowmobile moved out, slowly at first, and one by one they followed him. Across the snowy court-yard, their headlamps shining through the falling snow, they quickly cut a line between the second and third domes, picked up speed, and left the camp behind. They rumbled out across a great plain of snow and ice into a blizzard of white, through thick-falling flakes under a dark gray sky.

Control room
Argentinean submarine ARA San Juan
Drake Passage
20 miles south of Cape Horn
depth 40 feet (periscope depth)

12:35 p.m. local time

It was true that a nuclear missile could kill a man.

By contrast, a small derringer, hidden in an assailant's pocket or purse, like the one used to assassinate Abraham Lincoln, was just as deadly.

Whether a victim was vaporized in a nuclear blast or shot with a .22-caliber bullet to the brain, he was no more or no less dead in one case than in the other. For the advantage that the derringer possessed, and had possessed for hundreds of years, was that it could be hidden in the secret crevices of a jacket or a purse or the pocket of a pair of trousers.

And while the more powerful British nuclear subs boasted more firepower, including nuclear-tipped torpedoes, than did the smaller and less potent diesel-electric Argentinean boats, if the British and American boats represented the power of the warhead, the Argentinean boats represented the lethal power of the derringer.

Just as John Wilkes Booth had murdered President Abraham Lincoln by concealing his derringer in the pocket of his cloak, the huge advantage possessed by the Argentinean submarines was their ability to remain concealed.

Carlos Almeyda had studied the assassination of Lincoln and applied it to his tactics as a sub commander. His goal: sneak up on his target, silently, as had John Wilkes Booth, and surprise his victim with a sudden and deadly shot to the head with a derringer.

"Range to target," Almeyda said.

"Range to target, one thousand yards."

"Scope's up, Skipper."

"Very well." Almeyda brought his eyes to the viewfinder and felt his mouth begin to salivate. "Mister Valera, you've got the best ears in the whole Navy! I've got three, count 'em, three British Type 45 *Daring*-class guided-missile destroyers in the bull's-eye! On my mark, I want three torps fired to the broadside! Stand by to fire torp one."

"Stand by to fire torp one. Aye, sir!"

"Navigator. Range to nearest target."

"Range to target, nine hundred yards."

"Very well. Fire torp one!"

"Firing torp one! Aye, sir!"

"Fire torp two!"

"Firing torp two! Aye, sir!"

"Fire torp three!"

"Firing torp three! Aye, sir!"

Bridge
HMS Daring
British guided-missile destroyer
Drake Passage
20 miles south of Cape Horn

12:36 p.m. local time

Captain! Inbound torpedoes! Five hundred yards and closing."

"Evasive maneuvers!" Captain Murray Atkinson, Royal Navy, shouted. "Right full rudder! All ahead full."

As HMS *Daring* cut hard to starboard, a fireball lit the sky, followed by a thunderous rumble across the water.

"Captain, the *Dauntless* has been hit, sir!" the executive officer said. Across the way, HMS *Dauntless*, the five-hundred-foot sister ship to the *Daring*, exploded in flames. The fireball on the *Dauntless* leaped above the ship's stern.

"Captain! Torpedoes still inbound. Range two-seven-five yards and closing."

"Left full rudder! Launch countermeasures!"

"Left full rudder! Launch countermeasures! Aye, sir."

As the *Daring* started her hard cut back to the left, another fireball. Another explosion.

"Captain! They've hit the *Diamond*!"

A second British guided-missile destroyer exploded in flames.

"Sir, torpedo, one hundred yards and closing!"

"XO, warn the crew! Brace for impact!"

"All hands! This is the executive officer. Inbound torpedo! Brace for impact! Brace for impact!"

The explosion rocked the ship so hard that it knocked the captain off his feet. Atkinson pushed up and saw the ship's entire foresection ablaze, flames leaping higher than the superstructure of the bridge, more than forty feet in the air. The bow was already sinking from water gushing in the huge hole cut by the explosion.

Atkinson had to save his crew. Any delay would cost more lives. He knew what he had to do.

"XO, alert the crew! Abandon ship!"

10 miles outside Belgrano II base camp
Antarctic Peninsula
Antarctica

1:05 p.m. local time

Plowing through a blinding white world of snow and ice, a sight that could pass for a peaceful postcard were it not for the roar of gas-powered engines that sounded like a half-breed cross between a Harley-Davidson and a lawn mower, Rivers pulled his hand off the left handlebar of the lead snowmobile and checked his watch, 1:05 p.m.

They had been running through snowy conditions for thirty minutes now, long enough, in his opinion, to have opened up a safe working distance ahead of the enemy. Their head start, enhanced by the blizzard conditions, seemed like an act of a God whom Rivers was still trying to decide if he believed in.

As long as the blizzard hid their position, Rivers leaned toward believing in God, a philosophical position of which Bach, no doubt, would approve.

But it wasn't enough to escape and drive blindly in a blizzard in the coldest place on earth to hide from an enemy. Even in the spring seasons in Antarctica, with twenty-four-hour daylight, and even with a survival tent, a portable heater, and numerous MRE military food packs obtained from the Argentineans, eventually they would run out of gas and supplies.

He needed to set a course for their final destination.

Rivers held up his right hand, motioning for the other snowmobiles to slow down. All eight snowmobiles, their headlights beaming through falling snow, all pulling sleds, came to a stop for the first time since leaving Belgrano II camp.

Rivers gave the throat-slash gesture, signaling his men to cut their engines.

The loud roar of the engines was replaced by the eerie howl of the ice-filled wind.

Rivers took a moment to absorb the near magic of the tranquility of the cold wonderland, a peaceful respite miles away from the mortal danger they had left.

Enough reflection.

"Bach."

"Yes, Leftenant."

"Check on our two guests. Make sure they're still breathing. Adjust their blankets if you need to. I want Montes tried for war crimes for murdering Anderson. I don't want him dying of frostbite."

"Yes, Leftenant."

"Dunn."

"Yes, sir."

Rivers got off the snowmobile and stepped out into the deep snow, his boots crunching into it as he walked toward Dunn's snowmobile. "Pull the GPS devices out. Let me know when you have one up and running. It's time to mark our bearings."

"Yes, sir. They're tied down on my pull sled."

"Very well," Rivers said. "Anyone who wants to get off and take a stretch, go ahead. Walk around. Take care of your business. It will be awhile before we stop again."

"Bloody good idea."

"Good idea, mate."

"Got it, Leftenant," Dunn said. "GPS is working like a charm."

Rivers walked over and stood beside Dunn as the GPS displayed a map of the Antarctic Peninsula.

"We left in such a rush, Leftenant, that I never heard you say where we're going."

"Ya know," Rivers said, "I could use a stogie right about now. I should've made those Argentineans load ten fine cigars in our stash. Bach!"

"Yes, sir."

"Ask Montes if he has a cigar in his pocket. Tell him if he does, I'll let him sit up and we can split it."

"Yes, sir."

"The Halley Research Station. That's where we're headed, Dunn."

"Montes says no cigars, Leftenant," Bach said.

"Figures," Rivers said.

"The Halley Research Station?"

"Exactly. Now that Camp Churchill has been occupied, that's the closest British research station. Let's have a look."

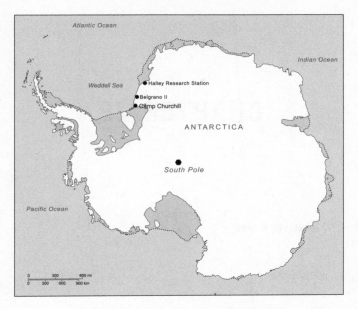

"We can see Belgrano II clearly marked. And to the north and a bit east of that, the Halley Station, the closest permanent British facility. It's an atmospheric and weather facility with seventy scientists stationed there.

"We'll set a course paralleling the Weddell Sea. With any luck, we should arrive by tomorrow. Once inside, we should be safe for the time being unless the enemy decides to strike at Halley. Maybe we will have British military reinforcements by then."

"Question," Dunn said.

"Fire away."

"This weather has been a godsend for us. What if it breaks?"

"Depends on when it breaks," Rivers said. "If it breaks anytime soon, they'll have aircraft from Ushuaia Air Base in Tierra del Fuego scouring the area. You and I know that could be a bloody mess."

"Yes, sir."

"In any event, we shall deal with that situation if it arises. Meantime, we set a course for Halley Station and move out."

"Yes, sir."

"Gentlemen, mount your machines and start your engines! Prepare to move out."

CHAPTER 28

Prime Minister Mulvaney stood behind his desk and removed his glasses. "Let me see if I understand this correctly, Admiral. Are you telling me that in the last thirty minutes we have lost three of His Majesty's warships in addition to the freighter we lost yesterday, and we're about to lose the *Queen Elizabeth*, and all this destruction is the result of one single solitary diesel-electric Argentinean submarine that does not even have a nuclear reactor?"

"Prime Minister, I remind you that we still have not yet lost the *Queen Elizabeth*. If we can beach her, our naval engineers can repair her, although the situation remains bleak," Admiral Sir Mark Ellington said.

"Perhaps I should submit my resignation to His Majesty," Mulvaney said. He began to crave a spot of brandy.

"With respect, Prime Minister," Sir John Gosling, the foreign secretary, said, "we were attacked first by enemy forces, not the other way around, sir. What the British people need is your leadership. Now more than ever. Not your resignation."

Sir John was right. The prime minister needed to be atop his game at this crucial hour, not wallowing in self-pity.

"So today we've lost the *Daring*, the *Dauntless*, and the *Diamond*. Do we have any survivors?"

"Prime Minister," Admiral Ellington said, "the sinkings took place twenty miles off the tip of South America off Cape Horn. Chile has dispatched a small armada of boats and helicopters from their naval station across the inlet from Cape Horn. They have already plucked some survivors from the water.

"Their facilities are rather small at their Cape Horn naval station, so they are erecting large hospital tents for MASH units to provide emergency treatment for our sailors being pulled from the water until they are ready to be transported."

"Sir John, when we've completed the meeting, please place a call to President Mendoza of Chile so that I can thank him."

"Certainly, Prime Minister."

"Now then. We've suffered a major blow to the fleet, but by no means is it the end. We shall continue to reinforce the area with naval firepower and overwhelm them with numbers. But the damage done by this one Argentinean submarine is troubling. Have we determined which sub it is?"

"Based on message traffic intercepted, we're convinced it's the ARA *San Juan*, the sister sub of the *Santa Cruz*, the sub we sank, sir."

"I want that sub sunk. Admiral Ellington, I am holding you personally responsible. Sink the *San Juan*."

"Yes, Prime Minister."

Bridge
HMS Queen Elizabeth
South Atlantic Ocean
approaching the Falkland Islands
course 90 degrees

1:50 p.m. local time

S o close, so close, and yet so far."
     The lyrics of the twentieth-century pop ballad danced in Captain Jones-Landry's mind as he looked down on the flight deck. Along with her air wing, HMS *Queen Elizabeth* carried a complement of 1,600 officers and enlisted men, most of whom had evacuated up to the flight

deck because of rapid flooding belowdecks. They stood there, all with life preservers on, awaiting the "abandon ship" order.

Five helicopters from Port Stanley circled the great carrier, and a number of small boats had come out to pick up crew members when the carrier went down.

"Depth sixty feet, Captain. Distance to shore, one-half mile. Distance to beachable depth, if these depth charts are correct, approximately one-quarter mile," Commander Donald Parrott said.

"XO. Order the chaplain to the bridge."

"Aye, Captain." Commander Parrott picked up the 1-MC. "Reverend Honeycutt to the Bridge."

An order to abandon ship was the hardest order for any captain to make. Not only was such an order an admission that his ship was lost, but the timing of the order was crucial.

If Jones-Landry waited too long to issue the order, he ran the risk that his crew, even if they were wearing life jackets or were in small lifeboats, could be sucked down with the ship.

"Leftenant Commander Honeycutt reporting as ordered, sir."

Jones-Landry turned around and saw the ship's senior Christian chaplain, the Rev. Daniel Honeycutt, ordained by the Church of England and wearing the rank of leftenant commander, Royal Navy, standing at attention.

"At ease, Reverend."

"How may I be of service, sir?"

"Reverend, I once watched the old American war movie *Patton*. At the Battle of the Bulge, at Christmas of 1944, General Patton's Third Army needed better weather for its tanks to advance.

"General Patton didn't know how to pray, so he ordered his chaplain to write out a prayer to the Almighty for better weather. Well, I don't know how to pray either, and we don't have time to write out a prayer. So I'm ordering you, right here and right now, to beseech the Almighty that he would spare the ship from sinking. Do it on the 1-MC so all the crew can hear. But make it fast or we'll all be swimming in the South Atlantic."

"Aye, Captain." Honeycutt took the 1-MC from the XO. "Now hear this. This is the ship's chaplain. Please bow your heads as I pray. Almighty Father, Maker of all heaven and earth, in this perilous time of trouble, we beseech thy help. We are grateful for thy divine providence and apologize for our sins and for the fact that this prayer cannot, because of these circumstances, last longer than a moment. We beseech thee now. Reach down from heaven with thy miraculous and powerful hand and save this ship. In the name of Christ our Redeemer we pray. Amen."

"Thank you, Reverend. Now get back down to the men."

"Yes, sir."

Jones-Landry looked at Parrott. "That was a gallant effort by the chaplain, but too late, I'm afraid."

"You tried, Captain. Nothing wrong with a little prayer, I suppose."

"Perhaps. But now I must focus on the crew's safety. Alert the crew. Stand by to abandon ship. We'll give this another sixty seconds, but we're sinking too fast. I can't wait any longer."

"Aye, Captain." The XO spoke into the 1-MC. "This is the executive officer. Prepare to abandon ship. I repeat, prepare to abandon ship in approximately one minute. Stand by for further orders. This is the executive officer."

Jones-Landry locked eyes with Commander Parrott. The end was near.

Hopefully their close proximity to the Falklands would minimize the massive loss of life. But even that depended, in part, on not delaying too long in issuing the abandon ship order.

The massive thud rocked the great ship. Papers flew to the floor and glass rattled. Anything not buckled down moved.

"Captain!" the ship's navigator shouted. "Water depth thirty-six feet! We've grounded on an uncharted sandbar! And this is high tide!"

"All engines stop! Belay that abandon ship order, XO! We aren't going anywhere! In fact, give me the 1-MC."

"With pleasure, sir."

"Now hear this. This is the commanding officer! I am pleased to report that the *Queen Elizabeth* is stuck in the mud! Belay the order to abandon ship. We aren't going anywhere until naval engineers from London arrive and patch the holes in our lower compartments."

Cheering from a thousand-plus crewmen rose from the flight deck.

"And a special thanks to Reverend Honeycutt, the ship's chaplain, whose prayer to the Almighty worked! I am going to personally promote Reverend Honeycutt to full commander in a ceremony on the flight deck later this afternoon!"

CHAPTER 29

CS Miro
Drake Passage
20 miles south of Cape Horn
depth 100 feet

7:00 a.m. local time

S kipper, FLASH Top Secret message from Fourth Fleet."

"Very well." Pete took the message from the *Miro*'s communications officer.

FROM: Commander, US 4th Fleet
TO: Commanding Officer, CS *Miro* (FKA USS *City of Corpus Christi*)
RE: Operational Orders—Drake Passage and Antarctic Region

1. Recent naval intelligence shows increased Argentinean/Venezuelan naval vessels in the waters of Drake Passage within fifty miles of Cape Horn, Chile.
2. Argentinean/Venezuelan forces have shown hostile intent to Britain.
3. Rules of engagement require that you attack and destroy all Argentinean/Venezuelan naval vessels in the area.
4. Be further advised that an Argentinean submarine, believed to be ARA *San Juan*, is believed to be responsible for sinking three British warships, one British freighter, and the near sinking of the carrier HMS *Queen Elizabeth*.

5. The location, sinking, and destruction of ARA *San Juan* is your top priority.
6. These rules of engagement shall remain in effect until further notice.

Respectfully,
KA Foster
RADM, USN
COMMANDER FOURTH FLEET

"Check this out, XO." Pete handed the orders to Lieutenant Commander Norman Rodman.

"Unbelievable. A single Argentinean submarine with four sinkings and a near sinking of the *Queen Elizabeth*."

"It is amazing, isn't it?" Pete admired, secretly, the war-waging abilities of a worthy opponent. "The skipper of that boat has some talent."

"Perhaps, Captain, but I'll put my money on you."

"I've got a feeling your skills as a riverboat gambler will be tested before this is over with," Pete said. "We'll see how good you are. I have a feeling this is headed to an old-fashioned sub duel to determine the outcome of this war. And in that kind of a duel, there can be only one winner. One captain will die. Only one will survive."

Comodoro Arturo Merino Benítez International Airport
British Airways terminal
Santiago, Chile

8:30 a.m. local time

Mommy! Mommy!"

The boy's sweet voice melted Meg's heart even before she saw him running with open arms across the terminal. He jumped into her arms, and she kissed him on the cheeks and forehead.

With her arms wrapped around Aussie, Meg felt another pair of arms wrap around her.

"Shelley!" She put Aussie down and wiped her eyes. "Thank you for coming."

"How couldn't I?" Shelley smiled. "Besides, you paid for it."

"Yes, and remind me to retain the first bankruptcy lawyer that I can find when we return to London."

That brought a chuckle from Shelley. Then a serious look. "Have you heard anything?"

Meg shook her head. "Nothing. But our embassy personnel here have been wonderful. They've invited me to call or stop in every day until we know something."

Shelley nodded. "Have you heard about Bob's ship?"

"Yes, I have. Why do you suppose I wanted you here?"

"How did you know?" Shelley said.

"How did I know what? That deep down you still carry a torch for him?"

Shelley nodded. "How did you know?"

"How long have we been best friends?"

"A long time."

"Look," Meg said, "no one knows what will happen. But no matter what, we have each other. We must have faith that no matter what storms we are facing, God will lead us through and provide us comfort and the strength we need."

A stunned look crossed Shelley's face. She stared into space, like she had seen a ghost.

"Shelley? Are you all right?"

"Yes . . . I . . . Sorry. It's . . . well, I recently heard someone else tell me the same thing."

"That's odd. Someone told me the same thing yesterday . . . here in Chile. Let's get your baggage, get something to eat, and get to the room. You must be exhausted."

St. James Catholic Church
Santo Domingo 36
Valparaiso, Chile

11:30 a.m. local time

Why?
       Why had she driven out to the peninsula again today? For the second day in a row. Before yesterday, she had not been out here in years.

Yet she knew why. She last saw him here. Perhaps this was the last place anyone would see him.

The city, in fact the country, was ablaze with the news of the attack by enemy submarines and the sinking of four British ships, including a British freighter, and the near sinking of Britain's newest aircraft carrier.

She barely remembered the Falklands War, when Chile sided with Britain against Argentina. But the old-timers and the news media claimed that this war could erupt into something much larger, since Britain and Chile had collaborated on the oil drilling in Antarctica that led to the first attack.

America and Russia might even get involved, according to the news reports.

Maria already knew that America was involved. Pete had sailed off in a submarine that was Chilean in name only, manned by an American crew.

War fever in the last twenty-four hours had swept Chile, especially this Navy town. She looked out at the spot in the bay where she last saw him. That day, the calm water looked glassy. Now, as the noon hour approached, choppy waves covered the bay, and boats and ships criss-crossed back and forth.

War fever. She'd not sensed it when he left. But now it was like the bay had been ignited with newfound electricity.

She had to pull it together and get back to work.

She started her car and started driving back toward downtown along Errázuriz Boulevard, paralleling the bay to her left. But as she took her eyes off the water, a sign caught her eye and instinctively caused her to tap her brakes.

St. James at Santa Domingo—Next Right

She turned off the main road, winding her way up the twisted road toward the basilica. Minutes later, high atop a hill at the top of the narrow road, she stopped the car at the basilica and got out.

A sign in the entryway announced that midday confessional hours were from 11:00 a.m. to 1:00 p.m.

Good. Perhaps she had gotten lucky.

She followed the signs to the confessional booths behind the sanctuary. No one was there, so she stepped into the first booth. "Forgive me,

Father, for I have sinned. It has been . . . I don't know how many days since my last confessional. I accuse myself of . . . of attempting to seduce a man that I just met, of loving a man that I barely know, and of wanting a man who may be about to die."

Nothing.

Then a kind elderly voice. "The first part, the seduction part, or the attempted seduction, may have been a sin, but I am not convinced that the other matters you have confessed are sinful."

"I don't know, Father. I feel torn inside. I feel so worried."

"It appears that your principal motive for coming to confession might not be to confess at all, but rather to seek prayer for this friend of yours whose life is in danger."

"Yes, Father. And if I have come to confession with an improper motive, forgive me for my improper motivations."

A chuckle from behind the curtain. "I don't think our Father views a desire for prayer to be an improper motive."

"Thank you, Father."

"Tell me, how may I pray for you, my daughter?"

"Pray for the safety of my friend. That he would return safely and that . . ."

"That the two of you would be together?"

"I . . . I don't know, Father. I don't know what to say."

"What is your friend's name?"

"Peter."

"Aah. A wonderful biblical name. Is he Catholic?"

"His father was Catholic. But he grew up in America and became Protestant."

"No matter. I will pray for him nonetheless."

"Oh, thank you, Father."

"But there is one thing that you should remember."

"What is it?"

"No matter what storms we are facing, God will lead us through and provide comfort."

"Thank you, Father."

"Go now knowing that this Peter is in my prayers. Go in peace, my daughter."

"Thanks be to God."

CHAPTER 30

CS Miro
Drake Passage
20 miles south of Cape Horn
depth 100 feet

11:50 a.m. local time

Like a cheetah waiting to pounce on an unsuspecting elephant, the nuclear attack submarine that had now been jointly designated, for purposes of this mission only, as CS *Miro* / USS *Corpus Christi* hovered in the dark under the cold sea lanes—waiting, listening.

With his sub's torpedoes cocked and ready to be fired, Commander Pete Miranda had learned that hunting ships, like hunting deer in the Carolinas or elk in Montana, depended on the dual elements of patience and surprise.

Checking the chronometer, as the clock approached the noon hour locally, Pete could not shake from his mind another sub commander. The Argentine captain of the ARA *San Juan* had, with four and a half kills in the past twenty-four hours, proven his worth as an opponent. Or had he merely proven his luck?

Until yesterday, Pete was convinced that he was the world's best sub commander. Today he remained convinced of that. But today, unlike yesterday, a challenger waited in the depths of the sea.

The thought of someone daring to challenge his supremacy brought a rush to his Chilean-American blood.

As the clock approached noon, Pete longed for a showdown with the Argentinean. If he could be so lucky!

"Skipper! Sonar showing enemy contact! Bearing two-seven-zero degrees!"

"Please tell me you've found me a sub to attack, Mister King."

"Stand by, Skipper." Sonarman Chief John "Bloodhound" King adjusted his frequencies. "Skipper, multiple screws in the water. Acoustics computer showing probability of Argentine warships!"

"Right full rudder. Let's try to slip in behind their wakes. They'll never hear us, never know what hit 'em."

"Right full rudder. Aye, Captain."

As the sub swung to the right through the cold waters of Drake Passage, Pete could not contain the rush surging through his body. Just like the rush a deer hunter feels before pulling the trigger on an eight-point buck. But not the same as having a twelve-point buck in the gun sight.

And for Pete, the enemy sub was the twelve-point buck.

"Captain! Counting four . . . repeat four screws in the water! Showing four *Almirante Brown*–class destroyers, and we're in behind 'em at point-blank range, sir! They don't have a clue."

"Four screws?"

"Four screws, sir."

Suddenly, the eight-point buck felt like a ten-pointer. "Go to periscope depth. Up scope. XO, take the boat to general quarters."

"Aye, Captain." Then on the loudspeaker, "General quarters. General quarters. General quarters. All hands to battle stations."

"Periscope depth. Up scope. Aye, sir."

Pete felt surging electricity throughout his body. With a little luck, he could even up the score with the Argentinean skipper before their showdown.

"Scope's up, Cap'n."

"Very well." Pete stepped to the periscope and looked through the viewfinder. "Yeah, baby!" Against blue-gray skies and gray waters, the sterns of four destroyers were steaming parallel to one another, in a line from left to right, spaced two hundred yards from ship to ship. The four warships were cutting a parallel course in the water that stretched about eight hundred yards from the ship on the far left to the ship on the far right.

Pete focused on the one in the right center and clicked on the zoom button. Then again. And then again.

The third click magnified the image so powerfully that he could see behind the stern the white churning water kicking up in the wake. Painted in black on the gray steel on the ship's stern, below the fantail, was the ship's name:

Almirante Brown

Flapping from an angled flagpole off the back, its light blue banner whipping in the wind off the water, the flag of the Argentine Republic!

The sight made Pete forget the sub. For he was a hunter and his prey was in sight. Nothing on the face of the planet could match the exhilarating rush of this very moment!

"Weapons Officer. Program four torps to lock onto each target. On my mark. Prepare to fire torp one."

"Prepare to fire torp one. Aye, Captain."

"Very well! Fire torp one!"

"Firing torp one! Aye, sir!"

"Fire torp two!"

"Firing torp two! Aye, sir!"

"Fire torp three!"

"Firing torp three! Aye, sir!"

"Fire torp four!"

"Firing torp four! Aye, sir!"

"Weapons Officer! Report status!"

"Four torps in the water, Captain! Torp one, time to impact, one minute, sir!"

Pete at this point would ordinarily order an emergency dive in case any of the torpedoes missed and the targets came looking for the submarine.

But these torps were not going to miss. Not with point-blank shots. He knew it in his gut.

"Sonar. Range to target."

"Range to target . . . thirty seconds."

Like a jet's vapor trail cutting through the skies, the four Mark-48 torpedoes painted long white streaks in the water, cutting under the surface, rushing as underwater missiles to a deadly collision with their unsuspecting targets.

"Range to target . . . ten seconds."

Pete gripped the scope handles hard.

The first fireball exploded in the back of the *Almirante Brown*. Then two . . . three . . . four fireballs lit the sky, leaping to the heavens in a perfect line from left to right. "We have four direct hits!" the XO reported over the 1-MC.

Spontaneous cheering and applause broke out all over the sub. But Pete could not cheer or applaud. He could only watch. The flames leaped high in the sky now, and black smoke billowed into the heavens.

The ship on the right began to list hard to starboard, and the left middle destroyer started sinking, stern down, her bow rising to the sky. The other two were burning out of control.

Pete had seen enough.

He had scored complete kills on every target, delivering a gut-wrenching blow to Argentina.

"Down scope."

"Down scope. Aye, Captain."

"Diving Officer. Take us down. Make your depth four hundred feet. Set course one-three-five degrees. All ahead half."

"Make my depth four hundred feet. Set course one-three-five degrees. All ahead half. Aye, sir."

CHAPTER 31

La Casa Rosada (the Pink House)
presidential palace
Buenos Aires, Argentina

3:15 p.m. local time

The president of the Argentine Republic, el Presidente Donato Suarez, stared down at the top secret memo announcing that four Argentinean warships had, earlier that day, been torpedoed and sunk in Drake Passage by an enemy submarine. Suarez felt his veins popping in his neck as he studied the list of ships:

ARA *Almirante Brown*
ARA *La Argentina*
ARA *Heroína*
ARA *Sarandi*

The president stood up, pulled off his designer navy blue pinstripe jacket, and flung it down on his chair. "Are you telling me, Admiral Blanco, that we have lost four destroyers in one swoop, all attacked by one sole, solitary submarine?"

"I regret that this is the case, Mister President." Admiral Victor Blanco, commander of the Navy of Argentina, sat in a leather wingback chair across from the presidential desk.

"How many casualties, Admiral?"

"We're trying to determine. A Chilean fishing boat picked up a couple dozen. The rest are believed to be lost."

"You didn't answer my question, Admiral. How many?"

Blanco hesitated. "Each ship carried a crew of 224. Times four ships. We're missing almost 900 sailors, Mister President. Most are believed to be lost."

Domingo Ramos, the Argentinean foreign minister, sat in the other wingback chair next to Blanco. Ramos had said nothing and winced when told that the Argentinean Navy had lost hundreds of sailors.

"But I would also respectfully remind you, sir," Admiral Blanco said, "that we, likewise, have sunk three of Britain's *Daring*-class guided-missile destroyers, and we also sank one of their merchant vessels, and, most importantly, we have attacked and disabled the most powerful vessel in the history of their Navy. We have beached a great and powerful nuclear supercarrier, which would have changed the balance of power in this war. We are winning the naval war, sir."

Suarez folded his arms. "I realize that we've gotten the best of the British. But they also have a lot more ships and submarines to lose than we do. We're down to two submarines, and only one of those is a *Santa Cruz*–class sub, and all four of our *Almirante Brown*–class destroyers are lost. Where were these ships when they were sunk?"

"Just south of Cape Horn, sir. We had sent them to intercept and deter British and Chilean ships coming into Drake Passage from the Pacific."

"They were bunched close together? Close enough for one sub to attack? Wasn't that the Americans' mistake at Pearl Harbor? Bunching ships together? Making it easy for the Japanese to target them? And in our case, would it not have been better for these destroyers to have been separated? Miles apart?"

Admiral Blanco looked at Foreign Minister Domingo, then looked back at the president. "Mister President, I regret to say that I do not have a good answer to that question, and I agree that under these circumstances, the ships should not have been bunched so closely together."

"Admiral," Suarez said, "we cannot make any more tactical mistakes like this. I am the one who must notify the families. I am the one who must face the press as bodies are recovered. I am holding you responsible for any more mistakes. Foreign Minister?"

"Yes, Mister President?"

"The Venezuelans got us into this. Where is their Navy? They presented this as a joint military operation, and yet we seem to be bearing the brunt of the naval operations."

"Mister President, their ships are on the way. Their foreign minister asked me to assure you, sir, that they are committing naval forces and to remind you that their commandos are on the ground, in control of Camp Churchill, sitting on the oil fields that we will split when this is over."

Suarez shook his head. "Sounds like a lot of big talk to me. I want you to tell their foreign minister that if they don't get more involved in the naval war, and fast, I shall advocate a quick diplomatic solution."

"Yes, sir."

Suarez turned his attention back to Blanco. "You would agree, would you not, Admiral, that we cannot sustain any additional losses of this proportion."

"Mister President, I agree."

"What about this submarine that sank our ships?"

"Sir, in the seconds before they were struck by torpedoes, passive sonar on board both ARA *La Argentina* and ARA *Heroína* picked up the sound of a *Los Angeles*–class submarine. Both ships broadcast that report in the seconds before they sank."

"A *Los Angeles*–class submarine? You think the Americans did this?"

"We know the Americans' sympathies lie with Britain. But as you know, the Americans recently sold a *Los Angeles*–class submarine to Chile, renamed the CS *Miro*. We suspect Chile is behind this, and CS *Miro* launched this attack."

Suarez sat back down. "All right, Admiral. I want you to find this CS *Miro*, and I want you to sink it. Is that clear?"

"Yes, Mister President."

CS Miro
Drake Passage
80 miles southeast of Cape Horn
depth 400 feet

4:05 p.m. local time

Navigator, display our current position on the screen."
    "Aye, Captain."
Pete waited, and then the active navigational display popped onto
the screen.

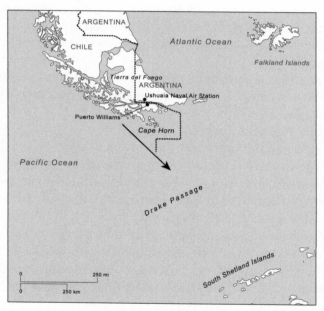

"Captain, the arrow shows course trajectory since our attack on the
enemy ships. The tip of the arrow is our current position. We're still
bearing course one-three-five degrees per your order, sir—due southeast—cutting a course headed to South Shetland Islands and the tip of
the Antarctic Peninsula. We are approaching 60 degrees west longitude,
58 degrees south latitude.

    "Here's another shot, drawn back, to give you a better picture of our
position, sir.

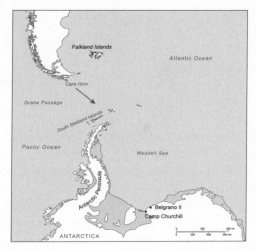

"As you can see, our current course will take us north of the tip of the Antarctic Peninsula and into the Weddell Sea. The British base camp, Camp Churchill, and the Argentinean base camp, Belgrano II, are located inland, near the Weddell Sea.

"Here is a third shot, a different perspective. You can see the Weddell Sea, Camp Churchill, and the Argentine base, Belgrano II. Right now, our trajectory will take us past the tip of the peninsula into the Weddell Sea, where we expect to find enemy naval traffic in support of the joint Venezuelan-Argentine ground forces."

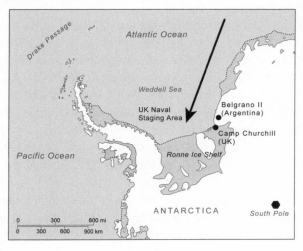

"Very well," Pete said. "I've seen enough. You can remove the navigational screens."

"Aye, sir."

"Steady as she goes."

"Steady as she goes. Aye, sir."

Pete stood up and stepped over to the duty station manned by the chief of the boat.

"Made a pot ten minutes ago, Captain. Fresh, strong, and black."

"You never cease to amaze, COB."

"Doing my job, Skipper," the chief of the boat said, "which is to take care of my captain and make him look good."

"That—you're the best at, Chief." Pete poured a stream of steaming coffee into a white mug that had the official US Navy emblem for the USS *City of Corpus Christi* on the front, and on the back, the silver oak leaf of a full commander in the US Navy and the title "Commanding Officer."

Pete sipped the battery-acid coffee that only a COB could brew. Just what the doctor ordered to restart his batteries after coming down from the adrenaline rush of a four-ship kill. He returned to the captain's chair.

The four-hour sonar silence since the big ship sinking, as the sub had passed southeast through waters of the Drake Passage, felt strange. Pete thought his submarine's passive sonar would have picked up some traffic as they crossed under active shipping lanes.

So far, nothing.

The public did not comprehend the enormity of the oceans, and even a narrow body of water like Drake Passage, with hundreds of miles of open water, could at times make finding another ship like looking for a needle in a haystack. During the Cold War, Russian submarines would camp outside Hampton Rhodes and San Diego and wait for a ship to leave port. Then they'd tail them all over the world. And if the sub lost track of the ship, the sub might never find it again.

The inactivity from the sonar, however, had given Pete time to think, and for better or worse, his thoughts had returned to her.

Why?

Why did she have this spell on him, even here, 1,500 miles away and 400 feet under some of the coldest and most dangerous waters in the world, in the midst of an exploding naval war?

What was it about her?

Whatever it was, he could not let his men know. For to be distracted by a woman in an atmosphere of combat, where correct or incorrect decision making made the difference between life and death, was a sign of weakness. Delilah brought down Samson, and David succumbed to Bathsheba, his grandmother had told him.

And Pete Miranda would not be weakened by some Delilah. Not even a red-hot Latin Chilean Delilah with nuclear-hot legs, a magnetic smile, and the ability to make him melt like wax under a candle flame. No woman, no matter how hot, no matter how attractive, no matter how seductive, would distract him from his mission or distract him from his work.

All this "get in touch with your feelings" garbage was for wusses masquerading as men who liked to go on stupid "get in touch with your feelings" talk shows that nonthinking, nonworking women spent their days lapping up.

He'd seen reruns of these "talk about your feelings" feminine sideshows like *The View* and *Oprah* and *Dr. Phil.*

No thanks. The World War II generation didn't talk like that, and that "talk about your feelings" stuff wasn't his cup of tea.

Never would be.

Besides. He'd tried marriage once. He'd gotten two beautiful children, but besides that, nothing but heartache.

Never again.

Besides, he-men kept their affection for women in the proper place.

Beep-beep-beep-beep-beep-beep-beep.

The collision alarm sounded.

Pete looked up. "What the—?"

"Captain! Inbound torpedo! One-eight-zero degrees. Range two hundred yards! Time to impact . . . thirty seconds!"

"Left full rudder! Launch countermeasures! Warn the crew! Brace for impact!"

"This is the XO! Brace for impact! Brace for impact!"

The explosion jolted the submarine like a Mack truck slamming into a brick wall, knocking Pete to the deck with a hard thud, sloshing hot coffee all over the deck. Others fell to the deck as lights flickered and warning bells sounded.

Pete tried standing up, but as the sub rolled hard to her left, he lost his balance and fell again. He reached up and grabbed the captain's chair and pulled himself back to his feet.

The control room went dark.

"Helmsman! Right full rudder!" Pete said. "Somebody get a flashlight! Let's see if we can get this baby stabilized."

"Working on it, Captain," a voice said from the dark.

The sub continued slowly rolling to the left. When the lights flicked back on, Pete hung on to the captain's chair to maintain balance. Lieutenant Curt Foster, having been knocked to his knees, struggled to regain his position at the helmsman's station.

A second later Foster pulled himself back into place, announced, "Right full rudder. Aye, Captain," and began to turn the submarine's steering wheel all the way back to the right. The *Miro* responded, making a slow turn back to the right. As she turned, she leveled out.

"Thank God." Pete picked up the 1-MC. "Control Room to all departments. This is the captain. I want damage reports. Now."

"Control. Engineering. Sir, all systems operational."

"Control. Sonar. We're banged up, but all is operational."

"Control. Weapons. All operational."

"Control. Radio Room. All systems operational."

"Control. Sick Bay. No reported injuries. At least not yet."

"It appears that the torpedo struck the countermeasures, sir," the sonar officer said. "We escaped with a near miss, and thank God we did."

"Very well," Pete said. "XO, sound general quarters."

"Aye, aye, Captain. General quarters! General quarters! General quarters! All hands to battle stations. All hands to battle stations."

"Control. Weapons," Pete said. " I want all tubes loaded and ready to fire. When we find this sucker, we're going to unload on him."

"Roger that, Skipper."

"Captain, all hands are at general quarters, sir," the XO reported. "All hands are at battle stations."

"Sir," the sonar officer said. "I've played back the acoustical tape of the inbound torp we picked up. We were only able to track it for thirty seconds or so. But for ten seconds or so before that, if you go back and listen to the tape, you can hear a faint diesel-electric motor. ARA *Santa Cruz*–class. You hear him for ten seconds on the tape, and then he's gone. Then, just the sound of the torp."

Pete stood and crossed his arms. "So we didn't get a read on him because he appeared just for a second and then vanished like a ghost." He sucked in his breath and thought. "How did this happen?"

No response.

Control room
Argentinean submarine ARA **San Juan**
Drake Passage
80 miles southeast of Cape Horn
depth 275 feet

4:12 p.m. local time

That was quite an explosion, Capitán," the executive officer said. "Not even the thermal layer could fully brunt its intensity. No one could have survived that blast. I compliment you on such an impressive maneuver, sir. Brilliant, in fact. Let me be the first to congratulate you for defeating the American captain! You are now undisputedly the world's greatest sub commander!"

Commander Carlos Almeyda nodded his head at the excited monologue oozing from the mouth of his exuberant executive officer.

"You continue to assume that the captain was American, XO."

"*Mi* capitán. We just attacked a *Los Angeles*–class submarine. The Americans may have turned the boat over to Chile this week, but there is no way that the Chileans could have trained a commander to take her to sea and display such deft war-fighting skills in so short a period of time."

The XO was right about one thing, Carlos decided. The skipper of the *LA*-class boat was surely American.

"You know, XO, as a student at the academy, I spent a semester studying abroad in America. I learned that the Americans have a saying. 'Don't count your chickens before they hatch.' All we know is that the torpedo we fired exploded.

"That torpedo could have exploded as a result of a direct strike on the American sub. If that is the case, then yes, I would agree with you that we have probably defeated the American captain.

"On the other hand, the torpedo could have exploded as a result of a collision with countermeasures fired by the American captain. If that is the case, then it is too early to tell what damage we have inflicted. Perhaps we sank him. Perhaps not. Perhaps we only wounded him. Perhaps not. All that depends on how quickly he got his boat away from the point of explosion."

"But, Capitán," the XO protested, "you maneuvered us in for a point-blank shot from the rear. It would have been virtually impossible for the American captain to have evaded that attack."

"My maneuvering was a combination of guts and blind luck," Almeyda said. "Sometimes there is little difference between the two. Besides, there's another American saying, 'Some cats have nine lives.'"

"We could always go down there and see if anything is left, Capitán."

"And suppose there *is* something down there? Suppose our torp missed? If the American captain is down there and he has survived, do you think he will not be watching and waiting, loaded and ready to fire if we descend again?"

"I see your point, Capitán."

"This captain we face is good. Very good. If he is still alive, he understands that being a great sub commander, hunting ships, like hunting puma in Santiago del Estero or wild boar in the forest of La Pampa, depends on the dual elements of patience and surprise.

"We have already used the element of surprise. Now we rely on patience. This captain that we face is like a puma. Fast. Intelligent. Deadly. If he is wounded and not yet dead, he is most dangerous. For the time being, we watch, wait, and see.

"Steady as she goes."

"Steady as she goes. Aye, Capitán."

CS Miro
Drake Passage
80 miles southeast of Cape Horn
depth 400 feet

4:15 p.m. local time

So how did this guy get in and get off this shot without us ever detecting him? And where is he now?"

Still no answer.

"Son of a gun!" Pete said.

"What, Skipper?"

"Sonar, where's the thermal layer above us?"

"Stand by, Skipper." The sonar officer punched the search query into his computer. "Three hundred fifty feet, sir."

"That's what he did!"

"I don't follow you, sir."

"Sonar, where's the next thermal below us?"

"Six-five-zero feet, sir."

"Diving Officer. Make our depth six hundred feet."

"Make my depth six-zero-zero. Aye, Captain."

"Sonar. Take that acoustics match of the ten seconds of the diesel-electric. Track it back three hours. See if you come up with anything."

"Aye, sir. Stand by." The sonar officer punched more numbers into the computer. "Wow!" His eyes widened. "Sir, he's been doing this every thirty minutes for the last four hours. Popping down below the layer for five to ten seconds and then popping back up. Just little bursts down below for short enough times so he's lost in the wash to the naked ear, and then back up above the thermal layer again."

Pete shook his head. "This guy is good. Really good. Somehow he got a bead on us, probably because he was nearby when we sank those destroyers. He uses the thermal blanket as a shield against our passive sonar, then every thirty minutes, he pops down under the thermal layer for five to ten seconds, long enough to get updated bearings on our speed and direction but not long enough for us to hear him in the wash, since he's trailing behind us.

"He closes the gap, and when he closes it enough for a point-blank shot, he pops down again and unloads a torp, hoping our sonar won't pick it up in time for an evasive maneuver. It almost worked. Brilliant."

"Do you think he'll try it again, Captain?"

"My guess is that he's still up there. But he won't venture back down here for a while. Right now, he's trying to figure out whether he sank us or not. If he sank us, he knows he's in good shape. But if he didn't sink us, he knows we'll be watching for him. A diesel-electric can beat an *LA*-class if it gets off the first shot and if that shot lands. But it becomes more problematic for him if we get into a shootout at the OK Corral.

"Besides, he took advantage of the fact that we were cutting a course just fifty feet below the thermal ceiling. He didn't have to pop down too far to get a bead on us. But now that we're diving down to six hundred, 250 feet below the layer, it will be harder for him to pop down here without us nabbing him." Pete thought some more. "The question isn't whether he's coming down here after us. The question is whether we're going up there after him."

"What are you thinking, Skipper?" the XO asked.

"I'm thinking about popping up above the thermal and giving this Argentinean cowboy a taste of his own medicine. Of course that's risky, depending on where we break the thermal. If we break in behind him, we've got him in our gun sights, and we can put a torp up his rear. But if we break the plane in front of him, then he gets another point-blank shot at us, and we could be toast. But know this: we're not here to let enemy submarines take potshots at us and get away with it."

Pete looked around the bridge.

"Skipper, depth is now six hundred feet," the diving officer said.

"Very well," Pete said. He looked at his men in the control room. "Gentlemen, are you ready to get back into the fight?"

"Ready, Skipper."

"Let's do this, sir."

"Let's give him a taste of his own medicine."

Pete looked at Commander Pedro Romero, the only Chilean officer on board and the man designated to become the first Chilean commanding officer of CS *Miro* after they returned to base. If they returned. "Commander Romero, you and I both know that technically, I'm designated as commanding officer for this mission. But this boat now belongs to your government, and you'll be taking the reins of command when we get back . . . if we get back.

"I want you to understand, sir, that we're about to execute a dangerous maneuver. When we pop up above that thermal, there will be a firefight, and that guy is good. One of two submarines is going to the bottom. I'd say there's a fifty-fifty chance that could be us, depending on where we pop up in relation to the Argentinean boat. So there's a chance this could be the first and last mission by CS *Miro*. I want you to understand the danger we're facing, and I'd appreciate your support."

The Chilean hesitated. "Would it matter one way or the other if I told you that the idea is crazy? And that, having accomplished four sinkings already, we should remain down here below the thermal layer, play it conservative, and ensure that the boat is returned safely to my country?"

Pete looked the Chilean in the eye, trying to gauge whether he was serious. "No, Commander, it would not matter if you said all that . . . or any of that. Because a great sub commander would rather fight and die than run and hide and live."

A smile broke across the Chilean's face. "I think you are a great sub commander, Captain Miranda. And I too would rather fight and die than run and hide and live." Romero extended his hand. "Besides, I know you have Chilean blood in you. I will always put my money on Chilean blood over Argentinean blood." The two men hugged, patting each other on the back.

"Good. Let's get to work," Pete said. "XO. On the 1-MC. I want to address the crew."

"Aye, Captain."

"Now hear this. This is the captain speaking. As you know, we took a sucker-punch in the gut from the Argentinean submarine *San Juan*. But, gentlemen, we're getting ready to punch back. Their captain is good. Very good. He's taken out four British ships and disabled their new supercarrier, the HMS *Queen Elizabeth*. He nearly took us out. This will be dangerous. But each and every one of us has volunteered for the submarine service of the United States Navy. And when we did, we volunteered for danger.

"Here's what we're going to do. We're going to ascend up to three-five-zero feet, breaking through the thermal lawyer above us. And when we break the thermal layer, we're gonna do something that captain won't be expecting. We're gonna light him up with active sonar. We'll know where he is, and he'll know where we are, instantly. And the fight will be on.

"One sub will live. One sub will die. Be ready, gentlemen. This is the captain."

Pete gave the microphone back to the XO and spoke to his officers in the control room. "All right, gentlemen. Remember the twin characteristics of a great hunter—patience and surprise. We're going to be patient for a few minutes. Make him think he's got us. And then it's game on, baby. Be prepared for battle."

Control room
Argentinean submarine ARA San Juan
Drake Passage
82 miles southeast of Cape Horn
depth 275 feet

4:32 p.m. local time

Commander Carlos Almeyda checked the chronometer. Twenty minutes had passed since he had attacked the *Los Angeles*–class boat.

In the silence of his control room, with his men sitting at their stations wearing sensitive headphones, monitoring the sound of every bubble and every fish and every whale that might pass within five miles of his submarine, Almeyda watched the green passive sonar screen.

Nothing.

For the first time, he entertained the thought that his executive officer was correct.

Perhaps he had defeated the American.

It was possible. Was it not?

The American had not returned to fight.

Yet something nagged at him.

The *Los Angeles*–class boat possessed superior technology and more firepower than the *San Juan* or any other boat Argentina owned or would own in the foreseeable future. Its acquisition by Chile shifted the balance of naval power in South America in favor of Argentina's most hated regional rival.

Perhaps his XO was right.

The improbable sometimes happens in warfare. David had defeated Goliath.

Still, Almeyda remained cautious. What would Capitán Gomez do? What would he say?

Alberto Gomez, his friend and mentor who died as commander of the *Santa Cruz*, was the dean of the Argentine submarine fleet. Yet in the last forty-eight hours, Almeyda had scored more kills than any other sub commander in the history of the Argentine Navy and accomplished far more than Commander Gomez ever had in his lifetime. Almeyda remained awed by the memory of his friend and pained by the freshness of his loss. He owed everything to the man who trained him and prepared him in every way for the victories he had achieved on this mission.

Through it all, he had discovered that he loved being a sub commander. This love of combat saturated his blood. He was born for this. But he would relinquish command of this mission to Gomez in a heartbeat if he could. That was how much he respected the man. He would dedicate the remainder of this mission, and indeed, the remainder of his career, to his beloved mentor.

"Sonar. Report," Almeyda said.

"Still nothing, Capitán. All is quiet."

"Stay alert, Sonar. We cannot let our guard down. Not yet. Not if there is any chance that the American captain is still alive. If he comes, he will try to slip up passively."

"*Si*, Capitán."

"What are your thoughts, Capitán?" the XO asked. "Are you beginning to believe that we have defeated the American captain?"

"I would like to believe, XO, but I cannot afford to believe. Perhaps you should ask me this question in an hour."

The XO smiled. "With respect, *mi* capitán, I suspect that even if I ask you this an hour from now, or in two, three, or even four hours, your answer will remain the same."

"Or perhaps in twenty-four hours?" Almeyda smiled. "You learn quickly, XO."

"Thank you, sir. But at some point, do we slip below the thermal layer again to look for him?"

"Eventually," Almeyda said. "If he pops up, it will be quietly, using passive sonar to try to catch us asleep so he can get off a shot before we can react. Like we did to him. And if we go down, we will go quietly to hide our presence for as long as possible. The American nuclear boat can dive to a test depth of 1,600 feet, with a crush depth of 2,400 feet. We, on the other hand, can dive to only 700 feet, with a crush depth of 890 feet.

"The American can dive twice as deep as we can. If he is alive, he would want us to chase him down deeper, where he has an advantage. He can duck down below our maximum crush depth, where we cannot reach him, and then pop up and take shots at us.

"We prefer to fight at shallower depths, above the first thermal layer, thus neutralizing his crush depth advantage. Certainly I would chase him down there under the right circumstances, but I prefer to fight where we have the advantage."

"Capitán, you sound as if you expect to fight this American captain again."

Almeyda looked at his second in command. "XO, my mind tells me that every minute that passes increases the likelihood that we'll never see him again. But my gut tells me that soon we shall be in a fight for our lives."

CS Miro
Drake Passage
83 miles southeast of Cape Horn, Chile
depth 600 feet

4:40 p.m. local time

The pounding inside his chest told him. The electrical surge in his veins screamed out.

For a great warrior, like a great hunter, the clock, the time, the weather . . . all these things were of secondary importance. Hunting was about instinct. That's why the greatest hunters drank the blood of their first kill. At the end of the day, it was about the gut.

Around the control room, men bore stern looks on their faces, manning their duty stations with marked determination and professionalism.

The XO looked at Pete and, without saying a word, gave him a confident thumbs-up.

"Diving Officer. Make your depth three hundred feet."

"Make my depth three-zero-zero feet. Aye, Captain."

Pete watched as the depth meter reflected the sub's rise through the water.

580 feet . . .

500 feet . . .

Pete took the 1-MC.

"This is the captain speaking. We're beginning our ascent and rising into attack position. Once we break through the thermal, in another

200 feet, we're gonna light him up with active sonar. Expect the torps to start flying. Stand by and be ready. This is the captain."

450 feet . . .

422 feet . . .

397 feet . . .

"Approaching the thermal layer, Captain."

"Prepare to initiate active sonar on my command."

362 feet . . .

340 feet . . .

328 feet . . .

310 feet . . .

300 feet . . .

"Captain, the sub has reached target depth of three hundred feet."

"Very well! Sonar! Light 'em up!"

"Initiate active sonar! Aye, Captain!"

The first *ping* shot through the water in a powerful, deafening, high-energy burst.

Two seconds later, the second *ping* followed the first.

"Captain. Contact! Enemy sub's three hundred yards to our rear!"

"Evasive maneuvers! Right full rudder! All ahead full!"

Control room
Argentinean submarine ARA San Juan
Drake Passage
82 miles southeast of Cape Horn, Chile
depth 275 feet

4:32 p.m. local time

Capitán!" the sonar officer shouted as the third earsplitting *ping* from the enemy submarine knifed its way through the *San Juan*. "The American's gone active sonar. Enemy submarine is three hundred yards dead ahead of us, sir."

Almeyda stood in front of the captain's chair, stunned that the American would be so brazenly bold. Then instinct kicked in. "Fire torps one and two! Now!"

"Fire torps one and two! Aye, Capitán!"

"Range to target?"

"Range to target . . . two hundred fifty yards, sir!"

CS Miro
Drake Passage
83 miles southeast of Cape Horn, Chile
depth 300 feet

4:33 p.m. local time

Captain! Two torps in the water! Two hundred yards and closing on our tail, sir!"

"Stand by to launch countermeasures! Stand by for emergency dive."

"Stand by. Aye, sir!"

"Range now one-five-zero yards and closing, sir!"

"Hang a few more seconds," Pete said.

"Range one hundred yards, sir!"

"Launch countermeasures!"

"Launch countermeasures! Aye!"

A *puff* sound . . . like the release of pressurized air pockets.

"Countermeasures launched! Range fifty yards!"

"Emergency dive!"

"Emergency dive! Aye, Captain!"

"Hang on, gentlemen!"

Like a roller-coaster car dropping from the highest peak of a towering track, *Miro*'s bulb nose dipped in response to the emergency dive maneuver, dropping her quickly through the water.

The explosion sent shock waves through the boat. But this explosion was not as close as the near miss that nearly took out the *Miro* forty minutes ago.

Hanging tight to the captain's chair to avoid falling again, Pete watched the depth gauge dropping.

425 feet . . .

450 feet . . .

"Revert to passive sonar. Level at five hundred."

"Revert to passive. Level at five hundred."

A second later, the boat had again leveled out, once again below the thermal layer, its active sonar turned off.

"Everybody okay?"

"Yes, sir."

"You bet, Skipper."

"Good. Because we're going back up after him."

Silence.

"Helmsman."

"Aye, Captain."

"I want you to turn us around, mark your point on GPS, and be prepared to bring us up through the thermal at a point four hundred yards behind our last break point. Unless he's turned around, that should bring us in behind him this time. And even if he has turned around, I've got no problem facing him head-on. Advise me when we reach the ascension point."

"Aye, Skipper. Executing turn in the water now, sir."

"Weapons Officer."

"Aye, Captain."

"This cat has gotten three torps off against us so far, and we haven't lit him up once except with active sonar. I want four torps ready to fire in rapid succession. We're gonna light him up this time, come hell or high water. Ya got that, Lieutenant?"

"Got it, sir."

They say that instinct makes a man think of family in the moments before his death, and when those thoughts begin pouring in a rush, a man can know that death is at the door.

As the boat turned, headed for a final showdown with a great warrior whose skills had proved formidable, Pete could not shake the thoughts about his teenage girls, Kelsey and Gracie. One month ago, he was headed back to Dallas to retire, to reengage in the family business, and his most important task, he knew, was to make up for lost time as a daddy to his two blond-haired, blue-eyed bundles of joy.

He should have learned. Any "easy assignment" in the Navy usually proved to be the hardest.

Now, at the bottom of the world, five hundred feet under the surface of the sea, he faced death in one of the coldest and darkest spots on the planet, unable to make up for that lost time as a daddy.

"Captain, we've reached the ascension point."

"Very well. Set course one-three-five degrees."

"Set course one-three-five degrees. Aye, Captain."

Miro made a silent turn until she was back on the same course to the southeast as before the attack.

"Diving Officer, make your depth three hundred feet. Prepare to go active sonar on my command. Prepare to fire on my command."

"Make my depth three hundred, aye, sir."

Pete watched as the sub rose in the water.

460 feet . . .

412 feet . . .

392 feet . . .

"Approaching the thermal layer, Skipper."

"Prepare to initiate active sonar."

360 feet . . .

328 feet . . .

311 feet . . .

300 feet . . .

"Captain, we've reached target depth."

"Sonar! Light 'em up!"

"Initiate active sonar! Aye, Captain!"

The first *ping* shot through the water, followed quickly by the second.

"Skipper, enemy sub's two hundred yards out front of us!"

"Fire torp one! Fire torp two!"

"Firing torps one and two!"

"Fire torp three!"

"Firing torp three. Aye, Captain."

"Range to target, fifty yards and closing!"

"Sir, he's attempting evasive maneuvers!"

"I'm not surprised."

"Sir, we have an explosion! Sir, we have a second explosion!"

A moment passed.

"Sir, he's dived down below the thermal layer!"

Another moment passed.

"The question is," Pete said, "whether he's dived under the thermal layer or whether he's sunk under the thermal layer."

"Sir, what are we going to do?"

"I don't want him popping up on our tail and taking another pot-shot at us. We're going down after him." A pause. "WEPS. I want three more torps on the racks, ready to fire."

"Aye, Captain."

"Diving Officer, make your depth five hundred feet. Passive sonar until destination depth. Then active sonar at destination depth. Be ready to fire. If he wants to play ball under the thermal, I'm game."

"Make my depth five-zero-zero. Aye, sir."

Pete watched as the sub again began descending through the water. His gut told him one thing, but he had to be sure.

300 feet . . .

332 feet . . .

"Approaching thermal, sir."

380 feet . . .

420 feet . . .

480 feet . . .

"Sub is at destination depth, sir. Five hundred feet."

"Very well. Light him up. Active sonar."

"Active sonar. Aye, Skipper."

Ping . . .

Ping . . .

Ping . . .

Ping . . .

"Captain. Active sonar reveals enemy sub—"

A pause . . . "Enemy sub has broken in half, sir."

Cheers erupted on the bridge.

"No! Quiet!" Pete motioned for silence. "Switch to passive sonar. Put it on the loudspeaker."

"Passive sonar. Aye, sir."

At first the sloshing sound of bubbles. Then, amplified throughout the control room, the long, eerie, grinding sound of metal on metal as increased water pressure began to twist and crush steel and other metal components that were no longer pressurized.

"On the 1-MC, XO."

"Aye, sir."

Pete took the shipwide microphone. "Now hear this. This is the captain speaking. Both active and passive sonar have verified that the enemy sub has been destroyed."

Cheering erupted throughout the sub.

"Silence!" Pete demanded.

The cheering stopped.

"There will be no cheering, no reveling, no applause for what we have done. For what we have done is our duty. We have defeated a worthy opponent and taken the life of a great warrior who, if he had an extra second or two on his side, would have killed us first. He battled gallantly, commanding a boat that is inferior to ours.

"There is no rejoicing at the death of a warrior. Only by the grace of God are we still alive, and only by his grace did we have weapons of war that were superior to the weapons of the enemy.

"Join me in a moment of silence and remembrance."

More sounds of grinding, whining metal over passive sonar—the death sounds of a sub falling to its watery grave.

"That is all. This is the captain."

CHAPTER 32

Antarctica
between Belgrano II base camp
and Halley Research Station
near the coast of Weddell Sea

5:00 p.m. local time

The sonorous roar of the snowmobile pack, each with a slightly different pitch, almost blended together over time as a mechanical musical chorus. In a strange way, the cacophonous chorus produced a near-tranquilizing effect that, if not for the cold wind whipping off the Weddell Sea, could nearly lull a man to sleep.

Two hundred miles of snow, ice, and howling wind separated the Belgrano II camp, where Austin Rivers and his ragtag group of British engineers had made their escape four hours ago, and the British Halley Research Station, where they hoped to be greeted with open arms by fellow countrymen.

Halfway between the two camps, a hundred miles either way from civilization, if one could call an isolated base camp at the frozen bottom of the world part of the civilized world, Austin Rivers' focus was on survival.

They had stopped to refuel minutes ago and to take a break and eat. As Rivers took a final bite out of a piece of awful beef jerky packed in an MRE, the weather started breaking.

The long trek across the snow triggered thoughts of men of the past. Antarctica had stories of men who survived expeditions across hundreds of miles of snow and ice in the world's harshest climate, and stories of many more men who died battling the elements.

For the great British explorer and Royal Naval Officer Robert Scott, who set out for the South Pole in 1911, fate and the Antarctic weather had not been kind. Scott started his trek in the Antarctic spring and summer months, with twenty-four hours of sunlight for the entire trip.

Early in the trip Scott's ponies died, forcing the members of the expedition to pull their own sleds. The team reached the South Pole on January 18, 1912, only to find Roald Amundsen's flag. Exhausted and low on food, Scott's team began the long trip home.

That trip back from the South Pole turned deadly. As winter approached, Scott confronted terrible blizzards—like the blizzard Rivers and his crew had battled. Starvation and frostbite took their toll. Scott wrote in his journal, "Amputation is the least I can hope for." Scott and his companions were found eight months later, frozen to death.

Yet even in death, the legend of Robert Scott, a Royal Navy officer, had inspired Rivers to volunteer for duty here when opportunity knocked.

Ironically, though harsh blizzard weather killed Scott, Rivers hoped that blizzard conditions would continue. With working GPS devices and snowmobiles and excellent thermal clothing, Rivers and his men could proceed through the weather, maintaining their course for Halley Station.

For Rivers and his men, a weather change for the better posed a dangerous opening in a curtain through which enemy helicopters could fly. Perhaps he should order Bach to pray for continued blizzard conditions.

Ten minutes later, the snow stopped.

Rivers recalculated the situation. He could stay put. Perhaps have his men dig holes in the snow and try to hide from aircraft. That would pose a calculated risk. What if the weather stayed clear for three or four days? That would give Argentina more time to get more aircraft in the sky. And what would they do with their snowmobiles? And their sleds? And their gas tanks? And everything else? Bury them?

In four hours they could reach Halley Station. Best not to wait. Best to keep moving and hope to reach Halley before anyone discovered them.

"Cut your headlights and move out!" he commanded.

The men cranked their snowmobiles, and when all eight were running, Rivers gripped the throttle on his and led the pack back out across a vast desert of ice, now under a sky turned gray with clouds high enough for fixed- and rotary-wing aircraft to operate beneath them.

Rivers held tight to the handlebars, steering the course laid out by the GPS. Just a few more hours. If they could avoid detection, just a few more hours.

The next thirty minutes proved uneventful. The weather continued to clear.

Rivers didn't notice anything wrong until out of the corner of his eye, he saw Dunn waving his hand and pointing to the horizon off to the left. Rivers raised his hands to halt the snowmobiles for a better look.

Three helicopters were flying side by side, about five hundred feet above the ground, each with black smoke trailing in the distance.

The choppers were flying straight in toward their position.

El Libro y la Taza
Santiago, Chile

5:01 p.m. local time

Shelley took Meg's hand and glanced over at Little Aussie playing at the next table with his iPod, earphones covering his ears. She lowered her voice.

"And when did you last have this dream?"

"Last night," Meg said. "It's the same dream. The honor guard bringing his body in a flag-draped casket at Northolt RAF base. I hoped the dream would stop when you and Aussie got here"—Meg bit her lip, trying to stop it from trembling—"but last night it seemed more real than ever. Something bad is about to happen. I can feel it." The tears welled up again.

"Come here." Shelley took Meg into her arms. "I don't understand what these dreams mean. But someone told me a couple of days ago that in him, there is hope for the future."

Meg pulled back with a curious look. "In him? Who is him?"

"I think she was referring to God," Shelley said.

"I could use some hope right now, Shelley. From God or from somebody."

Shelley held her arms out and embraced her friend again. Meg's body trembled like someone with an uncontrollable case of shivers. Shelley now knew why she had come to Chile—to provide comfort to Meg in the event of Austin's death.

Still, as she held her friend, hoping that love and comfort would flow from her body to Meg's, she could not help but wonder: Who will bring me comfort when news comes of Bob's death?

She had no answer, and the answer to that question did not matter.

Antarctica
between Belgrano II base camp
and Halley Research Station
near the coast of Weddell Sea

5:05 p.m. local time

The thunderous roar of helicopter gunships approaching rapidly from the gray skies to the left began to overpower the rumbling chorus of snowmobile engines speeding across the expansive field of ice.

The lead helicopter looked like a Sikorsky SH-3 Sea King, the type flown by the Royal Navy. Rivers looked over at Captain Dunn and exchanged a smile and a thumbs-up.

When the chopper swung out in front of the moving snowmobiles, Rivers' hope for rescue vanished. Painted on the fuselage of one of the lead choppers he saw the light blue flag of the Argentine Republic.

They hovered in the sky over the snowmobiles like giant angry locusts.

"Halt or you will be fired upon!" The voice boomed in English over the sound of the engines. When Rivers did not stop, the *crack-crack-crack-crack-crack* of machine-gun fire from one of the other gunships sprayed bullets along a straight line in the snow ahead of the moving snowmobiles.

Snow and ice sprayed up in cloud bursts, an effective intimidation tactic, announcing with an iron fist that superior firepower had arrived from the skies. The small arms they had taken from Belgrano were no match for a single fifty-caliber machine gun in one of those gunships.

If only he had a handheld Stinger antiaircraft missile. But "if onlys," at this point, would do them no good.

Rivers gave the halt signal with his hand, and all the snowmobiles stopped.

"Cut your engines!" the voice boomed from above.

Rivers turned and gave his men the throat-slash signal, then shut off the engine on his snowmobile.

"Get off the snowmobiles with your hands up or you will be shot."

Rivers nodded to his men and put his hands in the air.

"Move in a group over to the right."

Rivers walked over to the right of the snowmobiles, followed by Dunn, followed by Bach and then the others. As the British formed a circle of surrender to the right of the now-silent snowmobiles, one of the three gunships, a Eurocopter AS332 Super Puma, began to descend for landing.

Rivers recognized the Super Puma, which he had flown in many times. Unlike the Sea King, which carried only two pilots and three passengers, the Super Puma carried up to twenty-four passengers and was used for troop movements.

"Maintain your positions until the helicopter lands! When it lands, you will obey the orders of the officers on the ground who will be taking you into custody of the Republic of the Argentine."

The *thwack-thwack-thwack* of the landing chopper's rotary blade grew louder as it touched down a hundred yards away. The gunship's bay doors opened. Rifle-bearing soldiers, wearing thermal battle-clad fatigues with insulated face masks and helmets, jumped out of the chopper.

Four of them rushed over with guns pointed at the British, quickly surrounding them but saying nothing.

Four others jogged to the snowmobiles, two attending to Montes and two attending to Sosa.

"I am in command here!" Montes shouted the second the soldiers had freed him and gotten him on his feet. "These men are murderers and are enemies of the Argentine Republic!" He pointed his fingers at the group as he marched across the snow, accompanied by two soldiers.

The other two soldiers had gotten Sosa on his feet, and they too were walking back toward the group.

"That man is a murderer!" Montes pointed at Rivers. "Lieutenant, I order you to take him aside and shoot him now!"

"I am sorry, *mi* capitán, but our orders are to transport the prisoners to sea."

"To sea? What do you mean to sea?" Montes fumed. "I am in command. I am Capitán José Montes, Comando de Aviación Naval Argentina. I am commander of the Belgrano II base camp. These are my prisoners! They are under my authority and my command and my jurisdiction! Now you will execute the one I have ordered executed, and you will fly the others back to my base, where they will stand trial on multiple charges before they too are executed!"

The Argentinean lieutenant hesitated, as if uncertain of how to handle Montes' forceful demands. "I am sorry, *mi* capitán. Our orders are to transport all the prisoners to the transport ship ARA *Hercules*, and from there the prisoners will be transported to the Argentine mainland to be turned over to military authorities. Those are our orders. That is all I know."

"Lieutenant, I demand that you fly me to my command at once. We are at war. And I can assure you that our nation needs me in command at my post at this crucial time!"

"I would be pleased to accommodate your request, sir—"

"My request!" Montes shouted. "Lieutenant, I am not requesting anything. I am ordering you, as an inferior-ranking officer, to transport me back to Belgrano II at once."

"I am sorry, Capitán, but we must follow the orders of the officers over us in our direct chain of command. And with respect, sir, you are not in our chain of command."

Montes' face reddened. Veins bulged in his temples. "You can be assured, Lieutenant, that I will be filing a report on this situation upon my return to high command headquarters and will report you for insubordination."

"I understand, Capitán. But I urge you to get aboard the helicopter. If you do not, sir, you will be left out here all alone. The pilot would be honored to have you sit in the cockpit for the flight out to the ship."

Montes huffed and grumbled under his breath as he walked to the chopper. "I'll have you court-martialed, Lieutenant!" Montes stepped into the helicopter.

"Are you okay?" The Argentinean lieutenant directed this question to Sosa, who was being escorted by two Argentine soldiers.

"Yes, I am fine," Sosa said.

"What happened?"

"There was a prisoner insurrection at the camp. Somehow the prisoners confiscated guns and took me and the capitán hostage."

"How did they manage to get guns?"

"That is uncertain. A security lapse, I suppose. I'm an intel officer. I have nothing to do with security."

"Well, our orders are to transfer everyone to the *Hercules*, which is waiting offshore. The ship will set course for Buenos Aires, where, as I understand it, a court of inquiry will be held concerning the security breach at the camp, with a focus on the capitán's leadership in the affair. Now if you would please get into the chopper, we must get moving."

"Very well." Sosa saluted his rescuer.

The lieutenant turned away from Sosa. "Which of you is Leftenant Austin Rivers?"

"I am Rivers."

"And you are the leader of this group?"

Rivers studied the officer's face. In it, he saw neither evil nor vengeance. Only an officer carrying out his duties. "I suppose that leadership, like beauty, is in the eye of the beholder. All these men but one are civilians. They are not in my chain of command nor anyone's chain of command, to my knowledge. They report to their employer."

"And their employer is one of the largest petroleum companies in the world, whose headquarters happens to be in London?"

"That I cannot comment on," Rivers said.

"I must say that your reputation precedes you, Leftenant."

Rivers did not respond.

"What happened, Leftenant? How did you get the weapons to orchestrate your great escape?"

Rivers hesitated. "I have already given you more information than the Geneva Accords require."

"Fair enough," the lieutenant said. He turned away, then turned back. "As you know, Leftenant, we are taking you and your men to an Argentinean naval vessel, the ARA *Hercules*. In my judgment, there is no need for more bloodshed. Can I trust that you and your men will do nothing stupid that will lead to that?"

"I suppose that depends," Rivers said.

A raised eyebrow. "Oh really? And what does it depend on?"

"It depends on whether you and your men treat these men humanely. If you or your men start anything like summary executions, like your Capitán Montes is guilty of, then no, I cannot and will not promise cooperation."

"Step over here with me." The officer motioned for Rivers to join him off to the side. "Off the record, we have received reports from Lieutenant Colonel Sanchez, who has already reported the alleged incident of which you are speaking. Others have corroborated the report. These allegations will be investigated by a full court of inquiry in Buenos Aries. If the incident is true, I can assure you that this does not represent the conduct or standards of the Argentine Republic, and it will be dealt with. I can also assure you that under my watch, your men will be treated humanely and in accordance with the Geneva Accords. You have my word as an officer."

Rivers looked into the man's eyes. "As long as these civilians are treated humanely, then you have our cooperation, supported by my word as an officer."

The lieutenant nodded. "Excellent. Then the first thing we must do, as a matter of routine, is to cuff you and your men for the flight to the ship. The handcuffs will be removed after our arrival on board the *Hercules*. You promised your cooperation. I would like to start with you."

"Very well," Rivers said. "I gave my word as an officer." He held his hands out.

"We are required to cuff from the back, Leftenant."

Rivers turned around. "Have at it, Lieutenant."

Click.

Click.

"Thank you, Leftenant."

"My pleasure."

"By the way, Leftenant, my name is Nuñez. Alberto Nuñez. Navy of the Argentine Republic."

"A pleasure to meet you, Lieutenant Nuñez."

CHAPTER 33

As he quickstepped down the corridor toward his office, surrounded by aides and guards, President Suarez fumed about having been pulled from his early dinner with the ambassador from the Republic of Lithuania. They had been discussing Lithuania's decision to close its embassy in Buenos Aires to pour more resources into Brazil and a prospective state visit by Suarez to Vilnius. Being snatched from the meeting would perpetuate the Lithuanians' perception that Argentina did not accord them proper respect.

When Suarez walked into his office and saw Admiral Victor Blanco and Domingo Ramos, the Argentinean foreign minister, he forgot all about Lithuania and its ambassador.

"I have a feeling you have not called me out of my meeting with the Lithuanians to bring me good news."

Admiral Blanco said, "Mister President, I am concerned that we may have lost the *San Juan*."

Suarez sat down at his desk, half stunned. "What do you mean you are concerned that we may have lost the *San Juan*?"

"Mister President, *San Juan* was scheduled to float a communications buoy at 5:00 p.m. local time for a daily status report and to receive

325

new orders. We received no communications at the designated time. If, for operational reasons, such as engagement in combat, the sub cannot broadcast at the appointed time, then the capitán is required to broadcast at thirty-minute intervals after that until communication is established. The next scheduled broadcast would have been at 5:30. And then again at 6:00 p.m. Sir, she has missed three mandatory broadcast periods. Our protocol calls for a declaration that the sub is missing after the third missed mandatory broadcast period."

"Is it possible that she is having broadcast problems?"

"Possible but unlikely, sir," Blanco said. "The sub has a primary transmitter and two backups. It's highly unlikely that all three transmitters are out."

"I had a bad feeling about this the last time we talked," Suarez said. "We're down to one sub? Is that correct?"

"Yes, sir. ARA *Salta* is the only sub we have left. She just entered Drake Passage."

Suarez leaned back in his chair. "What about the Venezuelan ships we were promised?"

"We expect six Venezuelan surface ships and one sub to enter the passage within four hours."

"Within four hours? Are you telling me no Venezuelan ships are there yet?"

"Not yet, sir. But four Russian frigates entered the passage from the Pacific side. The Russians have offered antisubmarine warfare assistance against the sub that has caused all the damage to our fleet, sir."

Suarez slammed his desk. "That's nice of the Russians, but I'm not going to lose my last submarine. Not until Venezuela contributes more. Foreign Minister Domingo. Send a communiqué to Caracas. Remind them that they got us into this and promised military assistance. Tell them that we expect them to contribute to the replacement of the two subs we've lost. They're OPEC members. They can afford it."

"Yes, sir."

"Admiral, where are our ships currently located?"

"If you could give me a second, sir, I can pull a regional map up on the laptop to demonstrate general locations of our naval forces."

"Very well."

Blanco opened his laptop and hit several keys.

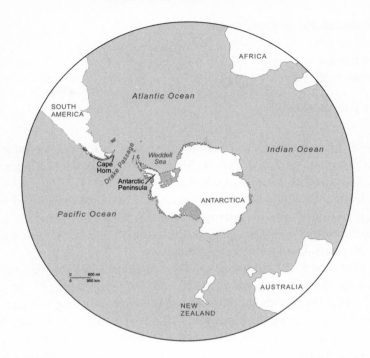

"As you can see here, Mister President, most of our surface combatants and subs have been moved into Drake Passage to deter the attempt by Britain and Chile to support the joint oil-drilling expedition that started all this.

"We also have naval forces here, in the Weddell Sea, off the Antarctic Peninsula, to support our base camp at Belgrano II and to further check the British attempts to recapture their base at Camp Churchill, which is now controlled by our Venezuelan allies. We've moved the ARA *Hercules* into the Weddell Sea to pick up some British prisoners who escaped from Belgrano II and to pick up the former commander of the Belgrano II base camp, who, as you know, has been accused by his second in command of war crimes."

Suarez nodded and studied the map. "Admiral Blanco, I want you to pull the ARA *Salta* out of Drake Passage. You can leave the other ships in the area for the time being, but keep me posted on an hourly basis until further notice."

"Yes, Mister President."

Argentinean AS332 Super Puma
"Eurocopter"
Weddell Sea
altitude 1,000 feet

6:20 p.m. local time

From his position in the webbed jump seat inside the Argentinean helicopter, Leftenant Austin Rivers turned and looked over his shoulder and out the nearest window.

Even with handcuffs clasping his hands behind his back and even when crammed into an enemy helicopter, the sight of the sea from above some of the coldest waters in the world brought a jolt to his veins.

Moments later, a ship came into view.

From the air, the ship had the familiar shape of a British destroyer. The Argentinean naval vessel known as ARA *Hercules*, built in Britain by the Vickers Shipbuilding Company, had the same hull design of a British Type 42 guided-missile destroyer. Britain sold the ship to Argentina during a rare period of thawed relations between the countries.

How ironic that the Argentineans would transport British prisoners on a ship they had purchased from Britain, a ship identical in hull design to the ship that represented one of the most devastating losses in the modern history of the Royal Navy—the Royal Navy destroyer *Sheffield*, set ablaze and sunk by Argentinean Exocet missiles in the Falklands War with Britain fought over a generation ago.

Rivers looked out as the chopper came to a hover high over the helo landing pad of the ship's fantail.

"Okay, listen up, gentlemen." This was Lieutenant Nuñez. "The pilot is about to land the chopper on the ship. When he does, we will lead you out by twos, under guard, into the ship's superstructure. You will be taken down to the ship's brig, where we will secure you until we can process paperwork to ensure that you are accounted for under the Geneva Accords.

"After that, you will be uncuffed, and I will arrange a rotation schedule so that you can come up on deck in shifts, two or three at a time, under armed guard. I've given my word to the leftenant that you will be treated humanely, and I intend to keep my word."

"You are being too soft on these animals!" Montes snarled. "I intend to include this in my report as well!"

"If you can be patient with us a bit longer, we will work to make your voyage to Buenos Aires as comfortable as possible."

The helicopter began descending toward the ship.

Montes snarled. "Never have I seen such softness from an officer in an atmosphere of combat."

Rivers watched Nuñez, who made no eye contact with Montes, nor did he respond, nor did his facial expression change.

"I shall see to it that you are prosecuted for rendering aid to the enemy."

A bump. Then another bump. Rivers looked around.

The Super Puma had touched down on the ship. The cargo bay opened and with it entered a bluster of cold salty sea air. "*Mi* capitán." Nuñez looked at Montes. "The commanding officer of this ship is Capitán Silva. Perhaps you wish to leave the helicopter first and head up to the bridge and begin the process of reporting my actions up through the chain of command. As a naval commander yourself, I am sure you will be able to find your way to the bridge."

Nuñez then looked at Rivers. "Leftenant, please lead the way."

Rivers stepped out onto the steel helo pad into whipping winds and dull sunlight.

A sailor, armed with a pistol in holster, took Rivers by the arm. "This way, Leftenant."

Dunn stepped out next, followed by Bach and the rest, each accompanied by armed sailors. They stepped into the steel superstructure and were led into the tight-quartered helicopter hangar bay, where they walked past a gray Sea King chopper moored in the hangar.

They then stepped into a large black steel freight elevator in front of the nose of the Sea King, all ten of them plus four security guards.

The elevator dropped down one deck, where they were led down a long passageway.

The ship's brig consisted of three steel-barred jail cells, each with a single open toilet in the back.

Rivers and Dunn were directed into the first cell, the door locking closed with a loud *clang*.

The rest were locked in two groups in the other two cells.

"Well, Leftenant," Dunn said, "handcuffed and locked inside a small prison cell on a ship. Apparently they don't want us to go anywhere."

"Or they don't want us to take over their bloody ship."

"Hope they come to remove these cuffs and get us out of these thermals. Well, look on the bright side, sir. At least it's warm in here."

"Let's hope it doesn't get too bloody hot in here."

CS Miro
Weddell Sea
depth 100 feet

6:40 p.m. local time

C aptain! I have contact. Single screw. Bearing zero-one-zero degrees. Speed twelve knots. Acoustical computers indicate probability of Type 42 *Sheffield*-class destroyer."

"*Sheffield* class?" Pete said. "I thought the Brits retired all those. We're talking Cold War vintage. And as I recall, Argentina is using *Almirante Brown*–class destroyers now."

"Seems right, Skipper," the XO said.

"Periscope depth. Up scope."

"Periscope depth. Up scope. Aye, Captain."

"XO, while we're approaching periscope depth, run a database search on any *Sheffield*-class ships that may still be active."

"Aye, Captain."

Bridge
ARA Hercules
Weddell Sea

6:42 p.m. local time

L ieutenant Alberto Nuñez, in regular winter uniform after having removed his Antarctic thermal gear, had been summoned to the ship's bridge by his commanding officer. He stood at parade rest as the two senior naval officers argued.

"Capitán, I know that you are commanding officer of this ship, but as a fellow senior officer in the Navy of the Argentine, having been a ship commander myself, I insist that you arrest this officer." Montes pointed his finger at Nuñez.

"On what grounds, Capitán? He has executed his orders to fly into Antarctica, to capture British prisoners who had escaped from your camp, and to bring them . . . and you . . . back to this ship. That he has done," the ship's commanding officer, Capitán Roberto Silva, said.

"To the contrary, Capitán," Montes said, "he has rendered aid to the enemy. He has embarrassed and humiliated a senior officer of the Argentine military in the presence of enemy captives, thus not only embarrassing our nation but undermining good order and discipline in the process."

"And how else has he rendered aid? By not shooting one of the prisoners in the head for no apparent reason?"

"I resent that comment, Capitán! I can assure that any action I have taken in my role as base commander was for good reason and is legally justifiable under the laws of war." Montes snorted to show his disgust.

"Your second in command, Lieutenant Colonel Sanchez, disagrees with that. Based on his report, I would say that you, Capitán, are fortunate that I have not arrested you and thrown you in the brig pending our arrival in Buenos Aires."

"Sanchez is a soft, power-hungry traitor to his country! A backstabbing liar seeking revenge because I replaced him as base commander because of his own ineffectiveness and inability to lead!" Montes' face reddened. Veins bulged on his neck. "Now, with respect, Capitán, if you are not going to arrest this man"—he pointed at Nuñez—"then I insist upon my right to file a report!"

Ship's brig
ARA Hercules
Weddell Sea

6:44 p.m. local time

Where is our newfound chum, Mister Nuñez?" Dunn asked. "He promised he would remove these handcuffs as soon as he finished some paperwork. Seems like a jolly long time to complete paperwork."

"It is getting uncomfortable," Rivers said. "And with these cuffs behind the back, awfully hard to take a leak. I don't know about you, but I'm feeling the urge rather vigorously."

"I'm beginning to wonder if we can trust this guy," Dunn said.

"I hope you're wrong, Dunn," Rivers said. "But I'm afraid you're right."

CS Miro
Weddell Sea
depth 40 feet

6:45 p.m. local time

W e're at periscope depth, Captain. Scope's up, sir."

"Very well," Pete said. He grabbed the handlebars alongside the periscope column and put his eyes against the eyepiece.

Against fading pale blue skies and choppy grayish seas, the long formidable image of a naval destroyer appeared in the viewfinder, cutting through the water from left to right.

From his studies of naval ship design in the late twentieth and early twenty-first centuries, Pete recognized the ship as a Type 42 destroyer hull, *Sheffield* class.

But the light blue flag, flying from the back, revealed that she was anything but British.

"Range to target?"

"Range to target, five hundred yards, Captain."

"XO, how's that data check? I want a rundown on any *Sheffield*-class destroyers Argentina has in its fleet."

"Skipper, data check's in. The last *Sheffield*-class destroyer operated by the Royal Navy was HMS *Edinburgh*, which the Brits decommissioned in 2013. The Argentinian Navy bought several of these destroyers a number of years ago. They have decommissioned all but one, the ARA *Hercules*, which they converted into a multipurpose transport ship capable of carrying two helicopters.

"Captain, if you're going to do what I think you're going to do, you're about to sink the last *Sheffield*-class ship on the high seas."

"No fun shooting ducks in a barrel, XO, but hey. The mundane is part of the job." Pete took another look at the *Hercules*. "Too bad for her she's not flying the Union Jack. It'd save me a Mark-48. Fire torp one!"

"Fire torp one. Aye, Captain."

Bridge
ARA Hercules
Weddell Sea

6:46 p.m. local time

A ll right! All right!" Capitán Roberto Silva threw his arms in the air, clearly fed up with the conversation. "We've wasted enough time on this. I refuse to arrest Lieutenant Nuñez, nor am I going to put any restrictions on him. From my perspective, he has done his duty.

"Capitán Montes, you may use the ship's communications facilities to file a report with Buenos Aires, as you have requested. You have that right. But I am instructing Lieutenant Nuñez to prepare a statement outlining his version of the events in question, and that will be filed and transmitted to high command along with your report."

"That's outrageous!" Montes protested. "You would take the word of a green, inexperienced junior officer over that of a widely respected senior capitán, on the verge of making admiral?"

"I'm not taking anyone's word. I'm making a decision. That is my decision."

"Capitán! Torpedo in the water! Inbound from starboard! Range, three hundred yards and closing!"

"What the— Left full rudder! All ahead full!"

"Left full rudder! All ahead full!"

Montes ran over to the left side of the bridge, away from the direction of the incoming torpedo as the ship swung hard to the left. Nuñez ran in the opposite direction, to the right side of the bridge, looking for a glimpse of the incoming torpedo.

There! A missile streaking through the water toward the ship, leaving a long white trail in its wake.

"Inbound torpedo one hundred yards and closing!"

"All hands. This is the XO! Brace for impact! Brace for impact!"

The explosion threw Nuñez so high that his head struck the ceiling of the bridge before slamming him to the deck under a shower of glass.

Alarm bells, sirens, the ceiling of the bridge whirling—first slowly, then faster, then in a lightning-fast blur. These were his last sights and images before he blacked out.

CS **Miro**
Weddell Sea
depth 40 feet

6:48 p.m. local time

H is eyes still pressed to the eyepiece of the periscope, Pete watched as towering black smoke and flames rose from the bow of the ARA *Hercules*.

"Put the image on the big screen."

"Aye, Captain."

A second later, every eye in the control room latched onto the image of the out-of-control fire burning at the forward section of the enemy vessel.

"You don't realize the destructive power of one torpedo until you personally witness the effects of it," the chief of the boat said.

"That's a fact, COB," Pete said, "and we've wreaked a ton of destruction with these torpedoes in the last twenty-four hours."

"Should we pop 'em with another one for good measure, sir?" the XO asked.

"Not necessary, XO. That's wasting good ammo. That ship's at the bottom of the sea in less than thirty minutes."

"Agreed, sir," the COB said.

"Radio. Float the communication buoy. Notify Fourth Fleet. Successful attack upon ARA *Hercules* at 1850 hours local time. Attack appears devastating and fatal to enemy ship. Updates to follow. Respectfully submitted, PC Miranda, Commander US Navy, Commanding Officer."

Ship's brig
ARA Hercules
Weddell Sea

6:50 p.m. local time

Hey! Hey! Let us out of here!" Rivers shouted through the bars at the panicked Argentinean sailors running up and down the passageway.

Some of the sailors grabbed life preservers. Others tossed life preservers along the passageway. Others, like a thundering herd trampling across the steel deck, took off running from in front of the brig.

The British engineers in the two cells adjacent to Rivers and Dunn, their hands cuffed behind their backs, kicked against their cell doors. "Let us out!"

But the passageway outside the ship's brig was a traffic jam of panicked humanity. The rumbling boots of sailors stampeding to get out of the ship as fearful voices yelled in Spanish neutralized the sound of the British desperately kicking against the steel bars.

None of the Argentineans even looked at the British prisoners locked behind in the cells.

An announcement in Spanish over the 1-MC.

"*¡Atención! Hemos sido alcanzados por un torpedo. La situación es irreparable. Abandonen el barco inmediatamente. Repito. Abandonen el barco. El barco se hunde y tenemos poco tiempo. Este es el capitán.*"

"Did anybody understand that?" Rivers yelled.

"It's an abandon ship order, Leftenant! The captain said the ship has been struck by a torpedo and is sinking fast."

Rivers and Dunn exchanged glances. For the first time, a glimpse of fear appeared in the eyes of the Royal Marine.

"Look, Leftenant." Dunn nodded down at the deck. "Water."

Rivers turned and saw a sheet of water moving along the deck, which set off an accelerated panic among the Argentinean sailors rushing to get out.

For the first time, Rivers began to believe that death was imminent.

CS **Miro**
Weddell Sea
depth 40 feet

6:55 p.m. local time

The magnified image on the big screen, which cast a spell of stunned silence over every man in the sub's control room, showed a warship still burning out of control, flames leaping fifty feet into the air, its bow sinking under the water, its stern rising up out of the water.

Along both sides of the ship, men leaped overboard, to their deaths. Even with life preservers, no man could survive long in the frigid waters of the Weddell Sea.

Sub commanders, fighter pilots, drone pilots, and missile operators—warriors who fought using highly sophisticated equipment from far away—rarely saw the up-close-and-personal face of war as did the soldiers on the ground, where one saw the blood drawn from an enemy soldier shot in the stomach or in the head, or retrieved the body of a buddy hit in the chest by a mortar.

For a flash, the sight reminded Pete of stories of men leaping from high above the World Trade Center on 9/11. The duel with the enemy sub commander, and now this . . . it was all sobering in a way that Pete had never experienced.

Still, Pete would remain on station long enough to watch the ship go down in order to transmit an accurate final report to Fourth Fleet on the fate of the *Hercules*. That fate should be final within the next few minutes.

Ship's brig
ARA **Hercules**
Weddell Sea

7:12 p.m. local time

The freezing-cold water sloshed up to their knees, soaking through their thermal gear and into their boots. Outside the steel bars, the passageway that only minutes ago held a sea of panicked humanity rushing to escape had emptied. They heard only the sound of rushing water against distant cries of men injured by the blast, men trapped and, like them, facing inevitable death.

The silence of the men trapped inside the brig Rivers found surreal. They had given up and were listening to Bach quoting words, perhaps from the Bible. Perhaps from some philosopher. Not that it mattered now.

"*Come to me, all who are weary and heavy-laden, and I will give you rest.*

"*Take my yoke upon you, and learn from me, for I am gentle and humble in heart; and you shall find rest for your souls. For my yoke is easy, and my load is light.*"

Bach's words seemed to have a strange tranquilizing effect at a time when the men should have been wailing and beating on the bars. As Bach droned on, Rivers' mind turned to Little Aussie. And yes, to Meg. So many regrets. If there was a God, he hoped God would forgive him.

"*And he shall wipe away every tear from their eyes; and there shall no longer be any death; there shall no longer be any mourning, or crying, or pain; the first things have passed away.*"

The water level had reached their waists. In the adjacent cells, some of the men started to wipe tears. In the face of death, Rivers could not bring himself to cry. Only wonder.

Who would provide for Aussie?

Would he ever have a father figure?

Even if God forgave him, would Aussie?

Would Meg?

Would it even matter?

"*God is our refuge and strength, a very present help in trouble. Therefore we will not fear, though the earth should change, and though the mountains slip into the heart of the sea—*"

"Rivers!"

Rivers looked around. "Rivers!" The voice came from down the passageway.

"Here! In here!" Rivers strained to look down the passageway. He saw a figure wading through the water.

"Nuñez! Is that you?"

"Sorry for the delay. I was detained. But nothing that a whiff of smelling salts from a quick-thinking medic couldn't cure."

"I didn't think you were coming."

"I gave my word." Nuñez put the key in the first cell door. "Remember?"

Rivers exchanged glances with Dunn.

"We must hurry." Nuñez opened the first cell door. "The ship is going down fast. Turn around, Rivers, and I'll get your cuffs."

Rivers complied. "That feels better."

"Here's the master key. Unlock your buddies and I'll unclasp Dunn."

"Got it." Rivers sloshed over and unlocked the next barred door. Then the next.

The British engineers rushed into the flooding passageway.

"I've got two master keys. Turn around and we'll get you uncuffed. Quick. Here. You take these guys and I'll take the rest." He handed Rivers one of the master keys. "Drop the cuffs in the water. Hurry."

One by one, the steel handcuffs were dropped into the rapidly rising water, each *plop* of falling handcuffs the sound of liberation.

By the time they had shed their shackles, the water had risen above their waists and kept rising.

"Follow me!" Nuñez said.

They sloshed down the passageway a few yards, away from the direction of the water flow.

"This way." Nuñez turned left and moved over toward a ladder leading topside. "This way."

"You go, Leftenant," Dunn said. "I'll bring up the rear."

Rivers was first up the ladder, right behind Nuñez. He stepped to the main deck into a strong, cold breeze and looked around. The front two-thirds of the ship had already sunk underwater, while the back third and the ship's superstructure remained above the waterline, sinking, but at a shallow angle.

Out beyond the sinking ship, in the choppy gray swells of the Weddell Sea, dozens of sailors, fighting for their lives, flailed and splashed in the water. Some floated facedown, apparently unconscious. Some had life preservers. Others did not. In the few seconds that he waited for the others coming up the ladder, Rivers saw three sailors slip under the surface. "This way!" Nuñez motioned as Dunn brought up the rear.

They moved in a single line up the raised deck toward the stern, away from the advancing line of water.

They reached the heliport on the fantail at the ship's rear, which was rising at a steeper angle as the bow section sank deeper. Under whipping winds and with the eerie loneliness of a ghost town, they realized the back of the ship had been abandoned. Every sailor who could get off the ship had already abandoned ship.

"This way! Inside the hangar!"

They followed Nuñez inside the ship's helo hangars, where two choppers, the Super Puma that had flown them in from Antarctica and a Sea King, were crammed inside and had rolled forward against the bulkhead as the ship's bow angled down.

"Are you going to try to fly us off this rust bucket, Lieutenant?"

"Hang on." Nuñez stepped inside the Super Puma.

"Leftenant, this ship is sinking fast, we need to get out of here," one of the engineers, Walter Turner, said, his voice shaking.

"Hang on a second, Turner," Rivers said.

"We may not have a second," Turner protested. "I can feel the deck angling down and he's in there wasting time."

"Not there." Nuñez exited the Super Puma, then disappeared inside the Sea King.

"Sorry, Leftenant, but I'm not staying in here with the ship sinking around us." Turner turned and ran outside the hangar toward the stern.

"Follow him, Dunn."

"Yes, sir."

Dunn followed him out onto the fantail. But Turner had a point. The sharpness of the deck angle had become much steeper in the last few seconds as the bow sank deeper into the water and the stern climbed higher into the air, rising toward the last fatal angle before the ship disappeared into the sea.

"People, don't panic," Rivers said.

"We're with you, sir," one said.

"We live together or we die together," another said.

"The Lord be with us," Bach said.

Dunn returned to the hangar. "Terrible news, sir."

"What is it?"

"Turner just jumped off the ship."

Rivers cursed under his breath.

"Lord, receive his soul into your bosom," Bach said.

"Rivers, give me a hand?" Nuñez from inside the chopper.

"Dunn, don't let anyone else get out of the hangar."

"Yes, sir."

Rivers stepped into the Sea King and, as he did, the stern rose another two or three degrees so abruptly that he almost lost his balance.

"I had a feeling this might be here," Nuñez said. "The pilot and co-pilot were killed in the blast, and nobody remembered it in the rushed panic to get off the ship. We'll have to throw it over the back and hope it deploys."

"The chopper's life raft?"

"It holds six. There are nine of you left. But if it deploys, it's better than nothing. Give me a hand."

"Bloody good."

The raft, undeployed, was housed in an orange cylindrical container that resembled a fat garbage can. Rivers stepped down from the chopper, gripping the handle at one end of the cylinder. Nuñez followed him, holding the other.

"Okay, I counted three or four life preservers in the chopper. Dunn, can you grab them?"

"You bet."

"Let's go, men."

Rivers and Nuñez stepped out onto the fantail into the daylight, holding the orange cylinder between them. Both men were Navy men. Both knew that the raft was designed to deploy on impact with the water.

Dropped from a chopper at five hundred feet, no problem. Dropped from forty feet off the rising stern of a sinking ship . . . who knew if that would be sufficient impact to deploy it?

They walked to the stern and looked down. "What do you think?" Rivers stared at the swirling water behind the ship.

"Fifty-fifty that it deploys from here," Nuñez said.

"Sir, we have five life preservers." Dunn emerged from the helo hangar, holding the orange life jackets in his arms.

"Okay, if you can't swim or are a weak swimmer, raise your hand."

One hand went up. "I can't swim at all," Lawrence Respess said.

Another hand up. "I'm not so hot at it." This was John McArthur.

Then another hand. Then another. And another.

"Perfect," Rivers said. The cold wind whipped up harder. "Five hands up. Five life jackets. Respess, McArthur, Meredith, Awe, Holt. See Captain Dunn. Get those jackets on! Now!"

"Yes, sir."

"The more the stern rises," Nuñez said, "the greater the distance to the water, and the greater the chance it deploys when it hits the water."

"True," Rivers said. "But if we wait too long, the ship goes down anyway, and we're about to lose our footing because of the angle. It's like standing on a steep hill."

"Sir, the men have their life jackets on."

"Okay, listen. We'll toss the raft overboard. We don't know if it will deploy. Whether it deploys or not, we're going overboard. We have no choice. Everyone remove your boots. Dunn, Bach, Edwards. Remove your thermals and your boots. The water weight will bog you down. If the raft deploys, swim to it. If it does not, swim together and make a human circle in the water, locking arms in the water. The five of you with life preservers can help the three who don't to stay afloat a bit longer."

"The three who don't have life preservers?" Bach asked. "There are five without life jackets. What about you, sir? And Lieutenant Nuñez?"

"Just follow instructions," Rivers snapped. He looked over to Nuñez. "Okay, let's do this. On my count . . . one . . . two . . ."

They heaved the orange barrel into the sky off the back of the stern and watched as it fell down to the surface, splashing water in every direction as it landed. It disappeared. Then, like a floatable fishing cork, it popped back to the surface.

Nothing.

"Men! In the water! Move! Move! Guys with life jackets first. Remember to form a circle and interlock arms."

"Leftenant, will that do any good?" Meredith asked. "Aren't we going to freeze in the water anyway?"

"Meredith, if you don't want the life jacket, then take it off and I'll give it to Bach."

"Okay. I'm sorry."

"In the water!"

Meredith volunteered first. He hesitated a second, then crawled over the back and jumped. Then Awe. Then Respess hesitated. "I don't know, Leftenant."

"Go, Lawrence."

Respess held his nose and leaped off the stern.

"Look, Leftenant!" Dunn pointed out to sea. "The raft! It's deploying!"

Like an orange flower coming to full bloom in the spring, the orange raft, its automatic air pump activated, unfolded onto the water, complete with a sheltered canopy. An orange floating tent rolled on the waves behind the sinking ship!

"Let's go! Everybody in the water!"

Bach and Dunn were last over the back, leaving only Rivers and Nuñez. "Are you coming?"

"Not enough room in the raft," Nuñez said. "I'll make do."

"Then you go," Rivers said.

"There's no time to argue, Leftenant. Your men need you! Now! Go!"

Rivers clasped Nuñez's hand. "You're a good man, Lieutenant."

"Go, Rivers!"

Rivers turned and leaped over the stern.

A second later he splashed butt first into the Weddell Sea, sank under the surface, and came up shivering.

"Leftenant!"

He turned and saw Dunn and Meredith, who had already managed to swim to the raft. "Over here!"

Rivers put his head in the water and started a furious crawl stroke. A minute later a hand grasped him. "Everyone is here except Respess," Dunn said.

"Where's Respess?"

"Don't know, sir, but please get out of the water."

Rivers' arms and legs ached and quickly stiffened from the cold. "Okay."

Rivers pulled up into the canvas floor of the large rubber life raft and looked around. Men were sprawled all over the canvas. Choking. Coughing.

"Anyone seen Respess?" No response. More coughing. In freezing wet clothes, the cold would be a problem. Even in a covered raft.

"Leftenant! Look!" Dunn pointed out into the water.

Floating on the water. A life preserver. Empty. The life preserver

Respess had been wearing. Rivers winced. First Anderson, then Turner, now Respess.

"Hey, wait for me! Wait!"

"Look!" Dunn said. "On the ship!"

The stern had risen much higher. One man stood alone at the top. "Wait for me!"

"Is that Nuñez?" Rivers squinted, trying to get the salt water from his eyes.

"Not Nuñez. It's Montes."

"Leftenant! He's jumping!"

Rivers cleared his eyes in time to see a man fall from the back of the sinking ship.

"Help! Help me! I'm drowning!"

Rivers hesitated. "I'm going for him."

"No! Leftenant! This guy murdered Anderson and he tried to execute you. It's over a hundred yards. You'll never make it in this cold water."

"I'm going. It's the right thing to go." Rivers dove headfirst from the raft into the frigid waters of the Antarctic.

CS Miro
Weddell Sea
depth 40 feet

7:20 p.m. local time

Pete watched, his eyes glued on the large screen as the stern of ARA *Hercules* slipped under the water.

Now, in the place of the mighty ship that moments ago had steamed across the water, only dark gray seas and pale blue skies.

Out of his respect for the dead, he allowed himself a self-imposed moment of silence.

"Radio. Notify Fourth Fleet. ARA *Hercules* has been sunk. Mark that at 1920 hours local time."

"Mark 1920 hours local time. Aye, Captain."

Silence.

"Captain! FLASH message in from Fourth Fleet. Radio traffic inter-cepted reveals British prisoners believed to be on board ARA *Hercules*!"

"What?" Pete's throat closed. "Let me see that!" He snatched the FLASH message from the radio officer and glanced at it. "Down scope! Surface the sub! Now!"

"Surface the sub! Aye, Captain!"

Meg Alexander's suite
Bellas Artes Suites
Mac Iver 551
Santiago, Chile

10:14 p.m. local time

Part of the problem with waiting on the unknown was finding a con-structive use of one's time during the waiting process.

Shelley needed to keep Meg's mind occupied, and with their hotel so close to Chile's most famous landmarks, they had spent the day taking in the Modena presidential palace, where Pinochet had staged his famous coup against Allende, and then the Basilica de la Merced Catholic Church.

Neither the palace nor the church were open to tourists, so they hired a cabdriver to drive them by each location and then drop the three of them—Shelley, Meg, and Aussie—off at the Santiago Town Square, where luscious flowers and greenery, sun-drenched palm trees, and European architecture made for a charming blend that integrated the flair of Paris with a semitropical atmosphere.

The strategy of occupying Meg's mind with sightseeing had helped, at least somewhat. For a little while anyway, Meg seemed distracted with small talk and commentary on the wonders of the great South American capital.

But now, approaching 10:15 p.m., having retired to Meg's suite for a cocktail, Shelley finally understood her duty. She would wait with her friend, be with her friend, support her friend and her friend's son no matter how long it took, no matter what the outcome.

Little Aussie had long since gone to bed, and she sat alone with Meg at the small hotel table in Meg's suite, sipping red wine and reminiscing and hoping for brighter days to come.

"To brighter days." Shelley held her glass high and smiled.

"I shall drink to that." Meg flashed a smile, the only one Shelley had seen since their arrival in Chile. "You know, Shelley, we may never find Rivers. We're spinning our wheels. Perhaps we should return to London. What can we accomplish here anyway?" She sipped her wine.

Shelley smiled. "I can't answer that because I don't know the answer. But if you are asking what good you are doing here, then my answer is that you're following your heart. You're following it wherever it may lead you. And that, I would say, is a good thing."

"You have such a way with words, Shelley. What would I do without you?"

The phone rang.

"Hello . . . This is Miss Alexander . . . What? . . . What?" Meg's hands shook and she began to weep. "Please, Captain. Talk to my friend." She handed the phone to Shelley.

"Hello?"

"Yes. This is Commander John Gordon from the British Embassy. With whom am I speaking?"

"I'm Shelley Washington. Meg's friend from London."

"Yes, Miss Washington. She mentioned that you were coming."

"What is it, Captain?"

"We promised to keep Miss Austin apprised regarding Leftenant Austin Rivers."

"What about Mister Rivers?"

"As I told Miss Alexander, an Argentinean ship was torpedoed in the Antarctic, and Leftenant Rivers and several other British subjects were prisoners on that ship. An allied submarine picked up some survivors . . . and some bodies. We believe that Leftenant Rivers was among those picked up, but we do not know yet if he survived.

"They are being transported to a mobile hospital facility that the Chileans set up at Cape Horn. I told Miss Alexander that she would be welcome to come and check on Leftenant Rivers, but this could be traumatic for her if he did not survive. Because she is the mother of the leftenant's son, the British government will pay for her transportation and lodging and for her son's transportation and lodging.

I can also arrange for your transportation and lodging to be covered as well."

"Can you hang on a second, Captain?"

"Certainly."

Meg began to sob softly.

"Captain, why is the information so spotty? Why don't we have a definite answer?"

"Because the injured and the bodies are being transported by an allied submarine, not a British sub, and our communication with the submarine is spotty. We may not know anything more until tomorrow morning."

Shelley held her hand over the phone. "Do you want to go, Meg?"

Meg nodded. "Yes."

"When, Captain?"

"I can arrange for a plane at six. You'll be flown from Santiago to Puerto Williams, a Chilean naval station at the tip of the continent, then by helicopter over to the Cape Horn Naval Station. I'm flying down tonight. But if you can call me at four in the morning, I will have all your transportation details."

"Thank you, Captain. We'll be there."

Chilean naval station
Cape Horn, Chile

11:00 a.m. local time

The helicopter banked to the left, providing a clear view of a raging blue sea swirling around the mountainous rock called Cape Horn. The sight of the great mountain jutting into the sea proved awe-inspiring and meant that the nail-biting flight and the harrowing experience of battling gusty crosswinds on the last leg of it was almost over.

The landing proved even bumpier, prompting an apology from the Royal Navy pilot in command of the chopper. Indeed, the flight had seemed like a horrible roller-coaster ride.

Shelley hated roller coasters.

"Welcome to the Chilean naval station at Cape Horn," the Royal Navy pilot announced as he shut down the helicopter engines. "If you will give us a moment for these overhead blades to stop swirling, we will get you safely off the aircraft."

Shelley looked out the helicopter's window, out across the windswept tarmac and across the large expanse of blue choppy water. Her eyes affixed on the huge monolithic mountain of a rock, protruding like a giant nose out into the rough waters of the sea.

From its base, where angry swells and whitecaps lashed it with an ineffective fury, to its towering peak rising at an angle 1,400 feet above the sea, Cape Horn reminded her of the great Rock of Gibraltar at the entrance to the Mediterranean, a place she had visited twice.

This great rock, along with Gibraltar, had to be among the natural wonders of the world.

The copilot slid open the back passenger door of the helicopter, and the blustery ocean breeze, with the cutting power of a sharp knife, dislodged her gaze from the rock. "You'll note it's cooler here than in Santiago," he said and smiled.

"So I've noticed," Meg said.

By this time, the pilot had joined the copilot standing outside the passenger door. "If you ladies would step out and follow me, the copilot will attend to your baggage."

"Thank you."

"Thank you, Leftenant."

They stepped onto the asphalt tarmac, and the wind caught Shelley's hair. She pushed the locks from her face.

The pilot said, "Follow me. There is a large hospital tent that the Chileans have set up for the reasons I believe Commander Gordon has already explained."

He led them off to the left. Aussie walked between Meg and Shelley, gripping their hands.

Not a word was uttered as they walked, surrounded by the sound of the wind and the breakers crashing against the rocky seawall.

Theirs was a march to an uncertain fate. Still guessing. Still not knowing.

They saw the lighthouse, and then they saw a large green Army tent, so large that it could have passed for a huge canvas warehouse.

Three flags flew in front of the tent. The British flag. The Chilean flag. The flag of the Red Cross.

"Before we go in, ladies," the pilot said, "would you like me to check first on Leftenant Rivers?" He looked down at Aussie.

"These men inside were pulled from Drake Passage and the Antarctic. Many are British. Some are Argentinean. Some are Venezuelan. All of them were plucked from the water when their ships were sunk. Please wait here. I shall go to find Commander Gordon."

"Mommy, is this a hospital?"

"Yes, Aussie." Meg wiped tears from her eyes. She turned to Shelley. "I may need you to stay with him out here. Perhaps I should have left him in London."

"Of course. We can wait over there, out on the walk to the light-house. Aussie might like to see the lighthouse."

Meg looked inside the tent at a scene that resembled something from the movie *MASH*. Dozens of portable cots were lined up in rows. Nurses and doctors, clad in white jackets and white uniforms, moved up and down the rows of men. She saw a cot with the sheet pulled over the face.

Meg turned away and buried her head on Shelley's shoulder.

Just then the pilot walked up with another British naval officer.

"This is Dr. Medina," the pilot said. "He will explain what happened to Leftenant Rivers."

"Oh, dear God, please." Meg buried her hands in her face. "Shelley, please take Aussie outside."

"It's okay, Miss Alexander," Dr. Medina said. He smiled. "He's alive. And very lucky. We're treating him for hypothermia."

"You mean . . ."

"He and his men were picked up by an American submarine. Actually, a Chilean submarine with an American crew. He dove into some near-freezing waters to try to save an Argentinean officer. He never found the Argentinean, but his men were in a life raft and got to him before he drowned. It was a close call. But he received excellent treatment on board the submarine, and that made a huge difference."

"Austin is alive?"

"Very much so. I'll take you to him."

Meg, trembling, hugged Shelley, then kissed the top of Aussie's head.

"He's alive, Meg. Our prayers have been answered," Shelley said.

"Follow me," the doctor said.

They headed down a row of cots. Little Aussie spotted him first. "Daddy!" He took off running the final stretch, arms open.

"Aussie? What are you doing here? How did you get here?"

"A little surprise for you, Leftenant," Dr. Medina said. He smiled and then walked away unnoticed.

"Meggie! Both of you! You are all here!"

"Mommy and I came to take you home, Daddy!"

He first kissed Aussie on the head and forehead, and then he kissed Meg in a manner that was not at all platonic. "The doc says three more days and then I go home. And this time, I'm never leaving you again."

More hugs. More kisses.

Shelley knew from the excitement in Austin's eyes the moment he saw them that all of Meg's prayers were being answered.

There is a God after all. She stepped back to give them some privacy, then turned toward the entrance to the tent.

That's when she saw her. Over by the entrance where they had come in. The nun. Wearing the same kind of black habit of the nun who had talked to her that day in Kensington Gardens. The nun had said God would lead her through any storm. Would be there to comfort her. And then the nun had simply vanished. How could this be? Was this the same nun? Here? Shelley hurried toward her. She had to find out. "Sister!"

The nun walked out of the tent.

Shelley ran to catch up with her, pushing her way through the tent door. The nun was a short distance away, still walking. "Sister!"

The nun stopped and turned around. "Yes? Do I know you?"

Her smile was beatific, her eyes were blue, but her face looked young. Not a wrinkle on it.

"Oh, forgive me, Sister. I thought you were someone else. I'm sorry to have bothered you."

The nun smiled but said nothing.

Shelley felt foolish, almost embarrassed, and walked back inside the tent to join Meg.

"Shelley? Is that you?"

She turned and felt her heart stop. There was Bob. She had walked right by him before. "Oh, thank God! Thank God you're alive!"

"How did you get here? Why?"

"I came with Meg. She was looking for Austin Rivers, her son's father. He's alive. Right over there. But we didn't know that when we got here. I heard on the BBC about your ship. I was so worried! They said that your ship had been sunk. I thought . . ."

"They torpedoed my ship. A Chilean fishing trawler scooped me up with some of my men. Brought us here. Hypothermia. Feeling much better now."

"Thank God. I was worried sick . . . Oh, Bob, I'm so sorry . . . so sorry . . . that I broke the engagement. I—"

"That was long ago," he said. "We were both much younger."

"I made a mistake, Bob. A huge mistake . . . Will you . . . can you ever forgive me?"

"Forgive you?" A smile crossed his face. "For the record, I still have your photo in my wallet. Never thought I'd see you again."

She sat down on his bed and reached for his hand. "Bob, I wish we could start over. I was foolish."

He did not respond. He didn't know what to say. He wanted to say something, but what? All those years. All those dreams. The hurt. Rejected by the Royal Navy and by the woman he loved. The wasted years. And now? Now what? Did she still want the life of an officer's wife? Or did she want him?

"I . . . I just thought—"

"Look at me." He smiled. "What if . . . we start with a cup of tea."

She smiled.

"To rekindled friendship."

"To rekindled friendship," she said. "I'll drink to that."

She bent down and he hugged her tight.

"Oh, Bob, I have missed you so."

Then she remembered the nun in Kensington Gardens, the nun who said God would lead her through any storm, would be with her to comfort her. Had God brought her all the way to Cape Horn to find the only man she had ever loved? Could God do that? She put her head down, closed her eyes, and whispered, "Thank you, God. Thank you."

10 Downing Street
London

5:00 p.m. local time

Prime Minister David Mulvaney sat at his desk, alone, staring at the bronze bust of Churchill on the corner of the desk. Had he done the right thing? Had the lost lives been worth it? He reminded himself that Britain was not the aggressor. Britain had only defended herself.

Churchill would have defended Britain.

The telephone buzzed on the desk.

"Prime Minister."

"The foreign secretary is here for you, sir."

"Send him in."

Mulvaney stood as Foreign Secretary John Gosling walked into the office.

"Good news, Prime Minister," Gosling said. "We got word that the British engineer who was shot, Mister Gaylord, has been handed over by Argentina to the Red Cross. His condition is still critical, but the doctors expect him to survive."

Mulvaney nodded. "Mister Gaylord has family, does he not?"

"Yes, sir. A wife and two children."

"Make sure his wife is notified, and make sure she is provided accommodations at government expense to be able to meet the plane when it arrives back in Britain with her husband."

"Yes, sir."

"And more good news. Just in. The Americans have negotiated a cease-fire. Terms of an accord are to be discussed at Camp David next week."

Mulvaney felt a wave of relief flood his body as he sat back down in his chair. "Bloody good. God bless President Surber. Now this is the kind of news that I can cheerfully take to the king."

EPILOGUE

The sleek black submarine cut through the waters of the bay, steaming back to port instead of heading out to sea as it had been when she last saw it.

Along the deck of the sub, American sailors and officers stood at parade rest, decked out handsomely in their white uniforms. At the back of the sub, the flags of both the Republic of Chile and the United States of America flapped in the wind.

Fireboats and tugboats formed a nautical parade in front of and behind the sub, spraying water high into the warm sun-drenched sky.

With a cease-fire having been announced yesterday, and with the countries of Chile, Britain, Russia, Argentina, Venezuela, and the USA agreeing to terms for division of the massive Antarctic oil fields, Pete Miranda was returning with Chile's prized new warship as a national hero.

Some were calling him Chile's "modern-day Lafayette."

Others, preferring a more appropriate naval analogy, had gone to the airways to call him "Chile's modern-day John Paul Jones."

Would he even remember her? Why would he? Their politics were too different. And with his newfound celebrity, he could—

Her phone buzzed. A text message.

Meet me at La Concepción in one hour. Pete

She checked her watch. She needed to leave. Now.

She took one last look at the sub returning to port in triumphant glory. Then she saw him, the handsome captain on the bridge, waving at well-wishers in a flotilla of powerboats.

Time to go.

Pier 2
Valparaiso naval station
Valparaiso, Chile

10:45 a.m. local time

Under the sunny skies of a gorgeous Pacific morning, CS *Miro* pulled alongside Pier 2 of the Valparaiso naval station to a throng of flashing lights, cameras, and hundreds of well-wishers on the pier.

As dockworkers threw lines at the sub for sailors to secure her and Chilean sailors moved the catwalk into position to connect the sub to the pier, the Chilean Navy band struck up a brassy rendition of "Anchors Aweigh," the famous theme song of the US Navy.

As commanding officer, Pete Miranda would be the first to walk off the sub. With the band still playing, he stepped onto the platform, turned, and saluted the American flag flying at the back of the sub, and then stepped down the catwalk to the pier.

The first to greet him at the base was a smiling Admiral Carlos Delapaz. Pete shot a salute, which Delapaz returned.

"Great work, Commander. You've made both America and Chile very proud."

"Thank you, sir."

"Pete, I know you're ready to get out of here ASAP, but there's someone who wants to meet you."

"Certainly, Admiral."

As other members of the *Miro* disembarked, Delapaz escorted Pete toward the end of the pier, where a group of Chilean Marines stood next to a British naval officer, an attractive woman, and a young boy.

"Pete, I'd like you to meet Leftenant Austin Rivers, SBS, Royal Navy."

The officer threw a sharp open-handed British salute. "Sir, I wanted to come and express my appreciation to you and your crew."

Pete returned the salute. "You look familiar, Leftenant."

"That's probably because the last time you saw me, I was stiff as an iceberg, unable to utter a word. You blokes fished me out of the chilly waters of the Antarctic."

"Ah, now I remember you. You dove in for a swim. Good to see you, Leftenant."

"Sir, I'd like you to meet two special people." He put his hand on the woman's back. "This is Meggie. She's the mother of my son and the finest woman in the world."

"A pleasure, ma'am," Pete said.

"And this is my son, Aussie."

The boy looked up and shot Pete a salute. "Thank you for bringing my daddy home."

Pete swallowed hard and returned the salute, trying to suppress his emotions. He thought of his daughters, Kelsey and Grace. What life is really about. "Glad to be of service to you and your family, young man."

"Sir, I wanted to be here to personally thank you. Without you . . . I wouldn't . . ."

"My pleasure, Leftenant. I appreciate your coming here. All of you. Thank you. Means a lot to me."

Restaurant La Concepción
Papudo 541
Valparaiso, Chile

11:30 a.m. local time

This way, Ms. Vasquez." Fernando met Maria with a broad smile and directed her to a table with a bottle of pinot noir, a vase with a dozen roses, and two glasses. "Commander Miranda called ahead with an order for the flowers and your favorite bottle of wine."

"Thank you, Fernando," she said as the waiter got her chair for her.

"And if I may? Commander Miranda insisted that I go ahead and pour you a glass. He insists that you have a sample, in the event that he is detained by his military duties."

"Thank you." She watched the glass fill with wine. When Fernando finished pouring the wine and left, she looked up and saw Pete standing there, stunning and handsome in the summer-white uniform of a US naval officer.

"I didn't think you would come back."

"I told you I'd come back. I do what I say I'm going to do."

"Yes. I remember. You're a conservative. You do what you say you will do. And now you're a national hero of Chile."

A Cheshire grin crossed his face. "So may I sit?"

"You invited me. Remember?"

"That doesn't mean you want me to stay and sit," he said.

"No. You think I might have a better idea? Like blowing this joint and coming to my place for a piece of peach pie?"

"Hmm. Sounds intriguing." Pete sat down. "But I've got a better idea." He poured a glass of the pinot.

"Oh? What could be better than my place and peach pie?"

"My place and barbecue ribs."

"Your place?" She felt herself blush. "Down on the waterfront?"

"I'm not talking about the waterfront. I've seen enough water for a while. And I've seen enough death for a lifetime. I've learned that life is all too short to let stupid stuff like politics get in the way."

"So if you're not talking about my place, and you're not talking about your place on the waterfront, then what are you proposing?"

He smiled. "What I'm proposing is Texas."

"Texas?"

"Ever been to America?"

"No, but I've always wanted to."

"Then we need to make that happen. You should come meet the family. My dad makes the greatest beef brisket, and my mom has her own personal art gallery with fabulous Chilean landscapes that she'd love to show you. And you'll love Kelsey and Grace. My daughters. You would have a blast. And who knows where it might lead."

That brought a smile to her face. She scooted her chair over next to his and threw her arms around his neck. "I would love to go to Texas."

Her lips met his and much later, their lips still glued together, applause broke out.

Fernando returned with a bottle of champagne. "Dom Perignon for the lucky couple?"

"Ship it to Dallas for me, Fernando," Pete said. "I'll get you the address. Right now, we're going out to finish a slice of peach pie."